THE

DRY

LANDS

BOOKS By Emma Howl

~*~

THE SECTOR SERIES

The Dry Lands
The Great Divide
The Sky Lanes
The Shadows

THE
DRY
LANDS

By Emma Howl

ISBN: 978-1-0687210-2-1 (paperback)

FOR INFORMATION CONTACT
Emma Howl
Email: emmahowlauthor@gmail.com
TikTok: @emmahowlauthor
Spotify Playlist: THE DRY LANDS

Cover, Interior & Map design by Emma Howl

1st edition 2024 paperback (self–publish)

To those who read to escape this world, welcome to the world of Sorn.

PROLOGUE

~*~

The screams of pain from the princess had cut into the night like a blade and echoed down the palace halls throughout the kingdom of *Versai*. No matter how the servant elves of the *High Peaks* tried to calm her down and cool her with purified water from the *Great Divide*, it did not dampen the agony that the princess was going through as her body arched off of the silk–bound bed, releasing another painful cry into the night. Her body attempted to force the small child that was inside her out into the world.

Outside the door of the princess's chambers stood her worried father, pacing the length of the corridor before he turned and stalked back. He repeated the action multiple times to try and smother his worry from listening to the cries of his daughter – who was only now nearing the end of her labour. The screaming had gone on for more than half of the day, having started at sundown. It was now nightfall as the pale moon shone through the curtains of the palace.

As much as the king worried about his daughter, his heart constricted with every cry, he was also angry.

He was informed that his daughter would not be joining him that evening for supper – due to a 'bug', he remembered the servant girl saying. The sickness his daughter, Fhara, had picked up on her daily stroll through the garden had resulted in her early retirement to bed.

He wasn't daft, he noticed how their relationship had become strained. Interactions with Fhara were less frequent in the past few months. He saw so little of her, having an inkling that his daughter held resentment towards him but he didn't so much as entertain the notion that his daughter could potentially be with child.

Frustrated by the fact that his daughter had managed to hide her pregnancy from him for so long, he felt blindsided and had nothing to do but go over the small details he had missed in his head. He should have noticed a growing bump under her layered garments or how her cheeks now possessed a rosy tint. He only assumed it was from the crisp winter air. The king only found out she was pregnant a few hours earlier when a servant rushed into the dining hall, disturbing him from his evening meal to alert him that his daughter had gone into labour.

Although he was hurt that everyone around him kept this secret, he was more hurt Fhara decided not to share her pregnancy with him. He thought of how lonely and frightening it must have been for her without a mother to help guide her, with what should have been a joyous and exciting time was laced with fear and the unknown.

The king decided right there and then that whatever his daughter was going through, whatever situation she had gotten herself tangled up in, he would support her. He could deal with it – but he could not deal with some lower–class elf wielding his way into his daughter's heart and forcing her to bear his child. The thought of some peasant male sullying his daughter made the king slam his tight fist down onto a small table, causing the wood to split from the strength that he forced out in his temper.

Running a hand through his quickly whitening hair in frustration, his blood boiled at the thoughts.

His beautiful, pure daughter was too young to hold the responsibilities that came with raising a child in this world. If willing, he could only think of how foolish Fhara was to have gone and done something like this behind his back, having known that she was going to be betrothed to a neighbouring elven prince from across the river only weeks from then. It dawned on him that this could have been a rebellious act.

The painful screams continued along with the king's pacing for another several minutes until they finally stopped and the cries of a newborn child rippled through the air. The sound alone made the king's anxiety ease and his heart stuttered. The terrible pain his daughter endured finally came to an end and brought with it, new life. Only one thing was for certain.

He had to meet his grandchild.

One of his daughter's servants quickly opened the door

to the bedroom. Their eyes found the king, and she smiled warmly at him, yet the smile did not reach her eyes. She almost looked afraid for some reason, cheeks and ears tinted pink ever so slightly as a small part of her blonde hair fell into her eyes.

The king immediately noticed this and his stomach dropped in fear. His eyes welled up as his worried gaze trapped that of the servant and he predicted the worst.

"What is it?" He asked in a whisper. Voice fragile, he feared for his daughter's life. He had lost so much in the past that the sheer thought of losing his beautiful daughter brought him to despair.

"My king. You can come in now." The servant's voice was monotone, the fear had reached her eyes as she opened the door wider to reveal his daughter, alive and holding her newborn close to her chest.

Fhara gazed down lovingly at the small child wrapped up in her arms, quietly assessing in adoration as the child stared up at her calmly. Its small hands reached up to grab a small piece of her blonde – almost silver – hair which fell over her shoulder. Fhara smiled down at her beautiful child, not shifting her gaze even as her father stepped in.

The king's eyes welled with joy as he brought his eyes over the child, with its white hair similar to Fhara's, he watched the newborn gurgled up happily at his daughter.

"Thank the Gods you are alright my child." The king whispered in thanks as he made his way over to the bed where his daughter and grandchild sat.

Fhara's glanced up at him when he moved closer in fear. The king didn't notice and continued towards his daughter, his eyes set on his grandchild wanting to have a closer look at the new addition to the family – to the elven city of *Versai*. The birth of a child, destined for greatness.

"Father, wait," Fhara spoke in a rush. "You should know–"

The king's large hand reached out for the tiny one, noticing how small and perfect it was. He wanted nothing more than to cradle his grandchild in his arms as he smiled down at the little life. His other hand reached up to rest on Fhara's shoulder.

"You bear a son." The king observed pleasantly, clearly distinguishing the different ears male elves possessed. They were less rounded compared to females – more pointed. Fhara, taking notice of the king's sharp eyes, clutched the small boy closer to her in an attempt to hide the boy's features from him. She nodded.

"May I hold him?"

The shift in the atmosphere went unnoticed and the king's gaze softened upon looking at the child who wiggled around in his daughter's embrace on the verge of crying.

Fhara opened her mouth to protest but quickly shut it, only to reopen it with a look that could only be identified as pure fear with a slight edge to it.

"You will not like what you see, Father, please forgive me."

Fhara looked weaker now as the king observed her. As if the challenges that came with giving birth had only started to take effect.

'She has been through a lot', the king noted to himself.

'She deserves to sleep.'

Her words, sounding grave, made the king pale. He quickly took the child with shaky hands and lifted him towards the light to assess him, afraid of what he might find when looking upon the child. His heart pumped with worry for a flaw upon his perfect grandson.

The child started to wail in discomfort and the king brought him down, hiding him in his firm chest as he looked down at the child. The worry started to fade as he realised what it was that his daughter was worried about. It didn't faze him that much.

"He is not as pale as the others." The king mused and Fhara held her breath before turning to her with a reassuring smile.

"His skin should be fine, but his eyebrows look like they will grow dark. We can have them lightened–"

"Father I–"

The child made a happy sound and pulled on the king's long, fair hair that was just within reach of the child and caught the baby's attention. It made the king look down in slight amusement. The king gasped upon seeing the child's features. From a distance, it wasn't noticeable, and the boy's complexion could be that of a normal child within the elven kingdom of the *High Peaks.* But upon closer inspection of the boy's eyes, it was clear.

This child was far from normal.

His eyes were a striking green instead of the multitudes of blue all elves possessed. It was seen as a flaw to be an elf without the blue. It was uncommon and tragic. Efforts to produce the sector trait were challenging at times due to genetics and things were guaranteed to go wrong; it was merely unfortunate. All elves who didn't possess the eye colour associated with their sector were to be exiled from the community. Most were banished, whether they chose to go or not. Others would only have a taste of life before it would be taken from them. Their parents knew the risk if their child were unfortunately given the characteristics no elven creature had. They were given no choice in the matter but to be rid of the child that threatened their very existence.

The king could not fathom words, nor could he look away from the enchanting eyes of his grandchild. Undecided himself on if he loathed or cherished the small, curious eyes.

"Father!" Fhara exclaimed weakly. Her eyes clogged up with unshed tears as she looked upon the king holding her son. He debated, going back and forth with himself mentally before finally deciding on how he felt about her son's features. He realised that this was no unfortunate occurrence of genetics and looked down at the child in disgust.

At that moment there was no point in crying or pleading with her father to spare the child. She sensed that he had already made his decision on what to do with her son, even though the decision was not his to make. The child belonged to Fhara, and the gods would fall before anything happened to him.

"He is *my* son. He is *your* grandson," Fhara tried to reason and show sense. Although the determination was there in her gaze, it did not withstand in her voice that was strained from labour. The longer she stayed awake, the more tired she became. She wanted nothing more than to close her eyes and drift into sleep.

"He is a prince–"

"He is no grandson of mine!" The king bellowed and caused a few of the servants to squeak in fright from where they were washing the red stains from the bedsheets. The king only sent them a glare and they scurried to the door to leave. This was a personal matter between the king and his daughter that needed complete privacy. They would be whispering about it the next day. Soon enough word would spread throughout the *High Peaks*, alerting everyone of the news.

The news of the elven prince with green eyes.

The king glared at his daughter. The child had been passed to one of the servants to care for as he argued with Fhara. Frightened, the child quickly became teary–eyed at the sudden loud voice.

"It would have been acceptable if it was with another elf... but Fhara, *my sweet child.* With a Dry Lander? You know the consequences of what has to be done–"

The *Dry Lands* were home to the barbaric savages of the neighbouring sector. The same sector that the *High Peaks* had been at war with for as long as the king could remember. He could not think of a time in all of his forty years on Sorn where the two sectors were not at each other's throats. A lower–class elf would have been a welcomed blessing in comparison to a Dry Lander.

"I love him, father," Fhara whispered out. Her features grew pale, yet she tried to hold on.

"Why is he not here then if he loves you so?"

"Something must have happened..." Fhara panted. "He would have been here."

'There is no way the soldiers would have let the outsider slip through.,' The king thought to himself before running through the possibilities. *'What if he did sneak in? What if that was how the rat had weaselled his way into the sector? If something happened to him...'*

"Don't hurt him," She breathed out in panic. "Don't hurt my son. Don't hurt my *Keylin*. He will grow up strong, just like *his*–"

With her last words, Fhara's heart stopped.

Of course, it wasn't uncommon for women to die during childbirth. It was just unfortunate that the gods decided to bless the elves with two devastations that day. A birth, and a death.

The king's eyes widened at the sight of his daughter, her beautiful blue eyes now lifeless and without the glint they once held.

"Fhara?" His voice was small as his eyes fell upon his daughter's still body.

A servant, who had made her way back in with more blankets for the princess spotted the scene in front of her. Her eyes grew wide before her horrified scream ripped through the room. She brought her hand up to her mouth as the king let out a heartbreaking sob, knees giving out as he was finally shaken out of his daze to the realisation that this was not a dream, this was real and his daughter was gone.

He stumbled forward to his daughter's body and

caressed her cheek whilst shaking her cold hands.

"Fhara! Wake up. This isn't funny–" The king shook her harshly, believing that this was all some sick joke in an attempt to soften the king and his decision.

After a while, he realised that this wasn't a joke, his daughter had already passed on. He sobbed into her hands, his cries echoing throughout the palace and to the sleeping city of *Versai*, where any elf still awake at this hour could hear.

It was only when the grieving servants were coming to clean up the mess around Fhara's body that the king stumbled his way out and into the corridor, away from the horrors of his dead child before him. He slid down the wall adjacent to her bedroom slowly, in a daze, while servants quickly ran into the room.

It was a while before someone approached him.

He looked up at the servant with red–rimmed eyes ready to shout at the female who leaned over him to *'leave him to mourn'*; when his eyes softened upon the sleeping boy in her arms. His blonde hair reminded him deeply of his daughter. Now that he could see the child in the lit hallway with the sun on the verge of rising, he noticed how similar in looks he was to his mother when she was once as old as him.

"What do you wish to do with the child sir?"

The servant, Mara – understanding it was a bad moment, asked quietly as she looked down at the king who broke his stare of the child.

He held his hands up for the servant to give him the child. His eyes never left the only thing that reminded him of his beloved daughter.

"Give him to me. I wish to hold my grandson." He demanded huskily. His voice filled with emotion.

The servant pressed her lips into a thin line, almost hesitant in case the king were to hurt the child but realised her position and knew better than to go against the wishes of the king and placed the sleeping boy gently into the king's arms.

She watched, a sad smile forming on her lips as the king held his grandson with such softness. Afraid that his large hands would somehow disturb the sleeping boy or hurt him but the last thing on the king's mind was to cause any more harm to his family.

The king took in a shaky breath, his eyes never left the sleeping form curled up in his arms. It was only when he held his breath that the small child shuffled closer to him in his sleep, his mouth falling open in the process. This made the king's heart fill with warmth and the love in his eyes radiated for the child, for his grandson.

"I will not banish him," The king broke the silence after several moments of staring at the sleeping boy in his hold. "I will not. He is my grandson and my heir. I do not care for his tanned skin and green eyes. All I see is my daughter. He is still an elf, and it was Fhara's wish, not to banish *him*–"

The king stopped to bite his lip as tears began to roll down his cheeks. The thought of his daughter in her last moments fighting him, fighting for her son. His heart broke all over again. As it would forevermore when he would think of her.

Mara nodded at this. Her heart broke at the sight of her king, so grief–stricken, so broken. There was never a time Mara had seen her leader look so defeated. Then again, Fhara was his only daughter. He gave her everything. Mara knew that the king would still give everything if only to have his daughter back. All that remained of her now was a memory.

A memory and her *legacy*.

"Sir, I think it is best that you rest," Mara suggested lightly. "I will take care of the child while you do."

The king looked up at Mara, his red and swollen eyes showed how tired he was. He nodded weakly before his gaze drifted back down to the sleeping newborn in his arms, and found himself unable to leave him. Mara smiled to herself upon witnessing the affection the young prince was receiving and couldn't help but ask.

"Has the child got a name sir, or shall we decide on a suitable name for him in the coming days?"

"*Keylin.*" The king interrupted in a whisper, remembering the last few words from his daughter. The boy's name was one of them.

The king caressed the small boy's tanned cheek. Although he wasn't pale, he was several shades of the common Dry Lander skin tone. It suited the child. His elven features dominated but the king knew that as the boy grew up, his unmistakable traits would eventually come to the surface, they would be harder to mask from peers. He also knew the boy would indeed encounter hardship. It was unsure what sector he truly belonged to or which would eventually claim the boy as theirs. He only hoped that when news eventually reached of a half Dry Lander elf from the mountains, the hunters would not seek him out and take advantage of him. He feared they would use him as a weapon, something to bring the sector to its knees, maybe even a martyr to shake the people of the *Dry Lands* to wage a war on Sorn itself. They wouldn't dare cross sectors. To do so would cause uproar and disturb the natural balance the world of Sorn was modelled on.

The king decided at that moment that he would do everything he could to protect the child and prevent the possibility of a whisper from escaping the sector. It wouldn't be easy but he would do it, for his daughter and his grandson.

"His name is Keylin."

~*~

6 Years Later

~*~

Keylin winced as the dirt scratched his palms. Cuts were made from dust and pebbles colliding with the ground, mixed with his blood and stung his palms.

He flinched from the pain as he turned on his side from where he had been pushed to the ground and glared up at the fair–haired elf he had known for a while now who wished nothing more than to bring him harm and torment from the very first day he started education. Today was like no other.

"What's wrong, freak?" The boy, Tobias, taunted Keylin from above as he looked down, disdain showing on his features.

"Too weak to get up and fight, *snake*?"

Tobias's minion friends snickered from behind at the nickname they had insisted on calling Keylin from the day they noticed the colour of his eyes. Keylin clenched his teeth at that, his eyes began to water at the sound of their laughter and so he shut them. They were the reason Keylin was in this mess in the first place. He hated them for it. The boy only wished to be the same as everyone else. Why did he have to be different?

Keylin's eyes were bright green with flecks of a lighter green around the outer part of his irises. Small flickers of gold ran along the fine line beside the black pupil, giving the eye an exotic look. This gave Keylin the nickname of snake, referring to the deadly and hypnotic eyes of the creature, much unlike the other elven children who possessed the majestic blue colour.

Keylin was unfortunate enough to be the only one with this eye colour and this didn't sit well with the other kids. He could understand why this would be; that green eyes were not something that the children would be used to seeing, they had never grown up with such a strange feature. If hate was not the obvious reaction at first, Keylin wouldn't know what to think. He had only hoped they would just leave him alone and carry on with their business, hopeful they'd grow tired of him. If anything, the bullying got worse and knowing that he wouldn't fight them back only made them angrier.

"I think he's going to cry!" Tobias exclaimed suddenly with a chuckle, causing his minions to react similarly.

He was startled out of his thoughts to find Tobias had moved closer to him and was now only mere inches from his face. Keylin took in a shaky breath.

"Stop it, Tobias."

Everyone's head turned to the voice while Keylin let out a small breath of relief.

The elves watched as Corrin made his way through Tobias's minion crowd with ease. His shaggy blonde hair was visible from where Keylin lay on the ground, only moving to get up knowing it was safe now that Corrin had arrived. Tobias rolled his eyes at the sight of him, nevertheless allowing Keylin to scurry to Corrin's side. Keylin did so with haste. His right ear twitched as he stood beside his friend and tried to keep the smile off of his face.

"*Of course,* you're here. The snake's *hero.*" Tobias sneered at Corrin who tensed beside the boy, fists clenching and unclenching.

"Leave him alone Tobias. He hasn't done anything to you and it's unfair to be treating him the way you do." Corrin stated strongly and Tobias muttered under his breath as he went to shoulder past Corrin.

"You can't protect him forever."

Corrin and Keylin both turned to glare at Tobias as he yelled from behind them, gaining Corrin's attention. He frowned at this before Tobias' soulful gaze focused on Keylin and he smiled sneakily.

"See you at school Keylin." Tobias taunted in reminder

as he and his minions left. Keylin took in a shaky breath as he tried not to let his words get to him.

"Sorry he's so mean to you."

Corrin muttered from beside the boy whose attention turned to him. Keylin sent him a small smile as he felt the rosy blush tinting his cheeks and the very tips of his ears.

"Thanks for saving me." The option of adding 'again' to the end of that statement only made Keylin's blush deepen. Corrin looked down at him with a softened smile before it was replaced by a smirk.

"What would my life be if I couldn't save my best friend from mean snot–nosed bullies like Tobias *huh*?"

Corrin was a friend.

Although he was a year older than Keylin, he liked to be around him for some reason. He didn't care for Keylin's peculiar looks and made the boy feel happy. Keylin was hesitant at first, believing for a time that it was a dare for Corrin to try and befriend him because it was not normal for the elven kids to be nice to him, contrary to their nature – they steered clear of Keylin, choosing not to interact with the boy whatsoever.

Corrin surprised him, however, when Tobias pushed the boy during the start of his schooling. Corrin immediately pushed Tobias back in retaliation making him fall and dislocate his shoulder. It was fair to say that any time Tobias saw Corrin after that encounter, he didn't aggravate the boy or cause trouble when he was around. Keylin liked to think knowing what Corrin was capable of scared him and took relief in knowing Tobias would never hurt him around Corrin.

"I don't know..." Keylin answered shyly as he looked down at his shifting feet, digging them around in the sand to make a pattern.

"Are you hurt?" Corrin worried and Keylin had to refrain from rolling his eyes at his constant fretting over him. He supposed he should be used to it as Corrin always wanted to know if he was hurt after a fight with Tobias – not that Keylin would call it a fair fight of course, more like an attack on a weak elf for being different than the rest – but at the end of the day, a part of Keylin liked the fact that Corrin worried about him. It made the boy happy knowing that there was somebody out there besides his grandfather, his *avus*, who cared for him.

Without saying a word, Keylin sighed and held up his bloody hands to Corrin in a form of surrender. The older boy frowned at this and there was a moment where he seemed mad, but he only let out a breath, coming closer to Keylin and taking him in for a hug. Avoiding his sore hands, he pulled the boy closer to him.

"I'm okay Corry–" Keylin giggled as he used the nickname he christened Corrin with a few days after the two had become friends, knowing that the older boy hated it.

Just as Keylin suspected, Corrin groaned in annoyance and gave the boy one last squeeze before pushing him away, smiling. Keylin laughed at that, looking at him with a small smirk on his features. His dimples poked out of his cheeks.

"Tobias is a wuss. He can't hurt me that easily. I'm tough!" Keylin stated, giving Corrin his most evil glare.

Corrin only burst into laughter at this, gasping for air after a few moments. Keylin rolled his eyes at him.

"Bono Malum Supsa."

'Overcome evil with good' Keylin quoted from his studies of the ancient scroll that day to him in their native tongue. Corrin stopped momentarily to nod at the younger boy, his eyes glinting before he continued to laugh. Keylin shook his head at his foolishness and looked down.

"Hey–" Corrin suddenly exclaimed once he regained himself and slung an arm over Keylin's shoulder, grabbing the boy's attention as they began to walk through the playground.

"Race you back?" Corrin lifted his eyebrow toward him in challenge and Keylin's eyes lit up.

Before he knew it, Keylin was pushing him back with his elbow as he quickly sprinted forward chuckling, leaving a slightly stunned Corrin behind. The older boy regained himself and began running, quickly catching up with Keylin.

They ran through the market street of *Versai*, ignoring the looks thrown their way by merchant elves and sellers while they weaved between stalls of fruit and nuts in the market area. Their laughter rang through the air as Keylin pushed himself faster, running beside Corrin.

It was not long before they were at the palace's gates, home to the prince.

Keylin touched the gates first, a few seconds before Corrin and turned to him with glee.

"I win!"

Corrin smiled down at him, panting for breath.

"You've gotten faster."

"I have been practising." Keylin smiled up at him, proud that his secret running around the palace grounds had paid off nicely. He could now keep up with – if not *beat* – Corrin.

His friend beamed down at him.

"discrio dandus."

'While teaching we learn'.

Keylin smiled, about to respond when the gates of the palace suddenly opened in front of him and one of the palace's servants moved from around it.

Mara frowned at Keylin as she tapped her wrist with her index finger knowingly, her brow lifted at the time it was that the two boys had spent being out so late – on a school night of all days. She let it go when she noticed the bright–eyed and dimpled smile of the six–year–old and scanned him for injury.

Keylin bit his lip as his pointed ears flattened against either side of his head from embarrassment. Knowing that he was late for supper, there was nothing he could do about it.

As the servant he knew well to be Mara, pulled him inside the gate, she didn't hold back her disapproving stare directed at Corrin, believing that it was him that had kept Keylin out so late.

Keylin heard Corrin shout a quote from the ancient scrolls, quotes that the elves studied as a way of life. This made the boy turn his head back as he was being pulled along by Mara. Keylin smiled at his friend, expression full of mischief.

"la tembio Keylin! Di quasi la momento per santo ani!"

'Take care of yourself, Keylin! Learn as if you're always going to live; live as if tomorrow you're going to die!'

I

KEYLIN

12 Years Later…

~*~

"Are you ready?"

I looked up at Corrin, seeing the glint of determination and adrenaline pump through his eyes as he looked down at me for confirmation, silently asking if I still wanted to go through with this. He was afraid I would be too scared to start something I wouldn't have the strength to finish.

I smirked at him, taking the moment to let my eyes rest upon the incoming targets; Tobias and his entourage of two – Theo and Darn. They were completely unaware of the bucket of fertiliser being held by some old rope I had found in the tool shed of the palace. As they quickly approached the small archway, Corrin and I hid in the bushes to the side of the archway waiting for them to walk under it so we could dump it on them – a form of retaliation for their latest pranks on me.

My eyes rested back on Corrin holding the same excitement and knowing what we were about to do could cost me my life and possibly Corrin's too. I knew I would take the brunt of the repercussions if Tobias found out it was me. He would go out of his way to make my life hell for it – not that he didn't already make my life hell in the first place, this prank would just give him a reason to hit me more and give me more bruises to cover up from my family and Corrin.

Yet, it didn't stop me from wanting to do it.

"Ready for anything," I replied, catching a glimpse of my green eyes on the silver blade Corrin had protruded from his satchel. He turned to me, offering a soft smile before holding out the dagger and bowing his head a little in greeting.

"Care to do the honours, my prince?"

I couldn't help but roll my eyes at his words, knowing that my status had never given me leeway with my bullies. Tobias didn't care if I was a prince destined to take over the kingdom one day. I was still weak in his eyes, unfit to even form a proper sentence without stuttering – let alone lead a sector.

My mother was a princess. My grandfather was the king who held power over the elven city of *Versai*. I was – *by title* – a prince but I have never given it much thought. I knew that this doubt and self–consciousness mainly came down to my odd complexion; tanned skin and striking green eyes. Even though I possessed my mother's blonde hair as a child – now having darkened to a light brown since I turned fifteen, I felt as though it wasn't enough to allow myself the urge to call myself a prince. A title that didn't feel right to me. One that deep down, I knew I wasn't worthy of.

Tobias' words echoed through my mind of how pathetic I was as an elf for years on end – that I would never belong here and no one would ever love me because I was hideous. His words were starting to finally break through to me and seeped into the back of my mind like a poison.

I made the mistake of breaking down in front of Corrin one day after Tobias had broken through the mental shield I had created. A shield I had put up to protect myself. His hurtful words managed to push through, and I let Corrin see me cry one time. I retold him the words used only for Corrin to take me by the shoulders and almost shake the doubt out of me, insisting that I was none of those things.

The next day, I saw Tobias in class sulking in his seat with a purple eye and broken nose. He glared at me silently with a newfound hatred unlocked.

From that day, it made me fearful of telling Corrin my thoughts ever again. The stares from Tobias were enough to scare me into silence, swearing to myself to never cry in front of Corrin again.

Overthinking his words like I always did, my heart fluttered at the mention of me being his prince but I ignored it. I grabbed the dagger from his outstretched hand and inched my body closer to the rope leading down the side wall of the arc.

I waited patiently as I heard Tobias and his minions' footsteps echo, indicating that they were getting closer to us and closer to their fate. All that could be heard around us was the buzzing of nature and Corrin and I's breathing.

I almost slipped up and cut the rope too early when Corrin's hand came to rest down on the spot between my shoulder blades and heard him inch closer to me so that he could get a better look at the scene, his hot breath washed over the tips of my pointed ears making them twitch uncontrollably.

'Damn you, Corrin. Why must you always make this difficult for me?'

With him distracting me, I almost missed my chance to cut the rope if it weren't for the visible head of Tobias coming into view. His hair was shoulder length with two small braids looping over each side of his temples before being pulled back and tied into a ponytail around the back of his head. His pale, white ears stuck out obnoxiously. I wanted to roll my eyes at his vanity.

Corrin's hair was not as long as Tobias' and my friend did not take pride in his appearance. He didn't care enough to spend hours braiding it or making it look presentable. Instead, he found comfort in throwing it back into a messy ponytail. There were two plaits on either side of his head, hanging halfway down his face from where I had braided them in boredom waiting for Tobias to finally walk his usual route upon leaving school.

My hair was short – shorter than Corrin's. I could not put mine in a ponytail or really braid it for that matter. It was a different texture that just sat atop my head sticking out at the ends, thick and obnoxiously shaggy. Sometimes it looked as if there were crows inhabiting my hair as a nest. No matter how much I brushed it, it was an impossible beast to tame.

Corrin only laughed at me when I told him this, reassuring me that my hair was not as I described and that he would still find it amusing, even if it were a nest to inhabit small creatures.

"Now is your chance Key." Corrin whispered, making my ear twitch and bringing me back to reality.

I took a breath as I looked up and noticed that Tobias and the others were standing almost directly under the bucket of fertiliser – formerly cow manure. I didn't hesitate in hacking at the rope that held up the bucket, knowing that when it did fall, Tobias would get the full blast of the fertiliser in all of its glory.

The moment was short–lived because as soon as the rope snapped, the ear–splitting sound of the bucket crashed to the ground. The horrified, oh–so–sweet screams of Tobias and his minions at the realisation of having cow manure dunked all over them filled our ears.

My eyes indulged in the sight before me. I got caught up in the moment of seeing my enemy in such a horrific situation – one he would definitely need an endless amount of bath soaks in order to get the lingering stench of dung from his body. It made me let out a small laugh.

It was quiet and short but Corrin's hands came around to clasp against my mouth to stop the sound from escaping but it didn't go unheard by Tobias.

His head quickly spun around him in search of the sound. His monstrous eyes suddenly turned and settled on me not too far away hiding in the bush. My eyes widened in fright.

"You!" Tobias screeched in a tone filled with such anger and disgust that it made me gulp.

I could sense my death nearing.

"Get the snake!" He screamed at Theo and Darn. Fortunately, by the time it took them all to stop sliding around in the fertiliser, Corrin had pulled me up to my feet and pushed me in front of him. We both turned around and ran through the small green forest near the archway, finally letting the laughter bubble from our chests as we ran from Tobias and company.

"Keep going, don't stop running, Key!" Corrin said through panting breaths as he came up to run beside me. This only made me push myself faster as I could hear the loud footsteps of our enemies running from behind us.

"You are so dead when I get you *half–mix* scum!" Came the threatening screams of Tobias from behind, making me let out a yell at the realisation of how close he actually was to us. I was starting to lag behind Corrin who was already making quick twists and turns, heading deeper into the forest. I started to feel slightly panicked, I didn't know this part of the forest well – *unlike Corrin.*

"Come on Key!" Corrin screamed from in front but I couldn't see him anymore. All I could do was keep running on the soft earth of the forest, in hopes that I was near to him.

"Cor–"

I tripped over a tree's root protruding from the earth. My body hurtled toward the ground at an inhuman speed which made me scream out.

I fell forward onto the forest floor, breaking a grass plant on the way down and banging my knee against something sharp – a small boulder.

I went to quickly get up but yelped at the warm stinging in my left leg. I slowly moved onto my back and looked down at the damage done. My knee had a large gash in it where blood was seeping out. The cut wasn't too deep, only partially grazed yet it still hurt to move on it.

There was suddenly rustling from above me and just as I was glancing up, Tobias – covered almost head to toe in manure – broke through the bushes. His eyes immediately trained on my hurt figure, glancing down at my leg.

He smirked at this, making my stomach lurch as Theo and Darn stumbled forward from behind him, also covered in manure.

"Dul inexpertia belus."

Tobias chuckled as he quoted one of the phrases from the scroll to me; referring to how I could find joy in the pranks I pull on my enemy because I don't do it very often. I was too scared to, so the small victory was sweet to me.

'War is sweet to the inexperienced.'

"It looks as though the person you counted on the most has left you," Tobias stated loudly, unable to control his patience as he clenched his teeth, looking down at me with disgust evident in his blue eyes.

"But I suppose you're used to that, right?"

My eyes widened as I took a shaky breath, inching backwards ever so slightly while my gaze stayed put on Tobias's looming figure. He resisted from making a move on me as of yet, but I knew that he wanted to wound me with his words first before going in for the kill.

"What–"

"Everyone knows the story of your mother Keylin," He interrupted with a roll of his eyes, and I froze up. "How she whored around with Dry Landers before getting herself pregnant with you. You were a mistake. You shouldn't have even been born to begin with! The gods only know how you're still here–"

"Stop it," I managed to grit out, my eyes beginning to sting with unshed tears. My fists clenched either side of my body as I looked up at Tobias.

"It's bad karma to talk ill of the dead. My mother was your queen, remember that."

Not once had Tobias mentioned my mother in all of the years that he had tormented me for being different. Everyone knew it was a touchy subject to begin with and they did not dare to talk lowly of their queen.

"She died before she became queen," Tobias pointed out, Theo and Darn chuckled to each other at the revelation. "My thoughts still stand."

My *Avus* had told me about my mother when I was younger, telling me how much she loved me and how I looked like the image of princess Fhara – my mother. I had seen her in old photographs and paintings and apart from my once blonde hair, there wasn't much resemblance to her. *Avus* said it was my spirit that reminded him of her, how my kindness towards others and selflessness shone through.

Tobias suddenly slapped me across the face, making my head lull to the side at the force he had put into the assault. My head spun from the slap as I tried to focus back on him, wincing through the stinging of skin right below my left eye on the padding of skin over bone.

Tobias grabbed a fistful of my hair and yanked my head back, making me look up with a strangled yelp of pain. I flinched away from him as he brought his head down closer to my ear and held my breath as the stench of fertiliser hit my nose.

"You're a murderer. You killed your own mater." Tobias whispered into my ear causing all of the blood to drain from my face.

I couldn't form words – let alone a snarky remark to throw back at Tobias. How could I reply to something like that? Having ignored it for so long, I didn't realise the pain that was bottled up for most of my life had led to this moment. To this realisation. I *was* a murderer because it was my fault my mother wasn't here right now. She would still be alive if it wasn't for me. I was beginning to think I would have saved everyone around me – *including myself* – a lot of hassle if I had just never been born in the first place.

"You are nothing but a Dry Lander savage. You don't belong here. In fact, do you know what we do to murderers Keylin?"

I didn't bother to answer him as I knew that it wouldn't lessen his blows or punches to my body.

"I know what I do to pathetic elves that don't know when to back off."

My eyes shot open and head spun around to look up at the voice behind me that cut Tobias off from what he was about to say next. This only made him more aggravated as his eyes fell on Corrin walking out from the bushes, an angered expression on his face. His eyes were ablaze with hate as he stared down Tobias.

"How many times has it been that I kicked your ass, Toby?" Corrin taunted with a knowing look which made me bite my lip to try and keep from smiling.

Tobias somehow noticed this and grabbed my shoulders, pushing me down to the ground with such force I couldn't help the groan that left my lips. I scrunched my eyes before another slap to my cheek made me cry out. The stinging in my left cheek only amplified as one of Tobias' long nails scratched under my eye, causing the skin to tear as blood slowly seeped out from the scratch.

I kept my eyes closed as I waited for the next hit. My breathing escalated at the anticipation but after several minutes, I peeked one eye open to look up at Tobias. His weight above me was still and unwavering.

Confused, I opened my eyes fully, scanning over Tobias's face only to find that his hateful gaze was not trained on me anymore. In fact, he looked worried; his eyes were now trained on the bushes behind me at Corrin.

I couldn't move out from under him and started to panic, not knowing what was going on or if he was ever going to get off of me.

An animalistic growl reached my ears from a few feet

away and my body stilled, eyes wide as I now sensed the presence of a powerful tiger making its way towards us. Its prints echoed with every step upon the ground as it moved towards us.

It gave another warning growl before Tobias' eyes were close to popping out of his skull and he scurried backwards, away from my body and finally setting me free. I quickly got up into a sitting position. My eyes didn't dare to look behind me when I could feel the tiger's hot breath fanning across my shoulder, it continued to growl at Tobias.

"T–That's not fair!" Tobias stammered as his gaze flickered between the animal and Corrin.

"We haven't learned how to control the animals to do what we want yet! You're older and using it to hurt minors–"

"Leave. *Now*." I heard Corrin's commanding voice not far from behind me. His voice sounded distorted as the power of the tiger coursed through his veins.

The tiger gave another warning growl from above me and I jumped slightly, forgetting it was towering over me. My eyes flew up to see it baring its teeth at Tobias and the others, its eyes a glowing purple.

I chanced a look back at Corrin to see that his eyes were that same glowing purple as the tiger's. He was crouched on the ground, his hands resting in front of him on the dirt–covered floor as he looked at Tobias. I looked down at the small string of purple light having made its way through the crevices in the dry ground, coming forward to connect with the paws of the tiger. The ground almost looked as though it had been hit by lightning. The purple light resembled the bolt that connected both elf and animal. I let out a shaky breath at how cool it actually looked.

"I'm informing the Trainor about this!" Tobias yelled in threat before quickly shutting his mouth at the warning growl the tiger made. I flinched inward from the sheer loudness and power radiating from it while myy ears rang in protest.

I didn't miss the colour draining from Tobias and his minions' faces as they quickly ran back the way they came, choosing to flee the scene and not make the tiger in any way angry.

I jolted forward as the tiger nuzzled into my shoulder with affection. A playful side came out of the animal due to Corrin's emotions being connected. It knew I wasn't a threat, unlike Tobias. When it started to lick my ears, however, I let out a strangled whine.

"Corrin – tell it to stop. Hey!–"

The tiger playfully bit at my hair. Corrin only chuckled from behind me at the sight as he made his way over to me. The connection had long been broken between the animal. In most cases when the connection was lost, the animal may still harbour the feelings of the bond, deciding whether the companion was still a threat to them or not. This tiger, however, I wasn't sure if I was being imagined as a big juicy steak or if they were just very playful.

"Down girl–" Corrin wrapped his hands around the tiger's neck, pulling her torso back playfully so that he could get to me. I sent him a relieved smile, noticing how his eyes were no longer purple and had returned to their deep blue colour. The tiger's eyes were also back to their natural colour – a piercing blue.

'Even the animals had blue eyes here. Just another example of why I was cursed to stick out like a sore thumb on this mountain.'

"Tobias is an idiot when it comes to the animals," Corrin brought me out of my thoughts as he pat the tiger's head. The tiger chuffed happily beside him.

"We don't control them. We connect with them. It gives them a greater understanding of our feelings and emotions. They can choose to break the connection at any time." Corrin explained seriously to me and I nodded at this, taking in the information before my smile suddenly began to fade. I could feel a sense of emptiness as I looked down at the dirt–covered ground. Tobias' words about me being a murderer and mentioning my mother played around in my mind.

I suddenly felt strong arms wrap around me from behind. Corrin took my hands in his as he nuzzled his head into the crook of my neck.

'Now I could see where the tiger gets it from.'

"I'm fine," I said as my throat dried up. "You don't have to worry about me. I'm used to his words by now."

Corrin held me against him as he brought his head up from my neck to let out a sigh.

"I'm sorry I wasn't here quicker." He whispered into my right ear causing it to violently twitch and almost hit him in the face. I silently cursed myself, Corrin chuckling at this only made my ear tips and nose turn red with

embarrassment.

"Your ears are always twitching around me. I can't even whisper to you anymore." Corrin stated between fits of laughter and I turned to him with a sour expression, managing to get out of his arms and push him backwards away from me. This didn't seize his laughter.

"It's not my fault – you know I have over–sensitive ears… it's not funny!"

"Okay, *okay* I'm sorry." Corrin finally admitted, regaining himself. My narrowed eyes made him smirk as he pushed himself off of the ground, patting himself of any excess dirt before holding out a hand to help me up. A charming, elvish smile now played on his features.

I took his hand in mine and got to my feet. A yelp from my lips caused me to stagger at the searing pain from my blood–covered leg, bringing me back to reality. Corrin's smile immediately faded as he turned in concern and his hand shot out to rest on my hip to steady me as he scanned my body for the injury he was looking for.

"Dammit Tobias," Corrin exhaled in frustration as he took in my injured leg before looking up to me, eyes filled with worry.

"He did this, didn't he?"

"I tripped and scraped my leg on something sharp shooting out of the ground. In the whole scheme of things, you can say it was his fault."

"Can you walk or..?"

"I think so. I mean it's not that deep–" I went to walk ahead, There was an obvious limp I failed to hide, but I continued to walk ahead unfazed, only stopping to wince every few steps. After a few moments of this pace we were going, Corrin realised that we would never get out of the forest at this speed before nightfall – he had enough.

"That's it." He stated suddenly making me stop in my tracks in confusion as I turned around to look at him perplexed.

"What? We can't stop now, or we won't get back before dark."

"I know that, and I don't want to be around here knowing it will be at your speed." I glared at him as he made his way in front of me, crouching down on his knees in front of my body. His arms reached out behind him in a ready position, looking back at me almost expectantly and I raised a brow at him.

"Hop on."

"What?"

"Come on Keylin. You need to patch that cut up and you seem in a lot of pain. Hop on my back."

"I–"

"My knees are falling asleep over here." Corrin sang sweetly and I rolled my eyes, climbing forward. My hands rested on his shoulders as my legs placed on either side of him.

He quickly grabbed hold of the backs of my thighs before I could back out, muttering a 'hold on tight' before his body lifted into the air. My eyes widened at the feeling of falling backwards and I grabbed a hold of his shoulders in fear. He quickly adjusted himself as my hands clasped tightly around his shoulders before I let them move down to plant on his chest. Pulling my thighs closer to his back, he was careful to touch my injured leg. I let my legs hang loosely.

We walked then – well *he* walked. I looked down with a wide–eyed smile, trying to keep the blush from tinting my cheeks.

Corrin was very tall, him being a contrasting six foot to my five–foot–eight frame. Needless to say, he was a tree with muscles. The fact that he could carry me on his back for so long only proved his strength and willpower. I was – *and knew* – that I could never be as strong as Corrin. Even though he was only a year older than me, the difference was remarkable, and I often felt like a child compared to him.

No wonder he had all of the girls swooning over him. With his striking good looks, he had girls lining up just to fall at his feet. But still, not as many as he should have had. That came with the downside of being friends with me. I repelled not only girls but also any creature in existence. Tobias may have had a minor impact on this but for the other part, it was true.

I didn't realise I was resting my chin on top of Corrin's head, sighing deeply until I felt his body shake. A small chuckle rumbled through his throat causing my teeth to chatter.

"What are you thinking about *pipsqueak*?"

"You do realise I'm only younger than you by one year right?" I countered with a raised brow. Corrin snorted at that, adjusting himself so that I wasn't slipping down.

"Oh, I know alright. And you can put that brow down Keylin, or it will get stuck up there."

I blushed at how well he knew me and lowered my brow, unable to contain my small chuckle. This in turn caused Corrin's ears to twitch at the sound.

"Do..." I paused, biting my lip in contemplation before deciding to ask Corrin a question that had been playing on my mind lately. "Do you think there is someone out there for everyone? That everyone gets a chance at love. But not the physical attraction kind of love but the kind of love that makes you feel warm inside. The kind that they write about in books?"

There was silence for a moment between Corrin and me. The longer the silence went on, the more I began to think that maybe I should have kept my thoughts to myself and not said anything at all.

Corrin adjusted me again on his back with a small grunt before letting out a breath.

"Was Tobias trying to get in your head again? I've told you before Keylin, don't let his words get to you. It only makes him feel better knowing he gets on your nerves."

"He gets on my nerves anyways," I muttered sadly before shaking my head. "And no, he... I was just curious I suppose."

"Well, what do you think, Key? What do you want?" Corrin prompted and I couldn't help but be confused by his words.

"Me?" I retorted. Corrin nodded in front of me and I took in a shaky breath.

"I–I don't know. I suppose I want someone to spend my life with. A *simple* life. Someone who makes me smile and laugh and... and doesn't care about my looks because it doesn't matter to them, all they see is me. The *real* me that not many people get to see. To them I... they don't see a Dry Lander or think of snakes–"

Corrin tensed at the word but relaxed when I continued.

"I'm not... I'm not a murderer." I whispered as though the words would assure me or confirm my thoughts but my bully's words seeped into my mind. My eyes began to sting as the cut from Tobias's slap under my eye made itself known again.

I jolted forward slightly when Corrin stopped in his tracks. Looking around, I could see we were out of the forest and near the gates of *Versai*. The sun was starting to set beyond the housing peaks.

Corrin didn't hesitate to lower me to the ground, turning around to place his hands on either side of my arms to keep me from going anywhere. I found his eyes fixed on me with determination. Concentration lines were evident along his forehead.

"Listen to me Keylin..." His serious tone made a cold shiver run down my spine.

"You are *not* a murderer. No matter what Tobias says to you. He's sour that you are more special than him. Keylin, you are the most kind, shy and selfless elf that I know. You could never kill someone."

"He's not far from the truth though right?" I interrupted shakily, biting down on my lip to keep from wobbling. "Everything would be better if I just wasn't born in the first place. At least then my *mater* would still be alive, my *avus* would be happy too."

"And what about me? Who would help me with my

46

Elvish High Lander?"

I sent him a small knowing smile.

'You would find someone who doesn't drag you down.'

"You would find someone better." I said quietly, avoiding his eyes.

"Are they hot?" Corrin asked casually as he kicked at stones in his tracks beside me.

"I don't know."

"Well, I need to know if my new Elvish High Lander tutor is going to be distracting or not–"

"Sure, she's hot." I entertained him and Corrin chuckled with a shake of his head. "Whatever you want Corrin."

"What I want is for my best friend to stop wishing his life away. A beautiful life, full of love and security that not many have the privilege of experiencing–"

"My life is *beautiful?*" I raised a brow at him. "The only reason I am even breathing is because of who my grandfather is. My mother is dead, I don't know who my father is – if he's even *alive*, only that he was s a Dry Lander and I'm tormented every second of every day because of how I look. What is beautiful about that?"

His silence only made the situation worse. I turned my head away and swallowed the sob that I had been trying to keep from slipping out for so long. I didn't want Corrin to see me cry so I angrily brought a hand up to wipe at my eyes.

Corrin quickly brought his hand up to rest around the back of my neck, pulling me into his chest as he held me tight. I let out a choked breath at this, trying to keep in my hurt as I clutched the piece of fabric around Corrin's chest. Corrin's hand slipped from my neck to run through my hair, tangling his fingers there as his other hand rubbed soothing circles that travelled from my shoulders to the small of my back, never stopping to rest as he tried desperately to calm me down.

"I'm fine." I assured him quietly.

"It's okay Keylin," Corrin whispered against my temple. "You can let it out. You don't have to be strong in front of me."

Those words were what I needed to hear in order to finally let go. My hands unravelled from their vice–like grip I held on Corrin's shirt, shakily moving them around his back to pull him closer to me. I cried silently into his chest. My tears stained his white shirt. I didn't know how long we had stood there in the street. Anyone could have walked by, sending us looks but I didn't care for once. In that moment, I let myself cry for the pain I had endured and the absence of my parents.

I never found out who my father was. I had asked *avus* about him, but he didn't know either. No one did. It wasn't something he really cared to look into and we all seemed to conclude that my father – *whoever he was* – was most likely dead due to the harsh conditions of the *Dry Lands*. Or worse, didn't want to know me. All I knew for sure was that he was an outsider, a Dry Lander, who my mother loved with all of her heart. She made that clear as she was dying. Grandfather told me once.

When the tears stopped falling Corrin pulled me back from his chest to look down at me. I blinked up at him, an embarrassing blush quickly rose to my cheeks when I pulled away and looked down at my shoes.

"I'm sorry."

"There's no need to be sorry, Key. You know I'm always here for you. I'm not going to run anytime soon knowing that you're hurting."

I exhaled as I looked up at him. A small smile cracked through my despair as I brought a hand up to wipe at my eyes beginning to itch.

"Thank you Corry. For everything–"

"Watch your eye," Corrin warned with a bite of his lip, grabbing my left hand from rubbing against the small cut on my face that Tobias had caused. Corrin pulled my hand down, away from the cut.

"That's going to bruise. You should get one of the servants to ice it for you."

"Don't worry. I'll be fine." I assured him with a dimpled smile. He rolled his eyes at me playfully.

"Telling me not to worry is hopeless, you know. I'm always going to worry about you."

I chuckled at this, not realising we had begun to walk towards the gates of my home. Corrin held me up slightly as he placed his arm under my far arm, allowing me to lean my weight on him as I hobbled along the small street.

"I know."

When we got to the gate, I let out a sigh of relief as the familiar servant's costume came into view. Mara stood with her arms crossed, foot tapping impatiently upon the ground as she looked around – most likely looking to scold me for being out so late on a school night.

"Alas, the shadow demon is here to take the soul of the innocent." Corrin muttered and I couldn't help but chuckle quietly at that, stopping when Mara's eyes immediately turned at the sound. Her eyes rested on me before they narrowed on Corrin. Her hate towards him was always evident on her face. She had never liked Corrin from the start, and I would never understand why.

"More like the predator finally catching its prey." I muttered back, glancing down at my leg with a wince.

"Keylin!" Mara exclaimed as she threw open the gates and hurried towards me, eyes ablaze with both concern and anger. Something I didn't know could happen.

"What happened to – you know what? Don't even answer that. I know for sure that he most likely had something to do with it." She narrowed her eyes purposely at Corrin as she took me from Corrin's hold. Corrin held up his now free arms in surrender with a wide–eyed look.

"Me? Mara if it wasn't for me–"

"Save it." She ordered and I chuckled at the gobsmacked look on Corrin's face.

All too quickly, I was being half–dragged, half–pulled inside the gates and through the small path leading up to the palace. From behind, I could hear the words being shouted by Corrin, the same words he had been shouting at me since we were six years old and I couldn't help the smile from gracing my features.

"Di quasi la momento per santo ani!"

'Learn as if you're always going to live; live as if tomorrow you're going to die!'

II

~*~

"Boys and their stupid games."

Mara muttered from where she sat on the chair in front of me as she dunked the white cloth into the water basin at her side. I looked around the small kitchen where the servants ate and spent most of their free time when not attending to my grandfather or me.

"Why can't you all be less violent to one another? It would save me from having to throw out all of the white linen cloth." She mumbled angrily to herself as she pressed the damp cloth to my cut cheek, making me flinch away. She quickly grabbed the uninjured part of my face and brought me back closer to her where she could clean the small wound. I opened my eyes and stared at her.

"I try, Mara, but they don't like me. Every time I try to talk to one of my classmates, they ignore me or throw things at me."

I sighed as I said these words. The words that I had been trying to tell Mara for a while now but she either chose not to listen or dwell on the fact that even if she wanted to do something, she couldn't, because she was only a servant. Going out of her way for me would result in her most likely losing her job. She needed the money to pay for her children's schooling. I could see why she couldn't risk it. I didn't blame her, nor did I blame any of the servants. They don't treat me like the other children but then again, they didn't really talk to me unless they had to. Mara was the only one who willingly talked to me and took care of me.

"Throw things back."

Mara mumbled after shushing me to keep my voice down.

I wasn't allowed to be in here because it was for servants only. Little did they know, I had been coming here for a while now with Mara as she cleaned my cuts and tried to help me hide the bruises from *avus*. The last thing we all needed was *avus* causing a commotion that could lead everyone to go against him as I was not what they expected a prince to look like.

My eyes widened as I looked up to Mara, not having expected her to actually encourage me to help myself. I supposed that was all she could do besides staying silent. I'm glad she doesn't though. It made me feel like she cared for me when in reality she probably didn't and only encouraged me so that she would have less work to do when cleaning my cuts.

"I can't, if I do it gets worse." I let out a sigh and when

I looked back up, I swore I saw a look of concern cross Mara's features but it was probably just a grimace, knowing any other eighteen–year–old could take Tobias and his minions on with no problem. I was weak, and apart from being so, I had no intention to fight them.

"*Besides*, I'm in enough trouble with them as it is." I muttered, remembering my cry–fest with Corrin. I knew he was going to get revenge on Tobias for this. I could expect a lot more pain to be inflicted in the coming days and my stomach felt uneasy just thinking about it.

"That Corrin boy brings you nothing but trouble." She took the cloth away from my cheek and threw it gracefully into the water basin to clean for later.

"*Transist la drima permatcha*." I quoted a verse from the ancient scrolls to her while she scoffed in displeasure, rolling her eyes at me.

'*Shadow passes, light remains*'

I supposed I was referring to how even the darkest of times with Tobias must come to an end and when it did, I had Corrin, my light through all of this.

It was silent for another few moments as Mara cleaned the dirt from my wounded leg, muttering to herself but I chose not to listen and distracted myself with my thoughts instead. A few minutes passed and Mara was quickly bandaging my leg with a thin layer of cloth before she was helping me down off of the table and practically shoving me towards the doors, ushering me out before someone could catch me.

I turned back with a smile, my dimples poking out as I quickly gave her a peck on the cheek.

"*Moa* Mara."

"You can thank me by buying me some more cloth child, now *shoo*." She ushered me out of the kitchen with her hands. I didn't miss the small smile that graced her features when I thanked her. I smiled at that, rolling my eyes at her stubbornness and limping out of the kitchen, making my way to the staircase where I awaited the struggles of climbing it in order to get to my bedroom.

When I – *finally* – made it up the stairs, I panted and puffed out of breath from the sudden upper body movement and strength that I needed to use. Although I was fit, I was not the strongest of boys. I felt as though the only reason I had some sort of stamina was because of all the running Corrin and I always did, mostly running for fun or running away from my problems; aka Tobias.

"Keylin?"

I turned at the sound of my grandfather's voice behind me, spotting his approaching form and walking over to me with furrowed eyebrows. His long white hair fell down over his shoulders, braid–less.

"Keylin son, you should be in bed. It is late."

I let out a tired sigh at my *avus's* worrying voice. The concern was evident in his striking features as he scanned my face. I apologised.

"*skoozat,* grandfather. I'm just heading there now."

"Keylin, what happened to your face?" He immediately came closer and took my chin in his large hand, turning my face to the side to examine the bruise forming under my eye despite my protests. My face scrunched up as I insisted it was nothing but a scratch, but he didn't believe me.

"*O mi sona...*" He worried and I let out a breath, closing my eyes briefly as he brought me in for a hug, his hair tickling my nose and I had to hold in my sneeze.

"*Avus*, I am fine." I tried to assure him but my words seemed to get lost somewhere in his hair as he crushed me with his bear hug.

"Was it another boy? Were you fighting over a girl?"

Oh, how I wished for nothing more than my life to be that simple. My grandfather really buried his head in the sand when it came to my personal life throughout the years, always being too busy to sit down and hear of my worries – that was Mara's job.

Avus had duties to attend. Important ones, seeing as he was a member of the elite sectoral supremacy, he was constantly being whisked into meetings or travel.

The sectoral supremacy existed for the sole purpose of trade between sectors, making sure that products and goods travelled between sectors and neither was cut off completely from another. People may not have had the luxury of travelling between sectors but that didn't mean spices from the *Dry Lands* could not wind up in the *Sky Lanes*, or the richest of fruits and jewellery from the *High Peaks* could not be traded for iron from the *Shadows*. Every sector had a purpose, a system in place. To go against a well–structured agenda would cause the ruination of multiple sectors.

My grandfather was an overseer in getting people what they needed. I couldn't hold such a responsibility against him. My struggles in making friends at the time were miniscule compared to his and I didn't want to burden him. Over time I learned to either deal with it on my own or leaned on Corrin and Mara for help. They were my only real friends apart from the castle guards and servants. My grandfather didn't particularly want me to have a social life as such. He believed it would be better if I stayed behind the castle walls, *safer*. I had everything I needed here.

Still, I wished for things to have been different. It would have been nice to be closer to my grandfather. Maybe I wouldn't have had to rely on Corrin for most of my life.

"Just a small altercation with a boy, *avus*, no need to worry."

"I should worry about who crosses you. You have a sharp tongue when angry *mi sona*." My grandfather's eyes crinkled at the sides when a smile stretched across his face in amusement.

'A sharp tongue like a Dry Lander. Just another foreign trait that made me different.'

My ear tips grew pink as did the small blush tinting my cheeks and nose as I tried to look anywhere besides my grandfather out of embarrassment.

"Keylin," My grandfather placed his hand on my shoulder in comfort. "Life has a strange way of challenging us, of moulding us into the person we are destined to be. You have it harder than other elves but that doesn't mean you are any less worthy. You were blessed with two paths of life. All I ask is you walk with pride down the one you choose."

"Thank you, *avus*." I said and bid goodnight to him before scurrying as fast as I could down the corridor to my room, hobbling like an injured animal in the process.

"You can talk to me, Keylin, I'm always here for you."

He started to call down the corridor and I could only sigh with both embarrassment and tiredness. Sleep was the only thing I needed right now as the calls from my grandfather echoed down the palace halls. His words of 'I love you' made me smile.

"Ch'io Keylin."

***

"I suppose it could be worse. At least when he shouts that he loves you for everyone in the city to hear, it's a good sign right?"

I lifted my head from my hands to look at Corrin, a small smile on my features as I considered his words.

"I don't know Corrin..." I bit my lip as my eyebrows furrowed. "He used to be so quiet around me and then a few years ago he started smiling more, telling me he loves me – he used to never do that. It's as if he thinks by doing so will bring us closer or like he's going to lose me or something." I voiced my thoughts looking down below at the elves walking along the streets, not realising that if they simply looked up they would see two misfit elves above them perched on the wall that protects the city of *Versai*.

"Maybe he's only now realising how much of a gem you really are and afraid to lose touch with you when you turn twenty–one."

It wasn't decided what would become of me when I turned twenty–one. I still had time to figure it out, I was near the end of my eighteenth year; the leaves were soon to change colour from their fresh bright green, and I was slowly coming onto my last winter before turning nineteen.

'It's not as if I have a choice, I am the heir to the *High Peaks* – the *only* heir.' It was a realistic thought – that the only reason I was alive was to continue my grandfather's bloodline. I would most likely marry a neighbouring princess when I finished my schooling. As much as *avus* insisted that wasn't true, the doubt remained at the back of my mind. I was alive for a purpose, to run the kingdom when it would pass to me.

For as little as we did see each other now, our interactions would be even more scarce when I became king.

Corrin lightly shoved me out of my thoughts, and I chuckled at this, turning to him and shoving him back, deciding at that moment it was probably best not to shove each other while perched on a wall side.

We continued to play–fight each other, completely forgetting about watching the quickly lowering sunset that Corrin insisted on doing. It was only when Corrin had me in a headlock and was shaking out my messy hair as he did so (as if it wasn't already messy enough) that I finally gave in.

"Okay *okay*! You win Corrin now let me go!" I stated in between fits of laughter. He always won our fights; I didn't know why he even attempted to let me win half of the time, from his muscles alone he could flatten me.

"Not until you tell me you love me." Corrin teased with a smirk. I couldn't stop my ears from twitching and a hot blush flooded my features at his random request.

"W–what?"

"You heard me." He smirked down at me. His breath fanned my ears making them twitch uncontrollably to the point where I just wanted out of this situation, to spare my ears at least.

"*Ch'io.*" I said, just audible for him to hear and he clicked his tongue at that. His smile and eyes glistened as he looked down at me.

"Louder."

"Ch'io."

"Come on you can do better–"

"*Ch'io! Ch'io* Corrin okay? Now let me go *peshla*!" I demanded at the top of my lungs.

I was not a violent person and never found the need to raise my voice. Somehow, Corrin always found a way to pull me out of my comfort zone, forcing me to experience things that normally I would have been too shy to do on my own. I was glad he did.

Corrin laughed lightly and released me from my hold. I turned my glaring gaze on him, watching him laugh softly.

"No need to shout Keylin, you'll wake everyone up."

"*Katcha.*" I cursed and he laughed at that before stopping to gasp, his eyes widening in feign hurt as he clutched his chest dramatically.

"I am wounded Keylin Degrassi."

"You deserve it Corrin Ruffelio." I played along and just to add to my point, I stuck my tongue out at him, causing him to raise his eyebrow at me before muttering how I was acting childish. I couldn't help but chuckle at that, shaking my head with a small smile and looking out at the quickly darkening streets leading to the market square of Versai, a feeling of contentment washed over me.

"*Moa.*" I thanked him when a comfortable silence encompassed us. I closed my eyes, letting out a breath I hadn't realised I was holding and finally felt relaxed. Corrin had that effect on me. He didn't follow the rules like everyone else. If rules were made of glass, Corrin would smash them to pieces with an axe. He didn't care what people thought of him in general. He was free–spirited. I was slowly learning his ways.

Learning how to be free.

Corrin's laughter died down soon after those words had left my mouth. He continued to focus his smile and attention on me, the glowing light of the moon now visible from where we both were perched on the wall. My feet dangled over the edge.

"What are you thanking me for?"

"For being my friend." I turned to him, dimples poking out from either side of my face as I smiled.

"When I'm with you… I forget who I am for a moment. There is no responsibility or doubt. I'm just happy. It makes me feel free. I like who I am when I'm with you."

There is a glint in Corrin's eyes as he looked down at

me. His ears twitched ever so slightly from my words before he looked away, letting out a small cough and settling his gaze on the moon above us. The smile still on his face illuminated from the light of the moon where a small rosy blush tinted his cheeks.

"I should get you home before Mara sends out a search party."

I chuckled at that, watching Corrin hop down the five–or–so–metre wall effortlessly. He quickly regained his footing before turning around to hold open his arms for me. I chuckled at that, rolling my eyes as I tried to land gracefully but almost fell forward due to my still injured – *but healing* – leg. Luckily, Corrin was there to catch me before I embarrassed myself further.

***

"How is the leg holding up? You're not limping as much."

My limp had lessened quickly in the past twenty–four hours to where the limp was almost non–existent. There was still a small bit of pain when I walked but nothing compared to how it was before when I couldn't even put pressure on my left leg without hissing. It was good that it was showing signs of quick healing. The bruises on my face however were still evident. The cut was becoming smaller, but I knew that the purple bruise would be there for a while.

"It's getting there. Doing things like jumping off walls is probably not making it any better though."

I said to Corrin pointedly who only raised his hands in

surrender, a smile spread across his face as he walked beside me.

"I suppose that is sort of my fault but *you,* on the other hand, are easily led."

I snorted at that, looking down at the dirt road in front of me. I kicked a small pebble in front of my line of vision and watched it skid forward until finally coming to a stop beside a well.

"Did you make up your mind yet on if you're going to the end of schooling party?" Corrin suddenly asked, making me frown and turn my head to look at him with a thoughtful expression.

"I don't know... Tobias is definitely going to be there, along with my classmates who hate me. If I go the night would most likely end with me in the river *liesion*."

Corrin scoffed at that, kicking my stone that had perched itself beside the well and sending it skipping in a different direction before landing a good distance ahead of us in a dark corner.

"I think you should go," Corrin said seriously, making me blink at him in confusion. I was about to ask if he, in fact, injured his head on the way down from the wall when he spoke what was playing on his mind.

"You shouldn't let your classmates intimidate you. They're all weak–minded beings who are forced into this society to think that having light hair and pale blue eyes is beautiful and the 'normal' look. How can we all be beautiful if we all look the same? Doesn't that mean no one is beautiful because we are being pushed to look a certain way, act a certain way. Feel a..."

Corrin trailed off, his voice dying in his throat as his gaze locked on something ahead of us.

I frowned up at him in confusion, wondering what it was that caused him to stop talking. My eyes shifted to where Corrin was looking, trying to figure out what it was that made him suddenly forget his words.

'An animal perhaps?'

"What is it?" I asked after a moment of silence, suddenly getting the feeling as if there were eyes on me, watching from the very depth of the dark as I walked down the dimly lit street. A cold shiver ran up my spine at the thought of eyes on us – like a predator watching its prey.

Feeling paranoid, I turned around. All of the blood drained from my face as I caught the end of something moving around in the dark.

Whatever it was, it didn't want to be found.

"C–Come on let's go," Corrin whispered just loud enough for me to hear. This didn't make me any less panicked now, knowing that Corrin was riddled with fear put me on edge. The best thing to do right now was to get home, maybe tell *avus* a wild animal was roaming the streets of *Versai*.

"Stay close to me Key." Corrin whispered as he turned his head, holding out his hand for me to take so that we wouldn't be separated in the dark.

"Okay."

I took his hand in mine, letting out a short breath as I looked around me. The street was familiar to me, even in the darkness, however... tonight felt different.

It was eerily quiet for some reason and I had a bad feeling that something terrible was going to happen.

As Corrin and I weaved our way through the dimly lit streets and alleyways littered with homes filled with sleeping elves, I couldn't help but begin to feel safer. Maybe it was knowing that we were getting closer to the palace gates or because Corrin was the one beside me, dragging me along so that we could get to safety. I knew I was safe with him. We didn't know if our lives were in danger as nothing bad ever really happened in *Versai*.

Murder was against the law and punishable by death.

That was until Corrin pulled me to a stop, pushing me behind an empty market cart before pulling me down into a crouching position. His eyes focused on something ahead in horror.

"What–"

Corrin quickly pulled me into his chest. His hands covered my mouth from uttering another word as he shushed me – motioning for me to stay quiet. I watched him in wide–eyed confusion as he pointed slowly ahead of him and I followed the direction of his pointed finger before looking up.

My eyes settled on what looked to be a man, dressed in black. His boots were black leather. A large fur coat hung off of his shoulders and was held onto his body by a clasp buckle across his chest. I almost gasped at his complexion if it wouldn't result in drawing unnecessary attention that we didn't need right now.

His hair was dark. It may be lighter in sunlight, but under the moon, the hair stood out as black as a raven. His skin was a deep golden brown. The only thing that made him visible in the night. It wasn't clear to see his eyes but thinking of what we were taught in school, I could only assume that they were dark brown, hazel or green.

A *Dry Lander*.

I watched as the foreign man held a weapon in his hands, only then did I realise the red paint around his eyes when the light from the moon shone down upon him, giving life to his menacing features. It looked as though he was wearing a mask over his eyes and his warm skin – like a canvas for the war paint.

I tried to keep my breathing even as I took the man in but my mind swirled with questions.

Who was this man?

But more importantly, why was a Dry Lander here – at *High Peaks*? It was forbidden to cross sectors. Did this man really wish for death to come to him?

A sinking feeling told me that this man wasn't alone and by him being here, it could only lead to destruction.

III

~*~

Once we made sure the man was out of sight, Corrin didn't waste time in grabbing my hand again and pulling me up and away from the cart we had been hiding behind.

We ran then, down the empty street where the Dry Lander had emerged from. It made me wonder how he got into our city in the first place. Versai had elven soldiers constantly guarding the entrance to our kingdom around the clock, patrolling the outskirts and along the perimeter of the wall. It was well protected to ensure something like this could never happen but really, it was all for show. No sector could ever cross into another. No one ever dared to challenge the rules that had been set in stone since the Great War happened. No one wanted to revisit a time of famine and bloodshed and *darkness*.

Somehow, the man managed to slip past the soldiers unnoticed, whether from pure luck or advanced planning. He must have known the exact time the soldiers switched to patrol the wall and entrance, taking care to know the moment in which a weakness in our defence would occur. This was the sort of planning that would set a person back months, of watching and waiting.

Or maybe he attacked the soldiers, going as far as to kill them to get inside.

We were not prepared for something like this – a raid, certainly not against Dry Landers. They were highly skilled barbarians — savages who were ruthless in battle. We were told that if we ever came across one, we would be lucky to leave with our lives. They were mercenaries while we were simple keepers of peace. It was against our beliefs and nature to engage in battle. What problem could the *Dry Lands* have with us?

The thought gave me shivers.

Corrin quickly stopped in our tracks to pull me behind the edge of a household, holding me close as he snuck a peak over the wall at another Dry Lander who was quickly coming down the way – the same way that we were heading with his axe in hand as he looked frantically around at the buildings.

'Was he looking for something?' I observed.

Corrin gripped my forearm tightly as the man passed by us, failing to notice us hidden within the dark only metres away from him. It was only when the man had turned a corner, disappearing out of view that I allowed myself to let out a sigh of relief. Corrin's body relaxed too from its tense stand and he let go of my forearm.

"You'll have to make a run for the gates when I tell you." Corrin breathed out and my eyes widened. He pointed down the street to where a small lamp was visible, casting over a set of jet–black gates.

The *palace*.

"You're not coming?" I turned to him in alarm.

"I can't," He gulped. "I have to get back home to my family. I need to make sure they're okay." Corrin replied, his lips pressed in a thin line as worry for his family was evident on his features. His little sister, Ava, was his main concern after having heard the remnants of a scream from around the housing areas. We hoped it was just our imagination playing tricks on us.

There was not only one outsider. It was clear now that there were more, a lot more. We were being attacked in the middle of the night for reasons I didn't know.

We both knew that we needed to start running to get to safety and fast. It wouldn't take long before everyone was waking up to the realisation that we were under attack from the Dry Landers. It was crucial to use the little time we had before elves started to litter the streets in chaos and pandemonium.

As much as I knew that Corrin couldn't come back to the safety of the palace with me – choosing to go to search for his family, I didn't want him to leave. I couldn't shake the feeling of something terrible happening if we were to separate. It played on my mind and I was lying if I said that I wasn't worried. If something terrible were to happen or if gods forbid, he was to have a run–in with one of the merciless Dry Landers...

"Peshla, es secura."

'Please, be safe.' I whispered out as I quickly rose on my toes to embrace him.

When I pulled back, he smiled down at me but it was a sad smile. The type of smile I knew him to give when he was afraid. He couldn't promise me anything. This could be our last time to see each other as far as I was aware.

"And you." He replied softly before he pushed me forward in the direction of the lamp post, telling me in Elvish High Lander to run.

I ran as fast as my feet could carry my injured body, running down the dark street in front of me and willing myself not to look back. My heart was beating erratically in my chest, my blood now coursing through my veins as I forced myself to run faster.

My eyes landed on the black gates, the gates of home. I was relieved when they came into view. My sprint slowed to a small jog as I approached them.

Mara wasn't there waiting for me this time tapping her wrist with her index finger to indicate how late it was. She must have given up when it turned shortly after midnight, sensing that I had probably stayed over at Corrin's house – as I usually did most nights that weren't school nights. However, this was no typical weekend night. The sun was not far away from rising and I was locked out of the palace. I shook the gate handles to confirm before cursing when I realised that I was indeed, locked out.

I started to do the only thing I believed was logical at that moment in time and climbed the gates.

It was not the first time that I was forced to climb the gates of my own home in order to get inside. The first time was several years ago, when Tobias and his minions had continued to chase me from school the entire way home.

This was a day when Corrin was sick and wasn't at the school gates to greet me like he always did before walking back with each other, as we always would.

I thought of the memory as the painted–over rust on the gate connected with my palms and I grimaced at the peeling texture. Nonetheless, I continued to climb, staying close to the high wall beside the gate for me to use as leverage instead of touching the sharp pointed spikes of metal at the top of the gates.

I lifted my arm over and up to rest on the smooth surface of the wall, hauling myself up as I readied to jump down.

I made the jump, my body plummeting to the ground where I landed on my feet. The sudden jolting feeling travelled up my foot and into my upper leg. I hissed at the pain riding up my injured leg but limped forward. I glanced momentarily back at the gates when I stopped in my tracks, trying to suppress the scream from leaving my mouth.

Right up behind the gates stood a dark–haired young hunter wearing almost exactly the same attire as the first Dry Lander Corrin and I came across back in the streets. Only this Dry Lander looked different. The fur coat wasn't as thick as the others – or the same mix of cool and warm–toned colours. It was jet black. I almost wouldn't have seen him if it weren't for the light of the lamp post capturing his figure. A large axe caught my eye that was positioned between the boy's belt.

'Easy access.' I thought.

I stared at him with wide eyes as I curiously took in his

features. His skin was not as dark as the others but still sun–kissed. His hair was the colour of rich chocolate and his eyes – a forest of green, almost mesmerising to look at if he weren't gazing at me with a look that would freeze over even the hottest of fires. His jaw clenched as both of his hands pressed on either side of the bars above his head.

He glowered at me before he stuck his hand out expectantly, uttering words to me in a language I didn't understand, voice deep and causing my blood to run cold.

"Otvis da gata."

I didn't understand what he was trying to say as he looked in at me with a sternness, impatiently making a gesture with his hand to come to him. I shook my head at him, trying to mask my fear but my heart rate accelerated as I took a step back.

'Where are the guards?'

He suddenly pushed the gate forward before quickly stepping back to assess its sturdiness. The gate responded with a worrying 'groan'. Its age was now its weakness. This was enough to make me jolt back to reality.

I turned back to the palace. My legs now woke up as I pushed forward in what was a half–jog half–limp.

I needed to warn *avus* and the servants – assuming they didn't already hear. They needed to know that we were under attack. They needed to know that Dry Landers were roaming the streets of *Versai*.

***

"Avus!" I burst through the front doors of the palace. My

fearful voice bounced off of the walls of my home. I staggered inside as servants looked out from their assigned rooms on the common floor, followed shortly after by Mara and *avus* who were quickly descending the master staircase. Mara, with a murderous expression on her face, struggled to tie her nightgown.

"Keylin Degrassi! Do you have any idea what tim–"

"Dry Landers are attacking *Versai*," I panted out, cutting Mara off from scolding me. My eyes – which always gave away more emotion than I often noticed – must have shown outright fear in them.

"They were wandering the streets – Corrin and I saw them!–"

I pointed behind me to the figure where I imagined he had followed my lead in climbing the gate but when I turned around, the only creaking of aged iron came from a breeze of air.

'Where did he go?'

My heart pounded in my ears, twitching furiously as I scanned the grounds for the fur–coated intruder.

"There was one just there, at the gate. He spoke to me in a foreign tongue."

Mara opened and closed her mouth before deciding to look at my grandfather with a strained expression.

"*Impossible…*" He muttered. Although my grandfather didn't see the Dry Lander behind the gate, he looked fearful and bellowed for Alfus, the head of patrol. A field mouse couldn't slip past him, certainly not a swarm of Dry Landers.

In my daze, I felt the gentleness of a hand caress my

face, scanning for signs of physical harm before it was pressed to my forehead. I met Mara's gaze.

"I don't have a fever Mara, I know what I saw."

Those forest–green eyes flashed in my mind and I turned back to the gate again, searching for a sign of him, anything that would prove that I was telling the truth.

A bright–eyed Alfus arrived not a moment later looking confused at the commotion so early in the morning. Before he could open his mouth, my grandfather spoke clearly.

"My grandson claims to have spotted Dry Landers roaming *Versai*. Wake everyone. Find the trespassers but do not kill them. They will answer to the *Sky Lanes* for breaking the sectoral code."

"Yes, my king." Alfus stiffened at the command from my grandfather, growing alert as he barked orders at the quickly appearing elven guards in silver tunics. They wore masks that looped around their ears. Only their mouth, forehead and eyes were visible. Their hair was tied back out of their faces that flowed majestically down their backs and over the pouch of silver–tipped arrows – their weapon of choice.

"Come Keylin."

My grandfather ushered me inside where servant elves were frantically scurrying around now that the alarm had been officially sounded. Dozens of guards littered the hallways, taking up positions both inside and outside the palace. Mara clung to my side, choosing to loop her arm through mine instead of joining the rest of the maids. I didn't question her on it. Even when my heart felt as though it was about to explode in my chest, it brought me comfort in knowing she was by my side.

My grandfather, Mara and I were accompanied by a few other servants and escorted to the basement of the palace where we would reside until the search was done and the Dry Landers were captured. No one knew how long it would take. The search could go on for days but if there was one thing the elves were good at, it was tracking.

Our sharpened hearing gave us an advantage over the Dry Landers even if physical skill was our weakness. We could be cunning and smart when we wanted to be. It was the only thing that we knew could prevail against Dry Landers if the worst came to battle. I didn't want to think of the possibility that the elves could become overpowered by the Dry Landers.

What then? Would they slaughter us? Take us prisoner? Torture us? A plethora of possibilities and 'what ifs' made me restless. Although sleep called for me, I was wide awake. I couldn't rest until these monsters were found.

***

I remember learning about the sectors when I was very young.

The Shadows were of the northern and furthest part of Sorn, known to be filled with creatures of evil. No elf was ever to find themselves there – for whatever reason. It was against everything the elves believed. Good does not and should never mix with evil. They taught us that it was wise to forget the sector even existed entirely.

But aside from those beings, there were the hunters from the *Dry Lands*. Mara told me that they were barbarians who had learned from a young age how to kill. That they wouldn't hesitate to kill us if they believed we were of no value to them.

I didn't know if I could defend myself if I ever came up against one – *a child I mean*, as all hope of going up against a fully–grown Dry Lander who has had a lifetime of experience would have the same outcome as throwing a rabbit into a nest of wolves, *starved* wolves.

Although I trained for years in archery, hunted rabbits and other small animals to improve my skill, I prayed today would not be the day that I would put that long–retired skill to use.

That was why when the basement door opened for the first time since being closed, everyone held their breath – only to release it a moment later when the familiar silver tunic came into view and a frowning Alfus strode in, dishevelled and sleep–deprived.

What time of day was it?

"Did you find them?" My grandfather wasted not a second in his search for answers, having spent the last hours silently pacing.

More guards filtered in through the basement door, helping elves get to their feet. I noticed Alfus' eyes dart to me before he sent my grandfather a tight–lipped shake of his head.

"There was no spotting of Dry Landers at the front gates. We scoured the city… it is possible that they may have retreated to their sector when the alarm was raised."

'Or possible that they were never here at all,' Is what I believed he truly felt.

My ears burned from embarrassment as I felt the judgemental stares linger on me from servants and guards alike. Mara clutched my hand when my grandfather scratched the back of his head.

"Thank you Alfus. Tell me, how startled are the elves?"

"*Very*, Your Highness." Alfus cleared his throat. 'It would be best, sir, to address them personally on the false–"

"Are you sure?"

Silence encompassed the room as all eyes trained on me.

"Are you sure they are gone? Corrin and I saw them – did you check the grounds? At the gate–"

"Everywhere has been searched, my prince." Alfus smiled, his lip curled ever so slightly upward in a smugness that made my blood boil.

"*Although*," Alfus pulled something out of his pocket and held it up clearly for everyone to see.

"When searching the palace, I did find mushroot in the prince's chambers. Hallucinations are common when under the influence."

I scoffed in astonishment at Alfus' attempt to discredit and accuse me of being out of my mind, somehow coming to dream up this belief that we were under attack by Dry Landers.

There was an echo of gasps from around the room before most servants and guards scurried to the exit, knowing that this was a familial matter not meant for curious ears.

"I don't take mushroot." I turned pleadingly to my grandfather. His silence made me worry that he would fall for this trick, knowing that he was embarrassed and less likely to trust my judgment now that it was proven wrong.

"I swear on this. Alfus is lying Avus–"

"That will be all Alfus, thank you."

Alfus gave a curt bow to my grandfather before exiting the basement, leaving only Mara, grandfather and I. Mara was the first to speak.

"I knew that Corrin boy was trouble from the start." Mara sniffled, taking her hand from me to rub tiredly over her face.

"No Mara – *neither of us* take mushroot. You know me. I'm telling you the *truth*, we saw Dry Landers–"

"That's enough Keylin." My grandfather finally spoke making me turn to him. The disappointment was clear on his face which made my heart sink.

"You don't believe me."

"I did believe you wholeheartedly but I began to wonder why you were outside in the middle of the night with this Corrin boy and not in your bed sleeping," He sighed tiredly. "Keylin, I have always given you your space but I fear that I have been neglectful as a parent to you. I have not fulfilled my duties as your guardian. For that, I am sorry."

I gulped as he met my gaze for the first time. Shame and betrayal filled his eyes.

"From now on, you are barred from interacting with

Corrin. He is not to enter the palace from this day forth."

***

Life continued in *Versai* the days following Corrin and I had spotted the Dry Landers. Soon, the tense air dissolved and everyone returned to their cheerful selves, well, almost everyone.

Corrin was disappointed when I broke the news to him that he couldn't come to the palace anymore but not nearly as disappointed when I told him that our late–night gallivanting was now no more. Until Avus had calmed down at least. He couldn't keep me from seeing Corrin. He was the only friend I had here.

When I told Corrin about Alfus lying to my grandfather's face and pulling out a bag of mushroot, he almost saw red.

"What a piece of trash elf! I know for a fact he only did that to hide his own love for mushroot. If your grandfather found out his top guard wasn't doing his job properly, he would be demoted. But to blame it on you? *Pathetic*."

"I'll figure something out." I bit my lip as I kicked a pebble at my feet. I had more pressing matters on my mind – Tobias being right up there.

We were yet to talk about what we saw.

"Don't worry about Tobias Key," Corrin sighed as he walked by my side with his hands in his pockets and schooling satchel over his shoulder.

"I'll make sure he–"

"*Corrin*." I stopped on our walk to school. "What if

they come back?"

Corrin ran a hand through his hair before turning to me, offering a tired smile.

"I'll beat them up."

"Please be serious, this is no time for joking," I frowned. "Do you not remember what we saw that night?"

"Of course, *yes*. I do. I just… it's been a week Key. If the Dry Landers wanted to attack, they would have done so that night, but they didn't. I'm starting to doubt myself if what we saw that night was even real. You know the rules, sectors can't cross."

"I just… I can't shake the feeling of being watched." I subconsciously covered my arms as a cold breeze blew, making my ears twitch.

"It wouldn't surprise me if your grandfather decided to have someone watch you from afar," Corrin chuckled before moving to sling an arm across my shoulder.

"Don't worry *pipsqueak*. All will be well again soon. For now, let's focus on getting back on your grandfather's good side."

***

All was in fact, not well with my grandfather. Grovelling needed to be made on my part – a lot of it.

That night, I couldn't sleep. I laid awake in bed mulling over the events in my mind from a week ago, wondering if it was all in my head. Had we imagined it, this sort of hallucination from lack of sleep? Was the noise that we heard only just that, an animal? One we dreamed of as something more?

I left my chambers and headed to the bathroom to wash my face. The feeling of cold water would clear my mind and help me sleep. I had schooling in the morning and needed all of the rest I could.

As I left the bathroom, a cold breeze flicked at my cheek making me turn in the direction of the large open bay window.

'Did one of the servants forget to close it?'

I didn't remember it being open when I first walked to the bathroom, then again, I was preoccupied with thoughts of animal fur and dark forest–green eyes. The more I thought of it, the more I started to believe that it was indeed an animal that Corrin and I saw that night. It had to be.

A drop in temperature from my room had my ears twitching and hairs standing upright on my body. My window that led onto my balcony was opened.

Stiffly and starting to doubt my own sanity – maybe I *was* on mushroot but wasn't aware, I hesitantly made my way to it. Even though it was still dark out, the moon illuminated a blue hue where I could just make out the pillars of the balcon–

Something glimmered on the wall tied above my balcony. *Rope.*

I inhaled sharply when I failed to notice it before. I thought it was the wind but *no.* The wind did not make a sound of weight being shifted across the floorboards.

I spun around, mouth dropping open to scream as I came face to face with those haunting eyes, dark forest green.

I only had a moment to register his strange attire. It blended into the night, only the bridge of his nose up was visible. The rest of his face was covered in a black mask but the fabric across his mouth was down as he held up his palm and blew dust into my face.

The dust caught in my throat and latched around my lungs, trapping the scream from leaving my throat. Everywhere burned. My eyes watered and my ears rang as I stumbled backwards away from the Dry Lander, feeling as though I was suffocating on hot dust.

My vision swam, I tried to focus my attention on breathing and the Dry Lander standing in the middle of my room.

A Dry Lander was standing in the middle of my room.

'Heh!' I tried to scream but it only came out as a hoarse whisper, one that still wouldn't wake sleeping elves to alert them of an attack from inside the palace.

My knees gave out from the lack of oxygen flowing to my brain. I only just registered the Dry Lander scuffling by me, not at all concerned. My ears twitched at an echo of noise he was making from the balcony and I took the chance, my only chance. With a laboured intake of air, I rushed to my bedroom door.

Hands latched around my stomach, pulling me back into the room. His hands caged my body and pulled me up over his shoulder as if I weighed nothing more than a sack of feathers. I kicked out, squirming in his grasp as I tried to reach for the door, coming to the realisation that I'd rather die than be taken from my home by these monsters

"Heh!"

I unleashed my frustration by lashing out against his back with my fists, hoping it would cause some sort of reaction from him. All I received was a grunt in reply.

Through my thrashing, I failed to realise he had taken me out onto the balcony until he was putting me down to sit on the ledge.

I managed to punch him right before he pushed me backwards.

With a gasp and a last–minute attempt to cling to him from falling to my death, I grazed his mask before tumbling from my balcony.

A moment of relief washed over me when the thought of this being a dream entered my mind. I would wake up from this nightmare when I hit the ground.

The nightmare only continued when I felt a prickly cushion of hay hit my back and foreign words were spoken in hushed tones around me.

My scream was the same level of a cough now. Another scream would alert–

A hand clamped over my mouth and pulled me to a corner of the small occupied wagon as another held something sharp to my neck. He wore the same attire as the kidnapper from my room only his hazel eyes were menacing, daring me to scream again so that he could see the colour of elven blood.

The Dry Lander from my room landed into the hay with a 'floof' before rolling to the side with ease.

Foreign words were exchanged between the hunters as I quickly scanned my surroundings.

There were six in total. One of them was in the middle of placing tape over my mouth when my vision went dark.

My heart hammered in my chest as I reached up to claw at the bag around my neck but a pair of hands prevented me from attempting to rip off the bag before my own were tied in front of me.

'No no no please this can't be happening please wake up!'

I lurched forward in my captor's arms as the wagon rolled away from the palace grounds. The men were soundless. I knew then that it wasn't their intention to raid the *High Peaks*. This was a kidnapping. One that was done in stealth and secret and not to draw attention to the breaking of the sectoral code. When the elves woke up to find me missing, they wouldn't know what had happened to me. Suspicion alone was not enough to charge a sector with trespassing, especially if no one witnessed it.

But Corrin and I did, a week ago. We saw them.

Memories of Corrin, My grandfather – my *childhood* flashed across my mind. Was this it? Was this what would become of me now? Here one minute, gone the next?

'I'm going to die. They are going to kill me. Please gods above, I need to live. Let me live.'

My squirming must have annoyed the Dry Landers as I felt a hand at my throat in what I suspected to be a warning, making me only thrash harder out of fear. Someone grabbed my legs as another restrained me. There was a heated conversation above me before the hand was replaced with the tip of a blade and I froze.

Silence engulfed us and I listened to the rhythmic trot

of the horse pulling the wagon. I listened to its hooves hitting the pavement of the bridge above the river Liesion, as it ventured through the square and listened as we approached the main gates of the kingdom, where I knew the soldiers would be.

All was not lost yet, I could still be saved.

The blade was heavy against my Adam's apple and I could tell the holder was nervous. Their breathing was quieter now and I knew right then that they weren't out of the woods yet. They still had to get out unscathed and unbeknownst to the elven soldiers.

I closed my eyes and focused on listening to my surroundings, envisioning the silver gates of the kingdom ahead. I waited to hear the Elvish High Lander.

And waited.

And waited until the horse rolled to a stop, indicating it was in front of the kingdom's gates. As the groaning of the iron being opened was harsh in my sensitive ears, I grew restless.

There should be soldiers – where are the–

Alfus's voice made my stomach feel heavy. Cold sweats littered my forehead from beneath the bag.

"They will be searching for him shortly after first light. Once you reach the cold pass you have the advantage. No elf will dare travel in cold conditions, at least not now. Make yourselves scarce and disappear."

Rage pooled within me as the tears threatened to escape my eyes. I was pulled up and pushed out of the wagon, into the arms of a Dry Lander. At that point, I didn't care. My ears twitched in the direction of the familiar sound of the silver tunic rubbing against skin and I lunged forward. Taking the Dry Lander and myself by surprise, I grabbed the hands around the knife at my throat and turned it to face outwards with a hoarse scream.

I felt the slicing of fabric before the knife was wedged and Alfus groaned.

The Dry Lander pulled me back but he wasn't quick enough to shield me from Alfus landing a punch to my face.

Chaos erupted.

The foreign voices shouted across the wagon but they weren't directed at me.

I screamed through the tape, the hot dust no longer had a hold of my voice as familiar hands dragged me forward by my bound wrists.

There was laughter from two Dry Landers. I felt as though they were laughing at my attempt to 'escape' but that wasn't my intention. Questions would be asked. Ones that would be directed at Alfus. How did he get that knife wound? Where were you when the prince went missing? How coincidental it was that you had a wound the same night the prince went missing.

I wasn't trying to escape. I was already lost. My plan was to leave a trace of me. The *only* trace of me…

Someone lifted me up onto a horse before settling behind me. The small grunt gave my captor away as to who I guessed it might be. I brought my bound hands around to hit him just as the horse moved forward but the sudden movement made me fall back.

I almost fell off the horse if not for the Dry Lander's

hands catching my waist. He tensed when I hit his chest, causing a few sniggers to erupt from around me. I froze at the sound – my ears picking up on multiple Dry Landers now outside the gates of the kingdom.

The Dry Lander's body tensed in what I could only assume to be anger as I felt his hands drag me upright. My ears flattened against the bag around my head.

He made a clicking sound and the horse began to canter forward. I jolted forward again but his hands kept me steady. I let my fingers grip the hair of the horse's mane to give me some leverage as I left my home, travelling to wherever it was that I was being forced to go.

A sinking feeling settled within the pit of my stomach as I left my home. I knew this was the last time I would most likely ever see my family again, ever see Corrin again.

I pushed my feelings to the deepest part of my mind, willing myself to stay strong as I held in my choked tears and gripped the horse's hair tightly in my hands.

IV

~*~

I didn't know how I came to fall asleep on the horse.

Maybe it was the pure exhaustion of not having slept last night or the crying that wore me out, but I awoke with a start from where I was leaning over the horse, bag and tape now removed. Only the rope around my wrist remained.

The boy's hands held onto me, holding me in place and not letting me fall off.

I pushed myself up with my bound hands as my eyes adjusted to the scenery around me, widening as I blinked repeatedly. My head spun around curiously taking in my surroundings.

We were descending the *High Peak* mountains slowly. The horses were taking extra care in their step as they travelled through the changing weather. I supposed it wasn't called the *High Peaks* for nothing. *Versai* stood at the top of the *High Peaks*, well above the skyline into the mountains. No one had ever descended the long trek down the sides of the mountain before – not that they could. It was dangerous. Someone could easily slip and fall.

Looking up to my disappointment, I noticed we had descended a good distance from *Versai*. The walls of my kingdom were only just visible but I knew they would soon disappear into the clouds. I cherished the view, taking it in one last time, for possibly a long time.

The Dry Lander did not make a sound as I stirred in front of him. Nor did he make any motion to speak. He stayed silent as did I whilst we travelled down the mountain at a steady speed.

It became a lot colder as the temperature drastically dropped the further down we rode and I shook, my teeth chattered and goose bumps rose on my arms. It didn't help that all I was wearing were my open–toed sandals, loose white shorts and a loose sleeveless brown top I often wore at night when it was particularly humid.

At the top of the mountain, it was hotter. The air was clammy due to the existence of a small tropical rainforest in the *High Peaks*, full of exotic animals.

This cold was new to me.

My ears flattened against either side of my head to preserve warmth. I knew that it was dangerous for elf ears in this temperature as it could possibly lead to frostbite, resulting luckily in one becoming deaf rather than the cruel fate of having an ear cut off.

I whimpered when a cold breeze blew through me, pushing my hair out of my eyes as we were now halfway down the mountain. The ground was littered with white snow in which the horses whinnied at the coldness under their hooves.

I could hear faint shouting from ahead and the horses in front of us stopped, in turn making the Dry Lander boy pull on the reins for our horse to stop. I watched through chattering teeth as the men began to climb down from their horses, shaking out their stiff bodies as some clustered together in groups, chatting and laughing to each other as if they were long–time friends. Most of them probably were.

The boy shifted from behind me before he, too, was climbing down from our horse. I watched him through hooded eyes as he shook out his stiff legs and clapped his hands in order to get the blood in his hands to circulate in the cold. He brought them up to his lips and blew into the crevices of his hands, warming them and looking up at me. I watched him take a breath before he reached up to help me down.

When my feet touched the snow ground, my legs almost gave way from beneath me and I let out a yelp. The boy held me up with a soft grunt before motioning for me to shake out my legs. I didn't understand him at first and it was only when he reproduced what he did when he stepped down from the horse I understood what he was trying to say and lifted my heavy legs.

The pins and needles stung but it was a good sign that I wasn't about to lose the feeling of my legs as the blood began to circulate. The boy held me up the whole time and when he believed that I could stand on my own two feet, that was when he let go, coming in front of me to pull my bound hands up to his vision.

My body and teeth shook from the cold as he looked down, unbinding my hands and bunching the rope up. He shoved it into his satchel attached to the horse.

He said something but I wasn't paying attention. I couldn't understand him so there was no point in even trying. My eyelids every few seconds fell shut as I zoned in and out of consciousness. I stayed upright though, to my relief.

There was a voice a small distance behind me that made the boy in front stop what he was doing to look in front of me. His eyes hardened and eyebrows furrowed in confusion – the only indication of emotion on his features. I turned around to the voice in confusion.

"Rain!"

One of them shouted over the wind and I looked up at the sky in confusion, finding no trace of any rain–bearing clouds threatening to spill and allow the gods to open their gates of silver. The boy behind me chuckled causing me to jump in surprise at his closeness and I turned around quickly. A look of amusement played on his features as he looked down at me. The edges of his lips were turned up into a smirk, but it was faint and his eyes crinkled slightly when he opened his mouth to speak.

"*A chwuyve se Raen.*"

I tilted my head at that.

What an unusual name. I had never come across someone by a name like that before. Like the weather, only spelt differently – as he took the time to enunciate and distinguish clearly between the two by writing his name in my hand with his finger. I couldn't help but think that it suited him. He was unusual as well as unpredictable. I would have never guessed that he was someone of importance until I heard how the others reacted upon me slapping him.

"*Raen.*" I tested the word on my lips and he watched me, nodding once.

As angry and hurt as I was, I wanted to blame this Raen for taking me from my home. I always struggled with forgiving people. It was an elf's nature to forgive. No matter how bad a person was or had done in the past, we must let go of our hatred and clear our minds. If we don't, we could become sick, with years of our lives shaved off.

He seemed to have no negative feelings towards me. He didn't hurt me physically, nor did he talk down to me. He treated me better than some of the elven kids I grew up with and I mentally scoffed at the irony. Of course, a kidnapping Dry Lander would show more kindness over a biased elf.

I was mostly afraid, fearful that if I didn't at least go with what this Dry Lander was saying, he might show a side to him that I didn't want to see. I couldn't risk it. I needed to do what I could to survive and hopefully find a way to escape from their clutches so that I could get back home.

I brought up my shaking hand and pointed to my chest, eyes looking up as I spoke through clattering teeth.

"K–Keylin. I–I am Keylin–n." He looked down at me with an unsure smile. His eyes twinkled at the sound of my voice.

***

He was staring at me.

I had felt his stare boring into my chest as I looked down at what they had said was food. By food, they made a hand motion of eating cereal. I said nothing as they handed me what I could only believe was stew.

As I brought the spoon up to my nose sceptical to sniff, I scrunched my nose at the smell before bringing the spoon back down to land in the stew with a small 'plop' and I ignored my stomach's protests.

It didn't smell like chicken. It smelt vile – almost like urine with floating chunks of carrot, leaf and some meat that *definitely* wasn't chicken.

"Keylin."

I looked up at the voice for my eyes to land on Raen who sat a few feet away from me, getting through the last of his stew. His lips were pressed into a thin line, his eyes hard but not harsh. That's what made Raen different from the others.

Raen motioned for me to eat using his fingers before pounding his chest once. I didn't know if he was trying to tell me that it would give me strength, or help me keep my strength – I wasn't sure.

The others said something to Raen making them all erupt in laughter as he frowned. I somehow had the sneaking suspicion that they were not telling Raen to give up, but mocking me.

I caught eyes with one of the Dry Landers laughing at

me and couldn't help but narrow my eyes at him. I looked down at the stew with a scowl before lifting the spoon up to my mouth. My hunger got the better of me and I swallowed it down, not taking a second for my thoughts to come up with possibilities as to what was in the stew. It tasted better than it smelled anyway. The feeling of the stew gliding down the back of my throat made me splutter slightly but I held it down. I even dared to look up at Raen as I went for another spoonful. I caught a ghost of a smile on his lips before it was quickly gone and his eyes were shifting away from me. A look of stone masked his expression.

I finished the stew, my insides feeling warmer but still cold in the freezing temperature. It began to snow just as everyone was loading back onto their horses, having rested for a bit and loaded their stomachs. They were ready to begin their descent again.

One of the younger males of the group that I had come to realise was purely men between what I believed to be the ages of eighteen to thirty, eighteen being a brown–eyed boy I had glimpsed at briefly from the wagon, now stood in front of me. He took my empty bowl from me without a word and stacked it away with the others.

"Thank you." I said quietly, not knowing why I said it as they didn't deserve my thanks. They deserved to burn for kidnapping me.

My natural obedient and kind nature was starting to get on my nerves. Besides, none of them spoke a word of English anyway. What did it matter if I threw a few curses their way?

He surprised me however when he turned his narrowed gaze on me, looking almost as if he was contemplating something before shrugging. His eyes softened from their hard gaze.

"You are welcome."

He had an accent. He wasn't fluent in English as it wasn't his mother tongue but just by him saying those words, he had reignited the quickly dwindling hope from within me and my eyes lit up. My mouth formed to speak but no words came out. I looked up at his curious gaze.

'You can understand me...'

"Malakei!"

The boy jolted in surprise before turning with a harsh glare that could have made eternal fires freeze over. He sent this glare to a boy not much older than him getting ready his horse. Looking at the other boy, it was blindingly obvious how much they looked alike. I knew right then that they were brothers. This 'Malakei' was the younger of the two and probably the youngest of the whole group.

The brother said something harshly to him before his sharp gaze turned to me but I quickly cast my gaze down to avoid it. Malakei, however, did not hold his tongue and yelled back at his brother with an accusing and angered tone. I looked up when Malakei was finished speaking, only to catch his brother rolling his eyes and turning around to climb onto his horse.

"*Esshole.*" He mused, making me snicker at the mispronounced word. He looked down at me, emotion in his eyes changing between being amused and curious as I corrected him quietly on the word.

"Asshole… The *'a'* is harsh."

"That's as I said. *Asshole*." He stated, this time referring to me as the asshole. My eyes grew wide and I went to step back in fear – afraid that he would pick a fight over this with me but he did something I would have never expected him to do.

He stuck his tongue out at me.

I couldn't help but blink up at him in confusion. Still expecting him to hit me or push me, to show hostility towards me. That was what I had learned about them my whole life, that these people were monsters. Savages that would murder you with their bare hands if you so much as looked at them strangely. He was childish for his age, with an obvious playful nature. Even though he was likely older than me, something about him made me believe that he was less frightening than the others.

"I'm Keylin."

"I know, Kaylin." He said and rolled his eyes at me, mispronouncing my name on purpose as if daring to challenge him on it like before but I was fixated on his words.

I didn't remember giving any of the Dry Landers my name – apart from Raen. Did he tell them?

"It's Keylin, *Key* not Kay." I couldn't help but to clarify. He smirked down at me, his raised brow never faltered.

"Whatever Kaylin."

"Whatever Malakay."

Malakei's eyes widened at that and he was about to say

something else when his brother's yell made him close his mouth

"Malakei!"

Malakei rolled his eyes, turning his gaze to where his brother was waiting for him expectantly from his horse. Malakei quickly made his way over to him, his shoulders tense and feet trudging through the snow, I couldn't help but find it amusing to watch.

"We talk again, yes?" He called out to me suddenly and I looked up to find he was already on his horse, slapping his brother's shoulder from behind which made his brother yelp in surprise before he turned around to try and slap Malakei.

He must have noticed the look of horror on my face when he asked me that question because a loud laugh left his lips before his eyes trailed back to me again, a smirk evident on his strikingly pleasant features.

"Okay! Talk to you later Kaylin."

I rolled my eyes as I watched them ride ahead, joining the small trail of horses beginning to leave. With the realisation that the remaining Dry Landers were busy packing up the horses and talking with one another, I decided that this was a perfect opportunity to make myself disappear.

I began to slowly walk backwards until I was out of sight of the talking Dry Landers. Just as I was about to turn around, however, I felt hooves make their way up behind me and a loud sneeze from the beast made me jump in surprise. I turned around to see Raen already on the horse and raising his eyebrow at me as if knowing exactly what I was thinking of doing.

My eyes widened but I suddenly frowned and my forehead creased.

"Can you speak English?" I asked him and he grunted in response – his response to mostly everything – he held out his hand to help me up onto the horse. I took it hesitantly and he half pulled me up before I settled into the familiar position in front of him. I clutched the horse's mane as I shifted on the horse. Raen did the same but instead shifted closer to me so that our bodies were touching each other, a way to preserve body heat. I couldn't help the small twitch from my ears as a blush rose on my cheeks.

"I–I'll take that as a yes."

V

~*~

It got colder.

I didn't know how that was even possible, seeing as it was so cold to begin with, but it did, and I felt it in my bones. Nightfall had approached quicker than expected as temperatures dropped further at night. There was also, of course, the fact that I was underdressed for the sudden weather change – but let's not go there.

I started to fall asleep from both the pure exhaustion of trying to stay awake and the immense cold. I was so drained that Raen had to grab onto me before I fell off of the horse completely, making the horse kick out its legs at the disruption. Sometimes the horse stood with its hind legs in the air while Raen pulled at the reins.

I outstretched a hand to steady myself against the horse and to help hold me upright but because of my shaking hands from the cold, they continued to slip forward weakly. I couldn't register when my numb hands touched the horse anymore which resulted in them almost missing the horse.

I let out a sharp breath when the desire to sleep and keep myself upright from falling off the horse battled in my mind until Raen sighed. His breath was cold on my neck.

Raen pulled me closer to him from behind, letting go of his hold on the horse momentarily to rest his hand on my forehead. He slowly brought my head back to lay on the crook of his shoulder. His hands reached for the reins again.

He could sense that I was quickly developing a fever. Small droplets of cold sweat formed on my forehead and my breathing was laboured, exhaling in small puffs. My eyes watered as I fought to keep them open through the blistering conditions.

I let out a whimper when another icy wind blew through me which resulted in any heat that my body was trying to preserve vanishing and I was back to feeling numb again.

This was bad. It had been a few hours since we had eaten any food and I didn't know if we were going to stop anytime soon. I only prayed we stopped to rest before sundown.

There was a shout a small distance ahead of us where we trailed near the back of the line and no sooner each of the horses stopped in their line. Raen didn't hesitate in pulling on the reins and jumped down from the horse. In the space of time that his body left, I could feel my eyes roll back and all I knew was that I was falling without the steady hands of Raen to prop me upright, my head felt suddenly light.

Raen caught me with a groan before he brought one hand to my back, the other scooped up my legs from under me and shifted me closer to his chest. He trudged through the snow briskly to carry me to the others while my hand grasped at his warm chest secured through a thick layer of clothing as my breathing shallowed. I allowed my eyes to close briefly only for him to shake me to consciousness, saying my name repeatedly to coax me awake and for my eyes to stay open.

I opened my eyes halfway as I strained to look up at him.

He shouted something suddenly towards the others and they stopped whatever they were doing. Their chatter died down as they noticed my shaking, weak form.

Raen shouted something else before someone took me from his arms and laid me down on something furry and warm. I didn't react and continued to shake as hands wrapped warm coats around me. Another coat was pressed to my front and from the familiar feel of it through my trembling fingers I knew it belonged to Raen.

There was suddenly something warm and wet placed on my forehead and I flinched away only to have my head turned back to someone placing a hot cloth on my forehead. My eyes rolled back at the burning sensitivity of the cloth. My fever only worsened and I cried out at how hot it was, screaming painfully as hands tried to assure me that I was fine.

I could hear the sound of arguing from above me as

someone pulled me closer to them. No doubt, someone's responsibility of making sure that I was properly clothed for the trek down the mountain was being questioned. It was difficult to assume if whoever was in charge, did it out of spite, lack of care or ignorance.

My head spun and I didn't notice when a man in front of me took the liberty of trying to prise my mouth open to pour something from a bottle into it. It looked like medicine and I let him. My throat gurgled at the foreign taste, making my face scrunch up and tears fall from my eyes.

The man said something to me that I didn't understand before he patted my shoulder with a sense of assurance. It only made me startle and grimace at his roughness. He said something again, but I seemed to black out for a second or two. My body only registered when I was back in someone's arms.

They carried me into a small makeshift tent that looked as though it had been put up in a hurry.

I was lowered onto what felt like a bed made out of blankets and fur coats, the person who carried me was quick to wrap me in.

I didn't know how I felt. I was cold and hot at the same time. Sweat formed on my forehead as I shivered under the mess of fur. Whatever they were trying to do wasn't working, and if they thought just warming me up with a few blankets was going to help me they were mistaken.

I had a bad fever that I knew I needed to either sweat out or be bedridden for the foreseeable future. Given that the latter was not an option – and at this stage of the fever

I was on the verge of hypothermia. I wasn't sure if the warmth from blankets alone could help with that.

I let out a sob as everywhere hurt. I wanted nothing more than to sleep, wishing the pain to ease. I knew by sleeping I should feel better and by morning, I hopefully would have slept the pain away. At least then, I could manage until we got off of this mountain.

There was a frustrated breath from somewhere inside the tent before the sound of something being dropped onto the ground reached my ears. I was lifted up by my elbow into a sitting position. My shirt and waistcoat were suddenly peeled from my body along with my sandals and shorts. I was stripped down until there was only the cloth around my private area.

It was when I felt the makeshift bed dip and arms pulling me into a strong chest that I gasped with relief as different kinds of warmth enveloped me under the fur coats. The type of warmth that could only be identified as body heat.

I thought it wouldn't work, that the fur from the coats would be enough with time but when I felt their hands rubbing up and down my cold back, a shiver escaped me. It sent a tingle down my spine as the blood began to circulate again.

Hands travelled up to close over my freezing and red–tinted ears while what wasn't covered, the stranger massaged with the tips of his fingers. I let out something between a protest and a sigh of relief as my ear tips were massaged. The heat brought to them made my eyelids flutter shut.

I was unable to keep my concentration on what was happening around me, all I could remember before I fell into unconsciousness was a hand coming up to tangle in my hair as – whoever it was, pulled my head into their chest and brought my trembling arms over themself. With the last of my strength, I moved to press them timidly on the person's back before falling under.

***

I could remember being shaken awake, making my eyes open before they fell shut with a grimace.
I let my eyes adjust to the brightness. My body was no longer trembling and my fever had fortunately depleted drastically. Although I was still very tired, I had to fight myself not to fall back into unconsciousness.

"Keylin?" Raen's voice from above was persistent in his attempts to get me to open my eyes and I sighed. Knowing that he wasn't going to stop, I poked an eye open to look at him. Both of my eyelids fully opened in confusion when I saw him so close to me.

When I meant so close, he was naked apart from the cloth around his lower region, with me – pressed against his chest. His hands were around my upper arms and our legs were entangled with each other's as he looked down at me seriously. I felt my ears twitch at the intimate position and a shiver running up my spine made me shake.

All too quickly, he pulled me back into his chest. My shiver most likely gave him the wrong impression that I still had 'the shakes' from the cold. A startled squeak left my throat in shock as his chest pressed fully against mine, his hands now running up and down my back in an attempt to generate body heat.

"R–Raen." I stammered out as I gasped into his broad chest. I noticed how strong he was when he pulled me into him. His chest rose and fell to the point I could almost hear his heartbeat. The intimacy made me blush and I pushed weakly at his chest to try and get him to stop. I had shut my eyes in embarrassment wanting to avoid eye contact and wished the fever had taken me then and there so I wouldn't have to face him.

Besides, it had started to become too warm.

"Raen, I'm okay. I'm not cold anymore."

Raen made a displeased sound from above me before scoffing. I felt his fingers tap at my closed eyelids and I flinched back, reopening my eyes to look up at him tiredly. He only glared at me.

"You didn't have to completely strip me," I said in a small voice, cheeks blushing a shade of rose. "This is embarrassing. I would have been okay with the blankets."

I spoke – even though it was pointless because he most likely didn't understand a word I was saying. I only talked to cover up the awkward situation between us, although I had a sneaking suspicion that he didn't care for our intimacy. His–

"You were dying."

Raen hissed lowly and my eyes flew open at this. A blush formed on my shocked face as I opened and closed my mouth, trying to form words.

'He could *speak English.'*

All of this time, he could speak English, yet he never spoke, not a single word.

I lifted myself up into a sitting position amongst the fur to look down at him, immediately seeing his expression as he looked up before he brought his body up into a sitting position, face red and about ready to explode with anger – I was taken aback by this and went to speak.

"I–"

"*Don't speak.*" He gritted out as he made his way to the edge of the bed, reaching down before coming back up to pull on his shirt quickly. I shut my mouth at this and immediately averted my gaze, not knowing how to feel.

"*I did what I had to do.*" He explained sourly with close to perfect English as he stood up, shoving his axe into his belt loop before leaving the tent without so much as a glance back.

I didn't know why that hurt as much as it did but I glared after him, narrowing my eyes at the entrance to the tent as I forced the lump in my throat to stay down.

Was he blaming me for almost dying of hypothermia? If it was anyone here that was to blame, it was *them*. They conspired with Alfus, turned him into a traitor and took me away from my home in the middle of the night against my will, forcing me onto a horse through a blizzard in nothing but my nightly attire.

As if it was all my fault for getting sick. He could have offered me a coat from the start and we probably wouldn't have been in this mess.

'*Too little, too late.*' I thought to myself when I was on the verge of going into cardiac arrest. It was inevitable from the get–go.

The realisation of everything that I had bottled for so long now threatened to spill over the surface around me. Was this why I got sick so suddenly? As much as I tried to shut out the feelings and keep my strength to leave them, it hit me that maybe that was the worst thing I could be doing right now. I was making myself sick from my anger.

I let out a frustrated growl as I pulled at my hair in an attempt to calm down.

"*Katcha, they all are.*" I said to myself, taking deep breaths and remembering what we were always told about the Dry Landers. What Mara used to tell me about them.

The thought of her made my eyes well up and I couldn't help but let the tears fall.

They were barbarians. They've known how to kill people from a young age. It came naturally to them. They didn't know the meaning of what it was to be kind or thoughtful. That was proven when the Malakei boy couldn't even accept my thanks as I handed him my empty bowl. He only looked at me, as if I was going to laugh in his face.

I remembered Mara's words and made a vow to myself there and then to survive and find my way back home. Even if it meant going against how I was truly feeling… I had to do it. For *Mara.* For my *grandfather, Corrin… for me.*

I had to believe that this was all happening for a reason and my thoughts couldn't help but stray to my father. I wondered if he had anything to do with this, but honestly?

I didn't know if he was even alive. He could be dead for all I knew. Or may not even know I existed in the first place. This could all just be a coincidence that they decided to take me but no one else – a sick joke of sorts perhaps seemed likely. My stomach twisted at the thought of encountering more beings like Tobias, only worse.

I couldn't believe I let my guard down around them for even a second, knowing that this would be my fate soon – a punching bag for the Dry Landers to take their stress out on.

I needed to start coming up with a plan to escape. I had to observe their habits, find out their weaknesses and just when they became comfortable around me, that's when I would be gone. I would be somewhere miles away.

I would be free.

I still didn't understand why I was here. Just as I was getting used to the idea of my soon–to–be life. I hated to say it but… I would have given anything to have Tobias punching me right then.

And Corrin saving me from Tobias.

It hurt to think about him. It hurt to think about my family and people. I wondered what they were doing right then. Were they looking for me? grieving the loss of their kin? angry? Were they going to try and rescue me? *Their prince…*

I scoffed at my naivety but doubt filling my gaze stopped my tears.

I wasn't very popular among the elves. I doubted they'd risk their lives for someone like me. Even if I was their prince, I was still a flawed elf, a stain on their culture.

They were most likely celebrating my riddance from the kingdom. I was the Dry Lander's problem now.

I sniffled in my wallowing before running my hands through my hair.

I debated on venturing outside in search of food or to turn around in the makeshift bed and sleep the last of the fever off. I decided against sleeping and with frustration, threw off the fur coats from around me and tiredly put on my clothes just as violently as Raen had done before quickly getting to my feet.

I ignored the dizzy spell as I made my way to the entrance of the tent. I ducked under the curtain that overhung the door and walked out into the crisp, cold mountain air. As I looked up, I noticed it was bright out. The morning had come already.

Many of the Dry Landers were eating breakfast beside a small man–made fire while some were in their makeshift tents, only stirring before committing to the journey ahead.

"Kaylin!"

Brought out of my thoughts, I turned to the man–made fire where beside it, Malakei and his brother sat with two other men.

Malakei waved me over to them with a genuine smile as his brother shoved him warningly. I watched Malakei send him a glare. His smile wiped off his face as he turned to shove his brother harshly to the side causing him to fall off his seat with a yelp.

"Kaylin come!" He shouted at me encouragingly.

'Comply and survive' I thought to myself with a gulp

as I made my way hesitantly over to them, not meeting any of their eyes as I sat down next to Malakei who wiggled his eyebrow at me suggestively. I blinked at him in confusion.

"You share bed with leader."

My eyes widened as my mouth fell open at Malakei's confident statement, suggesting a different form of bed–sharing between the *katcha* and myself.

"W–what?" I stuttered, cursing to myself as a blush formed on my cheeks at his direct words and I avoided his eyes. This only made Malakei's face light up in surprise and a smirk crossed his lips.

"I knew it!"

"Not when he was unconscious, Malakei." One of the other Dry Lander men stated with a slight 'twang' of an accent raising his brow at him, causing the last Dry Lander to snort just as he was taking a drink of something hot. Immediately cursing when the liquid burned his mouth.

"*And with fever!*" The man who was recovering from almost choking, scoffed and laughed boisterously.

I stayed quiet, looking down and feeling uncomfortable as they talked about me, assuming I was someone I was not. The mere thought of intimacy made me blush.

"You will need to excuse him–" The first Dry Lander began as he looked at me apologetically. His brown eyes warmed before they focused on an eye–rolling Malakei. "–He is *ah*... too confident in his skin and rude. He is nineteen. All boys turn to men by his age. *Him*, not so much. I am Caito and he is Bear." Caito introduced himself before turning to the Dry Lander who spilled his drink as Bear.

Bear gave a small wave before cackling loudly at Malakei's sharp look at Caito.

Caito looked to be in his early thirties. His brown curly hair, muscles and stubble gave him a defined look while Bear appeared a bit older with more muscle mass. The older Dry Lander resembled something from ancient scriptures where they talked of Vikings and their armour. Bear had his sword at his side, his animal fur coat hung over him.

"You look young," Caito observed making me turn to him, noticing a sort of pity in his eyes as he smiled at me warmly and I looked down biting my lip.

"How old are you?"

"Eighteen." I said quietly in between chattering teeth. Even though I was closer to my nineteenth year. The thought of not being in the *High Peaks* to share it with Corrin made me cast my gaze down gloomily.

There was silence after that and I looked up to see them all staring at me. Even Malakei, whose eyes held a stern gaze the majority of the time, had softened. His brother – whose name I still didn't know – was looking at me now without sending his usual glare my way.

They must be aware of the elven ways. Dry Landers came of age at sixteen, for elves it was twenty when growth was completed. This was when we were at our peak of youth. I would have been king the following year.

I let my eyes shut and took in a shaky breath of cold air, deciding right then and there that I didn't want to continue talking with them anymore. I was going to return to the tent to sleep off the last of my fever when Malakei caught my attention.

He took off his fur coat, walked over to where I sat on the ground and threw it over my shoulders. He put the clasp in place before retreating and sat back down beside his brother. I noticed his brother looked at him strangely as if he couldn't believe Malakei had just done that. Whether he made a kind gesture that he wasn't used to seeing his brother do or was unsure as to why he was helping me.

I bit my lip as I looked down at the warm texture of the fur between my fingers. I pushed the thought that this was once an animal far away as I looked up at Malakei.

"*T–Thank you.*" I said to him genuinely through chattering teeth as he poured something into a cup, rolling his eyes as he held out the steaming hot beverage to me. I took it gratefully.

"No more catching fever. Drink and you feel better." Malakei stated sternly as he looked at me, making a motion with his hand at me to drink. I nodded at him in a daze as I slowly lifted the hot drink to my lips, immediately coughing afterwards and spluttering. Everyone chuckled at this.

"What is that?" I couldn't help but grimace as I tried to look inside the cup, noticing something was floating at the top of it.

"*Goose fat*," Bear stated as he slugged out of his own without flinching. He licked his coated lips subconsciously and looked at me with a shrug. "It is nice while hot. Drink fast or it turn cold."

I took in a breath as I looked down, knowing it would be a while before we stopped to rest for food. My stomach was empty from yesterday. I clutched the cup tightly as I glared down at it before bringing the cup up to my lips and chugging down the drink, telling myself that it was 'chicken soup' as it dribbled down my chin. I let out a strangled cough when I dropped the cup, leaning over my knees as I coughed. I noticed Malakei wore a proud smile as he slapped my back.

"That's my boy! *See*, I knew you like him."

Malakei mused to his brother and friends as I continued to cough, feeling as though there was something stuck in my throat – something slimy that I didn't want to think of right now. As I pulled myself up with a groan, I could feel Caito's worry–filled eyes on me while Bear clapped in my direction, his head thrown back as he cackled loudly, definitely waking the remaining Dry Landers.

"I feel like something is crawling around in my throat."

"That might be the maggots. We found goose this morning and it was dead long time with bugs and beasties–"

I couldn't hold it in any longer as I quickly ran through the snow and around the side of one of the tents, throwing up the remnants of my stomach as I heard their laughter echo. Something told me they knew I would have a weak stomach and did that on purpose.

***

When it was time to leave again, to travel the remaining distance down the mountain; I didn't have the words to describe how I felt. Leaving the mountain meant leaving my home, the *High Peaks*, leaving everyone and everything behind.

Caito had offered me to ride with him on his horse when it looked as though Raen had already taken off without me. I wondered why he took on the responsibility of taking *'care'* of me. He wasn't doing a very good job of it and I could have probably died if we hadn't stopped for rest the last time.

"He's not very nice to be around when angry."

Caito stated out of the blue as he was leading me to his stallion, a cool mix of white and brown, grimacing as a memory popped into his mind.

"I ask him if he okay one time and he punch me in eye. I not see for week."

I winced at that, nodding my head along at the memory of Tobias's treatment over the years. It was definitely something I wasn't going to miss.

"I know how that feels."

Caito looked at me curiously then, a frown etching itself in between his eyebrows as he brought his finger up to touch the fading bruise under my eye. Now made even more distinct from Alfus's punch. I flinched back from him. Caito, noticing this – immediately drew his hand back and cleared his throat before climbing up and jumping onto his horse effortlessly.

He held out his hand to me and I reached up to take it as someone was quickly slapping my hand away, dragging me in the opposite direction of Caito and his horse.

"H–hey what–" I managed to gasp out before looking up into the hard eyes of Raen. My teeth clenched as he yanked me forward so that I fell in line with him. I almost stumbled but caught myself, throwing him a glare as we walked to his jet–black stallion.

'Still in his mood.' I took it.

Raen was quick to climb his horse, holding out a hand for me, his eyes daring me to refuse him as they bore into my soul.

"You can't just–"

"Come here. *Now.*"

His voice made a cold shiver run up my spine. My ears flattened as I timidly brought my hand up to his. I yelped as he pulled me up in front of him onto the horse, almost dislocating my arm as he did so from his strength. I tried not to hyperventilate as I shook out my arm at my side. My trembling hands came down to clutch the horse's mane but they weren't shaking because I was cold, I was angry.

I had been around people like him, hell – hurt by people like him. Tobias was a prime example of that. I knew that when Tobias was like this and took his anger out on me, it was best to just stay quiet and not say anything that would just put me in a worse position than I was already in.

'Comply and survive'

I took a deep breath, cleared my mind of all harmful thoughts and ignored the way his fingers dug into my sides to make sure I wouldn't fall off the horse.

I couldn't help but feel ticked off. He had nothing to be angry with me about. I should be the one angry in this situation. Over everything he had put me through.

"*Katcha.*" I cursed at him in my native tongue, knowing that he wouldn't understand me calling him an asshole because he didn't know the language. As expected, he didn't react and it made me smirk victoriously as the animal moved into the line of other horses, leaving the area

VI

~*~

I still wore the fur coat that Malakei had given me during breakfast.

It was warm and kept the cold at bay from getting under my skin. I planned to hand it back to Malakei before we began the journey to the *Dry Lands*, knowing he would be cold without it yet he insisted I keep it. He said he had many more at home and that he could battle the cold for the remaining few hours before we reached land.

Raen had refused to speak throughout the entire journey. I didn't mind it one bit as I battled with myself for holding a grudge against him. Knowing it would make me sick, I didn't want to entertain him with my words if it meant that I didn't run off was such a chore for him. I still didn't know who gave him the right.

By not talking to him I also refused to sleep, battling

with my exhaustion the whole journey just because I didn't want to be vulnerable when I slept. I didn't want to give him the satisfaction of knowing that I was still sick when I told him earlier that I wasn't.

I tried to keep a distance between us while on the horse. It was childish, I knew, but not feeling his body pressed against mine made me feel more in control. I didn't feel like I was being forced against my will to sit on a horse, which was how he made it feel all of the time.

He hopped down quickly when a shout in front of us to 'stop' was heard and the horses stopped their trek. Dry Landers hopped off, glad to be getting food and rest before we climbed back onto the horses.

It made me wonder why they would go through so much travelling and possible hypothermia; all for a single elf kid that they didn't know. If their goal was to kidnap an elf, why didn't they take more? It seemed an awful waste of time and resources to invade a neighbouring sector only to take one, not to mention if the other sectors were to find out what the Dry Landers did. Was all of this worth penalties, exile and possible multitudes of death for their sector to be made an example of? It didn't make any sense.

The short time spent away from our journey was uneventful. We ate quickly whatever we were given and repacked the belongings for the journey. I could only wonder how far more this journey was going to be. It was dangerous and I contemplated if I would make it through.

What would happen to me when we finally got to their destination?

What *would* happen to me?

I kept silent as I stared down at my food. It was the same stew we all ate yesterday. I brought the food up to my lips and ate slowly. My appetite had long gone ever since the 'goose fat' incident this morning, the thoughts of eating now made my stomach churn. The only reason I forced myself to eat was because of the green eyes boring into me.

Raen had scolded me once when he caught me not eating, only staring down at the food after one of the others had given it to me.

He helped me up onto the horse afterwards in silence, still refusing to talk, although his gaze was not as harsh as it once was. His fingers didn't dig into my sides as much. It didn't help that I bruised easily, my body seemed to welcome any infliction made to it.

Soon enough, the cold air started to lift until the fur coat over me was becoming too much as the horses made their way down one of the slopes. When I looked up, I gasped.

I could see the ground where we were descending to at a moderately fast pace. The mountain floor was not covered in snow anymore, but instead a grey stone. Tufts of grass that seeped through the fissures could be seen as we got closer to the earth. My heart pounded in my ears the closer we got to the flat ground until the horses were making small jumps down from a large overhang.

When we jumped down, I jolted forward with a gasp but Raen pulled me back to him, pressing me firmly against his chest as we made it safely onto the ground. I felt dizzy but I shook it off, allowing my wide eyes to look around me. I took in the overgrown greenery and small streams.

Raen muttered in his language from behind but I paid no attention to it as I looked around me. My head tilted back to gawk at the large trees, birds chirping as they flew between the winding layers of the trees. Looking down, I watched the small stream. My eyes followed it lead down into a large lake where above it, a waterfall stood.

"The Dry Lands." I whispered in awe. I heard a small grunt from Raen behind me in confirmation as our horse fell in line with the others who were about to cross the stream.

I didn't know what I was expecting when I would eventually arrive here. I thought it would be more barren and wasteful – *deserts* roaming for miles on end, nothing like this. This was what I would think of as *paradise*. However, my heart constricted at the thought of never finding my way back home again. I was so far away now that the possibility of escaping was becoming less and less. I was in a foreign land compared to the mountains. I didn't know my surroundings as well as I did in the *High Peaks* to navigate my way home and it scared me, coming to the overwhelming realisation that I *really was* kidnapped and if I didn't memorise my trail, I would never be able to return to it.

I hoped my family was okay. I didn't know if they were alive or dead but I knew if I thought about that possibility, I would shut down completely. I couldn't afford to do that right now. Up until now, I had barely cried about my situation. I was afraid to let my guard down. Gods knew what these... *people* would do. I didn't trust them.

The horse whinnied at the feel of the rushing water beneath its hooves as it walked across the small stream, leaving large steps as it trotted through the water before jumping onto a small bank and into the outskirts of a forest.

I looked up as we went through, noticing how the sun seemed to disappear ever so slightly but not to the extent that it had vanished completely.

Not a few minutes inside the dark forest, I felt Raen taking off his fur coat and laying it behind him on the horse, along with his dark brown leather jacket. His axe – now in view, was attached to his belt.

I followed suit in taking Malakei's coat from me and as soon as I had it off, Raen took it and threw it on top of his own.

I couldn't help but let out a sigh at the small heat from the air around us, the sounds of insects clicking and leaves swaying in the wind at a distance around us. A part of it was familiar to me, it felt like the forest from the *High Peaks* but visually, it was different.

It was only when there was a shout from in front that Raen's hands slid away from me altogether as he pulled on the reins quickly, causing the horse to whinny to a stop.

I looked up in confusion as to why they would be stopping for a break now after we just had one not too long ago, but the confusion dropped as the others stayed on their horses. I watched them look around frantically, saying something to each other. My ears picked up on their hushed and worried tones. One of them even threw an axe to the other who caught it with ease before huddling closer to their horses. I frowned at this, looking back to see them doing the same thing behind Raen and me.

"What's happening?" I couldn't help the concern that entered my tone, those words being the first words I had uttered to Raen since this morning.

"I… *don't know*..." He trailed off in confusion. His breathing was calm, however, as he spotted Malakei and his brother on their horse galloping down the outside of the line of horses looking around them alert, weapons drawn in the air.

"Malakei–" Raen asked calmly before continuing whatever he was going to say in his language. Malakei looked at him with a serious expression. One that I didn't realise the jokester from earlier could even muster. It cast a sense of graveness over the situation.

Malakei's eyes glanced to me momentarily before he replied shortly.

"Vûltsi."

Raen didn't say anything but merely nodded at Malakei, in turn Malakei rode back, continuing down the line of Dry Landers and their horses. When Malakei was out of sight I asked;

"Raen, what are..." I tried my best to pronounce the word and Raen let out a small breath at this, correcting me on its pronunciation before he jumped down off of the horse. His bare chest came into my line of view and I couldn't help but follow the ink on his body, tattoos covering scars and healed puncture wounds scattered over his chest. I followed one particularly painful–looking scar that seemed to have faded with age but I could only imagine the memory of the pain remained.

"*Wolves*." He replied shortly, piercing his lips together as he looked up at me.

At the revelation, I immediately looked around us fearfully before settling my gaze back on Raen taking his axe from his belt loop, he looked around him. His eyes and jaw were hard and set on finding its target.

"Stay here Keylin." He said sternly without looking back as he stalked away from his horse and me. I began to grow fearful as he did this. For the simple reason that he was the only one of us with a weapon and he had just left me defenceless. My breathing came out harsh as I went to call out to him but a howl drowned out my words from somewhere to my left, causing the horse to move backwards in fear.

I yelped as my hands shot out to take the reins but I was too slow. The horse stood on her back legs, her front two kicking out as she whinnied loudly, spooked from the sound.

I fell backwards and off of the horse completely, crashing to the ground on my back and causing the wind to leave me. I coughed painfully and watched as the horse came down on all fours again, fleeing me as it cantered off.

There were shouts as people got down from their horses, their axes swinging through the air around me, some missed whilst others struck their targets. I heard the wolves whimper when axes and swords impaled them. I could only guess that this was not just four wolves, but a whole pack of maybe eight or ten.

'This was my chance.' My thoughts screamed at me as I bit my lip, looking around at the occupied Dry Landers.

I decided not to hesitate then, grabbing a fur coat and ran.

I ran back in the direction of the waterfall towards the mountain, towards my *home*. My heart pounded loudly in my chest as I could hear the faint shouting of the Dry Landers but I had never felt more free than I did right then – running from them, running for home.

That free feeling left me when I tripped over my unused feet and face planted the dirt. The slight dull ache reminded me of my bad foot and I cursed at this, casting my head back to see how far away the Dry Landers were from reaching me.

'I could still make it.'

I had to get back up but as I turned, a low growling coming from in front of me made me freeze up. I slowly looked around to see a grey and white wolf baring its teeth at me, licking its lips as it began to come closer.

My thoughts ran wild and I quickly scrambled forward, sinking to my knees. My hands laid flat on the dirt in front of me as I thought of the only thing to do at that moment and willed the connection to happen between the wolf and me. My heartbeat escalated the longer it seemed to delay. The purple connection didn't show like it did for Corrin in the forest against Tobias. I could only watch in worried frustration as the wolf came closer to me, snarling, its eyes never changing to that vibrant purple.

"*Come on, peshla.*" I whispered as I took my hands away from the dirt–layered ground beneath me and placed them back down again, thinking that if I positioned them differently, the connection would work between us.

I closed my eyes tightly, bowed my head forward and tried to force the connection to work.

I didn't know how to summon the connection between an animal and me. I could only remember Corrin in this stance when he connected with that tiger to save me from Tobias. Only I had no proper way of knowing how to connect with an animal as I was too young to be trained in that sense. Corrin only knew because he was older. I knew I wasn't ever going to be trained and the only way that I could learn was to try and teach myself; through trial and error – or however that would be.

I opened my eyes to look up at the snapping wolf. Froth formed on either side of its mouth as it bared its teeth my way. I could tell by the visible ribs protruding from the wolf's side that it was hungry. Its eyes were set on me – it's next meal.

I held a breath as it did, refusing to back down as I watched it come forward.

I noticed a small flash of purple that sparked hope within me but it was soon distinguished as the wolf shook its head and continued forward towards me.

All too suddenly, there was an ear–splitting swooshing sound that rang through the air before an axe was lodged in the wolf's head. It whimpered as it fell forward and I let out a startled scream as hands pulled me back from the wolf.

"*No!*" I shouted back at the Dry Lander that found me and tried to cast my gaze on anything – *anywhere* but at the wolf. The image of blood seeping out quickly between the axe ingrained itself into my memory as the lifeless eyes of the wolf looked up at me, its body convulsed from the shock and sudden death. I could just about see the purple forming in its eyes, another moment and I would have connected with the animal.

"Get *off* of me!"

I looked back and saw the angered eyes of Raen – who had by now pulled me to my feet and was turning me around to face him. His face and eyes were filled with anger and frustration, all aimed down at me. His hands gripped either side of my shoulders, now shaking me violently. He started to yell at me in his language, most likely for leaving him and his *'protection'* from the wolves. I closed my eyes trying to keep my breathing even as he continued to scold me but the anger at what he just did bubbled inside of me. If he had just waited–

Raen pulled on my ear to get my attention when he noticed I was blocking him out, making me cry out in pain. My eyes narrowed into slits at this action. Throwing caution to the wind, I conveyed through my deadly serpent eyes to the Dry Lander *exactly* why the elves had called me *'snake'* in the first place. Looking up at him with such anger, I didn't know was possible, I slapped his hand away from me.

"I said, *get off of me."*

I noticed that a few of the Dry Landers had gathered

EMMA HOWL

around us, watching Raen and waiting for what he would decide to do next. No doubt entertained – that a small elf boy was standing up to their leader.

This made me mad, knowing that I was away from Tobias and the hurtful actions of my classmates, it was still the same here. I was still *different* and I didn't register my actions until I was letting out a scream, bringing my hands up to push Raen away from me harshly, causing him to stumble back and fall over a branch at my sudden unleashing of rage. His hands came out to grab at me and he pulled me down with him as he fell back.

I managed to bang my head as it came into contact with his hard chest and couldn't stop the groan from leaving my lips. I brought my hands up to plant down on his shoulders to use as leverage and pushed myself up.

Taking the opportunity when he was down, I drew my hand back before punching him square in the face. This caused a gasp from the onlookers, a silence casting over each of us.

I wasn't one for violence. It wasn't in an elf's nature, but I couldn't help the feeling of something snapping in me that time. All of my pent–up emotions started to come out and in a hateful rage, targeting my kidnapper, *targeting Raen.*

Then again, I was half Dry Lander.

Raen groaned at this, not expecting the punch. I managed to land another punch before he grabbed my wrists and rolled my body off of him so that I was the one being pinned to the forest ground. His legs cemented on either side of my body as his weight crushed my stomach.

I gasped up at this with a twinge of pain as his startled eyes looked down at me, observing my angered features.

"Calm yourself."

"G–Get off of me." I whimpered whilst tears of frustration began to leave my eyes. My hands went out to try and push him off of me but he pinned them either side of my face, looking down at me, his features conflicted. His eyes were fleeting and I realised too late that he was listening to other Dry Landers chatter quietly in their foreign language. They didn't sound pleased.

His eyes suddenly turned emotionless at something a Dry Lander shouted. He surprised me when his hands came down to wrap around my neck, squeezing lightly and causing me to choke out a strangled gasp as my wide eyes looked up at him. The chatter behind him died down as everyone watched me claw at his hands.

"Don't disobey me again, do you understand elf?" His loud voice made my ears flatten against my head, loud enough I realised for the others to hear him. It didn't stop the fear from coursing through my eyes as I looked up at him.

"Raen *Stop*! Just think what you are doing!" Malakei's voice came from somewhere behind Raen, shouting at him to get off of me before continuing to yell in their language.

Raen took this as a sign to remove his hand, shoving it off of where he sat on top of my stomach and pinned me to the ground.

I inhaled a painful breath. My hands flew to my throat where I knew if he had squeezed harder, it would have been enough to scare me into submission. It would have been enough to kill me. He had held back though, whether it be for my sake I didn't know. I wasn't sure what to make of this show of leadership in front of the other Dry Landers, something in particular that one Dry Lander said seemed to have struck a chord in him.

There was a hand at my back and I flinched away, thinking it was Raen but Malakei's concerned eyes came into view, frown lines creased his forehead before his eyes turned hard. He threw his head back to glare at a retreating Raen – probably to find his horse that I managed to lose.

Malakei's eyes fell back on me as I massaged my sore throat, eyes feeling glassy because I knew right then and there that I had just hit my breaking point. If Malakei noticed, he didn't say anything and guided my hand away from my neck, helping me to my feet before placing a somewhat comforting arm around my shoulder.

"Come now. You ride with me."

VII

~*~

Malakei's brother wasn't impressed that I took his spot from Malakei's horse but I had no say in the matter. Malakei shoved his brother off of his horse, saying something in his language to him before his brother's angry gaze flew to me in shock. They started to argue but in the end, it was Malakei that won – he seemed to always get what he wanted, come to think of it.

I sat in front of Malakei on his horse, much like the position Raen and I had been in before only it wasn't filled with tension. I liked riding with Malakei because of this, although I didn't know if I preferred Raen's silence over Malakei's constant chatter.

"So... *what happened*?" Malakei had asked not a moment after I got onto his horse. I should have known this conversation would come up and yet, couldn't help but shift uncomfortably looking down at my fingers gripping the horse's white mane.

"Nothing."

Malakei scoffed from behind me.

"It was not nothing. Raen save you from death."

This time I was the one to scoff, my face souring at the memory as my eyes narrowed down at my hands. Malakei stayed silent at that before taking a breath.

"You wanted to suicide?"

Malakei questioned quietly in my ear from behind, making it twitch. I shifted away from him. My eyes widened in shock at his words as I brought my head up, shaking it repeatedly trying to turn around to him.

"No. No that's not what I was doing–"

"So what? Your escape plan fails so you wish to die instead?" He raised an eyebrow. His mouth pressed into a thin line as he tried not to be disappointed in me. I searched his eyes for a moment, suddenly feeling small as I let out a breath and turned back around. My head fell slightly as I exhaled.

"You don't understand…" I whispered in defeat, lifting my head slightly. I focused on the fur coat over someone's back riding in front of us, frowning deeply.

"None of you do… *I'm*, I'm not like you Malakei. We don't see things with the same eye."

Malakei made a displeasing sound from behind me and shoved my shoulder forward.

"Tell me, Kaylin."

I sighed at this. "We can connect with animals."

There was a moment of silence as Malakei said nothing to my words before he was spluttering and snickering from behind me. Frowning at this, my hand came around to slap at his side and he yelped at that. His hands came to latch around my waist to balance himself on the horse.

I took in a shaky breath at the feel of his hands resting on top of my bruises but ignored it, instead continuing to glare ahead and I opened my mouth to speak.

"It's true you asshole."

"*So*... so you can talk with animal?" Malakei asked in between fits of laughter. I rolled my eyes at this, nodding my head before stopping to grimace.

"Well, I have never connected with them before because I'm too young and I don't know how. I saw my friend doing it – he saved my life when he connected with a tiger."

"So... control animal?" Malakei asked curiously, suddenly intrigued because I could feel his eyes bore into me from behind. I shook my head at that, frowning.

"No not control them... we can communicate through the connection, but we can't control them. It's their choice to help us, all we do is ask." I stated softly and Malakei hummed in understanding.

"That is cool but, not work because Kaylin not strong enough? Or too young to know how?"

Malakei questioned thoughtfully and I furrowed my brows at that before shrugging.

Maybe he was right, I hadn't eaten something proper in two days, so maybe my concentration was low. I did everything right that I saw Corrin do but it just didn't work for me, I needed practice. I was still recovering from a fever which would lead to a major part in the depletion of my strength, that could be my problem.

"I think you're right..." I muttered, looking ahead of me. A small silence enveloped Malakei and me momentarily before he was whispering in my ear again, making it twitch.

"Raen – he *stares* at me."

I frowned in confusion before an angered expression flashed across my features at the name, remembering what he did to me in front of the other Dry Landers, all because I punched him – something I should have done sooner.

"*He is angry with us. That is bad.*" Malakei whispered again with a sigh.

"*Why*? You did nothing wrong. I was the one who punched him." I scoffed, the anger clear in my voice as I went to turn around and glare at Raen who was on his horse a distance behind but Malakei pushed my head back to look forward.

"Don't look. *He* looks, and yes, I did. I raise voice to him." Malakei replied with a small trace of a smirk, the playfulness coming back to his features. I, however, was only more confused by his words and scoffed in disbelief.

"What–"

"Raen is *strong*." Malakei interrupted me seriously. "He is best hunter but scary. No one dare challenge him. Everyone is afraid of him–" He stopped to lean forward and whisper in my ear.

"*You are not afraid of leader. You are elf with fire.*" He nodded once at me and leaned away with a sigh, probably fearful of catching Raen looking at him, he smiled at me thoughtfully.

"He likes you."

I almost laughed at Malakei's statement, thinking that I could add *'funny'* to the list I had conjured up describing this boy only for he was so sure of his declaration. I shook my head in disbelief and looked down at my hands, frowning before letting out a breath.

"Likes me? Are we talking about the same Raen? He strangled me Malakei, he probably would have killed me if you didn't say something–" Malakei winced at the memory of what happened but shook his head at it, frowning. I turned around to look at him. A small, tired smile tugged at my lips as I did and sincerity poured from my eyes.

"Thank you for helping me."

Malakei narrowed his eyes at me when I said that and I realised that every time I thanked him for something, he didn't know if I was being serious or if I was going to laugh in his face, as if he didn't believe that I was actually thanking him and waited for me to throw it back in his face. It made me feel bad for him and think of how it must have been harsh for him growing up.

He nodded once at this, eyes tearing away from me to focus on the journey ahead. His face didn't show any emotion or give me any indication of his acknowledgement apart from nodding at me in silence. I sighed and turned around to look down at my hands, thinking he was finished with our conversation when he spoke again.

"He still likes you."

Malakei declared in a knowing voice before a trapped

whine fell from his lips at the sudden realisation of something. He snickered then, at the thoughts of an inside joke perhaps.

"I hope I don't get axe in back tonight for helping cute elf boy."

***

Nightfall came quickly due to the trees above sheltering us all from the harsh rays of the sun. When the sun went down, it made the forest seem a lot darker during the night. The only light came from the man–made fire the Dry Landers had created before they started to set up camp for the night. As the night grew closer, I noticed small flying bugs started to appear, they seemed to illuminate in the dark.

Malakei had hopped off of his horse and left me to find his brother. I was getting down from his horse, noticing them start to appear out of the blue and my eyes widened with wonder as I looked up at them, dancing in the night above me.

I moved my hand slowly out to touch one, it landed on my index finger softly fluttering its wings slightly before flying away.

I smiled at that, looking up at the small lights that they created. There were some clustered together above me and some lone wandering ones near my body. It amazed me how beautiful they looked.

"Schetchi."

I jumped at the voice, turning around to see Raen

standing with his arms crossed over his bare chest and looking at me with his brow raised in curiosity. His eyes were thoughtful as he considered me.

My eyes dragged over his smooth as sand skin, taking in the multiple scars on his body that looked as though they were a reminder from battles, both man and animal alike. One particular scar that looked like a large cat's claw mark ran from his bicep and slanted over the left part of his chest below his left nipple. I blushed, noticing his eyes stayed on me. I moved my gaze that was shamelessly looking at his bare chest – up to meet his eyes. Frowning, I cleared my throat and decided to test Malakei's assumptions of the boy.

"What do you want?"

He took his arms away from their folded position and slowly came closer to me. My eyes widened at this as I began to step back from him, in fear that he might hurt me or worse; continue what he couldn't finish earlier.

"*S–Stay back.*" I stuttered out as I continued to step back blindly. His eyes never left mine, yet he didn't stop coming closer to me. His mouth pressed into a thin line and I gasped when I felt something hard against my back. My eyes fell shut at the realisation of being cornered against Malakei's unbothered horse and cursed to myself silently.

I peeked one eye open to look up at Raen when I sensed him stop in front of me, my other eye opened immediately afterwards to see him looking down at me calmly. All traces of anger that were clearly on his features earlier, now suddenly vanished as he looked down at my quickly dwindling fearful expression. He cleared his throat.

"*Schetchi*… fireflies." He said before looking up at the flying insects calmly.

My eyes drifted back to the flying bugs, smiling at the name given to them. I had never seen such creatures before. Most birds and insects did not reach as far as the *High Peaks* and I always wondered why.

"*Fireflies.*" The words fell from my lips in a whisper as I looked up at the lights around us. It suited them – flies protruding light like the glow from fire, maybe even some heat too as I noticed the air had become warmer when they arrived.

Raen looked back down at me, his eyes shining in the night's light as he reached forward to take a small bag from Malakei's horse. I turned and watched with a confused frown, not knowing what he was doing but when he turned back to me, he grabbed my hand.

My stomach rolled in fright as he pulled me closer to him, holding up my hand between both his chest and mine and pouring some of the contents from the bag onto my hand, a grainy substance. I scanned it curiously before looking back up at Raen, confused about what I should do with it. He blinked down at me before he slowly brought his fingers around my wrist, holding my hand up into the air.

My eyes lit up as one by one, fireflies landed on my hand until it was almost consumed in light. Raen's fingers slid from my wrist down my arm before resting on my shoulder to stand behind me and look up at what I was seeing. I could feel his eyes on me but I didn't look away from the fireflies eating at whatever the grain substance was off of my hand. My smile had come back to my cheeks as I took in the sight before me, dimples poking out as even a small laugh left my lips at the tickling sensation of the fireflies eating out of my palm.

I slowly brought my hand down to look closely, eyes glinting as the insects roamed my fingers and up my arm before disappearing back into the night above me.

I felt Raen's breath against my left ear while his fingers rested near the small hairs at the back of my neck. I sensed his eyes looking down over my shoulder at my palm before looking up at my face.

He exhaled with a breath I could only describe as relief.

Was this his way of saying sorry? Apologising for what he did earlier? I thought about what Malakei had told me a few hours ago. How almost everyone here was afraid of Raen. He was supposedly the best hunter and could take on the role of being the strongest here, so of course that gave him the reputation of never showing weakness, never showing heart. When I punched him, I must have really damaged not only his ego, but his reputation. I could see now how he was forced to do it to show power over the other Dry Landers. I didn't know what rules they had for attempting to overthrow a leader or disobeying an order but it made sense now. If it didn't, why would he even apologise to me in the first place if he hated me so much?

I frowned at my thoughts but shook them away quickly. I could see he was quick–tempered and had some anger issues, but just by him showing me this small act, it made me feel something other than loneliness and heartbreak. For the first time since I left my home, it made me thankful.

When the grain substance was completely eaten, I watched as the last of the fireflies left my palm and with it, a thought came into my head.

"You could understand me this whole time… why didn't you say something?"

I asked slightly nervous but determined to find out the reason for his silence at the start. He sighed at this, breath fanning my shoulder before his hand left the back of my neck. He stepped out from behind me, putting the small bag of grain back into Malakei's satchel on the horse.

"I didn't feel like talking."

He stated calmly although I could tell he was tense as he turned back to look down at me where I stood.

"O–Okay." I stuttered out as I let my gaze drop to my sandals, understanding what he meant, even though it sounded ridiculous but respected his decision. He wasn't much of a talker as I had come to realise and grunted more than used words.

With that said, he left. His footsteps echoed silently as he walked away from me and I let out a breath I didn't realise I was holding.

***

"Come here, boy!"

I jumped at the unfamiliar voice, head turning to one of the older Dry Lander men pointing in my direction and summoning me over to sit with him and his friends at the fire.

My heart pounded as I made my way over to them slowly, eyes wide and confused when all of their gazes seemed to lock on me, suddenly taking interest in me.

When I was close enough, the man pulled me into his chest making me gasp as I stumbled forward. The smell of alcohol hit my nose and almost made me gag. I could hear the other Dry Landers laugh and cheer at something but I ignored it, looking up at the man when he let me go and tapped me on the back roughly.

"We are celebrating! Join us."

The man cheered, already taking the liberty to pour a drink for me before shoving it into my chest. I stumbled back at his roughness, catching the drink and looking up at him wide–eyed.

'How could they celebrate right now? Oh right, They were celebrating successfully kidnapping me.'

"I–I don't drink."

"Drink boy, we celebrate together! We are almost home!" The man bellowed in his drunken state causing some of the other men to cheer loudly. I winced at that, ears flattening against my head at the sudden sensitivity. I shook my head at the man, wanting nothing more than to rest after the events of today. My fever was still there although I was recovering quicker now, it still seemed to take the energy out of me.

The man looked at me with a dark expression on his face.

"You think you are better than us?" The drunk man asked lowly, his eyes narrowing down at me. Almost challengingly as he staggered forward. My stomach sank at his change of mood and most of the others around the fire grew silent as they watched me. Knowing that I wasn't one to hold my tongue if the events from earlier were anything to go by, I took a step back shaking my head at the man's angered eyes.

"No, I–"

"How dare you refuse to drink with us! We risked our lives for you, and you refuse to celebrate? *Elf scum*!" The man shrieked as he threw his alcoholic drink at me.

I barely registered his words through my scream as the drink smashed against my chest into tiny pieces. I fell backwards onto the ground before looking up at him fearfully. My body was now drenched and smelt of alcohol.

He laughed from above me and so did a few of the others. The rest, however, either stayed silent or left before the scene could escalate further.

I looked down at my soaked clothes, wincing at the small cuts on my arm and chest from the smashed ceramic mug. My eyes quickly shot up at the staggering man coming towards me in worry. I tried to move backwards on the ground but winced at the stinging pain when I used my arms.

I felt a foot before my back crashed into someone's legs. I relaxed when I saw Malakei, his brother, Bear and Caito behind him, all looking at their drink comrade with disgust.

Malakei frowned as he took in my state and didn't hesitate to reach down and help me up, careful not to touch my cut arm. I sniffled as I stood up, feeling sticky and sore.

Caito's voice resembled that of a snake's as he hissed through the bubbling drunk laughter from the others in their mother tongue, making them all stop what they were doing and turn to Caito with alarm.

Malakei slung my arm over his shoulder carefully to help me walk as I winced, trying to break away from him to walk on my own but his grip was strong around my waist.

"We are celebrating!" The drunk man explained happily as he staggered forward but I flinched back from him.

Malakei pulled me behind him and glared sharply at the drunken man. His lip curled with disgust as he said something to him.

The man blinked before the anger resurfaced onto his features, his eyes turning to me where he pointed harshly, making my heart beat out of my chest.

"He refused to drink with us!"

"Keylin is young. He decides to drink or not. He will not be forced." Caito stated, loud enough for the other Dry Landers to hear and turn their gazes on me. I only lowered my gaze.

"You force drink on boy. Look what you did. Have you no shame?" Bear's voice was calm but the seriousness behind it was terrifying. He could explode at any minute.

Malakei stayed quiet beside me. The only time he did speak was when he turned to his brother to whisper something. His brother glanced at me pitifully before

Malakei pushed me carefully into his brother's arms. I grew fearful at this and reached out for Malakei. He was the only real person I trusted out of everyone here. I felt safer with him.

He frowned at me and said something to his brother before Bear stalked over to the man. I watched him ball his fist as if getting ready to hit the man. His dagger caught my eye from his back pocket and after a moment, he took it out, raising it to the man's neck in threat. I gasped in fright as my breathing came out harshly.

I didn't get to see what Bear did – if he killed the Dry Lander, nor did I want to watch. I was glad when Malakei's brother pulled me away from the bloody scene that I imagined would have given me nightmares if I had witnessed what Bear had done, knowing what he was capable of.

VIII

~*~

Malakei's brother dragged me through the makeshift camp roughly before pushing me forward into a tent, I staggered and fell forward onto my knees with a groan as I brought my blood–soaked hands out in front of me.

I could hear someone getting up from within the tent and Malakei's brother said only a few words to them before turning and leaving me alone with the stranger.

I gasped, looking down at my hands as the person knelt in front of me. Their hands moved under my legs and around my back. I went to protest but hesitated as I was being picked up into a familiar chest, a sense of deja vu overcoming me. I lifted my gaze to Raen with alert and slightly red–rimmed eyes.

Raen's eyes pooled with mixed emotions scattered across his face. He was frustrated, confused and worried all at once but the other emotions were not as prominent as the anger that shone through his eyes when he noticed my drenched, trembling and injured form.

I held in the lump in my throat and closed my eyes while my fingers clutched at his bare chest, slightly disappointed that he wasn't wearing a shirt for the sole reason I could have something to cling to and hide the tears from trying to escape my eyes.

I supposed I was angry with myself, for being so scared all of the time and knowing that life would come easier to me if I just stood my ground and *gods*, stopped crying as if I were a simple child for once in my life.

I looked up after a few moments with clenched teeth to see the trees of the forest. Growing confused as I turned to Raen, I wondered where he was taking me when the sound of a river filled my ears, making them twitch.

We were quickly approaching a river. Raen wasted no time in lowering my body down beside the bank. He knelt before me, hands moving down to take off my shirt.

"W–What are you doing?" I couldn't help but ask wide–eyed as my hands went around his, stopping him from what he was trying to do.

"Helping you take off your shirt," He rolled his eyes as he flipped me onto my front despite my protests. "Unless you want to wear–"

"I–I can take it off myself." I shoved away from him, bringing my knees up as I scooted backwards on the grass to create distance between us.

I couldn't help the blush rising on my features as I realised what exactly he was trying to do – albeit not in the most communicative way. The river behind me only indicated that this was a midnight soak to clean my body of the cuts and rid the stench of home–brewed alcohol.

"Okay," Raen replied cooly, blinking in confusion as he observed me, not understanding what I was making such a big deal about no doubt. To him, we were both males. We both shared the same anatomy. He may have even thought his gesture of taking off my shirt for me was a kind and helpful one. Absolutely *not*.

Raen held my gaze for another moment before rising to his feet, peeling his shirt from his body and revealing his ink–coated skin that almost glowed under the moonlight. My mouth dried up at the sight of him but before I could say anything, he cast his shirt towards me. It landed at my side next to the river.

"Take it off and get in." He commanded, looking down at me. He took off his belt and placed his axe down on the grass beside him before he pulled down his trousers.

I turned my head away from him as he had no problem stripping directly in front of me, gulping at his words when they dawned on me.

He was getting into the river too.

"Unless you are a shy little elf."

He snickered as he walked by me and I clenched my jaw at that, refusing to move until I heard him enter the river.

I glanced at his axe he had discarded a few feet away from me. He was almost too sure of himself that I wouldn't take it or try to kill him.

'Good luck trying to kill the leader of the Dry Landers that invaded your home. He could crush you with his

biceps alone and use your ears as decoration for his belt.'
My thoughts so cruelly reminded me of when he choked me earlier, not believing that his strength had any limitations.

I felt a wet hand touch my wrist from behind and I turned around, noticing him standing in the river behind me.

"I will not hurt you. You have my word."

"I suppose you choking me earlier was a sign of your good intentions?" I raised a brow at him. His eyes flickered at the memory before he took a breath and shook his head.

"No. That was… not my intention. My men were questioning my ability to lead our mission. I needed to remind them why our leader picked me for this. I used you as an example of what I could do to those who disobeyed me. I am sorry for that."

So he wasn't the leader of the Dry Landers per se – but a close second. His reasons only brought with it more questions. Questions I wanted answers to, but I knew he wouldn't give me so easily.

'Comply and survive.'

"You should wash up while we have time." He brought me out of my thoughts and I nodded at him in agreement, standing up from where I sat by the river bed and ever so carefully – began peeling my blood–stained wet shirt from my body. Taking care to avoid my stinging hands, I should have let him help take off my clothes when he did.

I could feel his eyes on me from behind as I stripped. A cold shiver ran up my spine from the night air that seemed to drop a few degrees as I stood bare under the pale moonlight.

I didn't dally – crouching down to jump into the river where I noticed Raen had averted his gaze, only turning to me when he heard the splash of water knowing that I was submerged in the river water then.

I gasped when the cold water engulfed my body and I tried to regulate my breathing at the sudden freezing temperature. My body felt as though it was being stabbed from multiple positions with ice–cold daggers.

"Keylin, come here." Raen's voice called from where he had ventured deeper into the middle of the river.

"This isn't where you finally murder me is it?" I called out in a joking tone all the while hoping he wouldn't reply to me. To my relief, he only chuckled.

As I walked over to him trembling furiously, he reached out and pulled me forward. I was beginning to get used to his rough ways, believing that was just how he was around me and probably people in general. All of the Dry Landers seemed to be like that.

I stumbled forward into his chest again as his cold hands came up to run over my cut arm. I winced as he washed the blood off before moving his wet hands to my back. I yelped quietly at the coldness of the water covering his hands trickling down my back and sending a cold shiver through my body.

His hands ran up around my shoulders and my ears flattened against my head while I gasped and reached out to touch his chest.

He made a displeased grunt at the feel of my cold

fingers and raised a brow at me.

"Really?"

"Your hands are cold."

"So are yours." His finger flicked at the edge of the water, sending droplets skirting in all directions towards me. I flinched to the side.

I didn't know why I smiled at this. A small laugh escaped my lips as I looked back at his curious gaze on me. A smirk crossed my features and I lifted my fingers to flick the water back at him.

He scrunched his nose at me, a glint in his eyes as he lifted his hand back and splashed some water at me, this time reaching as far as my hair and making my lips form an *'O'* as a cold shiver ran through me.

Raen chuckled from above me and his eyes crinkled at the sides as he took in my expression. A small smirk rested on his lips before it was wiped off by me splashing him, his hair becoming wet in the process.

I laughed at his expression as he wiped his face and pushed his wet hair back. His eyes fell on me with a mischievous glint.

Suddenly, his whole body dropped into the water and left me standing in the river confused. I started to panic when he didn't come up for air after a few moments.

"Raen?" I called out to him as I made my way over to where he disappeared under the water.

A hand suddenly pulled me back and I turned around to see Raen with a smirk on his face.

"What—"

He spat river water in my face, causing me to yell and

lurch away as some of the water got into my eyes.

"I can't believe you just did that." I muttered as I rubbed my eyes fiercely before looking up at him. Teeth clenched and ready to take this river battle to the next level.

I quickly reached out to his laughing form and shoved his shoulders under the water, only to yelp when I felt his arms latch around my waist. I let go of his shoulders as he submerged me in the river. I couldn't see anything as I thrashed in his grip but he didn't let go and quickly, we made our way to the surface.

I gulped in air and so did Raen when we broke the surface, panting heavily before looking down at our position.

His arms were still wrapped around me but he had pulled me closer to him underwater. My arms were around his shoulders holding me up above him, giving me a sense of feeling tall as I towered over him. Our eyes found each other in the night.

Malakei's words played on my mind then, confusing me further when I started to think that maybe there was some truth to his assumptions.

Raen didn't push me away, his hold around me didn't falter, it almost got tighter as he brought our heads closer, breathing heavily in the cold of night. He panted slightly out of breath as mine came out panicked at how close our lips were getting to each other. If one of us were to tilt our heads slightly, our lips would have touched.

His eyes flickered down to my lips in thought and a small gasp left my lips.

"Keylin?!"

Malakei's voice rang through the silence and Raen abruptly shoved me away from him, making me yelp in surprise and fall back into the water. I spluttered at the flavour of river water in my mouth.

I turned back to glare at Raen but frowned when I noticed he had already left the river completely and was throwing on his clothes, bringing his belt up to buckle around him.

I blinked at him in confusion, about to open my mouth when Malakei came into view, holding something in his hands.

"Kay–"

"*Keylin* is in the river." Raen growled out with sudden frustration making both Malakei and I jump. Malakei's eyes widened at Raen as he nodded. He was about to open his mouth when Raen abruptly left Malakei and me alone, darting through the bushes of the forest.

My heart suddenly began to race at the sight of Malakei, not having seen him since the incident with the drunk Dry Lander. I remembered Bear holding an axe as he went over to the drunk man, probably killing him for all I knew.

I dived under the water, faintly hearing my name being called and didn't break the surface until I needed to. I coughed, brushing the water off of my face.

When I looked up, I saw Malakei sitting down at the riverbank – holding what appeared to be a towel in his arms as he smiled at me.

"My brother said you wash up in river. You finish now

or need more time?"

He called out to me with a charming smile plastered on his face and I rolled my eyes at his sarcasm, slowly making my way to the bank of the river. Just as I was about to get out, a blush crept up my neck and onto my cheeks. I stiffly shook my head, refusing to get out and let him see my naked body.

Malakei frowned at me as he raised his brow.

"What?"

"I–uh, nothing–"

"Come now. *Out* elf boy, it's late and I am tired." Malakei commanded with a roll of his eyes before he suddenly stopped, eyes growing wide when he spotted my discarded clothes beside the river. He turned back to look down at me in amusement.

"Ha! You are naked!"

My eyes grew fearful before I let out a small breath and began to move back into the river. Malakei held up his hands as he smiled, taking the towel in both hands he held it outstretched.

"I won't peep!" He said over the towel and I bit my lip.

"Turn around and close your eyes." I called out, watching him carefully for the minute he turned his back to me, I would make a beeline for the towel. I only hoped he didn't turn around.

Malakei chuckled at that, shaking his head playfully as he turned around, towel outstretched in his hand behind him.

I quickly got out of the water, gasping at the cold night air but continued to walk hurriedly towards the towel in

Malakei's arms. Just as I was about to reach it, Malakei turned around and smirked down at me. I yelped and grabbed the towel from his hand, wrapping it around me tightly as my teeth chattered.

"You *asshole!*" I grumbled quietly and went to push past him, picking up my discarded clothes with an unimpressed huff. He chuckled behind me before slinging an arm over my shoulder, guiding me in the right direction back to the small camp.

"I'm sorry. You can wear my clothes when we get back to camp. You need new one anyways." He stated after his laughter died down. I rolled my eyes in response and shoved him away.

"You're an idiot."

"I love you too *dimples.*"

I rolled my eyes at his joking statement as we continued to walk through the forest ground back to the camp. It was only after a moment that Malakei let out a muffled laugh.

"What?" I turned to him with irritation clear on my face.

"You have small penis."

My mouth fell open in shock at his words, narrowing my gaze into slits – I reached forward and slapped him on the shoulder. He chuckled at that.

"N–No, I don't!"

I *didn't.* Honestly, it was average for its size, being a little over five and a half inches but Malakei only smirked as he shook his head at me.

"It is the smallest I ever saw–"

"Do you have a list or something that you keep? Don't tell me Dry Landers have measuring contents." I raised my brow at him, making him immediately stop laughing and turn to me, his eyes cast down in amusement and a small smirk formed on his features. There was a mischievous look in his eyes.

"*And you*? Do not think I not see *Raen* coming out of river. He naked too. *Both of you*!"

"Shut up Malakei." I grumbled under my breath as I furrowed my eyebrows at the ground.

"Shut up Malakei." He imitated me in a high–pitched voice. Offended, and tired of listening to him – I shoved his laughing ass hard, smiling to myself in victory as he stumbled and rolled into a nearby ditch.

IX

~*~

Malakei gave me some cloth, wool–brown trousers followed by a white, long–sleeved shirt that had a large dip on the front. I frowned at a large stain on one of the sleeves before looking back with a raised brow at Malakei. The guilty Dry Lander only raised his hands in surrender.

"I don't know – blame *Charon*."

"Who?" I frowned.

"My brother."

A look of realisation made its way onto my face before I glared at Malakei spread out on his makeshift bed, twiddling his pocketknife in his hands as he stared down at it thoughtfully. He motioned for me to come over to him.

"Come now."

I walked over as he brought his body up into a sitting position on the bed; glancing up at me, he then grabbed my wrist and pulled me down to sit beside him on the bed. When I did, he held out my hand flat and placed the small pocket knife in my hand.

"Keep this." He croaked and placed his hand over mine.

"Kill bad men when I not there to kill them."

He told me firmly and I frowned, about to comment only to see that he was deadly serious. I gasped and shook my head, trying to give him back the knife but he insisted I take it.

"I–I can't. I don't want to kill anyone. It's not... it's not who I am–"

Malakei looked at me as if I had two heads before he shook his. His hand came up to ruffle my hair. I protested at this and shoved the loose hair out of my face with a frown.

"You know how to fight yes?" Malakei wondered, his voice laced with concern and I scrunched my face at that.

"Sort of, *but I always lose.*"

I muttered the last part hoping he didn't hear me. He considered this and nodded as if in a daze. A small smirk crept onto his face and I was almost frightened to know what he was thinking of. Oddly enough, his smirk faded and he smiled.

Okay, *now* I was worried.

"Come now, let's sleep." He disregarded our conversation after a moment, reaching forward to blow out the small candle on the ground, I let out a sigh.

"Goodnight then Malakei."

I got up from his bed, about to make my way to the tent's entrance. Thoughts of where I was going to sleep ran through my head when his hands suddenly came up to wrap around my middle, pulling me back into his chest and we both fell back on his bed.

"*Stay.*" He whispered in my ear, making it twitch profoundly and I shivered, releasing a small breath. Malakei rolled us over so that he was pressed up against my back, his hands clutching me close as he nuzzled his head into the crook of my neck. He let out a breath which made me all but combust in sensitivity at the feeling he sent through me.

"We are friends, *yes*? We protect each other? Like *brothers*?" He asked suddenly into my neck and my heart panged at the memory of Corrin. With a shaky breath, my eyes began to sting. I had completely forgotten to respond to Malakei.

Malakei rolled me over until I was facing him. His concerned eyes scanned mine in fear of having said something he shouldn't have said and he gulped at my tearful gaze.

"Was something I said?"

"*No*," I smiled, a brief and tearful smile and I shut my eyes tightly, taking a breath.

"I had a brother in *Versai* and I just miss him. *I really miss him.*"

I whispered out as I rubbed my eyes. Malakei frowned, running a comforting hand over my back, smiling a small smile as he shifted on the bed to prop his head up on his arm and stare down at me curiously.

"Tell me about him."

"Well..." I smiled at the many memories we shared through our childhood.

"His name was Corrin and... he reminds me of you actually. Although he was older than me, he was a huge child."

I smiled when he scoffed, shoving me lightly before letting his head rest on the pillow, our faces only centimetres from each other as he motioned for me to continue.

"He used to save me from a boy called Tobias. He would push me, beat me and call me names like *'snake'* because of my eyes–"

"Why your *eyes*?" Malakei frowned at me in confusion. "They are strong green. That is good in *Dry Lands*."

"They're not blue," I whispered out.

Malakei made a face at this, not understanding why that would be the reason for someone to hurt me. This shocked me. I presumed every sector knew of each other's rules but then again maybe I was mistaken. Not everyone was as well educated or curious as the *High Peaks* or the *Sky Lanes*.

I tried to explain and keep it simple as best I could while not wanting to go into too much detail to the extent Mara taught me in the *High Peaks.*

"Elve's eyes are different shades of blue and nothing more. Anything else and it's said to be ugly–"

"You are not ugly," Malakei whispered in shock as his fingers came up to caress my cheek. *"They* are ugly ones. Inside *and* out."

I smiled at this before continuing.

"I guess because my mother was a princess and my

grandfather was the king, they let me stay."

They let me live.

Malakei nodded slowly, processing everything that I had just told him before he fell back onto the bed on his back and turned his body up to the ceiling. A few minutes of silence passed us and I began to think that he had fallen asleep but his voice whispered through the night.

"I can't wait for you to meet Tara. She loves elf ears."

My curiosity got the better of me and I glanced over at Malakei's face in confusion, about to open my mouth and question who this Tara person was when he continued.

"–And *Bow*. Something tells me he will not like you at start but once he gets to know you, he will love you."

This made my thoughts run wild at these new names and the idea of Malakei introducing me to his friends back at his camp. It only sent a sinking feeling as I wondered what would become of me when I finally arrived there. My initial thoughts were that they would kill me or that I'd become a Dry Lander's slave – but now, hearing Malakei talk about meeting his friends had me confused.

"Malakei, what will happen to me when I get to your home?" My voice was quiet in the dark tent. The glow of the moon was the only source of light, allowing us to see each other.

Malakei stayed quiet momentarily, choosing his words carefully as he turned on his side once again to face me.

"I am not allowed to say but... you have to pass a test."

"What test?" I furrowed my brows at this.

"I can't tell you that." Malakei sighed, closing his eyes. I could tell he didn't want to talk about this anymore, but

I needed to know one more thing before I went to sleep. Maybe his answer would ease my mind – or make it worse.

"*Am I going to die… if I don't pass this test?*" I whispered nervously looking at Malakei's closed eyelids. He poked an eye open towards me before sighing and closing it again. He pulled me closer to him so my head was buried in his chest, his face resting in my hair.

"I can't tell you that."

'*Yes,*' it sounded more like.

"Sleep now. We rise early at dawn."

***

I woke up to an empty bed with no trace of Malakei. I frowned when my hand reached out to touch the side where Malakei had slept only to feel – what I hoped would be his sleeping form – was only the ruffled sheets of the makeshift bed where Malakei once remained.

I sighed as I opened my eyes, blinking repeatedly and slowly getting up out of bed. Throwing on the black boots Malakei had given me, I tied the belt around my waist. My eyes locked onto the small dagger on the ground that Malakei had given me the night before. I picked it up thoughtfully before placing it in my belt loop.

I left the tent, eyes immediately falling on the fire not too far away. Shaking the memories from yesterday away, I made my way over to the small crowd gathered around it eating their breakfast.

I wondered if I would see the drunk man's dead body

lying there with an axe sticking out of his chest but when I got there, there was no trace of any murder being done. The body that I thought would have been there – simply wasn't.

"Keylin!"

I turned and saw Caito coming towards me with a small friendly smile. I smiled back but before I could say anything, Caito bet me to it.

"Malakei told me to tell you; he is waiting for you near horses."

"Oh. Okay. Thanks, Caito."

Caito moved forward to pat my shoulder. Eyes bright, he continued towards the fire, greeting the few men eating around it warmly.

As I turned and made my way to the horses, memories of the fireflies and Raen danced in my mind from last night and I couldn't help but frown as I wondered where Raen went after that time in the river. I remembered how close we were and if my eyes didn't trick me – almost kissed if we weren't interrupted. At least, *that's what I thought it was…*

I was so deep in my thoughts that I failed to pick up on a rustling that came from the bushes to my left until someone ran out of it with a scream.

I didn't turn around fast enough to see who it was and yelped as our bodies collided, sending us both toppling onto the hard ground. A choked groan escaped me.

I tried to get up but hands shoved me down by my shoulders. My attacker held mine in place while they lowered themself down so that their mouth was right against my ear. I whimpered at that, not understanding why someone was attacking me all of a sudden. My mind went to the drunk from last night, maybe Malakei's brother Charo–

When Malakei spoke in my ear, I let out a sigh of relief, knowing that he wouldn't hurt me.

Or so I thought.

"Rule one when fighting; never let guard down. Always be alert."

"Malakei! what are you–"

Malakei quickly got off of me and helped me to my feet. I shook out my shoulder as I turned to glare at him. His face held no emotion, the only indication of any that gave him away was in his voice and he sounded serious.

"Mal–"

He suddenly punched me in the face, making me gasp and stumble back in fright. My hand immediately flew to my throbbing nose to feel something wet starting to drop from it.

"Be alert Keylin."

He hissed at me seriously making me look up at him fearfully. I began to back away from him, shaking my head in fright at his towering form.

"What's gotten into you? Please stop this already, you're... kind of scaring me." I pleaded with him before gasping at the feeling of being cornered against a tree. My eyes stayed on Malakei's advancing form, almost resembling a predator, about to pounce on his prey.

"Act on your feet."

Malakei's voice rang through my mind just as he

brought his hand back to punch me again.

My eyes widened and I moved my head, not getting the timing right and he managed to clip my jaw. I cried out in pain at the force behind it.

Too focused on the pain in my jaw, Malakei sent a hard blow to my stomach and I lurched forward. My mouth fell open to yell but no sound came out.

He pushed me back upright against the tree, fingers digging into my shoulders causing a soft whimper to leave my lips as I tried to focus back on him.

"Malakei... stop–"

"*Fight me!*" Malakei screamed and I winced, ears flattening against my head. My eyes began to water from the pain and I looked up at him pleadingly. His eyes were full of confusion as he stared down at me in what looked to be something close to disappointment.

I yelped as Malakei shoved me to the side, resulting in my body stumbling forward and falling to the hard ground. Letting out a groan, I moved my hands in front of me to grip the dirt and pushed myself up onto all fours before taking a breath and holding it. I brought myself up to a full standing position and rushed forward, away from Malakei completely and made a dash through the forest.

"Running is useless when bad man chasing you Keylin!"

I heard him shout but that only made me run harder. Clutching my stomach with a wince, I managed to make my way back to the fire. There weren't as many Dry Landers around it now but that didn't stop me from screaming at them, hoping one of them would help me –

or stop Malakei.

Some of the men around the fire stood up in alarm but Malakei yelled something to them in their language from where he had quickly gained on me. I watched them frown at me before looking back at Malakei, nodding silently before lowering themselves back down to their seats.

No.

I clenched my teeth at that, ignoring the stinging in my jaw as Malakei reached me and pulled me back to him.

Before he could even have the chance to hit me again, my eyes locked on him menacingly and I grabbed a fistful of his shirt, pushing him back against a tree roughly. His body jolted at the sudden force and groaned in pain. I fisted his shirt in my hands.

"*Stop this now. Are you crazy*?!" I screamed in his face and Malakei, for a moment, was startled before he glared back at me, registering my words.

"I'm preparing you. You thank me later–"

"Preparing me?! You're *hurting* me! How is *this*–"

Malakei brought his knee up, quickly kneeing me in the stomach and I crumbled forward in pain. Whatever strength I had vanished as I tried to catch my breath.

Malakei pushed me back roughly and I stumbled onto my front. My face erupted in pain as I tried to move onto my side, only to scream in terror as Malakei took one of my legs and used it to push me onto my back, pulling me closer to him.

"No Malakei–" Malakei ignored me as he climbed up my body. His fingers bunched my shirt as he gripped my right shoulder harshly. He brought his hand back to punch me again.

And again.

And again, until I moved my hands down to clutch at my injured stomach.

I felt the dagger Malakei had given me when my fingers shook around its handle. I took it from my belt just as Malakei was getting ready to land another swing at me. I brought it up and held it to his neck, breathing heavily up at him.

"*Enough*." I managed to wheeze, taking the break greatly while Malakei jolted above me and out a relieved sigh before he smiled down at me. His eyes were now impressed and returned to their playful mischief.

"A bit late but good for first combat lesson."

At that he got off of me, allowing me to curl up on my side. I dropped the knife beside me and wretched violently onto the ground at what I was forced to do. Malakei's hand clapped down on my back in a sort of assurance before he pulled me up to my feet, patting the dirt from my clothes.

"G–Get off me!" I whimpered as I shoved him away. Malakei stumbled slightly at that, a look of hurt crossed his features before his lips pressed into a thin line, eyes hard.

"Key–"

"Stop it!" I yelled at him before wincing at the dull pain in my ribs. My eyes filled with anger.

"Why did you do that? Are you *insane*?! You could have seriously hurt me for no reason."

"You can't fight for shit Keylin. I was glad I witnessed it before someone else did. It is me who teach you to fight.

Every Dry Lander must know how...What if something happened to you and we not there *huh*? What if *I* was bad man?" Malakei raised his voice as mild concern played on his features but he remained calm. I was about ready to slam him to the ground.

I limped forward, eyes ablaze with unshed tears and anger fuelling me.

"You *are* the bad man," I informed him slowly. "The same bad man who helped kidnap me from my home. Who thinks just because I am still here and not trying to escape that I am willing to have friendships and pretend everything is fine – *like my whole world didn't just fall apart in one night*."

Malakei was silent as he watched the tears of frustration roll down my cheeks, gulping at my words and almost looking sorry for his actions. Other Dry Landers watched in silence from behind us.

"Keylin–"

"*I am not one of you*," I gritted out seriously. "And I *never* will be."

I made sure that Malakei understood every word as I watched his face fall. Confusion crossed his eyes before it was quickly covered up by slight frustration. He went to speak as I was walking backwards but just as I went to turn around, I found myself turning into someone's hard chest. I staggered and the stranger's hands immediately flew out to steady me but I winced bringing my hands up to push them away.

Raen looked down at me with an unreadable expression. His eyes didn't shift as he looked down at my bloody and bruised features while I limped away from both Malakei and him, trying not to let the mild embarrassment and utter hurt reach my eyes as I did.

I missed my home. I missed *Corrin*.

***

I let out a painful wince as I tried to pull my shirt up over my body, stopping for small breaks in between tugs when a wave of pain ran up my body at the smallest of movements. I had just managed to get one of my arms out of the shirt when I heard rustling from the bushes behind me.

I held my breath as I stopped trying to prise off my shirt and frustratingly tried to pull it back down over myself to cover my badly bruised body. A small grunt of pain left me when my hand brushed over a sensitive part just below my chest.

"M–Malakei?" I stuttered out, cursing myself for showing weakness before my eyes narrowed in anger at the thought of him coming to apologise or *worse*, coming for round two.

The worst of all was that the night before he decided to do this, I had told him that I had been bullied for being different, hurt repeatedly since I was young. Yet, he decided to take liberty and inflict even more pain.

Hadn't I suffered enough?

I knew I wasn't good at fighting but it was *my* choice. There was a reason I had allowed myself to go through Tobias's torture for so long – and it wasn't because I couldn't defend myself. I didn't see the point in being violent to others. Violence never solved anything and instead, only made situations worse. Call me a coward, but it was never my decision to fight – nor would it ever be. To spring a brutal fight on me like that was something I couldn't comprehend, let alone as a method of teaching. Was this the way it was here?

"Keylin?"

My eyes immediately darted up, chest tightening when the sight of Raen came through the bushes. I gulped and turned around, trying not to hiss as I pulled the rest of my shirt down to cover my body.

"Go away," I warned him. My voice shook ever so slightly when I heard Raen move closer to me, ignoring my warning.

'What was with these Dry Landers? Do they not understand the concept of 'no' or when someone just wants to be left alone? Gods…'

This only made me even more frustrated and I turned around to face him just as he was about to reach out to me with a concerned look. I slapped his hand away and pushed at his chest causing him to stumble back in surprise. He blinked down at me.

"I said go *away*!" I shouted, voice firm. "Do you not understand that I want to be alone?!"

"Malakei told me what he did to you." He noted calmly, grabbing my arm and pulling me forward. His eyes filled with a flicker of anger before it was quickly drowned out with concern. He looked down at me, grip tightening when I tried to pull away from him.

"Are you alright?"

"I'm fine," I grumbled. "Just let *go*."

Raen pulled me into his chest, hands coming around to grip tightly at my waist before he began to push me backwards until my back was pressed against a tree.

"What are you doing?" I gritted out as tears of pain pricked my eyes. Raen's hands moved from around my waist to lift my shirt.

My breathing hitched when his hand moved down to press against one of the black bruises and I squirmed under his cold yet gentle touch, one hand clutching his shoulder while the other reached for his wrist.

Before I could ask him again what he was doing, he cleared his throat, looked up at me and spoke.

"Not broken. Maybe sprained." He explained, I blinked up at him. "Come, you need rest."

"I'm fine." I took my hand from his shoulder and pulled my shirt down roughly, trying my best not to look away from his intense stare but cursed the blush creeping up my neck and cheeks, tinting the tips of my ears.

"No, you're hurting. You need rest. Do I have to pick you up?"

My eyes shot up at that, cheeks now burning. I shook my head furiously.

A small smirk formed on Raen's lips. A sense of victory washed over him at this while I let out a defeated breath and allowed him to drag me back to the camp.

"Why does it matter to you?" I couldn't help but ask.

He glanced at me over his shoulder.

"Why wouldn't it matter?"

"You *know* – you treating me this way just because I'm a prince. This doesn't feel like a normal captor and captive relationship."

When we crossed the small fire where most of the Dry Landers were gathered, I felt eyes on me. Looking up, I spotted Malakei's brother Charon glaring at me before he moved to Raen, a murderous expression on his face.

I gasped when I spotted Malakei beside him with a black eye and burst lip. After a moment of staring, he finally looked up and met my gaze.

He smiled apologetically and offered me a small wave, wincing when he spotted Raen before casting his gaze back down at his feet.

"That's because it's not." Raen replied, turning to me but I was too focused on Malakei's state.

"Did you hurt him?" I found myself asking after a moment. I turned to look up at Raen whose jaw clenched and eyes hardened as he walked in front. His hand remained around my wrist as he did but hummed back at me, giving me a small nod before turning back around to weave his way through tents.

"*Why?*" I whispered as my heart exploded out of my chest. He stopped at a tent that I believed was his and turned to me with a raised eyebrow.

"Why *not?*" He counteracted calmly. "He disobeyed orders and it didn't sit well with me that he hurt you."

He stated quickly and I blinked up at him in surprise, not believing that I had actually got an answer from him.

I nodded regardless. Unsure of how to respond. He brought a hand around the small of my back, ushering me into his tent.

I took a moment to look around me at his spacious tent, only grunting when he playfully nudged me forward from where I was blocking the entrance to the tent. I turned around to him with a raised brow and he only chuckled at my expression.

"Sit down on the bed."

My gaze shifted to the makeshift bed littered with fur coats. It looked so comfortable that all I wanted to do was fall asleep right there and then. All I could do was look at it longingly as my legs failed to carry me towards it. Raen gave me another nudge towards the bed, this time making me stumble. My hands flew out to land in the soft fur of the bed.

I turned around before lowering my body down carefully onto the bed, hands flying to clutch my stomach as I did.

After a moment, I heard rustling and spotted Raen dunking a small bowl into a large bucket of river water in the far corner. He grabbed a brown rag from his satchel before coming over to where I sat on his bed.

I watched him silently place the bowl and rag onto the floor and grab a small stool, pushing it under him to sit in front of me. He reached down to grab the now soaking rag and rang it so it wasn't dripping with water but still damp.

Without warning, he grabbed my chin and pulled me forward closer to him, bringing the rag up to my face to dab at the dried blood around my nose.

I flinched out of his grip only for him to bring his hand around the back of my head, taking a fistful of my hair between his fingers and guiding me back closer to him.

I hissed at the feel of the wet rag under my sore bloody nose.

Sounds of displeasure left my lips as my fingers came up to wrap around his wrist meekly, not pushing him away but not fully accepting his cleaning of my cuts and dried blood from my face. I suppose it had to be done sooner or later. The last thing I needed was an infection setting in.

I didn't squirm or flinch away from him after a moment of getting used to the feeling. With nothing else to do, I watched him look down at my face with such concentration, his brow furrowed as he gently dabbed the rag at my temple and forehead.

"Malakei is an idiot." He spoke eventually, letting out a sigh.

"He is only trying to help you adjust to your new life here. I don't agree with his method of teaching, but I do agree that you should know how to fight. At least to defend yourself from another Dry Lander. I know Malakei, he's Charon's younger brother. I know he's lethal with a sword. He's a good fighter and a good person. He didn't think before acting today. He will apologise soon but will continue with training. I told him to wait until we get to camp before he does anything. It will give you time to heal and prepare as you will be expecting it next time." Raen stated as he concentrated on a rather deep cut under my eye. I flinched away at the sting of the wet rag but he held my head in place. His fingers ran through my blonde hair comfortingly. I couldn't help but let my eyelids fall shut at the feeling of his fingers in my hair and I leaned into his touch slightly, opening my eyes to find him looking down at me. His eyes held a glint of something that I couldn't pinpoint exactly. I didn't let it bother me and allowed a sigh to escape my lips.

"I guess I have no other choice but to fight then?"

"You could die instead, if that's what you prefer?"

I held back the snort as I searched his eyes but found he wasn't looking at me.

"Thank you... for helping me before."

A part of me understood that this was not all Malakei's fault. I was the one who refused to fight him or accept that I needed to learn how to train. It was clear now that I had no choice in the matter – unless one counts being murdered as a choice. If I had just cooperated with Malakei, I wouldn't be in this situation. Raen was right though; I wished Malakei had gone about it differently. An ambush in the forest – *although likely to happen* – was not the best strategy to help me learn. I needed a teacher, a patient one.

"You must think I'm an idiot for refusing to fight." I mused feeling self–conscious, remembering being told of how the Dry Landers were taught from a young age how to kill someone. All Dry Landers were born to either be warriors of the forest, tribesmen of the desert or protectors of the land. Not one of them proved more brutal than the other. These people were born fighters, forced to hunt for their food. If they didn't come home with a fortunate catch, they starved until the next opportunity to hunt came. That was how it was here. It made me wonder how Raen grew up here. Was his body littered with scars from fights with other Dry Landers or from simply trying to survive in the forest?

Raen's hand left my hair to rinse the rag into the bowl on the floor. He hummed in reply before he came back up to look at me.

"Take off your shirt." He told me, turning around and reaching beside his bed for something. I let out a shaky breath as I looked down at it, bringing my hands down to slowly peel off the material. I could feel Raen's hands helping me pull it over my head before he took my shirt from my fingers and placed it beside me on the bed. His eyes came down to take in my bruised body. Looking down closely now, I could see small scrapes from stones and other objects that ruptured my skin.

I looked away from him and focused my vision on the rag in his hands, watching as he pressed it to my skin gently, not as harsh as he was with my cuts on my face. He knew this was a sensitive area.

I jumped slightly at the feel of the cold rag. My hands on instinct flew to grip his forearm. I stayed in my tense position, only letting out small puffs of breath when he brushed over a tender area.

"You are not an idiot," Raen whispered eventually, not realising how close his mouth was to my ear causing them to twitch uncontrollably.

"You are not afraid to fight. Believe me, I know. You only fight when you need to, that is good. Malakei is a great fighter and he only wants to help you be great too."

"But what if I don't want to fight? I don't want to hurt people over something as simple as a scrap of bread." I protested slightly, looking up at him and hoping he would understand. He only lifted his lips in amusement, tilting his head at my statement.

"Bread? Now that is a crazed thought. I hope you don't either. That would be a pretty bold move," He pursed his lips in thought. "As for learning how to fight... wouldn't it be better to know how to defend yourself and decide what to do when the time comes? By refusing to learn, you are already at a disadvantage." He said with a hint of sternness in his voice that made me take in a weighted breath.

I had the feeling he was holding himself back from saying more. Instead, he shook his head and changed the topic of conversation as he took the rag from my body and dipped it into the bowl, his other hand pinched at my waist.

"Turn around. Lay on your front." I didn't miss the glint in his eyes before it was suddenly gone. He looked back down to rinse the rag. I turned around slowly, fingers digging into the fur as I clutched it between them. My front lowered onto the fur, trying not to put any pressure on my bruises.

My face finally scrunched up when I felt him press the rag down onto my back where a few scratches littered from being pushed up against the rough tree by both Malakei and Raen.

I let out a startled cry at the stinging pain and tensed my muscles. Raen didn't say anything but I felt the small caresses his thumb was making into my hip almost as if he didn't realise he was doing it.

It was soothing and a part of me wanted him to continue but another part of me wanted him to stop. To stop touching me because I was scared of where this could go.

The thing I was conflicted about, was not knowing if that was what I wanted or not.

I jumped slightly as his hand moved from my hip, travelling up my side to squeeze my waist.

"Turn around." His voice sent chills down my spine as he moved away from my body completely. I turned around slowly, eyes quickly flying to him as I did only to see he was now holding some bandage between his fingers, looking down with furrowed brows as he unravelled it from its packaging.

I couldn't help the small sigh of relief that escaped my mouth before swallowing. I didn't notice Raen lift his head. His narrowed and curious eyes fell on me before they turned back to the bandage between his hands.

"Do I frighten you?"

"Coming from the person who took me from my home, almost pulled my arm out of its socket and choked me to demonstrate authority to his tribe – naturally *yes*."

He seemed displeased at my answer. As if what I counteracted with wasn't the answer he was searching for. I couldn't help but notice the twinge of hurt on his features.

Looking at Raen now, he wasn't as Malakei described. He was strong but never weak. He was mean and cold always around the other Dry Landers but I got to see a side to him that I felt he didn't let anyone else see. This caring side of how he wanted to help me with my injuries and make sure I was okay both physically and mentally.

I looked down quickly, feeling ashamed for thinking little of him before. That he would be just like the others – a savage. Raen was more than that.

"*No*." My voice was above a whisper and lifting my shoulders, I brought my eyes up to him. His brows furrowed and forest–green eyes never left mine. He looked as though he was trying to solve a puzzle in his mind.

"Despite everything, you are *good*. You are thoughtful and warm."

I told him honestly. The memory of last night at the river filled my mind along with today. Although leaving abruptly, he still had a way to go in proving himself worthy enough of my trust. At least I hoped. I was still wary of him, but I wasn't going to tell him that.

"You are not what I thought you would be."

I watched as he seemed to consider this before nodding once at me in understanding. He then made his way closer to me, bandage in hand as he came back down to sit on the stool in front of me, pulling me closer by my waist before he began to help wrap the bandage around my middle, looping it across my shoulder and back around.

When he was done, I thanked him and he nodded at me silently, taking the bowl from his feet and moving to throw its contents outside onto the grass. I grabbed my shirt at my side and began to pull it over my head. Before I could get up, however, Raen's hands were on my shoulders, pushing me back down onto his bed softly. I looked up at him confused before he spoke, tone assuring.

"Rest here. We have a long journey tomorrow to our camp and you need your strength."

X

~*~

I bolted upright in a panting and sweaty mess as the vivid memory of my dream played in my vision.

I dreamt of Corrin calling my name as I was taken by the Dry Landers. I couldn't run to him, scream... I couldn't do anything.

It was only when I came to my senses and noticed Raen leaning over me with concern, his face only centimetres from mine. I was startled and fell back on the fur–coated bed in alarm, trying to control my breathing and brought a hand up to my chest.

"W–What were you doing?" I asked him, not knowing why he was leaning over my body like that and I immediately started to scurry backwards, away from him. Raen raised his eyebrow at me. Not amused in the slightest as he moved back to stand upright and folded his arms over his chest.

"You were having a nightmare. You were thrashing

and crying–"

My hands flew to my damp cheeks and eyes widened when I realised Raen was telling the truth. This made me pale at the comparison of how I had been crying in my dream and also managed to cry in my sleeping form.

"–I tried to calm you down but you kept shouting."

"I–I'm sorry," I spoke quickly, looking down at my hands in confusion. "I *uhm...* it won't happen again."

I assured him, still refusing to meet Raen's eyes as I moved to get up, resulting in me wincing and bringing a hand down to cradle my bandaged body.

"*Careful.*"

I flinched at Raen's firm voice while he came closer to me, pulling my hands away to touch my bandaged and sensitive area on inspection. Worried I may have ripped the binding.

My hands on reflex flew around his wrist and my eyes darted up to him worriedly. I panted slightly when I noticed him looking down at me as if he were searching for something within them.

Raen's hand over my bandages slowly slide across to rest on my left hipbone. His other hand came down to press against the small dip of my back. My breath hitched when I felt his hand begin to press my body closer to him, so close, that our faces were only centimetres from one another's.

Before anything could happen, a small cough from the entrance of the tent made both Raen and I's gazes fall on Malakei, looking conflicted between being completely frightened by the fact that he was standing in Raen's presence and thrilled that he had caught us in a somewhat intimate position.

I was the first to move away and narrowed my gaze on Malakei's smirking features.

"If you're here to hit me again then I think you should leave." I couldn't help but say glaring menacingly at him.

Malakei's face dropped at this before he looked at Raen almost pleadingly. A silent conversation went on between them. When Raen proved unresponsive, however, Malakei sighed and turned his sad gaze back to me, black eye shining as he did.

"I just wanted to say... *I'm sorry*. I'm very sorry for hurting you badly. I only want–wanted to help, but... I realised... *that*... was not the right thing to do." He paused and I couldn't help but be taken back by how he must have rehearsed his speech he would eventually say to me over and over again – to perfect his pronunciation for me.

"I understand that you are hurting. I do, and I am sorry I can–*can* no *can't* do more for you but I only work with what I know. And what I know is fight–*ing*." Malakei breathed out, the most words he had spoken to me since I met him.

"We still brothers, yes?" Malakei chanced his luck with a hopeful expression. I blinked at his odd request as I noticed Raen rolling his eyes from the corner of my eye.

I let out a breath and moved forward, making my way over to Malakei who didn't know what was happening, the obvious reaction being to flinch as he thought I was going to hit him.

He whined when I brought my hands up around him in

an embrace, letting my head rest on his chest lightly. I didn't know where else Raen had hurt him.

Malakei let out a sigh of relief and hesitantly brought his hands down around me, burying his head in my hair before blowing out hot air over my ear tips.

I let out a high–pitched whine at that as I moved my hands up to clutch my twitching ears and after a moment, brought one hand up to slap at his shoulder. Malakei chuckled at that as we broke apart, smiling down at me before remembering Raen stood behind me. His eyes widened as he looked up at Raen and cleared his throat.

"We eat breakfast then set out for home."

***

After breakfast – which consisted of berries picked from nearby bushes and leftover rabbit stew Raen forced me to eat, we were back on the horses after a long stop and carrying on the journey towards their camp.

I rolled my eyes at Malakei's attempts to make me laugh from where he and Charon rode on their horse not too far ahead of Raen and I. Malakei threw weird faces back at me out of boredom and tried to get my attention. I let a few snickers pass my lips at the start but as we began to journey deeper into the unfamiliar forest, my nerves rose, Malakei making faces at me was down the list of concerns on my mind.

"Raen?"

I eventually broke our silence when my thoughts started to eat me alive. I bit my lip afterwards, wondering if I should have said anything.

Raen shifted forward with a hum and I took this as him agreeing to listen to what I had to say.

"Why did you take me from my home? Why am I here?"

Raen was silent for a moment, I began to think that he wasn't going to answer me when he sighed in defeat, his breath fanning the back of my head.

"We have planned for years to invade the *High Peaks*. Counting the years and going over every detail of the plan to take you home."

My eyes widened at that, biting my lip and asked him a question that had been playing on my mind since Malakei told me about it. I knew it had to have something to do with it.

"Why me? Is this to do with your test? What is the test? Why are you hunting the outcasts?" I questioned frantically. "Have many people failed it before?"

Raen hesitated.

"You are the only one to do this test," He said seriously, avoiding the topic of hunting the outcasts that I believed they were doing, but for what reason?

"There was no one else before you."

"What?" I only grew more worried by his words. "What do you – Raen *wait*. Whatever you think I am, I'm not. okay? I'm not a Dry Lander – just because I have the traits. This place isn't my home. You took me from my home. My home is the *High Peaks, not* the *Dry Lands*." I tried to explain to him but Raen only grunted in response, leaning forward so that his mouth was close to my ear as he whispered.

"I guess we will have to see won't we?"

"And if I'm not who you think I am? If I fail the test, what then?"

I whispered back, not trusting my voice to be strong in that moment. My breath hitched as I felt his nose brush against the top of my ear. He chuckled in amusement and my ears flattened against my head at this, flinching at his loud voice being so close to my sensitive ears.

"I don't know. Death perhaps? We could torture you until you beg for death if you prefer. I might take your ears as a trophy to remember that I got to meet an elf for the first time in my life..."

He was mocking me.

I was silent for a moment and narrowed my eyes ahead, ignoring Malakei sticking his tongue out at me as I tried to think of something witty to say.

"Or you know – you could set me loose," I reminded sarcastically as another option other than death. Raen hummed in contemplation and I felt his chin rest on top of my head from behind.

"You haven't seen me run."

His throat rumbled at this, a laugh that made me feel small.

"I'd like to see you outrun me. I am fastest and strongest. You are smallest and youngest. I think I win."

My eyes narrowed at that, sensing him smirking behind me without even looking at him to know. I gritted my teeth and scoffed.

"I'm almost nineteen. I'm not that young. Malakei is

only twenty so you must be what? nineteen–"

"I am almost twenty–one." He copied me and I rolled my eyes at that.

"But for now you're twenty."

"Are you mocking me?" He whispered near my ear and I leaned back against his shoulder, looking up at him with a raised brow.

"That depends. Are you mocking *me*?"

He said nothing, only blinking down at me curiously. The glint reappeared once again in his eyes before they refocused on the journey ahead and I moved my head off his shoulder.

***

There was a shout from above us and I lifted my head curiously. Some Dry Landers cheered and gave shrill yells as they came to the edge of the forest. I looked ahead of them in confusion only to widen my eyes in realisation. My heart rate rose as what looked like wooden spikes came into view that travelled in a line at the edge of the forest. When we got closer, however, those spikes went around the perimeter of a camp filled with large tents and small wooden houses. They reminded me of log cabins built deep in the small jungle on the edge of *Versai*.

I took in a breath as I looked forward, noticing a Dry Lander from the campsite communicating with one of the Dry Landers at the front of the line on his horse. Words were shared between them before the Dry Lander on the ground began pulling aside the small barrier of spiked spears sticking up, allowing us to pass into the habitable camp.

My breath hitched as we began passing by him one by one. His eyes landed on me immediately with a sort of awestruck expression.

Raen grunted from behind before he leaned down to whisper in my ear.

"He has never seen yellow hair before."

"I–It's blonde. Not yellow." I whispered back, correcting him. I could sense him rolling his eyes above me before he let his hands guide the horse.

"Looks yellow to me." He mumbled. I didn't bother saying anything in response because as soon as we were through the makeshift spear gate, there were people suddenly everywhere looking at us curiously.

I sucked in air.

Their eyes somehow found mine and large gasps and murmurs could be heard from around the camp. I lowered my head at this. I was an outcast wherever I went.

A voice rang through the crowd and I brought my gaze up to see a boy a little older than me with raven black hair and bright green eyes. He stared at Raen with an expression that implied he was not happy with him over something. I furrowed my brows at this and tilting my head to the side, I studied the boy curiously.

Something about him was... unsettling and I couldn't quite place my finger on it.

A girl's laughter travelled to my ears from somewhere in front and I searched for her. My eyes widened when she stepped out, coming over to inspect us.

She looked frightening and exactly what we were taught a Dry Lander would look like. She had red paint on her face in a design that stretched above her cheekbone before curving up the side of her left temple. The red paint stood out against her darkened skin and almost cat–like eyes. Her hair – a frizzy brown, was pushed back with a light brown band over her face. She was striking, although I had never seen a female like her before in all my life. I couldn't deny the fact that she was beautiful.

As she stepped forward to speak, her eyes landed on me. There was a hardness to them that I never expected a girl to have. I knew right then that she had been through a lot more than the elven girls would have gone through in their entire lives. Those girls didn't hold a candle to her.

She said something to me and held her hand up. My eyes grew disinterested and I only blinked down at her in confusion.

Raen cleared his throat from behind me and said something to the girl. I only watched as she rolled her eyes at this before looking back up at me, her hand still outstretched.

"Are you just going to sit there or are you going to take my hand?"

She asked with a raised eyebrow. Her expression was so similar to Raen's that it made me do a double take as I stuttered for something to say.

"I–I oh, *uh*–"

She quickly rolled her eyes at my lack of words and grabbed my hand, pulling me down off of the horse but not as violently as I thought. She made sure that I wouldn't hurt myself as I got down. Raen must have told her about my injuries in their exchange of words, else she was gentler than Raen when helping me down from the horse.

When I was on the ground, the girl wasted no time in coming closer to me and brought her hands up to touch my ears.

I flinched back wide–eyed. Flattening my elven ears against my head as I looked at her shell–shocked. I didn't expect her to reach out and touch my ears. She was a stranger. To touch an elf's ears like that, the elf would want to be comfortable with the person. That person was usually a close friend or lover that they trusted. Not a strange girl I had just met all but a heartbeat ago.

She laughed at my reaction. Her eyes gleamed in amusement while I tried not to stare daggers into her at her rudeness all the while feeling the tips of my ears turning red.

"Come here elf boy, I will not hurt you. Let me see your ears."

I let out a strangled yelp as she came closer, immediately backing up into Raen who had now made his way down from the horse. He was looking at the girl with a frown, eyes hard.

"Stop scaring the boy Tara. You can touch him on your own time but for now, where is *Maekin*?"

Raen continued to say something to the girl, Tara, in his native tongue but I didn't listen. Raen's words rang in my mind. Fear bubbled to the surface as I muddled them over.

'You can touch him on your own time'

What was that supposed to mean? what happened to the Raen that didn't want me riding with Caito back in the mountains? The Raen that hurt Malakei because he had caused me harm previously? Did none of that matter now? Was he passing the job of taking care of me onto someone else now that he was back home?

My eyes found Malakei's friendly ones as he too, got off his horse a small distance away. Before I could venture over to him, however, there was a hand pulling me back. I turned to yank it away from Raen only to pale at the sight of the angry boy from earlier gripping my arm tightly. He started to drag me backwards passed a frowning Raen and Tara.

"R–Raen!"

I yelled back in his direction, meeting his gaze and not a moment later, Raen made his way passed Tara to run up to me, eyes quickly filling with frustration. He began speaking to the boy who dragged me through a small crowd of onlookers and curious faces.

I panicked as I was led behind numerous small and large tents before a massive open space filled my vision. A large pit for a fire sat in the centre of the space followed by a rather big tent not too far behind it. My eyes fell on some people around the area chatting to one another. Their laughter immediately died down when they spotted me from the corner of their eyes and came closer in curiosity.

When we were close to the large tent, the boy suddenly pulled my arm forward, his other hand coming behind my back to push me down onto the ground. I hissed as he pushed me into a kneeling position in front of the tent and how his hand dug into my right shoulder. It suddenly disappeared and Raen's voice was loud from behind me, anger directed at the boy making me flatten my ears as I turned to look up at him.

I saw Tara running up behind Raen only to quickly hold him back by his shoulders after Raen punched the boy square in the jaw. The boy staggered back as a result but quickly recovered, hurtling something in their language back at Raen.

A deep, booming voice stopped the three of them. It shocked them into silence and they all turned to the entrance of the large tent in front of me. With my ears still flattened against my head, I turned slowly around. My breathing hitched when I noticed a towering figure not too far from me, glaring at the three Dry Landers behind me.

He went to say something but his eyes immediately fell on me, words dying in his mouth only to be replaced by a look of utter shock and I gulped visibly at this. Not liking the attention being directed at me and in that moment, I wanted nothing more than for the ground to swallow me up.

XI

~*~

I watched with fearful eyes as the man made his way over to me. His strides were long and full of confidence. I stayed in my kneeling position because I felt that if I moved to get up, it would be wrong on my part.

When I sensed him standing directly above me, my breathing laboured.

I waited impatiently for him to say or do something – I couldn't help but notice how his nose was a lot like mine.

Or at least it was, before Malakei almost broke it. Now, it was a purple and red mess to go along with my cut–up face. A dark bruise and a cut formed under my left eye.

All of a sudden, the man sank to his knees. His eyes searched my own while his hand reached out to touch my skin. I wanted to flinch back but something stopped me. A feeling – maybe I was curious as to what the man would do. He didn't seem threatening to me, regardless of how the others seemed to cower and straighten their backs at his arrival. Everyone stood watching the silent encounter and held their breaths, afraid to speak in fear of disrupting something before it had a chance to begin.

My ears came away from the sides of my head and they twitched curiously as I looked at the bearded and sad–eyed man before me.

His eyes seemed to widen at my ears and I frowned at this, immediately flattening them again.

"No, *no*." His words tumbled out. His hands came out in front of him as he tried to assure me.

"I won't hurt you, there is no need to be afraid."

At that, I allowed my ears to slowly peel back out from my head until they were almost sticking out with curiosity at the ear tips. The man watched me with building tears before his hand moved up to run through my hair.

He mumbled to himself in their language and Raen spoke from above me. The man's eyes flew to him, listening intently to what he had to say. My ears twitched as Raen said my name in his words, getting the impression that he was telling this Dry Lander about me and what my name was. I watched his sad smile until he was looking down at me with tearful eyes.

"Keylin…do you know who I am?" He asked in a gruff but hopeful voice, only to frown when I shook my head slowly. His face fell at that as though he wanted nothing more than to hug me or even curl up in a corner. There was something about this man though… I just couldn't place what it was.

"*Keylin*, my name is Maekin."

196

The man took a breath as he ran his hand through my hair, the other now cradling the uninjured side of my face as he looked down at me. Tears fell from his eyes.

"I am your father Keylin."

I didn't know what to say. All I could do was let my mouth fall open in shock. The memories resurfaced of me at such a young age being told time and time again by the elves of *Versai* that my father was dead. That he was a scum of Sorn, a filthy Dry Lander who raped my mother...

None of it seemed true. The man before me stood powerful, I could tell he was an important figure by the way everyone reacted to his voice, maybe he was even higher in rank than Raen. He looked down at me like he had just been reunited with a part of himself he thought he would never see in his lifetime.

I had told myself that if my father were alive, he would never meet me – his *son* – because he didn't care enough. To him, I didn't exist. How could he have known about me when we had never met before?

This man sent his loyal men, trusting them dearly to cross sectors, punishable by death if caught, to climb the *High Peaks* and bring back his son – whom he had never discovered until now. Looking at his glassy eyes and hopeful expression, I believed that he didn't know I even existed until recently.

'This was the test. I was the test. Me'

It all suddenly made sense. Although the idea had crossed my mind, I didn't believe it until now. The Dry Landers were looking for me. They knew about me even then – but how?

Was this the secret I felt they were hiding from me? Could they not tell me about my father for fear it would disrupt the process of the test? I didn't understand…

I felt my father's thumb come under my eye and wipe away a stray tear that I didn't realise had fallen from it. Bringing my hand up to cover over his, I took in a shaky breath

I thought that this was all some sort of twisted joke but deeply hoped that it wasn't. That it was all true and I wasn't alone anymore because I had a father. A father who cared about me. *Finally*, someone I could call mine.

"It's *you*," Emotion filled his voice. "There were whispers of a Dry Lander elf soon to come of age, rumours that we couldn't ignore… you are mine. You have my eyes, my nose… you have *everything*."

"*Pato?*" The elvish word for father fell from my lips before they began to wobble. He nodded curiously at that, sniffling before all of a sudden he brought me into his chest, fell back into a sitting position and took me in his arms. He cried into my hair before kissing my head.

"*Keylin*… I am sorry for not being with you sooner. The last time I saw your mother… I didn't know she was pregnant with you. My *son*, I am so sorry. For *everything*, please forgive me…"

He continued in his language to himself and I let out a sob as I clutched him tighter. My face buried deeper into his chest.

"It's not your fault. Please don't blame yourself. How could you have known?" I asked, trying to make light of the situation.

"What matters now is that you're here. *You're alive*."

He looked as though he wanted to comment but decided against it, holding me closer to him as he ran his hand through my blonde hair. The time for talking could be postponed but not the moment we shared together, holding each other for the first time. The first of many times. In that moment, a part of me was silent as I cried, a part of me felt as though it was finally mending.

He brought my head closer so that he could kiss the side of my temple. My heart warmed in a way I never imagined it could.

***

It was a few hours later when I stood in the large tent, looking up curiously around me at the colourful designs that made up the room.

My father stood in the centre around a circular table accompanied by Raen, Tara, the angry boy from earlier, and another girl who I didn't know, Malakei and Charon. I shuffled on my feet to the side as I gawked around me. The girl found amusement in this and even giggled at me.

"Keylin?" My father asked softly, making me turn my attention to him. He smiled, knowing this was a serious situation that involved me and what was to become of me here. I didn't bother to listen before when they spoke between themselves in their language, I had felt left out of the conversation already.

"Come here Keylin. I need you to understand something." My father spoke up. His eyes flickered to the angry boy from earlier who glared at me, eyes full of hatred. I didn't understand why he disliked me so much.

"Keylin..." My father began but trailed off, not knowing how to put what he was trying to say into words.

"Before I ever met your mother, I was with another woman called Ana. We were together for a long time–"

"–And they had a kid together. Me."

My eyes flew up to the angry boy in astonishment and I opened my mouth to speak but it quickly shut in shock, allowing the boy's words to sink in. Now I knew why he hated me at least and how something about him felt familiar.

My father's fist suddenly slammed down onto the table and I jumped back at that. His eyes narrowed into slits as his attention trained on my so–called brother.

'My temper! He has my temper!' I couldn't help but think gleefully.

"Bow! For god's sake."

"He was going to find out eventually! Who better to tell him than his half–brother?!" The angry boy who went by Bow, raged at my – *our* father and I frowned at that. My father, now stressed, ran a hand through his hair.

"You made it sound like I was cheating on your mother which wasn't the case."

Bow scoffed at that, folding his arms over his chest. I grimaced at his attitude.

"Don't yell at him, he's only trying to explain." I found myself saying in a neutral tone, not trying to overstep but not trying to be entirely silent on the matter either.

Bow's eyes narrowed into slits when I spoke. Now I

understood the meaning behind the word 'snake' and why all of the elves called me that word. Our eyes were identical. It was the only thing that visibly made us brothers apart from our noses.

"No, he's *not*," Bow growled out. "He's trying to make light of a dangerous and foolish situation he got himself into long ago. Your mother being one of them."

"Bow that is enough!"

Father bellowed down the circular table and I bit my tongue from telling Bow how I truly felt about his attitude. Eventually, I let out a sigh and my gaze shifted to my father who looked even more stressed than he was a few minutes ago, unsure of what to do.

"What happens now?" I asked him quietly, to which he let out a small sigh.

"We adjust." My father let his anger go with his breath. "Ana is allowing you to stay with her because you are my son. She is… not thrilled but she will come around to the new adjustment. You will be sharing a room with your brother–"

"Half–brother." Bow interrupted with gritted teeth only for father to ignore him and continue speaking to me.

"–Until I can get the time to build a room for you. I think it will be a good chance for you too to get to know one another while I'm away on business."

"You're leaving?" I asked breathlessly, not believing that just as we met each other, he was leaving me all of a sudden.

"Do you expect the leader of the Eastern camp to abandon his duty?" Bow barked out in my direction making me frown.

"He's not around much because he's busy protecting us from invaders. You should be used to the absence–"

"Bowen." Father warned lowly. A hurt expression fell over his face when he turned to me.

"I had hoped we would have met a few days ago. I didn't factor in the time to find you once my men got to *Versai*, that was my mistake."

"One of many–"

Tara who stood beside Bow, stomped on his foot causing my brother's eyes to widen. He grew silent but I could tell he was holding in pain behind his cold eyes.

"It's only for a few days. I will be back as soon as I can. Then we have all the time in Sorn to get to know one another. Make up for lost time."

I nodded silently at that, looking down at the circular table in front of me.

"I'm leaving Raen in charge while I'm away–"

Tara groaned at this, throwing her spear down onto the circular table in a temper before she folded her arms stubbornly across her chest. Father only continued, ignoring Tara like he had ignored Bow. I found myself smiling at this in amusement.

I was never allowed to act out like this. It wasn't normal, seeing these Dry Landers throw fits when they didn't get their way was close to child–like and judging by my father's reaction, it was also common.

'What a dysfunctional bunch.' I thought to myself.

"–If I trust anyone to watch over my people as well as both of my sons, it's *him*." Father glanced at Raen who was already watching him seriously and nodded. Silent but obedient, not having said a word throughout the whole meeting as he took in my father's words.

I snuck a glance at him and watched as his jaw was set while his eyes trained forward. A perfect right hand to my father, I noticed. His words from the river played on my mind.

'My men were questioning my ability to lead our mission. I needed to remind them why our leader picked me for this.'

Raen glanced at me from the corner of his eye and I quickly averted my gaze, zoning out when the others continued the conversation in their language.

When father dismissed us, I walked out of the large tent. I felt a hand tug me to the side. Bow's harsh eyes glared down into mine.

"Come on elf. Unless you want to sleep outside like the dog you are."

I blinked up at him. Surprised that my tongue wasn't chewed off at this point, although I might have spoken too soon.

"Bow!" Malakei raised his voice, startling both of us as he walked up from behind me. His eyes trained menacingly on Bow.

"You say another bad thing to him and I make my fist ram down your throat and shove my foot up your ass, got it?"

Bow let his mouth fall shut at that, looking at Malakei with a sort of fear in his eyes before it was gone and he glared at me again. He mumbled something to Malakei before he grabbed my arm again and pulled me along with him.

"Keylin!" I heard Malakei yell and turned my head back, stumbling as Bow dragged me along.

"He is brat! Don't let him get to you, I see you tomorrow for training!"

***

"You sleep *there*."

Bow pointed to the far corner of the bedroom before he began to rummage through drawers in search of old fur coats to throw in the corner as, what I presumed, some sort of makeshift bed for me. I was surprised he even made me a bed in the first place, believing he would make me sleep on the floor or even outside – as he had threatened earlier.

"Thank you." I said softly, bowing my head slightly as I walked past him and began to gently lower myself onto the fur coats scattered on top of one another on the floor. Careful of my bruises, I could feel Bow's eyes on me as I did so and looked up to see him raising a brow at me before he shook his head. He made his way to his bed, peeling off his clothes as he did.

I struggled as I tried to take off my clothes but managed to get my shirt off, revealing the bandage that covered half of my upper body. I didn't bother taking off my trousers as it would have meant a lot of stooping and effort that I was just too tired and sore to do. I laid down on the fur coats, letting out a sigh at their softness.

Bow said nothing more to me as he curled up on his

bed, throwing the fur blankets over him before quickly drifting off to sleep. A few minutes later, I did the same and dreams of Raen made the night bearable.

It didn't seem long until my foot was being kicked awake and I hissed, retracting and bringing it closer to my body as I blinked awake. Of course, Bow was scowling down at me.

"Get up. *Maîka* wants to see you."

Bow informed seriously as he towered over me, already dressed in a light black shirt and black baggy trousers. He wore multiple bracelets around one of his wrists and one around his neck that stood out in resemblance to a tiger's tooth. His dark brown hair almost looked black against the attire while his piercing green eyes glared down at me.

"Maîka?" I questioned as I quickly got into a sitting position. My face scrunched up as I did and reached for my discarded shirt beside my makeshift bed. I let out a yelp when Bow suddenly threw clothes at me, hitting me square in the face before they fell onto my lap. I narrowed my eyes as he chuckled at this.

"Mother you idiot. Don't tell me you don't know *Fasik*?"

He frowned as I quickly put on the white shirt. It was tighter due to the material being old and I presumed it belonged to him from when he was younger as it just about fit me. I put on the trousers, socks and shoes he gave me. My eyebrows furrowed at his words.

"Fazeek? What's that?" I asked, trying to pronounce the foreign word and Bow sighed from above me.

"*Fasik*." He corrected and I looked up at him sheepishly. "And it's our native tongue. English is our second, *Timïr*, *Talamahï* also."

I blinked up at him in astonishment when he told me about these language names that I had never heard of in my history lessons. Those lessons I usually skipped because they were held directly before school ended. Corrin and I would skip them to get ahead of Tobias in his attempt at chasing me home.

I couldn't help but look at him in awe, knowing that he could speak so many languages.

"That's amazing." I tried to keep my awestruck expression to myself but he saw it and for a moment, I thought I spotted a ghost of a small proud smile form on his lips before he rolled his eyes and pulled me up by my arm.

"Yeah well. We all have to know the languages that make up the *Dry Lands*. That means you too now." He looked back pointedly and I nodded in understanding, not knowing how I was going to accomplish learning these languages, but I supposed with time I would pick them up.

In the *High Peaks*, we were told that besides Elvish High Lander, our native tongue; we were taught English because it was a common language to resort to if there was ever a language barrier between sectors. I was fortunate to have had my grandfather hire a tutor for me in Spéirtail – the language of the folk who lived above in the *Sky Lanes*. It was an important language to have when dealing with trade. My grandfather made sure I was educated in that aspect if something were to ever happen to him. He needed a successor.

As Bow dragged me down the narrow stairs of his home, I trained my gaze along the walls to pictures of Bow when he was small followed by a family picture that made my heart sink for some reason. Maybe it was knowing that Bow grew up with his father and mother to care for him which made me feel sad or knowing that my father had loved another woman before my mother fell pregnant with Bow.

It wasn't common for something like this to happen in the *High Peaks*, nor was cheating acceptable. It wasn't at all common that brothers would come from the same father, but separate mothers. Only in special cases where one of the parents had passed on young. My bloodline was something of a special case within the impossible special cases.

My father told me the story shortly after we met and I remember soaking up the little details of my parent's encounter. How he had been heartbroken after ending the relationship with Bow's mother, Ana. He had ventured too far west to the borderline between the *Dry Lands* and the *High Peaks* one summer's day. *'Hunting a stag'*, he had said, when he spotted her picking flowers outside of the kingdom's walls.

'She said that they bloomed better there because they got more sunshine.' I saw how his face became less shadowed as he recalled the memory.

Like the flowers, their love blossomed.

Over time, they grew closer until one day, my mother stopped showing up to their secret meeting spot. He was heartbroken but continued to wait there every day for her. Six months went by and he began to lose hope until eventually, he made his way home.

That was when Ana showed up on his doorstep, handing him a newborn Bow, having kept her pregnancy to herself out of stubbornness before realising the work that came with raising a child. She went back to my father. My father – who was unaware that my mother had ever been pregnant, I presumed had stopped meeting him when she began to show in her pregnancy, finding it more difficult to venture outside of the kingdom.

She didn't abandon him like he had believed all of those years. I shook the sad thoughts from my mind.

This was my home for now.

To stay with my father, I needed to make a hard choice. One that I wasn't sure if I was strong enough and knew would be a difficult decision to make. But for the time being, I was stuck here, physically and mentally stuck. I needed to learn to accept that I had a brother who most likely hated me and was only putting up with me because our father told him to. This didn't bother me, even if he didn't at least care that I was his younger brother, he was *mine*, and I would make it my job not to let anything happen to him. We needed to stick together.

I tried to push the feelings of betrayal from entering my mind for Corrin, my grandfather and even Mara – my true family.

I promised myself that I would see them again, even if I had to make my way back to them. I would travel if it meant crossing every sector of Sorn – I would, a thousand times over.

As Bow dragged me into a small kitchen area, my eyes landed on a figure at the sink where she appeared to be washing up cutlery, unaware of our sudden entrance.

Bow said something to her in Fasik and she froze, her cold eyes landed on me as she turned around, throwing the towel in her hands over her shoulder. Her eyes narrowed as she looked me up and down.

It made me uncomfortable so I decided to clear the air and speak first as it was starting to look like all she wanted to do was stare and frown at me.

"H–Hello," I greeted and she snapped her eyes to me in surprise. I took a hesitant step forward.

"I'm Keylin. You must be–"

She cut me off, saying something to Bow in Fasik which made Bow freeze and rub the back of his head nervously. I frowned and was about to open my mouth to speak when she suddenly turned around to continue with her washing up.

"She doesn't like you."

Bow informed from behind me and I let out a breath, trying to ignore my mind replaying the image of her piercing eyes that bore holes into me with distaste.

"Oh." I breathed out in disappointment. She didn't turn back around. "I see how it is."

I stepped back from her, getting the feeling that my presence only angered her more. After all, I was the child of another woman. She wasn't my mother, nor was I her son, and the only reason she was somewhat tolerating me was because my father was the leader of the camp – her husband.

I felt Bow's hand around my arm as he dragged me out of the house.

"Why did she want to see me if she already hated me?"

I asked him, keeping the hurt from my voice as I glared at the back of his head.

"She wanted to see if it was true. She was also curious and wanted to know what you looked like – *very ugly* by the way. Maybe that's why she ignored you–"

"I get it." I growled out looking down, not knowing whether to feel ashamed of myself for being who I was, or angry at everyone else for treating me less than a person.

Bow glanced back at me with a raised eyebrow and looked like he wanted to say something else but decided against it. I was relieved at that, I wasn't in the mood for any more of his sarcasm and just allowed him to drag me to wherever it was he intended to go.

XII

~*~

"Why does everyone hate me here?"

"Come now, *dimples* – I don't hate you. Raen don't hate you and your father don't hate you. Everyone's happy *yes*?"

I let out a breath as I looked up from where I was sitting on the ground.

Malakei stood a few metres away, a sword in hand as he practised a few attack stances. I watched for a few moments before looking back to the ground.

"Not everyone. *I'm* not happy." I mumbled to myself, glad that Malakei didn't hear it as he continued with his stances. I sighed, taking in the forest before us with a frown.

"Why did you bring me out here?" I asked curiously. Just as he was throwing down his sword, he grabbed a water pouch at his feet.

"We train today." He said too cheerily after taking a mouthful of water.

My eyes widened and he noticed the terror washing over my face, holding up his index finger to point at me seriously.

"Yes." He insisted. "If you run, I catch you and you don't want to do that because I will go harder on you with training, understand?"

I let out a whine as I rolled my eyes, falling back onto the golden leaf–covered ground.

"You will go hard on me anyway. It's not fair when I can't really protect myself."

He tapped the sole of my foot with his shoe and I saw he held out a hand to me, no weapon in sight as he smiled genuinely.

"That is why we train today. I see what you do and teach you to protect yourself."

I debated for a moment as I looked up at his outstretched hand before taking it in mine. He pulled me up with little effort and it was moments like that where I underestimated Malakei and how strong he was.

After we walked over and passed the discarded swords, he stopped and turned to me, taking hold of my wrists with a seriousness on his features.

"Okay, we start with hands–" He held up my wrists in front of him, almost blocking my vision of him completely.

"Hands are good to use during fist fight. Sometimes hands block better than shield."

He moved my hands into a wall formation in front of

my face, curling my fingers downward into fists.

"Watch."

He glanced at me momentarily before he suddenly aimed a punch at my face. I flinched but kept my arms up as he continued to hit my forearms repeatedly, but not hard enough to hurt badly. He learned that from experience.

I observed him carefully as he threw mock punches at my wall–formed arms before he stopped and nodded at me.

"Good but you need to watch hands Keylin. I move them down and bam–"

He moved his fist under my wall–formed hands and poked at my still–healing bandaged stomach. I frowned, taking in what he was saying and nodded silently at this. I fisted my hands tighter in determination.

He nodded and started to hit my arms. I watched him make a move to go under and brought my hands down to block him, smiling when I did, only for him to bring his other hand up to curl along my jaw.

"*Bam*." He whispered knowingly with a smirk before pinching my cheek. I pushed his hand away with a grimace.

"That was unexpected."

"Life is unexpected." He snorted and I narrowed my eyes at him, shaking off my hands.

"Watch *dimples*." He instructed and brought his hands up in a swing. I flinched, thinking he was going to hit me but he didn't. I peeled open my eyes to see him punching air, ducking down to throw low punches and just by watching him, I could see what he meant. I could tell every move he was going to make just by the way he held his arms and curled them back, whether he was going to punch low or high.

"It is about finding weak spot and knowing your partner." He stated and my eyes flew up to him as I nodded in understanding.

"I got it."

He nodded at that and quickly threw a punch to try and catch me off guard but I was alert. I brought my hands up to block him and watched as he dragged his other hand up to punch my face but I ducked, immediately straightening when he recoiled his hand. I stepped back to give distance between us and he smiled at that.

"Very good. You are learning fast."

He made a quick jab to my stomach but I brought my hands down and blocked him which made him smirk.

"Now, instead of using arms. Use hands and grab fists."

I nodded hesitantly, taking a breath before he started over, throwing punches at my chest.

I grabbed his fist, immediately seeing his other coming up to punch my stomach again but I grabbed it and pushed it away. Malakei's eyes widened in happiness.

"Yes!"

I looked up in time to see him bring his hand up, he twisted my arm painfully so that I was forced to turn around. Malakei pressed against my back as he breathed in my ear and my eyes widened in awe when he let my arm go. I turned to him.

"Can you teach me that?"

Malakei chuckled at my eagerness but nodded

nonetheless.

"In time you will learn lots of things and maybe even overpower me one day."

I smirked at this, looking forward to the day when Malakei wouldn't be able to hit me so easily and I would be able to finally defend myself.

The thought made me more determined than before as I realised fighting wasn't just about hurting people. It could be used to defend one's own and protect others. That is what I wanted to do and I would train hard to get there.

Suddenly, Malakei landed a punch to my chest and I winced.

"Focus *dimples*." He instructed with a frown and I brought my hands up to block my face from his next punch.

This was going to take a lot longer than I had hoped.

***

Bow's mother threw down the dinner plate which consisted of mixed vegetables, potatoes and some sort of meat – in front of me, almost making the contents spill over the table by the force with which she threw it.

"T–Thank you." I said in a small voice causing her to snort and say something under her breath in Fasik.

My ears flattened at this – knowing she was most likely cursing my existence, just like she had been doing ever since I got here.

Bow sat in front of me, not bothering to look up as he moved his vegetables around the plate with his fork. Only once did he seem interested enough to lift his head when greeting me with a scowl, but nothing more. The longer I stayed here with them, the more I felt like an unwanted guest in their home, like someone who just came in and invaded their space. In reality, that was what I did, only it was against my own will.

This made me mad. To think that I was ripped away from my home in the middle of the night and taken from my only family at the time, not knowing why or what was going on. Almost dying of hypothermia, I was strangled, alcohol was thrown at me and my friend – *whom I trusted at the time* – hurt me for my 'protection'. Only to come face to face with a father who I was told was nothing but a scum Dry Lander that didn't even know I existed until however long it took for him to find out about me.

How could they treat me like this? They looked at me like I was some sort of monster but really, *they* were the monsters.

Of course, I said none of this and ate silently, only glaring down at my food in the process before Ana was conversing with Bow.

Bow only nodded and got up from his seat, coming around to pull me up and drag me upstairs.

'Time for bed.' I took it.

Bow all but flung me into his room and I stumbled slightly as I turned to glare at him. He paid no attention to me and he began to take his clothes off to get ready for bed.

I stood there, my fists clenching and unclenching as I felt the remnants of frustrated tears start to sting my eyes.

I blinked them away, choosing to glare at him instead.

"How long do you plan on treating me like this?" I found my voice, confidence weakened from their constant abuse.

He stopped what he was doing and turned to me, raising his eyebrow innocently.

"Treating you like what?"

"You know what." I gritted out and Bow tilted his head at this in amusement, a smirk slowly crept onto his features as his eyes looked torn between wanting to rip my head off and keeping the false pretence of innocence plastered on his face.

"Just go to sleep. I don't want to talk to you." He eventually sighed and turned back around to continue what he was doing, I let my shoulders fall at his hurtful words.

"What have I done to deserve this?" I asked as the tears started to form again in my eyes. "Why do you hate me? My own bro–"

He quickly turned around, a menacing look in his eye before he stalked over to me, pushing me backwards and causing me to stumble against the corner wall. I didn't make a sound as he fisted my shirt in his hands, shoving me deeper into the wall to stare down at me. His eyes turned to slits.

"*Listen* to me. You are not and will never be my brother. I have no brother. We may be related but you will *never* be one of us no matter how much Malakei helps you train or my father treats you like you're the gem of his life. You are a snot–nosed little elf, *not* a Dry Lander. You could never be one of us. You're an *out–*"

"*Outsider.*" I finished for him. "Mistake, scum, flawed elf, mix, snake... Take your pick. I've heard them all. If you think that your words will affect how I see you, you're wrong. I've been reminded of how I look since the day I was born but here it's because of who my father is. So if you're just going to yell at me for being taken from my home and brought here against my will because my father found out I existed and wants to replace all the years of missing out on my childhood without a father, a mother... then you're going to have to do better than that. In fact, why don't you just punch me? It will get your message across better."

Bow only stared, an unreadable emotion swam in his eyes before he suddenly pushed away from me with a grunt.

"I can kick your ass blindfolded, but I won't. I'm not an idiot. The last thing I need is Malakei or even Raen coming after me for hurting their precious little elf boy."

I frowned at that, wanting to retaliate but Bow sighed tiredly.

"Go to sleep Keylin."

I watched, unmoving as Bow walked back over to his bed and got under the fur coats. My heart beat fast as I realised that was the first time he had said my name since we met. I made my way over to my makeshift bed in silence, finding it hard to settle my thoughts as I shifted in my sleep.

***

Bow's mother threw down the breakfast – a white lumpy texture resembling porridge, but it looked far from it. Something bubbled within it and I was pretty sure she spat in it.

Taking a breath, I looked up to watch her handing Bow his share with a small smile on her ageing features. She ruffled his dark hair as he thanked her before diving in. She sat down between us and began eating in silence.

I didn't touch my food.

I felt Bow's eyes bore into me like daggers, noticing how I only stared down at my food.

He kicked me under the table.

I didn't react and only continued to stare at my porridge with a clenched jaw, ignoring Bow's warning kicks to eat the food before Ana could notice.

I let out a breath as I pushed the bowl away from me. The scraping sound of the pottery–designed bowl filled the air as I pushed it along the table, mentally wincing when I did.

Bow's mother stopped eating and her eyes narrowed when they fell on me, but I was done with playing nice when all I got in return was monstrous looks and something not even close to courtesy.

"Eat." She demanded. It was the first word she had uttered to me that I could understand since I got here, not even a welcome or even bothering to ask me my name.

I shook my head at her slowly, refusing to look up as my ears flattened against my head.

"Keylin," Bow warned, the edge evident in his voice

gone as he all but pleaded with me.

"Eat the food. Don't upset her please."

I let out a dry laugh at that, startling both of them. I could feel how drained my eyes were, now replaced with a dark twinge to them.

"She's already upset. She doesn't fail to show me that when she looks at me with disgust." I stated seriously and Bow gritted his teeth at this.

Ana didn't say anything and only glared at me. She recoiled slightly when my frustrated gaze turned to her. My eyes – that no doubt – reminded her of her husband.

"I don't want to be here as much as you don't want me in your home," I said bluntly. "I'm sorry that things have to be this way and if I could reverse everything... I would, but I'm sick of people treating me like I'm some sort of monster that killed someone close to them."

I took a breath and swallowed the lump in my throat. Her eyes seemed to soften at that as something resembling a look of pity – or was it sympathy? – crossed her face.

"I know you're not my mother, I'm not expecting you to change or shower me with love – or whatever you people think love is." I blinked before looking back at her, determination filled my voice.

"All I'm asking, is you give me the respect that I deserve and if that means staying out of your way or making sure you don't have to look at me then so be it. Don't treat me like I'm nothing. I am the *prince* of the *High Peaks*. I have a purpose." I finished, biting my lip. I pushed my chair out from the table and stood up, already done with the conversation – or clearing the air in my case.

At least my mind would rest easy knowing that I had said my peace and could be free of the bubbling cold setting in my chest.

Just as I was about to walk away and leave her and Bow to their demise, I felt small hands wrap around my wrist, keeping me in place.

Ana got up, her fingers were still around my wrist as she came closer and for a moment I thought she was going to hit me.

My suspicions were confirmed when she lifted her hand to my cheek and I closed my eyes awaiting her slap, but it never came.

I peeled open my eyes when her hand softly pressed on my cheek. Looking up at me now, she analysed every part of my features before settling on my eyes. They were the only thing apart from skin tone and light brown hair that identified me as a Dry Lander. My eyes were familiar to her because they belonged to my father, her lover.

"I was so angry," She began. "When I found out Maekin had another child, one that was not Dry Lander. I forgot you were hurting. I forgot a boy was trying his best to adapt to his new life just like us trying to adapt to you being here."

I stayed silent as she looked away from me now, afraid to meet my gaze. I knew it was from shame.

"*It must have been difficult for you…*"

She was embarrassed by her treatment of me. It was made clear when she offered to make me a different breakfast – thinking it would somehow rectify all of the mistreatment she did.

"Here, let me make you some fresh food. What would you like?" She asked, pulling back slightly as both of her hands came down to frantically pat her sides. She rolled the invisible creases out of her dress and looked up with a wobbly smile.

I stuttered. No words formed as I looked down at her. She found amusement at my lack of words and immediately walked towards the stove.

"How about eggs? Do you like eggs *yes*? I'll make you some eggs, you sit down now, good. Bow will wash your bowl won't you *Bow–*"

Bow groaned at the request from his mother and rolled his eyes but still took my untouched bowl of porridge and complied with his mother's wishes, walking over to the sink to wash both of our bowls.

I couldn't help but furrow my eyebrows at the accepting smirk on his face when he walked past.

"It's okay really," I assured but she frowned, looking back at me unsure.

"You don't have to do this..."

"*Ana*." She offered a smile to me as she began cracking an egg into a black frying pan.

"But if you want, I wouldn't mind if you call me *Maîka*."

XIII

~*~

"She what?!"

Malakei questioned in shock–filled delight when I told him what had happened with Bow's mother during our training a few hours later. Bow – who abandoned me after breakfast to meet up with his friends, in turn left me to walk around the camp freely until Malakei eventually found me. This led us to where we were currently training in the same place as yesterday. In the middle of the forest, Malakei insisted was more private for us to concentrate.

I chuckled at his response, blocking his fist when he tried to punch me. I shook my hand out as he recoiled. Malakei wasn't going as easy on me as he was yesterday, he thought stepping up the game a bit would help me. He believed that throwing really hard punches my way was stepping up the game a 'small' bit.

"I can't believe you *un–cold* the cold woman's heart ha! You are something else."

I smiled at that. The word he was probably looking for was 'thawed', that I thawed the cold woman's heart – but I didn't have the heart to correct him. Even though he preferred it when I corrected him on mispronounced or inaccurate grammar. He shared with me that it made him feel stupid and ridiculous when he spoke to me in broken English. I planned to help him improve, I knew he would get better with time but for now, it made me smile.

When Malakei had seen the ease in my step, he continued with his pestering until I gave in and told him what had happened at breakfast involving Ana and Bow.

I still wasn't completely sure how I felt about the situation with Ana. It was all so quick and slightly confusing. It was like a switch turned on in her head. It made me wonder was all of this just her way of testing me, trying to figure out what type of person I was and if I could prove myself worthy of being in the family. I was practically a stranger to her in her own home. Of course, it would make sense for her to assert some sort of control and authority... still, it was going to take some time to warm up to them, as they would me.

I also had time to understand more of how Bow and I came to become brothers.

My father was with Ana first, like any normal relationship it had its ups and downs. They eventually called it quits for a while and went their separate ways.

I was curious about my parent's interactions, wanting to know how they would meet up under the nose of my grandfather.

That was when Malakei told me about the cave

halfways up the mountain.

I had never stopped to think a cave connected to the drainage tunnels under the city of *Versai* until Malakei mentioned them but thinking about it now, it made sense. It was the perfect meetup spot for lovers.

And the perfect entrance into the city from below.

'That's how you disappeared that night so quickly.' I thought back to the night Corrin and I spotted them roaming the city, only to later vanish without a trace. If they didn't have help from Alfus, they most likely could have fled with me through there, albeit dangerous. I didn't know why they chose the extreme option of tackling the mountain head on but believed it slowed down the elves. Their decision proved advantageous.

At breakfast, Ana found the time to tell me her story about how around the period my father had met my mother and was falling in love with her, she realised she had fallen pregnant with baby Bowen.

She gave birth to Bow then. He was everything she never realised she needed in her life. She was determined to be fully capable of raising him alone until the pressures of parenthood started to sink in. She couldn't do it alone, not without help.

When Bow was over a year old, she told my father of his son, who all that time had no idea he was even a father. That was when he decided to step up and be there for Bow. He had no idea that I would soon come along, how could he? The only person who could tell him disappeared.

I didn't blame him in all of this and I didn't blame my mother, or grandfather – or Ana and Bow. Sometimes things happen that we can't understand, even when we want nothing more than to go back and rewrite our history. I was always a great believer in things happening for a reason and I guess I was always going to end up with my father one way or another. It was a lesson I learned in my schooling that had always stuck with me, even now.

Things could have been better, I admitted that. It would have been nicer to be with him whilst I was growing up and he wouldn't have had to outright *kidnap* me, but I was here now and it was better for my health to look to my newfound future with him rather than dwell and wallow in my past.

Even if it meant leaving a piece of me behind – leaving Corrin, my grandfather and Mara behind, leaving them in the past was something I was still trying to come to terms with.

Malakei and I continued training in silence before I frowned deeply at a pestering thought.

"Have you seen Raen recently?" I asked, my voice coming across a little too hopeful. He tilted his head to the side before brushing whatever it was he was going to say away.

"He is busy I suppose, with leader work, catching up with his sister Tara – *and Mila* of course."

"Who's Mila?" I couldn't help but ask, the numb and unsettling feeling appeared again in my stomach as I imagined Raen, finally relieved of his duties in capturing me and guiding the Dry Landers across the sectors in one piece. I had not seen him since that day in my father's official tent.

This made me frown and my concentration slipped letting a few of Malakei's punches through.

"She's friend of his," Malakei paused. "At first I thought they were together because they so close. Raen only likes her as friend. Everyone likes her. She is nice and friendly. You should meet her." He said with a smile before his foot came up to kick me. A small grunt left his lips when I caught it and twisted it to the side making him whine.

"Ow *ow* okay *ow* let go *please*!"

I chuckled and let go but only for him to wrap his arm around my neck in a sneaky headlock. His leg came up to twist around my ankle just before he could fall to the ground, in turn, causing me to lose my balance and fall backwards. I landed on top of Malakei and a painful grunt escaped both of us.

I managed to turn around in his grip, slapping him playfully on the shoulder.

"You asshole!" I stated with furrowed eyebrows although it was hard to keep from smiling down at him. "That wasn't a move."

"Yes it–" He hissed when I shifted on top of him, my knee accidentally coming down onto his crotch which in turn made his hands reach out to grab my hips. He pulled me back down with a groan and writhed in pain from under me. I bit my lip as I looked down at him innocently.

"Oops."

Malakei poked an eye open to look up at me. His eyes visibly widened before he let them shut again.

"You traitor. I feel you did that on purpose."

He croaked through the pain and I rolled my eyes, shifting to get off of him but his hands on my hips kept me grounded, he groaned.

I lost my balance trying to get up and my hands flew out either side of his head, I glared down at him.

"*Ow* don't move, please. I am still recovering."

"Don't be such a baby, it was an accident. It's your fault anyways."

"I do not plan for you to hit me in weak spot."

He opened his eyes finally to look up at me. His pupils dilated at how close we were before he shut his eyes tightly again, refusing to look up at me. I frowned at this and tilted my head to the side.

"You are not helping my problem being so close." He whispered between us and I frowned at him confused. I raised my brow and pushed myself up into a sitting position.

"What are you – *oh*."

I gasped when I felt something hard push against my trousers and immediately scrambled off of him, feeling my face and ears burn as I tried to avoid looking at his 'problem'.

"*Okay*." Malakei's voice cracked. He still refused to look at me and a light blush coated the apples of his cheeks, proving this.

"I think we done for today."

I walked forward and held out my hand to him, feeling awful now that I kneed him in his 'weak spot', as he called it.

Malakei took my hand and reddened up at me in

embarrassment, shifting his trousers as we walked through the forest in silence.

"Well." I cleared my throat to try and break the silence. A smirk crept onto my face as I looked ahead of us.

"You were right... when you said you were bigger than me."

"Shut up." Malakei growled out and I laughed loudly for a split moment before I noticed his hand came out to slap me in my own weak spot.

***

Bow glared at me.

Not that it was anything new – but he hadn't stopped narrowing his eyes whenever I looked at him.

I supposed it was slightly awkward when he opened the door and in I walked, limping slightly. Bow only glanced at Malakei before looking down at his slightly lessening erection.

I could hear Bow muttering to himself as he grumbled something at Malakei before shutting the door in his face and following me up the stairs.

"Stop staring at me." I protested, feeling uncomfortable under Bow's scrutinising stare. I was lying down with my eyes closed on my makeshift bed, trying to rest the pain in my lower region but Bow's glares made it hard to do so.

"I'm not staring at you." He defended and I turned my head, opening my eyes to look at him. He was looking down at his hands in his lap, trying to look like he wasn't just staring at me a moment before I called him out. He looked up at me then and raised his brow.

"Stop staring at me." He counteracted and I rolled my eyes at his childish antics, shifting my body slightly and yelping as I did.

"Did you both do – you know…?" He tried to ask with an almost ashamed look towards me and my eyes flew open at that. I blushed at his suggestion and shook my head repeatedly.

"No no, you've got it wrong. We didn't have sex. I don't know about here but where I'm from, that would be considered illegal–"

"What? *sex*? Or two boys having sex?" Bow raised a brow at this and I frowned at him seriously, wincing as I moved my body into a sitting position to look at him properly.

"No." I strained with concerned eyes that he would think of me so little. Then again, I would expect it from him. He was not particularly fond of me.

"I'm eighteen–"

"So? You are old enough here. You're part Dry Lander. Malakei has been a walking disease for as long as I can remember–"

I winced at his words, feeling sick as he talked about Malakei being with multitudes of people but I tried to push these thoughts away.

"It's not something we do young in the *High Peaks*," I tried to explain as best as I could. "It is a punishable offence if found out. Elves are shunned from their community, they go through stonings and if the offence

230

was particularly... gruesome... punishable by death." I told him and he furrowed his brows at this, not agreeing with what I had to say.

"Which is why elves wait until they are older to marry and have children–"

"How much older?"

"Usually... twenties–"

"What?!" Bow couldn't help but hold back his laughter at hearing this but I bit my lip and stayed silent.

"Wait, you're telling me that you all stay virgins until you're twenty, do you simply marry someone just to have sex with them?"

"It's our law..." I frowned at him, feeling uncomfortable with the conversation and his judgemental stare on me as he bit his lip and looked at me thoughtfully.

"And no... we don't have to be married to... *engage* in activities. We can start as early as after we finish our schooling, but it is frowned upon. When we find our life partner, it is more upsetting for them to find out."

"So you and Malakei didn't have sex–"

"No." I groaned as I brought my hands up to cover my eyes, not appreciating the accusations of him talking about me and Malakei in that way.

"We are just close friends, nothing more okay? I accidentally hit him in the balls and he got me back Nothing else happened. For the love of gods *please* stop talking about *sex*."

Bow chuckled at that as he looked at my face now red with embarrassment before a thought struck his features and the smile started to slip from his face.

"So you've really never…"

"I'm sorry – did you forget everything I just said about elves being ex–communicated if they're caught having sex young? Or do I need to explain in graphic detail–"

"*Virgin*, got it," He interrupted, making my jaw clench angrily. His eyes, however, held a hint of worry.

"Maybe it's best not to mention that detail to anyone. Don't want certain Dry Landers finding out."

I gulped at that and subconsciously nodded my head at him. He was right.

"I guess there is one good thing about being a half–elf, half–Dry Lander though. And since you're in the *Dry Lands*, you don't have to worry about those ridiculous rules anymore. If you want to, go for it. You don't know what will happen to you in the future and no one wants to die a virgin." Bow chuckled and I furrowed my brows at that. The loophole that was my life – I had never thought of before. Not that I ever saw a reason to.

The *High Peaks* was my home – *it still was*. If I let myself be tempted by Dry Lander culture, I felt as though I may as well be turning my back on the elves and on everything I believed in growing up. I didn't want to pick sides, especially over something minuscule. Maybe it would be a simple decision if circumstances were different but for now… it wasn't something I would worry about. Sex didn't interest me.

It didn't stop me from messing with Bow, especially over Malakei. Now that I knew he wasn't too fond of him.

"So you're saying… that I should have sex with Malakei?" I bit my lip to hide the smile as I asked, noticing how Bow seemed to go rigid at the mention of my friend's name.

"No. Not Malakei. *Gods* anyone but Malakei."

"Why? What's wrong with Malakei?" I frowned at this, ears pricking up.

"He's an idiot!" Bow scoffed. "He can hardly speak English because he's lazy and he whores around with almost everything that moves. Trust me, you don't want to be around someone like that."

"He treats me better than anyone else here. He understands what I'm going through. We're brothers, he said so himself."

I noticed how Bow winced when I said the word 'brothers', moving his eyes off of me as he got up from his bed and began to make his way out the door.

"*Whatever.*" He mumbled and slammed it, causing me to jump in fright. He left me alone and I sighed, lowering my body gently back onto the bed so that I could try and sleep the dwindling pain in my lower region away.

***

It was a few days after breakfast one sunny morning that Bow and I were walking behind the small tents I had come to know were used as sleeping quarters for Dry Landers. Some were simply stored for food supplies or used for other purposes.

As we were walking back home, we came across some Dry Landers around Bow's age that made Bow freeze in his stride. His eyes were fixated on the boisterous males and caused me to walk into him from behind – a small 'umph' left my lips as I did.

Bow turned around quickly. I was about to apologise when I noticed the sheer panic taking over his eyes.

"You have to hide."

He whispered lowly while pushing at my chest, sending me backwards until I was standing in one of those supply tents.

"What? Why?" I grew alarmed. He cursed however when he heard the laughter of the other boys growing closer by the second. He pushed me back, causing me to stumble onto the ground. I cried out at this and glared up at him, about to question his motives.

"J–Just stay here and be quiet okay? I'll come back to get you. Don't move."

He let the curtain at the entrance of the tent fall, enclosing me in the small confinement of the supply tent and I frowned in confusion, getting up to my feet and brushing the dirt from my clothes with a huff.

I heard voices close by, not knowing what they were saying as they were talking in Fasik – a tongue I had yet to master.

I crept closer to the entrance of the tent, hoping that I could get a look at the faces that were talking.

I froze. Just as my hand was about to pull back the curtain of the tent, I heard Bow's panicked voice.

The sound of punching suddenly filled the air and I quickly pulled back the curtain and ran outside.

I gasped when my eyes landed on the three Dry Landers. Two of them held Bow up as one of them punched him mercilessly. Blood had already started to coat his face.

"Hey!" I screamed at them, causing the one who was punching Bow to stop and turn his head towards me, his eyes blinking in surprise as he looked me over.

"Stop it!"

My face fell as I saw Bow lift his head to me. His nose bloodied and trickling into his mouth. I winced as he spat red out in front of him.

"...Run." He tried to say to me but I only clenched my fists, keeping my gaze on the three eyes now set on me. Excitement danced in their eyes as if they had been starved of the opportunity to draw blood, *fresh* blood.

I zeroed in on the one closest to me who began to inch closer. I stood my ground as he went to punch me but I blocked him, twisting his arm the way Malakei had shown me in our training sessions over the last few days. The boy cried out in pain.

The small victory was short–lived and I groaned when he sent a blow to my stomach using his foot, kicking away from me and we both stumbled away from each other. We looked up at one another again, our eyes too alike but for all the wrong reasons.

"Stay away from him." I hissed at the boy. This seemed to have the opposite effect and made the Dry Lander fume visibly before he charged at me with a scream.

I managed to sidestep him just in time, turning around to him and holding up my fists in a wall formation to block his incoming punches, like Malakei had taught me, wincing as his hard hits that I knew would leave bruises on my arms tomorrow.

In frustration, the boy pushed me and I gasped when my back collided with the hard ground, knocking the wind out of me. I heard Bow scream at the boy in Fasik but the boy didn't listen and walked towards me.

I shuffled back in fear as I noticed him take what looked to be a knife out of his pocket.

My hand reached back on the grass as I moved away until I felt something that I thought resembled a horse's hoof. I jerked my hand away and turned to look up.

A horse's head came into view. Behind it was none other than Raen, glaring down in disgust at the boy who clutched the dagger.

The horse moved its head down to lick me and I quickly shuffled to the side as Raen's boots hit the ground. He glanced at me briefly before his gaze snapped back to the quickly retreating boy.

"Oh no you don't big shot."

I heard Malakei's voice just as the boy was making a break for it in the opposite direction of Raen. Only then did I realise the utter terror on the boy's face – but not at being caught.

It was at the sight of Raen.

The boy yelped when Malakei's hand grabbed him, battling with the boy for a moment before not long Malakei overpowered him. The boy gasped and dropped the dagger in his hands while Malakei shoved him forward and I looked up at the sound of more horses coming closer.

Tara was looking down in amusement. Eyes on me from where she sat on her horse followed by the girl from the meeting the other day. I thought she could be the one Malakei was talking about. Mila.

Mila looked down at me from her horse and I noticed a look of remembrance cross her features as she scanned me before sending me a soft but beautiful smile.

I didn't have time to organise my thoughts when I heard Bow groan from a few metres behind me and my eyes immediately looked over to see him on the floor, clutching his middle as the other two boys started to make a break for it.

"Bow!" I screamed as I got up from the ground and made my way over to him, ignoring the slight dull pain in my abdomen, I knelt beside him. My hands immediately flew out to comfort him but he slapped them away. He slowly got into a sitting position and took deep breaths through his nose before his frustrated eyes fell on me, anger set in them and all directed towards me.

"Why did you do that?!"

He yelled suddenly in my face and I blinked at his outburst, not understanding what I did wrong.

"I told you to stay in the tent where they couldn't see you. Now look what you've done!"

I got up and backed away from him slowly, not understanding why it was such a big deal. I was only doing what I thought was right – which was to help him. He didn't have a Corrin to swoop in and save him from the bullies.

He just had me.

I didn't think he would react like this and I didn't bother to mask the hurt on my features.

"I'm sorry," I croaked out. "I was just trying to help–"

"You didn't!" He screamed back. A shrill pain echoed throughout my eardrums causing them to flatten. My face scrunched up in pain both from my ears and Bow's words as my eyes started to blur.

"All you do is make my life harder. Gods above, I wish you were *never* born. *I hate you*!"

I winced and cowered away from him, letting out a sob at his words, not able to hold it in anymore.

I found myself backing up into a hard chest but I didn't acknowledge it as my eyes were solely trained down on Bow's hateful gaze, my bottom lip wobbled.

"Hey *hey*! don't say that," Tara came forward with a raised brow. "You are brothers–"

"He is *not* my *brother*!" Bow screamed at her as he struggled to get to his feet.

"Bow calm down yes? You're hurt–" Malakei tried but this only caused sparks to fly from Bow as his gaze flew to him. Anger now directed upon the boy he despised – apart from me.

"You stay away from him. I know where your true intentions lie and it's not going to be with him–"

"What is that supposed to mean?!"

I let out a whimper at the painful throbbing setting deep within my ears as my hands moved up to cover them and shook my head as if to drown out the noise. I shut my eyes tightly, backing passed Raen – whose attention I failed to notice was on me the entire time instead of on the screaming match ahead. He frowned down at me and held his hand out for me to take.

'Comply and survive. Comply and survive.'

I began to panic as my eyes went from Raen's, over to where Malakei and Bow looked as though a brawl was about to begin between the two.

'Survive. Survive.'

I shook my head slightly out of fear at Raen, in turn backing further away from him.

'Survive.'

Hurt flashed across his face at my refusal and he began to come closer to me.

'Run.'

Before he could touch me, I let out a startled breath and set off.

I ran, ignoring my name being called as I darted as fast as I could through the tents of the camp, until I was running through the spiked entrance gates and into the dark forest ahead of me.

Corrin's words rang in my mind from when I was younger and running from Tobias. It felt like I was running from multiple Tobias'.

Everything I did was wrong and when I felt like I was doing right by putting myself in danger for the person I cared for, it was still wrong. I didn't know what to do anymore but I knew I couldn't stay here, no matter how much I wanted to build a relationship with my father and brother.

I just wanted to go home. Home to the *High Peaks* because that was my true home, not here.

XIV

~*~

I ran through the forest, not taking so much as a fraction of a second to stop as I weaved through vines and ducked under low–hanging branches. My heart pounded in my chest as the sound of untiring footsteps from behind me reached my ears. They only made me push forward.

Some of the others had stopped running. I didn't know if that was because they knew they couldn't catch me or if he told them to stop. The only footsteps I could hear now were his as they thundered behind me, ever so quickly coming closer and closer like a predator closing in on its prey and–

I cried out when I felt strong arms suddenly latch around me from behind, sending us both hurtling towards the ground. His body was now on top of mine as he knelt on either side of me, his hand squeezing one of my shoulders as the other propped himself up from the ground from letting his weight completely fall on top of me.

I groaned at the feeling of being crushed. My left cheek pressed into the dirt.

He was making it harder for me to breathe as I tried to catch my breath. He had no problem showing how much the chase affected him when he panted heavily down onto my neck and even closer to my ear.

"You were right." He suddenly spoke. A note of surprise appeared in his tone.

"You *are* fast." He panted out before pulling us both up from the ground. I let out a strangled cry and began thrashing in his grip, screaming wildly when he suddenly picked me up and threw me over his shoulder.

"Not fast enough."

"Let me go!" I yelled at the top of my voice as I began to thrash at his back, sending punch after punch and not stopping anytime soon. He seemed to show no irritation towards me doing this and let me continue hitting his back as he walked through the forest with me over his shoulder. It was long into our journey back to the camp when my breath hitched and a stray tear rolled down my cheek. I stopped throwing punches at him because we both knew it was useless. It was clear I had lost and he was taking me back.

"*Raen*," I sobbed. "Don't bring me back there, *please*."

He didn't listen to my cries as he continued to carry me back to the camp over his shoulders. I hit him in frustration and let out a heart–wrenching scream.

"I want to go home!"

"This is your home now." Raen said in a calm voice

and I shook my head at this, letting out a strangled breath.

"This is not home. This is *hell*." I said lowly as I noticed after a while the trees began to fade as we came to the edge of the forest – meaning that we were getting closer to the camp; the awful place I tried to run from that held demons within it.

As we made our way past the spiked barrier, I tried to fight the fatigue from creeping in but it was proving difficult. It didn't help that my resentment and anger was accelerating my sickness.

Raen noticed this as I unknowingly grew heavy in his arms. He brought my legs to the side and let the upper portion of my body slide down his shoulder until my head was resting tiredly against his chest.

I blinked slowly up at him. My eyes – now red–rimmed and puffy from crying, I watched his emotionless expression stare forward as he continued to carry me past white tents. I brought a hand up to clutch his chest in fear of having to face my brother. I didn't think I could deal with what else he had to say to me.

"Please don't bring me back to Ana. Bow will–"

"Bow is with Mila. He is staying with her tonight, and you will stay with me."

He stated and after a moment he sighed but didn't look down.

"You both need to get along with one another. As much as he hates the situation, you both are brothers. Sons of the most feared warrior in all of the *Dry Lands*."

"He hates me," I spat the words out in both hurt and anger, remembering his words clearly in my mind.

"And I *have* tried. I tried being *nice* to him. I tried to *reason* with him – I even tried to give him space but it didn't *work*. I tried to save him from those boys and you saw how he threw it back in my face. Everything I do is a mistake in his eyes. I've been living with him for *weeks* now. Even Ana couldn't stand to look at me until recently. Everyone either hates me or pities me. *I'm sick of it. I just want to go home."*

Raen suddenly glanced down at me with furrowed brows, he pulled me closer to his chest to the point where he was almost crushing me against him.

"You should have left me alone that day," I couldn't help but voice my thoughts. Tears threatened to spill out of my eyes. "I don't belong here."

"That is not true." He said in disbelief.

He looked as though he wanted to say something else but refrained from doing so. Instead, his eyes narrowed ahead of him and I sniffled, looking up at him.

"Yes, it is. Just because I'm a son of a great warrior, does not mean I am destined to be one too."

"No one is expecting you to be anyone but yourself," Raen paused. "No one. Not even your father."

I thought of how he avoided the subject of that day in the *High Peaks*. How he seemed conflicted with even his own beliefs and I wondered what he would have said to me. I wondered if he agreed with me, that he should have never kidnapped me to save me from this turmoil.

"And you?" I questioned him, feeling bold and he raised an amused brow at this.

"And me what?"

"You expect me to be a warrior. Become a weapon for my father, an ace to use in battle strategy when it comes down to sector trade. I'm not a fool Raen. I know my position in all of this." I admitted, knowing that was most likely all I was here for. A pawn for my father to move along the chessboard as he pleased, wielding me to his advantage in the trade of goods between sectors.

Raen seemed taken back by my statement, eyebrows knitting together in thought.

"That is an evil thought. Did the elves teach you to always look down your nose and think the worst of us?"

"I could say the same for you. You don't seem all that fond of elves either."

"I'm not." He admitted making my heart skip a beat. "I believed they were heartless creatures that only cared for appearances and gold. If it came down to it, they would sooner take off running than help a brother or sister in need. They are cowards."

My face turned pink with embarrassment and I refused to answer him. He eventually sighed.

"You are not a warrior," He admitted. "You are also not a coward. You are both brave and afraid. Strong but lacking strength. A fearless hunter and gentle elf."

"What's your point?"

"You are not what I expected either." He adjusted me in his arms.

I let his words wash over me. His words somehow lulled me into a sleep–filled daze as I let my cheek fall back against his warm chest.

"I think we were both wrong about one another."

It began to grow cold due to the now quickly setting sun. I didn't even realise the time had gone by as everything happened this morning. I wondered how long I had been running for and how long Raen was chasing me. He was the only one who didn't give up and as much as my heart leapt in my chest at the thought, I really wanted him to just turn around and give up, to just forget about me like the others had done.

"How is he?"

I heard a girl's voice from in front and I didn't bother nor have the strength to lift my head, keeping my cheek pressed against Raen's chest.

"He is tired *Tara*. He has been running for long, he needs rest."

"Poor little thing," She cooed "I'm going to rip Bow's face off next time I see him. How could he be so cruel to him?"

I could feel her eyes on me and my body grew rigid when I felt her hand in my hair, relaxing and un–tensing when she ran her fingers through my messy dark golden strands.

I clutched my eyes tightly when her fingers travelled down to touch my ears and I held my breath as she massaged them in comfort, making them twitch in her grip. She giggled at this and Raen sighed at her.

"Tara, let him rest." He reminded her.

"Yes okay," She immediately retracted her hand and I let out a breath, pressing my cheek closer to Raen's chest as I clung to his shirt.

"He is precious. I can see why you care for him the way

you do."

I heard her say in a fond voice. My heart stuttered at her words as Raen let out a frustrated sigh and began walking away from her. I lifted my head slightly to look at her over Raen's shoulder. Opening my eyes, I blushed when she caught me peeking at her and waved at me.

I dug my face back into Raen's shoulder and I could hear her laughter as Raen continued to walk away from her.

"Ignore her," Raen sighed and I regained my position with my head on his chest gazing up at him.

"She is crazy."

"I like her." I found myself saying.

Raen glanced down at me slightly, raising a brow before looking up again.

After a moment of silence, he brought me into a tent. I went to sneak a glance around me at the spacious tent that was given to higher–up warriors. A wardrobe, a storage chest at the end of his bed and a small seating area fit into his tent. When he laid me down on his soft bed, I turned back to look at him. He met my eyes for a brief moment before he pulled me up into a sitting position and peeled the clothes from my body.

I didn't bother to fight him as he did this, only wincing when I felt another bruise forming around my middle from where the boy had kicked me earlier. The other bruises were still prominent but I didn't need the bandage anymore.

I opened my eyes when he was finished to look up at him.

He took off his shirt to reveal his toned abs and muscles, there was a tattoo under his arm that I failed to notice before, along with one on his side. As he removed his trousers, I noticed he had another, larger one on the inside of his thigh and I swallowed as I looked at them.

"Are you staring at me?"

My eyes grew wide as they snapped up to him and I immediately sat up, startled as I tried to find words. Raen only raised his brow at me, a small smirk forming on his lips as his eyes shone with that mischievous glint.

"I–I no! I... I didn't know you had tattoos."

"Not many people do."

I blushed as I looked up, trying to keep the smile from my cheeks but felt my dimples protruding.

My eyes suddenly caught something odd and I looked down wide–eyed. Raen watched me in amusement as I did this and furrowed his brows at me in confusion.

"What–"

"How did you just do that?" I interrupted him with excitement and curiosity.

"This?" He raised a brow as he flexed his left nipple again and I chuckled at this, finding the secret talent hilarious. Raen kept doing it for a moment, raising his brow as he tried to keep the smile from his lips but failed miserably as he watched me wheeze for air.

I brought my hands up to cover my stomach as I let my head fall back onto his pillow, panting as I tried to contain my laughter.

"I don't know why you are laughing," He stated in amusement moving to the other side of the bed.

"When you can do the same with your ears."

"I've never seen that happen before," I chuckled as I looked up at the ceiling of the tent. My laughter slowly died in my throat as my eyes grew sad.

"Besides, I was cursed with over–sensitive ears. When they twitch too much – they start to hurt. It can become dangerous."

"Over–sensitive?" He questioned and I turned my head, heart beating out of my chest to see him lying beside me looking over with a curious glance. His eyebrows furrowed.

"They uhm.. twitch a lot," I tried to explain, frowning at the memory of this morning when I felt trapped and covered my ears at the loud voices of Malakei and Bow. I swallowed and let my eyes shut briefly.

"They get painful around loud noises. This morning…"

"You were afraid of getting hurt and ran. I understand Keylin."

Raen's voice was soft and I opened my eyes to look over at him, breath hitching slightly at the look in his eyes, not harsh or judgmental.

"We all do it," He said in a daze before sighing and letting his head rest on the pillow next to me, his eyes shut lazily.

"It's instinct."

I frowned at this and went to speak when he was suddenly speaking again.

"You should get some sleep."

I let out a small breath and turned on my side, my legs curled slightly as I clutched the soft bed, letting my fingers tangle in the fur and I sighed at the feeling.

I couldn't help but feel ashamed for hurting Raen earlier when I let my anger get the better of me. He stuck his neck out for me – on more than one occasion and I was glad he did. It meant a lot to me and I wished I could say this to him but I didn't want to feel more vulnerable than I already felt.

I didn't know when I fell asleep but I remembered it being one of the best sleeps I had in a long while.

***

When I woke up, I felt extremely warm but it wasn't because of the sun's rays shining through the ajar fabrics of the tent or the fur blankets.

It was because of Raen's arms encasing me.

His soft hands rested lightly over my middle. His body was pressed up against mine – where most of the heat was coming from. Our legs tangled with one another's and I felt the small exhaling of breaths from above me where his head rested on the pillow. His chin perched on my head as he slept and I could feel the steady rise and fall of his heartbeat.

My ears twitched furiously as I sighed, letting my eyes close for a moment only to drift off back to sleep in his arms.

The next time I woke was to a girl's giggle and I immediately winced as I dug my face further into the mattress, feeling Raen now stir in his sleep to glance up at whoever was at the entrance to the tent, grunting in greeting before burying his face back in my hair.

"That is the rudest, yet cutest thing I've ever witnessed in my life."

I opened my sleepy eyes, blinking my blurry vision away so that I could tilt my head up to look at Tara. She cooed at me.

"Go away, Tara." Raen said and to my disappointment untangled our limbs and brought his head up from my hair to move his body into a sitting position on the bed. He glared pointedly at the giggling girl. My ears twitched at his deep morning voice before I yawned, shaking my head slightly as I tried to wake up.

Tara looked torn between coming over and wrapping me in her arms and scoffing at her brother. Instead, she sighed and looked up at the ceiling, saying something in *Fasik* before looking down at us seriously.

"As much as I would love to let my older brother spoon a puppy, you both need to get dressed. There's a problem."

At that, Raen was immediately on alert and I felt his warmth leave me, he immediately got up and started throwing on clothes.

I frowned at this and opened my eyes again before sitting up on the bed. Tara threw my discarded clothes toward me, hitting me square in the face. She giggled apologetically when I glared at her.

"Come on little one. Hurry up." She smirked at me as Raen was putting on his belt, reaching down to the floor for his axe. He twirled it in his hand subconsciously before shoving it in his belt loop, jaw clenched.

After I quickly got dressed, Raen and I followed Tara

as we all hastily made our way out of Raen's tent. Raen walked ahead as he asked Tara questions in Fasik. I rolled my eyes at them, zoning out of the conversation I wasn't a part of and looked ahead while I walked.

It was only when I gasped at the scene in front of me Raen looked up from his and Tara's conversation, eyes hardening at the scene in front of him.

The spiked barrier had been left open last night. Allowing for someone, or something, to come into the camp, leaving a mess as it raided the food tent where what looked like most of the food that had been stored there to be shared amongst the villagers – had been raided of its contents.

The food that many of the Dry Landers relied on for the following days was gone.

I slowly lifted my head to look at Raen. Memories of last night flooded my vision of him carrying me through the barrier, but no memory of us closing it surfaced. This was likely our doing.

His stormy eyes landed on me.

"Some are saying they heard voices late last night," Tara began. "We're thinking it's another tribe that took the opportunity when most of our soldiers were away to steal from us." Tara explained and Raen cast his gaze over the empty food tent in a daze, nodding slowly.

"Why would they steal food and not weapons?" I questioned quietly.

"Because they are lazy bastards who can't catch their own food. Why bother when we did all of the hard work?" Tara seethed at her own words and I stepped back slightly.

She suddenly let out a frustrated scream and I jumped in surprise.

"Now I have to go out and catch food on top of my other duties. Damn the gods!"

"I will help," Raen volunteered. "I need time to think."

Tara frowned at her brother and went to say something when Malakei's cheerful voice filled the air.

"Not this idiot," She mumbled to herself before turning around with a raised brow. I followed her gaze and my stomach dropped when I spotted Malakei coming over to us, Mila and Bow behind him not too far away.

"Go annoy Charon, Malakei." Tara stated seriously, causing Malakei to roll his eyes.

"We thought you might need some help because you know, there is no food for us to eat. We catch with you."

When Malakei was close, he slung an arm over my shoulder, nuzzling his head against mine as he pulled me closer to him in greeting. This caused my dimples to poke out as a soft laugh left my lips.

Raen turned around from in front of us at the sound. His eyes settled on me in confusion, only for him to spot Malakei. I swore I saw his jaw clench before he quickly turned his attention away from us.

I froze at the sudden feeling of eyes on me and turned to spot Bow, glaring at me and Malakei.

Mila rested a hand of comfort on Bow's arm before looking up at Tara confidently.

"Tell us how we can help."

XV

~*~

I didn't know how I ended up strolling through the forest floor, carrying a large sword in my right hand with Bow beside me as he trudged in silence, refusing to talk to me.

When Tara had mentioned us splitting up into groups, I didn't expect three hands to immediately grab for me. Those hands belonged to Raen, Malakei and of course Tara. Before I could be pulled apart however, in what could only be described as a tug–o–war for my companionship – Mila stopped them and suggested for Bow to be my partner, reminding them that we still needed to work on patching things up between us.

I didn't know whether I liked her for saving my arms from being ripped from their sockets, or despised her for suggesting Bow and I go into the forest, alone and armed while she on the other hand, was paired up with Raen.

Bow wasn't the only one sulking.

"I just want you to know that I don't hate you,"

My eyes flew up in astonishment when I heard Bow

say those words. He avoided eye contact with me as he tried to keep his eyes on the ground in front of him.

"Although you are a pain in my ass, I don't think I could ever hate you."

My face scrunched in confusion.

"But you said–"

"I know what I said alright?" He lifted his head and narrowed his gaze at me before I could interrupt further. He walked ahead and I couldn't help but sigh sadly at the realisation that there was not going to be much talking – *more tiptoeing* – around the issue, instead of using the time to actually resolve our differences, maybe delve into some underlying childhood trauma if we had the time.

I fell back in line with him, looking down at my feet as I walked and decided to keep my mouth shut to prevent any further arguments or disagreements from erupting between us.

It was only when I noticed a small trail of blood start to appear at my feet in my line of vision that I stopped suddenly, eyes widening as I looked up. Bow noticed this and cast a sideways glance, scoffing.

"What did–"

"Shut up." I told him seriously, bringing a hand out over his chest and stopping him from moving any further to the bloody scene in front of us. Chunks of red meat littered the ground before I noticed a rather large striped tiger in front of us not too far away.

"Don't move." I whispered out, eyes never leaving the beast. I watched it chomp down on something tender, ripping the flesh away from the once–alive animal.

It didn't notice us yet.

Bow, who failed to notice the tiger several metres away, scoffed at me, causing the tiger to immediately twitch its ears in our direction. My hand flew up to cover Bow's mouth before his eyes fell on the sight of the tiger lifting its nuzzle in the air before him.

There was a moment when both of us were frozen in our spots, with only our breathing and heartbeats echoing around the forest.

Bow timidly reached down for his axe at his side, his fingers only grazed the handle when the tiger got up and turned around. Its dangerous eyes landed on us just as it went to sniff the air, growling in warning.

As the tiger had gotten up, I immediately spotted the cowering twin cubs at its feet and my eyes widened. Turning to Bow, I grabbed his hand just in time before he could throw his axe at the tigress. The sight of the weapon made her roar and I stumbled forward, pulling Bow down with me.

"Are you insane?!" Bow screamed from above me as he tried to prise the weapon from my grip, eyes darting up at the now–approaching tiger.

"Keylin. Give me–"

"Stop shouting you're making her nervous." I stated in a calming tone so as not to disrupt the tiger. She growled lowly and I knew the only way we would survive this encounter was to get rid of the weapon.

When Bow was preoccupied gawking at the animal, I took the distraction in my stride and threw the axe into the bushes a small distance away.

Bow looked as though he wanted to strangle me and quickly went to pull me to my feet in what I presumed was his last resort, going to bolt for it. But this would have only been a treat for the tiger. We would not have made it all that far before she caught up with us. We would have been no better off than the bloody meat she had been sinking her teeth into only several minutes ago.

"There's no time." I whispered urgently as I heard the tiger's paws indent on the forest floor, coming closer with a predatory growl.

I pulled Bow down to the ground level, shoving him forward so that he was in a crouching position and quickly got into the same position beside him, tilting my head to the side as I turned to him. Bow did the same. His breathing was erratic as fear seeped into his gaze.

"Copy me." I said simply.

My head crouched down between my knees as I brought my hands forward, demonstrating to the tiger I was of no harm to her or her cubs. I could only hope that Bow did the same. If he didn't... I couldn't save him without dying in the process. If there was one thing I did know from my years of study in the *High Peaks*, it was the way of nature and how to interact with animals, and how we were similar to them in spirit.

I could feel the tiger's presence when she growled lowly. Bow took in a shaky breath when the tiger sniffed at his hair.

I held my breath as the tiger made her way over to me, walking over Bow's back. He bit his tongue at the action but didn't make a sound.

I felt the tiger sniff at my right arm. Her wet snout travelled up before burying deep into my neck, getting a whiff of my scent. I let out a shaky breath as her snout trailed over my ears, stopping to sniff at them before she sneezed violently.

She sniffed my hair tentatively before licking it and I shut my eyes tightly at this. All too quickly, she made a small chuffing noise and I let out a relieved breath, bringing my hands back slowly from their position in front of me. I smiled when I noticed her retreating to her whining cubs as they cried out for her.

I turned to Bow clutching his eyes tightly as he stayed in his crouching position, afraid to move a muscle in fear of the tiger returning. My eyes softened at this.

"It's okay." I breathed out as I brought my head up to see the tiger sinking back down on her side, swatting the bloody meat in her hands playfully.

"She won't hurt us once she knows we're no longer a threat to her and her cubs." I panted out, suddenly feeling exhausted and I brought my hand up to wipe at my wet ear, cringing as I did.

All too abruptly, I was pulled into Bow's arms and dragged back down onto the ground. I let out a small huff of breath as my head collided with his chest.

Bow brought his trembling arms around me as he buried his face into my neck, closing his eyes and taking deep breaths.

"Don't fucking scare me like that again." He said into my shoulder and I swore I could feel something wet seep into my shirt.

"I thought it was going to kill you Keylin." His voice raised slightly while his arms clutched onto me tightly. "I'm going to fucking kill you after this. I swear–"

"We're okay *see*? I'm okay," I tried to assure him, gulping. "We should get going though, before she changes her mind."

I felt Bow's body stiffen before he was nodding all too quickly into my shoulder, releasing me to get up. His eyes fixed on the tiger in caution while he held out a hand for me.

I furrowed my brows up at him at this but accepted his outstretched hand. He pulled me up and immediately put a hand on my shoulders, guiding us quickly out of the presence of the tiger. He even failed to notice that he had left his axe behind as he only focused now on getting us back to safety.

***

"I think… I'm finally finished scolding you for doing such a risky thing–"

I groaned at that, narrowed eyes turning to him.

"No no go ahead. We might as well spend the remainder of the journey talking about how stupid I was and how I could've died–" I winced at the idea and quickly shook my head.

"Actually, no. Please don't say anything. I've learned my lesson."

"Good," Bow said flatly before biting away the smile on his lips, his arm came to rub against mine as we walked out of the forest, walking up to the spiked barrier of the camp I had slowly grown accustomed to.

"What you did back there... it was cool. *Thank you*. You saved me. You saved both of us."

I frowned at this as I brought my head up in confusion.

"It's my job to protect you, is it not?"

Bow looked to the floor at this and a heavy sigh left his lips before he looked back up, his hands came up to ruffle my hair and I whined in protest making him chuckle. A small smirk played on the corners of his lips.

"No, you idiot. It's *mine*. I'm the older one here. It should be my job to protect you. Not the other way round."

I stopped in my tracks when we were inside the camp, not believing what I was hearing. Bow paid no attention to me and sighed with relief at being home before frowning when he realised I wasn't walking beside him anymore. He turned to me then.

My vision blurred as I looked at him and he was about to speak but I didn't waste any more time. I ran forward, my hands going around his back as I buried my head in his chest. It was clear I took him by surprise when he stumbled slightly but held his stance. I tried to choke out a 'thank you' through my tears but Bow shushed me, bringing his hands around my back and patting me in assurance.

"It's okay Keylin... I'm sorry for treating you badly before." I inhaled sharply at that and Bow looked down at me in alarm.

"*Hey*, don't cry. I'm not going anywhere, and I promise

you. From now on, I won't let anything happen to you. We're family now. Which means you're stuck with me."

When I looked up from his chest, wiping my eyes, I noticed the others had made it back.

Tara and Malakei were looking at Bow and me a few metres away, both with smiles on their faces as they watched us hug from where they currently sat amongst the grass, finally relieved that Bow accepted me now as his brother.

Bow surprised me when he brought the cloth of his sleeve up, wiping the stray tears from under my eyes before bringing my head closer and placing a quick kiss to the back of my head.

"I think I'm going to cry." I heard Tara say from where she sat on the grass, wiping at her eyes. Malakei threw her an unimpressed look before turning back to me and rolling his eyes to show his annoyance with the girl. I couldn't help but chuckle at that while Bow groaned in irritation. His eyes found me again with a small smile before he nudged me in their direction.

"Stay with them while I go find Mila–"

Malakei made a suggestive face at the mention of Mila, throwing sloppy air kisses Bow's way. My brother only turned to him with a narrowed gaze, lifting his finger in a warning.

"I'm giving you a chance because Keylin likes you. Other than that, I would have knocked your pathetic ass to the ground."

Malakei rolled his eyes at that as Tara let out an amused laugh on hearing this, causing my ears to twitch.

"Whatever kid. I'm still older than you. You not even make it to patrol. Come back to me when you earn wings yes?"

The muscles in Bow's face tightened at Malakei's words, definitely hitting a nerve, with my brother looking as though he wanted to say something but thought against it. He reached forward to ruffle my hair instead and left me with the two Dry Landers looking up at me from the ground.

A mischievous look settled behind their dark eyes and I knew nothing good could come from being with them.

***

I was right when I said nothing good could come from being with them because I was currently in Tara's tent – which looked a lot similar to Raen's. Malakei practised his jabbing techniques on a bolted punching bag that hung in the corner where Tara kept all of her training gear together.

While I laid on the couch with Tara behind me running a hand through my hair, her thumb sometimes dipped down to brush along my ear tips and I whined when she did this. She only chuckled at me in response, looking down with a fondness in her mesmerising eyes similar to Raen's.

"You know, if you didn't like someone – I would have ravished you the minute you appeared at the camp." She sighed out of the blue to herself and my eyes flew open at her words. I moved to get up but she pulled me back to her chest, chuckling.

"W–What makes you think I like someone?" I stuttered out in slight panic but she only hummed from above me, continuing to twirl my dark blonde hair between her fingers.

"*Oh honey*, the way you look at my brother; it's obvious–" She noticed the panic on my face. "Of course, it's nothing to be ashamed of. No one cares here–"

"–But I..." I trailed off and eventually sighed, letting my head fall back against Tara's shoulder with a frustrated huff. She giggled at this and I closed my eyes in exhaustion.

"You're starting to sound like him too."

"Sound like who?"

My eyes flew open at the familiar voice only to see Raen at the entrance of the tent. He spotted Tara before doing a double take at our position and frowned.

"You aren't holding him hostage are you?"

"That's rich coming from you." Tara judged with a lifted brow.

"Yes." I interrupted seriously not waiting for him to continue his banter with his sister. I yelped when Tara suddenly pulled at my hair.

"Shhh say nothing little one–"

"Tara!" Raen's voice made both Tara and I jump before she was sighing loudly in frustration.

"Fine." Tara huffed before she moved her arms that were keeping me from getting up, allowing me to freely move away from her and stand up. I stretched my arms out as I did.

"We will finish this later." She suddenly said with a

knowing smile and I let out a shaky breath as I nodded at her, figuring that she was talking about me and her brother. Raen looked between us in confusion before shaking his head.

"Malakei come here."

Raen called over to the boy in the corner who was quickly stopping his punching and looking up curiously. He threw a sweat towel over his shoulders from beside him before coming closer to us. Tara got up too, now on alert of what Raen had to say, knowing it was something serious.

"The food has been stocked up but we don't have nearly as much as we did before. Just enough to pass a few days maybe," Raen sighed and my mind suddenly went back to the tiger, remembering how there was so much blood and raw meat littered around her where it looked like she was gathering food to feed her and her cubs.

"As for the thieving tribe. The only thing to do is to journey to neighbouring–"

"It was an animal."

I found myself saying, causing Raen to fall silent. I felt everyone's eyes on me and I looked up to see them staring at me curiously. My ear tips blushed and Raen frowned at this.

"An animal?"

"A tiger–"

"A tiger would not do this."

"She was stocking up to feed her cubs." I stated in slight defence, not understanding myself as to why I was defending a dangerous animal. Raen narrowed his eyes at me in doubt.

"How do you know this? Are you making this up?"

"No," I assured him seriously before taking a breath. "Bow and I ran into her and her cubs. The ground around her was filled with raw bloody meat and she looked like she had been snacking for a while – come to think of it, maybe that was the main reason she didn't kill us."

I said the last part quietly as I thought about it. Of course, it didn't go unnoticed and Tara's eyes widened, as did Malakei and Raen's.

"What?!" Tara questioned in shock from beside me and I winced at her loud voice.

"Didn't kill you… How is that even possible you're alive right now?" Malakei repeated my words in exasperation as he looked down at me with an angered and concerned expression that made me flatten my ears against my head.

The only one that didn't say anything was Raen and as I peeked up at him, I couldn't help the squeak that left me when I took in his close–eyed expression. His fingers pinched the bridge of his nose in frustration while his jaw clenched tightly.

"I–It's okay. I'm fine and so is Bow. She didn't hurt us."

A look of recognition crossed Malakei's face as he seemed to remember something. He let out a relieved breath and looked up at me with a confused smile. His eyes lightened off of their intensity.

"You do connection thing?" He wondered and I frowned slightly at that, about to speak when both Tara and Raen's eyes flew to Malakei's in confusion.

"What?" Raen questioned.

Malakei snorted, rolling his eyes as he went to explain to them what I had tried to tell them. I didn't listen to him however as I ran my hand through my hair and went to sit down on the couch.

I felt Raen's eyes glance to me every few minutes watching me carefully. A look crossed his face that resembled regret, but he quickly shook it off.

'Was he thinking back to the incident with the wolf perhaps?'

"Fine, so the tiger got the food but... who let it in? Someone must have left the barrier open last night for her to wander in." Tara frowned and I turned to Raen.

Raen sensed my stare and quickly turned to me. A silent message travelled between us before Raen looked at Tara.

"That was–"

"I left it open."

I cut Raen off, having all of the eyes in the room turn to me with a disappointed frown. My head cast downwards as I fed them the lie.

"I forgot to close it when I ran away yesterday. I'm sorry. I wasn't thinking."

Malakei let out a frustrated sigh from above me and brought his hand up to run through his hair.

"It's okay Keylin. We understand but you need to help us get the food back."

I looked up at Malakei and nodded at him seriously.

"Of course."

***

"Tell Bow not to worry, that his brother is staying with me tonight."

My head moved up in curiosity and my eyes fell on Raen talking to Malakei, not bothering to whisper or talk privately amongst themselves although I felt like he wanted me to hear this too. I had no say in the matter and Raen hadn't uttered a word – not even so much as a glance in my direction since a few hours ago, instead insisting on helping Malakei with his fighting stances – much to Malakei's horror.

Tara made the move to pull me back into her chest at this to continue where she had left off twirling her fingers around my stray blonde strands.

Malakei glanced at me before looking back at Raen with a raised brow. A knowing smirk formed on his lips and he nodded silently, not saying anything as he turned and left the tent. He sent me a visible wink before he did.

This made me uncomfortable and I quickly got to my feet, despite Tara's protests. She had somehow fallen asleep on the couch in our position and her grip slackened, allowing me to escape her. She grumbled something under her breath in Fasik before turning her body into a more comfortable position on the couch.

"I–I should probably be getting home."

"*After*," Raen said sharply, still refusing to look at me before grabbing my shoulder.

His fingers dug into my skin as he all but pushed me out of the tent in front of him. I hissed as he moved his grip down to my upper arm. His hold was tight as he began dragging me towards his tent.

"We need to talk." He insisted lowly.

I gulped at that, knowing exactly what he was upset over.

When he pushed me inside his tent, he quickly reached for me and grabbed me by my shirt, lifting me against his wardrobe with one hand and I couldn't help but gasp at that, taken off guard.

"You think you are funny when you go around and throw your life on the line? With wolves it was concerning but *tigers* Keylin…" He questioned with prominent frustration and worry about his features. He pushed me further back into the wardrobe and I let out a strangled breath shutting my eyes tightly.

"*Look at me.*" He growled out, gripping my shirt tighter.

My back dug against the splintering wood causing my eyes to fly open and I looked down at him through my blurry vision. His eyes tried to convey how my reckless actions could have backfired.

"They are wild animal! What would your father say if I told him you were mauled to death by tigers? He would skin me alive Keylin. Do you not realise the danger of what could have happened?"

"I'm sorry." I choked out in desperation. "It's not like we planned for it to happen. We walked into her den by accident!"

I brought my shaking hands down to wrap around his clutching my shirt. I bit the inside of my lip, drawing blood as I looked down at his slowly deflating eyes pleadingly. His anger quickly left him as he looked at how shaken I was and he panted coming to his senses.

"I'm sorry. It won't happen again, I promise you just please, put me down."

He seemed conflicted by this for a moment as he fought a mental battle with himself, deciding whether to let me go or not. In the end, he dropped my dangling feet to the floor but caged me against the wood breathing heavily, trying to contain his rage.

"I don't know what it is about you Keylin, you make me crazy sometimes that I can't think straight."

My cheeks burned red at his words.

"Other times..." He trailed off as his hands came up to brush over my reddened cheeks. I flinched back, for a moment washed over me of Tobias, copying the small action and thinking he was going to hit me on instinct but he only stared down at me with furrowed brows and sad eyes.

"Other times I want to keep you from harm. Protect you from Sorn itself and every evil thing that lurks in the shadows... I could never live with myself knowing that I let you slip through my fingers."

I watched him as he spoke. His eyes filled with that glint they usually possessed around me and I processed his words as his thumb caught a stray tear falling from under my eye.

"I just want to protect you. Why can't you see that?"

"I can protect myself," I whispered out to him. "I'm fine. You don't have to take on the responsibility–"

"*No.*" Raen shook his head at this, not getting at what

he was trying to say. He suddenly slammed his hand on the wooden wardrobe door right beside my head in frustration and I flattened my ears at that. His eyes looked tired now but quickly turned sad as he stared down at me with pleading eyes.

"Keylin, I–"

"Raen."

Mila's voice was stern yet held a calming tone to it, almost soothing.

I peeked over Raen's shoulder to spot her and Bow at the entrance. My brother looked like he wanted to rip Raen's head right off of his body when he took in my shaking form.

"You're frightening the boy. Let him go."

Raen let his eyes fall shut from above me, taking a deep calming breath before slowly and surely backing away from me. He opened his eyes and cast them down to the floor, showing no emotion as he deliberately avoided my gaze.

"Come on Keylin."

My red–rimmed eyes met Bow's concerned ones. His hand outstretched towards me carefully from behind Raen. As if Raen was a ticking bomb that could detonate at any sudden movement, I snuck a glance at Raen before reaching out with shaking hands to Bow. Bow immediately pulled me into his chest when we touched and not realising it, I let out a shaky breath of relief.

"It's okay." Bow assured me as he took me in his arms and I brought my hands around his back loosely while he rubbed soothing circles into mine.

"You're okay Key. I'm taking you home. You're trembling…"

I heard Mila's footsteps moving to Raen and tilted my head up in time to see her rubbing his shoulders, whispering words of comfort to him in Fasik.

"What's going on?" I asked quietly.

"She's calming him down," Bow whispered to me, afraid as if speaking the words would disrupt Mila's work. *"We are lucky we found you… when he gets angry, there is no telling what he can do. I heard he killed people before who have crossed him for less."*

Bow's words made the sudden realisation of how much danger I was truly in dawn upon me. This was why they feared Raen. He was unpredictable, like a dangerous animal.

Before I could say anything else, Mila brought her lips up to kiss Raen's cheek.

Something broke in me after hearing and seeing that. Something internal that made my eyes misty again as I gritted my teeth. I watched Raen – who although had eyes devoid of emotion, welcomed her embrace. The one that he trusted to calm him down. I believed their relationship dove deeper than friendship. It made me feel foolish for ever thinking he could value me as someone other than his leader's son. He didn't know me, not like he knew her. Even all of this time while he was trying to get close to me, opening up to me and getting me to slowly break down my walls and trust and *feel* something… was it all a lie?

"I trusted you."

I whispered out in disbelief, making Raen turn his head with tired eyes. The words flowed out of my mouth before I could even process what I was saying. He quickly pulled away from Mila, looking at me.

"Keylin–"

"I can't believe I let myself trust someone like you... *all of you...*" My eyes narrowed as I looked at them all in disbelief, turning to each of them.

Bow frowned, hurt at my words but I pulled back from his grip and began to back away. I turned back to Raen.

"You kidnapped me, strangled me, I almost got hypothermia because of you and I would be far away from here if it wasn't for you. *You* did this to me. This is *your fault*–"

"Keylin, *no*." Raen whispered out as I noticed his eyes became glassy. He blinked them away in frustration and moved away from Mila, immediately coming over to me but I shook my head and began to walk back, feeling drained as my cruel eyes met his.

"Don't *ever* touch me again. Don't talk to me or even look at me."

"Wait, Keylin!"

I ran out of the tent, my legs shaking with adrenaline as I finally let the tears fall from my eyes. My feet wanted to lead to Malakei because I knew he would find a way to make me feel better about what I just did but he couldn't understand what I was going through.

How could he? He was an accomplice in my kidnapping. He was there that night. This pain I felt was as much his fault.

I had never said anything so hurtful to anyone in my life and I didn't know why I was crying when I meant every word.

I meant every word that I said. I couldn't take it back. So why was I crying like my heart was being cut out of my chest?

I ran back to Bow's house, refusing to call it my home because it had never felt like one from the moment I got there. Opening and shutting the door hard, I didn't care about possibly waking Ana as I ran up the stairs, threw open the door and shut it quickly. I leaned back against it as I let out my body slide down the door until I was sitting on the floor in front of it. Curling my knees up close to my chest, I pulled my arms around them tight. My body shook as I let out violent cries.

I just wanted to go home.

XVI

~*~

I flinched in my sleep at the feeling of something hitting my back.
I curled up on the floor just as Bow opened the bedroom door from behind me, it opened just enough for someone to fit through the frame I was blocking, or for someone as slim as Bow to fit through.

I heard him sigh from above me cuddled against the door but I didn't open my eyes even as he picked me up in his arms. I made no sound as he did this, only letting out a sigh when the feeling of fur tickled my neck.

I curled up on my side in a foetal position when I felt the bed dip and Bow's body was lying down beside mine, his hand came around to the back of my head as he pulled me onto his chest.

That was the only thing I remembered before I woke

up the next morning in Bow's bed. Bow slept quietly beside me as I let out a shaky sigh. My hand combed through my messy hair and squinted my eyes in an attempt to prevent the sting from having cried so much last night.

"You know..." Bow shifted on the bed, stretching as he croaked sleepily at me. He blinked awake.

"I don't think I've ever seen Raen cry. Definitely not over someone younger yelling at him. You were like a small dog, barking up at a wolf."

I let my eyes shut at that and my face scrunched up at the memory. The familiar lump in my throat came back and I tried not to make a sound.

"Everything I have been piling up just sort of came out. I'm still upset."

"You have a right to be. I blame our father for how he handled the situation with you. He should have been here for you. Even if it meant upsetting other leaders across the land. If I was in your shoes, I would be too."

As much as I wanted to give my father the benefit of the doubt, Bow was right. He should have been here, if not to aid in the transition of living in this strange land and getting to know him, but to help me understand why I was here in the first place.

He would be home soon.

"Something happened with Raen, didn't it?" Bow asked hesitantly. "Otherwise you wouldn't have said what you did."

I opened my eyes at that and nodded sadly, bringing my hands up to press against my eyes in an attempt to rid the tears and sleep from them. Bow's face fell at the action.

"I'm so sorry Keylin. If I was there–"

"Don't," I said, slightly hoarse. My voice was filled with emotion bursting to be free, there was a dryness and vulnerability to it that I was beginning to really grow tired of. I looked up determined at Bow.

"Don't blame yourself. How could you have known he would snap at me like that? Shit happens."

"Yes, but they always happen to good people, like *you* Keylin. You don't deserve it."

I smiled weakly at that and shook my head at him.

"I'm not–"

"Keylin." He cut me off seriously. "You are a good person."

***

Bow insisted I stay home. He said I should take a break and just relax with him and Ana, get to know each other more. He told me father would be coming home tomorrow which made me relieved. I was starting to worry. It had felt like so long since I saw him last.

We talked about a lot of things such as our father. Bow told me all about him, what he liked, disliked and even shared some memorable experiences with me that Bow and his father shared when Bow was younger.

This made me smile, I pushed down all of the jealous and upset feelings regarding how I never really had a father who would spend time with me – besides *avus*.

My grandfather wasn't much of one, to be honest, running a kingdom and being the king of a sector had a part to play also.

I was glad that Bow got to cherish the memories with our father. In a way, his fun times with him going out hunting brought me happiness, even if it couldn't make up for lost time on my part.

The day after that, there was a knock on the front door early in the morning.

Bow told me to wait in our room while he went down and checked who it was. All the while, I hoped it wasn't Raen.

It was Malakei.

He had somehow got wind of what happened the other night and didn't hesitate in storming past a yelling Bow up the stairs to me. He sent me his familiar friendly smile before throwing me one of his spare swords, telling me that the both of us were going to clear our heads.

Malakei and I sparred with our swords in the forest, silence surrounded us along with the trees and mysteries of the forest. He didn't say a word to me after we left the house, leaving a frowning Bow as we travelled through the forest.

He wasn't going hard on me with sparring and I didn't like that. Mostly because he knew that I was going through some confusing stuff and even with him going easy on me, I was losing.

For the fifth time in a row, my back collided with the ground and I let out a frustrated sigh, dropping my sword to the side in defeat.

Malakei frowned as he looked over at my discarded sword. "Why you stop?"

"I think we're done for today," I began. "I thought I was up for it... but I'm not. I think I'm just going to go back to the house." I said as I sluggishly got to my feet.

Malakei sighed at this, he too, threw his sword down at his side before running a hand through his dark hair, eyes searching mine.

"Keylin... I don't know how to make you feel better..."

"You can't. I'm fine. I just need some time I guess to feel okay again. I'll get over it eventually. I just... want some space." I sighed and looked up. Malakei took in my words with a worried look on his face. His eyes suddenly widened as what I believed was a thought – popped into his head and I frowned at that, going to turn away when he scrambled forward to pull me back.

"Hit me."

"Wha–"

"Get it all out of system and you won't feel sad anymore. Go ahead. That is what we train for."

I shook my head at him as I looked at how he seemed to ready himself by closing his eyes. I watched him get into a position, shifting on his feet. He only opened his eyes in disappointment when I didn't hit him and continued to stare at him blankly.

"I'm not going to hit you because I'm not angry with you."

"I don't mind Keylin," He let out a breath, looking up at me sadly with a knowing look in his eyes.

"I don't mind you hitting me, if it means you don't hit yourself."

Those words stung and I opened my mouth to speak

but nothing came out. I closed it and shut my eyes tightly before looking up at the clear blue sky above me.

Malakei must have noticed my shift in mood as I felt him pull me into a warm hug. His hands went around my back as I let my head bury into his shoulder. No tears fell from my eyes however, they only misted up. I didn't feel like crying today.

"I think I'm all cried out." I whispered as I pulled away from his shoulder. Malakei moved back to look down at me, a small sad smile playing on his features.

"My gift to you," He stated lightly. "I take your tears away."

I chuckled at that. My dimples poked out almost painfully as the feeling of my skin stretching on my face for the first time in a few days came back to me. It scared me how I hadn't smiled a real smile until now. Even with Bow, it was small smiles or fake ones. No one could make me really smile here like Malakei could. He made this place bearable. I guessed that's why I wasn't crying around him because when I was with him, I felt like there was no need to cry about my problems. Malakei took my mind away from them by helping me fight.

"Thank you Mal."

***

I greeted my father with a small smile when Malakei and I got back from the forest but he insisted on taking me in a bone–crushing hug. Our training session was long over and I was happy to get out of there. I couldn't shake the feeling of eyes on Malakei and me the whole time we sword–fought, it was me who eventually suggested we leave after I thought my ears picked up on something strange not too far from us. Thinking of it now, it was probably just the wind. The air had become thick and cold, dropping with the colder temperatures. I was still getting used to this climate.

"You've gotten taller." My father noted with a smile, bringing a hand up to ruffle my hair.

"It's crazy what a few weeks can do." I raised a brow at him, remembering how he had said he would only be gone a few days.

Regret washed over my father's face, smile fading.

"Ah, I believe I said a few days." My father remembered, sending me a sorrowful look.

"I can't believe you left for so long this time. You really are father of the year." Bow rolled his eyes but I noticed the small flicker of playfulness behind them. When father reached a hand out to swot at Bow, my brother sidestepped him with a smirk.

'Their interaction is so strange… yet endearing.'

"I'm sorry Keylin." My father said sincerely, taking me in a warm hug that was more gentle this time around. I smiled at that.

When we both pulled back, I tried not to look at Raen who was making his way up behind him. An emotionless expression blanketed his face as he stared ahead, almost avoiding my eyes.

Malakei had told me on the way back that Raen was acting strange now. He barely spoke to Tara and when she mentioned me to him, he would avoid her and try to leave the conversation. He was like that over every little thing these past few days. He kept everything to himself and didn't so much as utter a word of anything to anyone, not even a hello most times.

The only person that knew anything was Mila apparently, but she didn't want to say anything to anyone, not that it was anyone else's business to begin with. She was a true friend who kept his secrets, and his respect.

Bow slung his arm around me when we were in touching distance, flashing his teeth at me. I returned the smile and my father raised his brow at our encounter.

"I see you two have gotten along. I hope he wasn't too much of a brat to be around Keylin."

I could sense Bow rolling his eyes as he scoffed at our father's playful teasing, making me chuckle lightly before shaking my head.

"I've never had a brother before. I was more than happy to get to know him." I stated with a shy smile.

From the corner of my eye, Bow looked down at me. A light smile crossed his lips before he frowned and turned back to our father, taking his hand from around my shoulder as he grew serious.

"I can only surmise there is a reason for your extended absence. Any news?" Bow asked and I watched silently as our father waited a moment before letting out a small exhale.

"We still don't know any more than we did weeks ago." Father replied and Bow cursed in frustration.

"Don't know what?" I frowned, confused and looked

up at my father in worry. He turned to Bow with a bewildered expression.

"You didn't tell him?"

"I–" Bow began and I turned to him. "I guess it slipped my mind. I didn't want to worry him."

Father didn't seem impressed by that but nodded in understanding. He turned to me with soft eyes as he explained this news.

"Other tribes have said that something is killing their people at night. We don't know if it's an animal or another Dry Lander. I have been working closely with other tribes in *Jhovst*. Helping them try and catch whatever this thing is but so far, we have had no luck,"

I blinked as I took in the information, nodding my head slowly to show that I understood before furrowing my brows at this.

"And it seems that the killings are only getting worse," My father continued. "More bodies are being found and they are starting to creep closer to home. *Too close* for comfort. I will be leaving again to meet back with the neighbouring Dry Landers for further news and so as of now, I'm putting the camp under watch. No one is to go into the forest after sunset." Father stated seriously before turning around to say something to Raen.

Raen nodded silently at whatever my father had said to him and began walking away, most likely to alert the patrol who watched the spiked barrier of the camp entrance, to make sure no one was to leave the camp after hours.

Malakei was soon enough pressing his hand on my

shoulder and I turned to him, knowing that the rest of the conversation would be left to the 'adults'. Malakei bid me farewell and I was about to walk away when I felt another hand stop me. My father looked down at me with a sad smile.

"I am sorry Keylin that this is cutting into us spending time with one another, but I promise you. After this – you, me, Bow and Ana are going to go somewhere we can relax and be a family."

I nodded, feeling as though it was all I could do, all I could offer him.

He pinched my cheek.

"Bow tells me you have been learning how to fight with Malakei. Care to show me what you've learnt before dinner?"

My eyes bulged. "N–Now? With you?"

His laugh was rough and genuine but his eyes gleamed with warmth. "Why not? Afraid to take me on?"

"Only because I don't want to bruise your ego when you lose." I smirked and he chuckled, clapping my back.

"Challenge accepted."

***

Father wasn't joking when he said that he was putting the camp on watch and monitoring the people who tried to leave after sundown.

His guards were strong and serious. They took on a typical Dry Lander stance from where I watched in the grass near the barrier. They looked at people passing them to leave the camp as if they were murderers. This confused me because it wasn't even dark out yet. They only had to watch out for people who would try to escape *after* dark, not stare them down as they left the camp during the day. Their stares gave me chills and I turned around to Malakei and Tara. Bow had left us only moments ago to spend time with Mila while Raen was... I didn't know where he was, and I didn't really care either.

I pulled at the grass from under me.

"They're trying to recognise the faces as they leave." Tara said all of a sudden from where she squinted at them. Her hair fell over her face because she didn't push it back with a hairband. It was uncanny how much she resembled Raen like this with the same colour hair, eyes and smooth skin tone.

"Why?"

"So that they know their own people coming back. Whoever this person or thing is, it's most likely slipping into camps unnoticed. I've heard it done before, many years ago."

My heart skipped nervously at that and Malakei scoffed from where he lay flat on his back, eyes closed as he rested. It almost looked like he was sleeping until he reacted to Tara's words.

"They not doing very good job if people know. I snuck out many times in middle of night, I never get caught."

"This is about murder, not a late–night booty call Mal." Tara rolled her eyes and chucked some grass in Malakei's face. She cackled when he sneezed at the sudden intrusion and rushed up into a sitting position. I couldn't help the smile as I watched him, dimples poking out slightly as I followed their playful encounter.

My gaze trailed back over to the guards with a frown and continued to watch them until I heard Malakei sigh in boredom.

"We should sneak out tonight. All three of us. For fun."

Our eyes flew to Malakei's unbothered ones and I frowned at his suggestion while Tara smacked him across the back of the head, a Fasik curse falling from her lips, causing him to yelp.

"You *idiot*. Do you not see how dangerous that is? We could get caught by the guards and punished for disobeying orders from Maekin – or not to mention, if we are *really* unlucky, get killed. If not by whatever this thing is, but by your brother and *mine*," She explained with narrowed eyes. "My brother would also never allow me to go. You know how he is."

Tara grumbled the last part and I knew exactly what she meant when referring to Raen.

Malakei only scoffed at this and glanced at me with a smirk, not taking Tara's words seriously.

"Fine. I'm not forcing you to come but Key will come with me, won't you Key–"

"No."

"*Dimples*." Malakei whined, face falling as he looked at me. I frowned at this and shook my head in disbelief.

"Tara's right Mal. What would we even do out there? Train in the dark?"

"It not stopped us before. It should not stop us now." Malakei tried to reason with a frown and I sighed, correcting him on his English vocabulary. He thanked me with the slightest tint of red colouring on his cheeks.

"That's only because I didn't know about what was happening. No one told me there were attacks going on. Besides, we would go during the light, not when it's dark. Training in the dark is useless."

"Well I'm going," Malakei spoke up with sudden determination and I frowned at his stubbornness.

"I dropped journal in forest and need to get it back. If you want to come with me, come. I not force you to."

Feeling the sudden urge to go with Malakei in case something did go wrong while out looking for his journal, I knew that if I refused to go with him and something happened to him, all because I was afraid. I wouldn't be able to have that sort of blame on my conscience.

"Fine. I'm going with you." I gritted out eventually, knowing that the reason for venturing out after hours was a genuine one because I saw Malakei discard his journal near his water bottle when we sparred together this morning, the same journal he used to doodle in and help him with his grammar.

He refused to let me see what he drew, out of either embarrassment or fear that I would laugh at him, I wasn't sure, but knew the journal was something he held dear to him. I would often notice him take freehand notes during the day before he would 'flesh them out on paper' at night, he said – or tried to say. I understood what he meant.

Malakei smiled warmly at my statement, sighing with relief at not having to go alone as he reached out and ruffled my hair. Tara looked at us as if we had just agreed to jump off a cliff together.

"You can't just get it in the morning? Like normal people?"

Malakei pointed a finger to the sky. "Tell rain man in sky to hold off, then I will be normal."

It was going to rain tonight if the grey clouds travelling east were indication enough, his journal would be soaked through. All his notes would disintegrate and the ink would bleed. In the *High Peaks*, one could easily get a new one but not here.

"Well, that's just great you two. While you both are out there looking for Malakei's diary, I'll be here, planning your funeral I guess."

"Keep watch for us yes?" Malakei asked her and she scrunched her nose up at this before giving in. She nodded her head in agreement.

"*Fine* – but if you go down don't drag me with you. I will have no part in your punishments."

Malakei scoffed at this, unable to keep the excited smile from his features as Tara narrowed her eyes at him, sighing loudly. I couldn't help but find myself asking;

"So what is this plan of yours anyways?"

XVII

~*~

It was an hour or so before sundown when Malakei and I crouched behind one of the barriers to the camp. The spiked objects held no cover from the guards above us as we waited for Tara to create her distraction that would allow Malakei and me to sneak out of the camp unbeknownst to the guards.

Malakei placed his hand on the centre of my back as he crouched down behind me, his breathing light on my ear yet the simple action made them twitch while we waited for the current guard to leave his post.

It reminded me of that time with Corrin, how we poured fertiliser on Tobias and his friends. It made my heart constrict at the thought of simpler times in my life.

"This is going to be so fun!" Malakei whispered to me, excitement clear in his voice. The words shook me from my thoughts. Of course Malakei would find something like this exhilarating. I couldn't wait to return.

I rolled my eyes playfully at this before letting out a sigh.

"If we don't find it by the time it gets dark, we come back and try again tomorrow okay?"

He hummed at that and I bit my lip, trying to contain the adrenaline that rushed through me as my heart pumped at the sudden thrill of what we were doing.

"You packed the swords right?"

"*Check.*"

"And the matches for light?"

"*Double check.*"

We may have been stupid for sneaking out, but we weren't completely hopeless in the sense that we remembered to pack weapons. Just in case we did come across something. We still needed to defend ourselves.

I bit my lip as I watched Tara make her appearance. Immediately, she brought the Dry Lander's attention away from his position by the barrier and he turned around to her.

"*Let's go!*" Malakei whispered loudly as he helped pull me up to my feet before moving back the barrier hastily. We winced when it made a piercing screeching noise but the small gesture thankfully didn't alert the guard.

Malakei pushed the opened barrier back into place and quickly gestured for me to run.

"Don't stop *dimples*!" Malakei shouted from behind as we both ran through the forest grounds. A laugh erupted from my throat as we did and for a moment, I felt free.

"Did you see Tara's face when she heard barrier noise?" Malakei asked as he curled over himself in laughter, clutching at his stomach when we finally came to a stop to breathe heavily.

We decided to walk the rest of the way to where we usually trained but made sure to cast our gazes down in hopes our eyes caught on Malakei's journal along the way. We were unlucky in our search.

"We are going to be in so much trouble when we get back." I winced at the thought of my father, brother – or Raen finding out what we just did but Mal's hand came down hard on my shoulder and a carefree look overtook his eyes.

"Live in the moment Keylin."

I shut my mouth at that. His words reminded me of Corrin.

I was surprised however when the feeling of missing him wasn't as crippling as it once was. I knew I would miss him – *I would worry if I didn't* – but I wasn't going to let the sorrow overshadow my life. I knew Corrin wouldn't want this for me. It only dawned on me that this was how Corrin always told me to live my life whenever I was upset about Tobias or my mother.

To live, not in sorrow and never in fear.

Although shadows passed, there was still some light in my life.

'I will see him again someday.' My thoughts were determined. It was the assurance I needed to grow.

I shook my thoughts out and smiled up at Malakei, pushing him back from me with a chuckle as I ran deeper into the forest. Malakei made a displeased scoff before he ran after me laughing.

***

"Mila is worried about Raen."

Malakei stated after twenty minutes or so of us scanning the ground for his journal. We took a water break and decided it would be best to head back to the camp before it got darker. The thoughts of being scolded by my father now started to seep into my mind, the thrill had long left me and anxiety filled its place, but I didn't regret any of it. I never did with Malakei.

I scrunched my nose up at that and took another gulp of my water before turning and placing it in the small bag Malakei had brought with him containing our swords. I hoisted it up and handed it to him with a sigh. Malakei frowned.

"I know you and Raen are still fighting. Want to talk?"

I winced as I remembered the words hurtled his way that night in his tent, going as far as to make him seem vulnerable by calling him out on his behaviour in front of his tribe. He must have been so embarrassed to have cried in front of both Mila and Bow, even to have the whole camp talking about how the small elf boy made Raen, the strong soldier cry. I was surprised he wasn't throwing daggers my way whenever I came within touching distance of him.

"I meant every word." I swallowed as Malakei and I walked back side by side. He trailed his sword over scattered bushes as if disinterested but his brows were furrowed, indicating that he was listening intently to what

I had to say.

"I don't blame him for ignoring me too. He has a right to hate me."

Malakei shook his head at me however and rolled his eyes.

"Raen likes you, *idiot*. He not cry easily because of few hurtful words. He not even cry when tiger slashes him and almost kills him."

I went to speak but Malakei continued.

"He cries… because *you* push him away when all he wants is to get close. He likes you a lot. We can see it. You make him happy."

"He… *wait*. Is that why he was so angry with me before? Does he have a fear of tigers or something?" I asked with confusion and crazily enough, an undertone of hope to which Malakei rolled his eyes before nodding with a frown.

"Raen was boy when found half–dead in forest. He fears the big cat. So much, he not let Tara go into forest without him. He knows forest is full of beasts that want to kill. He only goes into forest when he must do."

"When he has to" I offered gently.

"When he has to." Malakei repeated.

I processed Malakei's words as I came to the realisation why Raen had been so mad when he found out that I had come into contact with a tiger, was purely because of his fear of them. He was afraid that the same fate that happened to him, could've happened to me too.

"So he didn't hate me before?"

"He never did. You only think so and afraid but all he

do is protect and care for you."

I let out a yelp when Malakei flicked my forehead with a tut and I quickly realised that it wasn't just Raen who had a problem with my actions. It was a Dry Lander thing.

"You cute but very stupid *dimples*. Very st–"

"Okay *okay*." I couldn't help but chuckle at this. "You *should*–"

Malakei quickly pulled me back as something black – that I thought was a hanging vine – almost made contact with my face and I let out a whimper when what looked to be a paw came out to swipe at my head.

I fell back against Malakei's chest. He cursed at the animal perched in the tree above us.

"Fucking thing." He mumbled while I looked up wide–eyed at the black cat of sorts. Its white teeth bared as it snarled at us from where it lay across the sturdy tree branch. Its glowing green eyes looked down at us menacingly. It looked frightening.

"W–What is that?" I stuttered out in fear of moving. Afraid I would disrupt it any further than I already had, assuming that it wasn't happy when I almost walked into its tail that had hung over the branch. Now curled as it watched us, growling.

"Panther." He grumbled in annoyance. "*Shoo* wicked beast!" Malakei raised his voice which caused the panther to get up on all fours and I pushed back further into Malakei in fright.

"Don't Mal–"

"Wait..." Malakei stilled and squinted up at the beast, gripping my shoulder as his eyes widened in alert.

"Something is not right."

The panther continued to growl at us but didn't make any move to attack, I was glad. My blood ran cold when my ears picked up on rustling from within the forest. It was only then I suddenly sensed a presence and the eyes that I felt the last time Malakei and I were out here alone, had returned.

My heartbeat rose to my throat and I jumped when I heard rattling in the bushes to my right.

Before I could say anything, Malakei brought a hand over my mouth as we sank to the ground below the panther.

I looked to Malakei in question to see his index finger come up to his lips. He signalled for me to stay quiet as what sounded like footsteps crept closer to us.

The panther's warning growls above us grew quiet but its silhouette was still visible, but only just. Its glowing eyes were set on the person that now came towards us.

Malakei pulled me closer to him when the sound of gurgling hit our ears and a rotting stench filled my nostrils that made me want to gag. I clutched Malakei's hand that covered my mouth as he reached back silently for his sword, just in case he needed to use it.

The panther growled again and I looked up to see its eyes on–

I screamed when Malakei's hold on me suddenly slipped and a scale–covered hand pulled me from under him, dragging me by my foot into a nearby bush.

My neck whipped around to see a creature that couldn't be human – tilt its head as it croaked down and went to dive for me. I screamed again.

Malakei rushed forward and slashed at the creature. He managed to slash a diagonal cut across its face and the creature wailed in pain as it stumbled backwards.

I clutched my ears painfully at the shrill sound from where I sat frozen with fear on the ground. My heart pounded out of my chest as I watched Malakei battle the creature and my eyes found his.

He was struggling and it looked like he was losing. I could tell that he didn't have much fight left in him and quickly got to my feet, scrambling for the other sword.

"Keylin *no*! Stay back." He yelled in my direction. "I have–"

Malakei grunted when the creature managed to pull the sword from his grip, tilting its head at Malakei the same way it did to me before it brought its hand up and bent the sword.

I heard a small growl from behind me, just as the panther – now on the ground, reached out and swiped at my leg from behind, making me cry out in pain and quickly turn around.

I fell forward on one knee. My two hands firmly pressed on the ground that held me up as I looked at the animal with wide and fearful eyes. It growled lowly, baring its teeth.

Malakei fell to the ground with a scream and I could hear the jagged footsteps of the creature approaching him. A twisted snarl escaped its mouth as Malakei shuffled back on the forest floor, in hopes of finding me.

"Get out of here – *go*!"

"I'm not leaving you!"

My breath hitched and tears brimmed my eyes as the monster took out what looked to be a green weapon of some sort, towering over Malakei. My eyes widened.

No.

I didn't know what came over me then. It was as if I were possessed as my head cleared and turned my head back to the panther and bowed my head forward.

The panther roared in reply to my scream before a sudden jolt – of what felt like electricity – ran right through me. I felt the tingling sensation as it coursed through my veins.

The feeling left me as the glowing power surged forward towards the panther between the cracks in the forest floor. I felt weak for a moment before screaming, letting my head fall back as a burning sensation overtook me. It felt as though it was ripping right through me.

The panther wailed in front of me in pain right before a whimper fell from my lips and I dropped forward. The panther's body did the same but it caught itself before it could reach the hard ground.

Herself.

I opened my eyes and looked up at her. Her glowing purple eyes stared back. What felt like an eternity of pain, all happened in the space of a few seconds and with a blink, she quickly leapt forward and tackled the beast from Malakei.

Malakei took the opportunity while the creature was being attacked by the panther to get to his feet. I tried to stand when I suddenly felt arms scramble to catch me before I could fall to the ground.

I didn't even know that I was standing until Malakei's hands came under me.

He scooped me up in his arms and ran. Ran through the quickly darkening forest, not stopping to spare a glance back at the panther occupied in ripping the creature to pieces. The creature wailed in ear–splitting pain, its scream haunting.

I tried to clutch my ears but found I had no energy to move my arms. My breathing was erratic and I was hot. *Very* hot.

I was burning up.

A painful cry ripped through me when burning to my left side along my ribcage started and I was suddenly finding it hard to breathe. My eyes widened and I opened my mouth to speak but only a small gasp left my lips.

Malakei's worried eyes found mine as he took in the scene before him where I was choking on air. His eyes filled with fright and I knew he felt helpless at that moment.

"What's–"

"It burns!" I managed to cry out through the sizzle of pain before another burning sensation had me wailing, feeling like my blood was boiling at the overwhelming heat my body felt.

Malakei cursed from above me and ran harder with me in his arms. I could feel his heart racing in his chest before I resulted to cursing and rambling on in elvish due to my delirious state.

"I–It's okay, *dimples*. Just stay with m–me."

"Malakei!" I screamed out before cutting off into a sob. Another heart–wrenching scream made me freeze and I clutched his chest shakily, the burning only intensified.

I could feel my sweat cling to my body. My hair was matted to my forehead and around my neck. My head fell back so that it was lying over Malakei's arm, not having the energy to hold it up any longer.

My vision started to go in and out and I swore I could hear the quick thumps of the panther as her paws hit the forest floor, following us. The wails of the panther not too far away from us only proved my suspicions. Malakei looked like he heard them too when his breathing became heavy. He forced his feet forward harder, faster.

"Open the gate!" He suddenly screamed as I scrunched up my face in pain. Another wail left my lips as he shifted my body upwards for a better grip on me. I was weaker now.

The action caused my head to move upwards and fall onto the space above Malakei's collarbone, just below his chin. This gave me a greater view of my surroundings and my bleary eyes fell on the cluster of light in front of me.

The camp.

We were close.

"Open the gate!"

Malakei screamed at the top of his lungs as he ran the small distance between the edge of the forest and the spiked barrier gates.

Another sizzling sensation burned around my ribcage and my body arched upwards in pain. I screamed again after it subsided slightly. Scared, I started to sob and shake violently in Malakei's grip. My body wasn't strong enough to sustain the pain it was bearing.

"*Malakei…*"

"Hold on *dimples*, hold on." Malakei panted. His voice cracked as he called me by my nickname and I gritted my teeth, breathing heavily through my nose and letting my eyes scrunch closed.

I heard voices from above me before the barrier was torn back. I could sense the guards looking at me. Horror–filled gasps echoed around us as they took in my state.

I heard my brother's voice from somewhere ahead. If he said anything else, I didn't catch it because an agonising scream erupted from my throat.

Malakei sobbed into my hair as he pushed through the gawking guards. They broke out of their daze to barricade it again when the sound of the panther's roar cracked through the air from behind us.

"No!" I screamed. My eyes tore open and my head turned to look over Malakei's shoulder, hand quickly flying out in a weak attempt to reach the panther.

The connection was long gone between us but the withdrawals of the emotion that travelled between her and me had touched me on a spiritual level. I believed she felt the same.

My eyes found hers in the black of night. Her worrisome gaze darted between me and the barrier that separated us. She attempted to plough through them, roaring at the spikes when they hurt her and I sobbed.

"Baja!" I screamed for her as tears threatened to leave my eyes. She continued to wail into the night causing some of the guards to step back from the barrier, startled.

Malakei's breathing was heavy as he glanced back behind him, slowing down now that he was inside the safety of the camp, completely exhausted.

When his eyes landed on someone up ahead, however, he screamed at them.

"Raen!" He shouted up ahead just as a whimper fell from my lips. I clutched my burning ribcage, only to cry out when it burned my hand. Shaking it out, I screamed when it sizzled again.

"It's Keylin – he's hurt, *badly*!" Malakei shouted through my scream and it was not long before a familiar set of arms took me in their hold.

I felt Raen flinch back under my burning flesh, grunting as he took me in his arms from Malakei.

"He burns up quickly." Malakei stated out of breath. His red–rimmed eyes came into vision as he looked down at me, bringing a hand down to my forehead. He suddenly hissed and retracted his hand. Shaking it out as if he had touched pure fire.

I could sense Raen looking down at me and I forced my heavy lids open to look up at him, completely exhausted as I breathed heavily. My body felt as though it was on fire and he looked down at me with so much emotion pooling in his features that it made my head dizzy to focus on just one.

I pleaded in elvish, sensing the familiar burning coming on and scrunched my face in pain, letting out a painful howl and arching my body upwards.

Raen took in a frightened breath. His hold on me

tightened.

"Come with me," Raen said lowly to Malakei.

"We need to cool him."

"Don't hurt her!" I screamed suddenly after a pained wail left the panther. The guards resorted to nudging the panther with their weapons in an attempt to coax the animal away from the barrier and I sobbed at this. My head flailed rapidly in panic. "Stop it she's–"

My eyes rolled back in pain and for a few moments, I blacked out. Unaware of what was happening, I was suddenly laid on top of a table, its contents now scattered on the floor around me after being pushed aside to lay me down.

I arched my back up off of it, howling as another sizzling sensation made my hand come up and claw at my shirt.

"Mal – hand me your knife now!" Raen shouted from my right. I opened my eyes momentarily before shutting them again when his hot hands pulled at the cloth around my shirt collar.

I heard the ripping of material as Raen sliced open my shirt before gasping when he saw the source of my problem.

Malakei whispered something similar to a prayer in Fasik.

I forced my eyes open to bring my head up and look down at what they were staring at only to whimper when I saw a burning mark a little over halfway up the side of my body, on the left.

It was a mark in the shape of a paw print that seemed

to be burning itself into my flesh – no, not into my flesh. This mark was burning from the inside out.

I screamed and jerked my head back to fall on the wooden table when it sizzled. I couldn't help but bite my tongue as I tried to calm down, my heavy breathing rose and fell quickly.

"Baja..." I found myself deliriously whispering out, her wails travelled to the tent I was in and I could hear her call out to me in the dark of night.

"Is that elvish?" Raen asked as he turned his head to Malakei. Malakei swallowed nervously.

"It's the panther... It's at barrier wailing. I think... I think Keylin connect with it but something went wrong–"

"Why did he connect with a fucking wild panther– *Malakei*. I *swear*, if he–"

"I tell you everything later – just please help him!"

I managed to listen to their conversation through the pain but let out a sob when a cold, wet rag was placed on my forehead. I sighed in relief at the feeling but it didn't last long. It turned hot under my burning flesh and I flailed, shaking my head to get it off.

Raen went to press down on the cloth at my forehead, cursing when he realised it was now scolding hot. He took it off to dip in the cold water again before pressing it back onto my forehead.

I moaned at the coldness of the rag, relishing in its healing before sobbing when it turned hot again.

Raen seemed to understand this and turned to Malakei.

"Wet another towel when I put one on him. When I take it from his forehead, quickly hand me the new towel. He's burning up quicker than he has time to cool."

I didn't hear Malakei's reply and let out a sigh of relief when another cold towel was placed on my forehead. I whimpered when it went warm too quickly and scrunched my face up, crying out suddenly when my mark burned.

I didn't even feel Raen take the towel from my forehead before he grabbed another cold towel from Malakei and pressed it back gently onto my forehead.

The tears escaped my closed eyes and ran down my cheeks when the adjustment of hot and cold on my body began to lose its effect until I couldn't tell the difference between a hot and cold rag anymore.

Raen let out a frustrated breath and took the towel away from my forehead, scrunching it up to press on my red–hot cheeks.

"It's not working anymore."

"What can we–"

"Keylin!"

Bow's voice was loud as he entered the tent. His eyes landed on my position before paling, eyes turning on Malakei full of hate and disgust.

"What are you doing to him!"

"Bow wait. Let me–"

My scream silenced them and I didn't pay attention to their bickering as my vision began to blur. I felt like I would faint again, slipping in and out of consciousness.

"I gave you a chance Malakei. If my brother dies because of you I'm going to kill you with my bare hands–"

"Stop it!" Raen shouted from above me and yanked the

wet cloth from Malakei. This time, he pressed it gently onto the burning mark on my body.

Both Raen and Malakei's hands came around me in an attempt to hold me down when I suddenly rose from the table in pain, my body tensed up at the sensation. When they managed to get me to lie back down on the table, Raen squeezed the towel so that water could fall onto the mark that had managed to suddenly appear on my body. I sobbed from the pain and shook my head. I noticed Bow's face paled at the sight.

"What is that on his–"

"We don't know," Raen cut sharply, taking another outstretched cold towel from Malakei's hands and dabbing it down my sweat–glazed neck.

"All we know is that it's burning him badly. We can't get him to cool down. Something tells me putting him in an ice bath won't work either. He will just melt the ice."

Raen furrowed his eyebrows as he looked down at me, dragging the chilled towel up my cheek and forehead where he pressed lightly. I began to mumble again.

"We need to do something!" Bow exclaimed, "We can't just–"

"Quiet!"

I whimpered as Raen practically yelled from above me. His fingers pushed back my matted hair from my forehead as I breathed in and out, panicked.

"What is it Keylin? Get who?" He asked down to me and I screamed weakly before breaking into a fit of sobs.

"*Baja*! Baja *please*, get her. *I need to see her* … before–" I stopped myself short as I opened my eyes to Raen for the first time in a few minutes, even finding the small task of keeping them open was hard and I blinked to try and focus on his features that swam in and out of my vision.

Was I dying?

Raen's breath hitched as he took in a shaky breath. He turned to Malakei with a serious and defeated expression.

"Get the panther."

XVIII

~*~

Malakei's footsteps slammed hard on the ground of the camp as he ran back towards the barrier, back to where the commotion was happening with soldiers – along with Dry Lander folk, lighting torches in the dark of night to catch a glimpse of the black panther. To end this terror.

To *kill* it.

The panther was silent now, it knew exactly what the men were doing. She had studied them all her life, watching them take to the hunt and their cruel ways.

Malakei couldn't help but think that this panther was no ordinary panther. It knew when to keep quiet in times when other animals would fall victim to the death trap and get themselves killed. This panther was a survivor.

"Malakei!" Tara yelled from ahead when she immediately spotted the panting and red–eyed boy coming closer to where she stood at the barricade. She didn't have the faintest idea what was going on, only hearing mumblings from others that a wild animal was trying to break into their camp.

"Keylin is hurt bad. We need the panther."

Malakei stated seriously – cutting to the chase. He ignored Tara's worried and confused look as he walked straight past her to the barricade, stopping briefly only for his hands to rest on the sides of the wooden spears, ready to pull them back when he heard a low growl from somewhere before him.

"Baja?"

He immediately saw the green eyes of the panther spring open amidst the dark, before they narrowed at him.

Baja didn't trust the Dry Lander boy, even when the panther had saved his life from the creature yet Malakei felt in debt to this animal.

Malakei sighed as his head fell forward, eyes shutting briefly before he let out a strangled breath.

"Please save him." He whispered into the night before quickly pulling back the barricade, unbeknownst to the guard who turned and proceeded to yell at Malakei. Caught between trying to put the barrier back into place and reaching forward to grab Malakei – it was too late.

A flash of black darted forward and into the camp which resulted in many Dry Landers screaming in horror and shock but the panther paid no mind as it leapt forward, almost knowing exactly where it needed to go.

To the young elf boy who was on his last few breaths.

***

Bow's gaze drifted to the tent entrance when he heard the sound of someone approaching. He immediately jumped back when the panther made its way into the tent. Baja growled warningly before stopping in her tracks at the sight of the Dry Lander.

Bow let out a startled yelp and stood up on another table. He pulled his legs up from the ground only to fall back onto the table clumsily while Raen's head shot up at the arrival of the animal.

Tears threatened to fall as he held Keylin in his arms. The boy's breathing only became more shallow by the minute.

Keylin let out a small, hitched breath and the panther's ears twitched in his direction. Turning her head, her glowing green eyes rested on the dying boy in this stranger's arms.

Baja wasted no time in trotting over and jumping up onto the table with caution. Her eyes narrowed menacingly in warning upon Raen – who didn't show any signs of fear, only defeat towards the panther. Raen took his hands away from Keylin and moved back from the panther, wary of the Dry Lander for all of the right reasons.

Raen kept his distance from the side of the table but insisted on reaching out and holding Keylin's almost lifeless hand.

The Dry Lander's breath hitched when he watched the panther lay down over the boy's body. Its dark paw curled up over Keylin's side as she licked a long strip over his mark.

Keylin's eyes sprang open at that.

His eyes flickered purple before they disappeared. He suddenly went limp under the large cat. Raen could feel him slip away as he held his hand.

Whatever fight Keylin had left in him suddenly came to an end. His once warm hand now started to grow cold.

"*K–Keylin*?" Raen whispered, looking down at the boy. His eyes blurred at the sight of the elf unresponsive. "*Keylin please wake up.*"

Raen's breathing rose out of panic as he clenched and unclenched Keylin's hand, resulting in a whimper to escape his mouth.

He couldn't be dead. This wasn't how it was supposed to be.

"No." Raen gasped out allowing the tears to fall freely down his cheeks. This wasn't the first time he had shed tears over the boy, he knew it wouldn't be his last.

Raen's angered gaze flew down to the panther licking Keylin's face in an attempt to get the boy's attention, but the boy didn't stir.

"I allowed you in here to save Keylin and that is what you're going to do. Do you understand me?"

The panther bared its teeth at Raen who paid no mind, only growing angrier as precious moments ticked away that the panther could be using to save the boy, rather than spend it snarling at Raen.

"Save him!" Raen slammed his fist down onto the table as he yelled at the panther. He ignored the fear rising at the beast in front and how the last time he was this close, his world collapsed around him.

The animal got up on all fours and let out a bone–chilling roar in his face.

Keylin screamed awake.

His breathing came out in puffs as he adjusted to the sight in front of him but screamed in horror as he looked up and noticed the black panther above him.

KEYLIN

~*~

When I woke up, it was like waking up from a long sleep. The feeling would set in of not knowing where you were or what was going on around you, before you relaxed because then it all came rushing back, and you remembered everything.

I didn't remember anything.

I didn't know why I was on a table, with Raen looking down at me from my right, his eyes red from where he looked as though he had been crying.

I didn't know why there was an animal above me. Looking closely, a spark of recognition made its way onto my features.

This was the panther from the forest.

At that, everything overwhelmingly rushed back to me

and I could remember everything before I fell to the ground.

Had I passed out? How had I gotten here in the first place? Where was Malakei?

The minute the scream left my lips, the panther's bright, glowing green eyes cast down to me before it let out a small wail under its breath.

With a frightened breath, I turned on my side and tried to scramble away but the panther sank beside me, cementing me in place as it threw its elongated paw over my body, putting pressure on my middle as it pulled me back to it.

My eyes flew to Raen's at that. The fear was clear in them when I felt its wet snout nuzzle the side of my head, stopping at my neck to let its head rest in the crook of it. I held my breath, sensing the panther looking up at Raen from behind me almost tauntingly.

"Raen... *Raen* – I."

My voice broke as tears streamed down my face. Fearful that the animal would kill me or sink its sharp teeth into my neck at the slightest of movements.

Raen did not show signs of panic as he looked down at me. Although he seemed wary of stepping closer, he was also afraid he would upset the panther further than it already was.

"It's okay Keylin," He breathed out, flicking his gaze between me and the panther. "She won't hurt you, because she knows if she did, I would skin her alive and use her fur for the insides of my boots."

The panther growled. It understood Raen's warning

and I swallowed helplessly before shutting my eyes. Raen quickly reached out to grab my hand in comfort and gave it a gentle squeeze, ignoring the warning growls that came from the panther.

"What… Why is... " I couldn't come up with a question to ask about the ridiculous situation I was in. If I couldn't explain it, how could Raen?

"I don't know," Raen sighed and I noticed the hint of worry in his tone before his eyes met mine.

"But we will figure it out. I promise you."

I wanted to tell him I was sorry for what I said to him. How I appreciated him here in this moment, comforting me instead of being mad with me over the hurtful things I said to his face a few days ago.

I didn't mean any of what I had said. I was stubborn and hurt. He didn't deserve it and as much as he did wrong, he was a good person. I tried to say all of this with my eyes but instead went to speak.

"Raen, I–"

"Keylin!" Bow's voice rang out from inside the tent and I turned my gaze to look down the end of the table. I noticed my brother scramble to get down from where he was perched on another nearby table. It was only then that I realised where we were; in one of the many storage tents, this one was used to house spare furniture.

Bow came closer, not paying mind to the panther that was beside me, possibly thinking it was friendly when it decided not to feast on me all but seconds ago.

The animal, however, grew silent as it waited for Bow to come within touching distance before it would strike.

Its malicious thoughts flooded my mind as I received a glimpse of what was about to happen.

Raen noticed what the panther was doing before I could have a chance to react and immediately rose to full height, pushing Bow back a safe distance from the panther.

A startled gasp left Bow when the panther sprang up from where it laid over me and turned around to swipe a paw at my brother. The panther snarled at him.

I took that as an opportunity to move away from the panther, inching away slowly to the end of the table, immediately getting off and allowing my legs to stand on their own.

I forgot about the gash the panther had inflicted on my back calf and fell forward with a yelp onto the hard ground. The panther roared at this from where it leered down at me on the table, making me clutch my ears and bring my knees up to my chest.

"Shit." Raen cursed before turning to Bow. "Get back."

My eyes found the entrance of the tent when I noticed movement.

Malakei and Tara, followed shortly by my father and Mila, all but ran inside. Their eyes darted around them in alert only to quickly zero–in on the panther.

Malakei's eyes landed on my position on the ground before they widened at the sight of the panther, now on its feet and trying to make a swipe at Raen. Raen jumped back.

My father shouted my name through a mixture of emotions – fright, anger and relief. He looked between me and the panther who was quickly leaping off of the table, slowly coming closer to me.

"No!" Raen shouted, sticking his hand out just as my father took his axe from his back pouch, ready to throw it and kill the panther but faltered and turned his cold eyes on Raen.

Raen only nodded his head in the direction of the panther. I was confused when their eyes locked on mine, wide–eyed and worried but curious nonetheless.

My breath hitched when the panther made a noise in the back of its throat from behind me before nuzzling its head along my arm, making its way around to my back. Its head continued to nuzzle – this time against my cheek. My ears twitched when the panther suddenly sneezed and I flinched back slightly.

Tara giggled at this causing everyone to glare at her pointedly, afraid she would disrupt whatever this was occurring between the panther and me.

The panther made its way to my other shoulder, where it let its head rest and growled lowly at the people before it. I furrowed my brows at this. My breathing became lighter when I suddenly didn't feel as afraid anymore.

It was almost like it was protecting me, assuring me that everything was fine.

"That's..." Malakei trailed off looking down at us in astonishment. I looked up at him, letting out a quick breath when the panther nuzzled against my neck but didn't move its chin from my shoulder. Malakei smiled down at me, at the scene that was taking place before him.

"It is like she thinks you are her cub."

I frowned at this, taking this in and heard the panther

wail in disagreement. A word stuck out in my mind that made my eyes widen.

"No it's not that." I gulped noticeably. The fear and confusion appeared on my face.

"She thinks I'm her *Trainor*."

***

I listened to the others argue outside of Raen's tent. Everyone shouted over each other to try and get a word in over what they believed they should be doing that could help me, but they all knew their attempts at helping me were useless.

I wasn't a Trainor. A Trainor was more commonly used for those who possessed a special connection to animals. One that was far greater than someone like me could ever have.

Trainors could communicate in their mind with their chosen animal to protect, share their soul with and train; for whatever reason that may be. This would have to mean that this panther and I were both born to lead the same life, the same path. It was destiny that our paths crossed when they did.

It was not common at all for anyone – besides the people that lived in the *Sky Lanes* to be Trainors. They were connected to the dragons that roamed the skies and trained them to work and use as they wished. Their souls were bonded. This could be dangerous on most parts and it made me panic at the thought.

When this panther bonded its soul with me, this meant

that she was to remain at my side until whatever duty bestowed upon me was fulfilled. And if I died bonded to this animal, they would die also. If the panther died before me, a part of me would be lost and I would live out the rest of my days empty, part of my soul having died with my animal.

I let out a sigh as I shifted on Raen's bed. The panther's head laid across my chest, paw shifting over me protectively.

She didn't sleep. Her glowing green eyes were the only indication of that, instead, she resulted to narrowing her eyes at Raen who sat in a chair beside the bed.

He was the only one who hadn't left my side to argue. Instead, he remained silent, not saying anything only to sometimes grasp my hand in assurance.

I didn't want any of this. I couldn't understand why any of this was happening and hoped it was all a dream of sorts. One that I wanted nothing more than to wake up from in the morning but I knew that wasn't the case.

"You don't remember anything?" Raen eventually asked quietly and I turned my head to him, not getting up from my position on the bed, afraid to disrupt the panther.

"I don't know how it got to this." I whispered through the lump in my throat, swallowing nervously as the panther brought her head up to yawn. She dipped her head down to lick once at the mark on my ribcage that now bound us before she rested her head in the same position she got up from. Her eyes remained on their fixed position, watching Raen warily.

She didn't trust him.

317

"I tried to connect with it. It was the only thing I could think of to help Malakei. I didn't think that I would be so stupid to bond my soul with a–"

"Her name is *Baja*." Raen cut off softly. The panther's ears twitched and I furrowed my brows at him.

"You told me to get her when you were…" He stopped talking and gritted his teeth before shaking his head of the thoughts.

"It's going to be okay." He eventually sighed, reaching out to squeeze my hand in assurance and I shook my head at him.

"You can't say that. You don't know for sure," I bit my lip, trying not to let it wobble.

"I'm afraid Raen. Things like this don't happen, ever. Not to someone like me. What if the *Sky Lanes* find out about this? *They'll kill me*."

"Trust me Keylin," Raen silenced my rambling, determination clear in his eyes as he spoke.

"Everything is going to be fine, there is no need to be afraid. You have me. You have your brother, father, Malakei... we are all here for you."

"I don't want them to take me away. Not again." I couldn't help but whisper my fears into the tent. The light of the bedside candle kept them from being swallowed up entirely by the dark.

"Do you know what the people of the *Dry Lands* are known for?" Raen asked after a moment of silence.

"Their brutality." I responded truthfully, remembering all that I was told from my schooling. Being here for as long as I had, the difference in culture was still something

I was getting used to.

"Other sectors fear us because we are not afraid to stand up and fight for what is ours," Raen stated. "You will never find a Dry Lander without its tribe. We protect our own. We don't abandon them. That includes you now, Keylin,"

I blinked in confusion at his words but before I could say anything he turned his gaze to me. Sincerity fell from his bright green eyes.

"You are a part of this tribe. Wherever you go, the tribe will follow. If other sectors try to take you. It only means they have underestimated the will of the Dry Landers and what we will do to get you back. No one messes with family,"

I took in a shaky breath at his words while Baja lay her head down on my lap. Her eyes shut softly.

"We won't let anything bad happen to you or Baja. I promise you."

Raen bit his lip as he looked at me and taking the chance while Baja was starting to drift off to sleep, he slowly brought a hand up to brush back the hair at my forehead. I let my eyes close and sighed in exhaustion.

"Sleep Keylin. You're exhausted and overthinking."

His words played over in my mind. I was taken aback by his determination and how genuine he felt about it. I realised then that I had been completely wrong about not just Raen, but the Dry Landers as a sector. Everything I was taught and told to feel about these people may still be true, that was yet to be determined – but the elves had forgotten to teach us the most important thing about Dry

Landers. The thing that set them apart from other sectors.

It was their values around family.

The people they cared about. They would go to the ends of Sorn for one another – something that I couldn't say the same for the elves in the *High Peaks.*

I had been led by fear to believe that these people were nothing but cruel and not for a second did I think they cared about me.

'No one messes with family.'

"I'm sorry Raen." I whispered out, feeling a weight lifting from my chest as I released what I had been holding onto this entire time. Now knowing that I was free to let it go.

Tiredness started to get the better of me and I felt myself slipping into unconsciousness quickly. I let out a breath.

Raen's hand never left my forehead as I fell asleep. Baja now let out soft puffs of air as she slept below me.

XIX

~*~

When I woke up the next morning it was bright. The sun was shining down on the tent and illuminating the room in light that I had no choice but to open my eyes, as tired as they were.

Raen was no longer at my side and I couldn't keep the frown from my lips, heart sinking slightly.

Baja was still sleeping beside me, never leaving my side as her head now slept on my shoulder. She – having moved around in her sleep during the night so that her arm was no longer around me – now meant it was easier to slip away and off the bed unnoticed.

I quickly scrambled for my shirt on the floor with shaky hands only to realise it had been cut open. A frown settled on my lips as I touched the ripped open fabric, holding it in my hands and it looked as if a knife had done this damage but I had no recollection of it.

I left my torn shirt behind and got off the bed carefully, slowly creeping over to Raen's wardrobe. I put on a plain black shirt that was a few sizes too big for me before making my way to the entrance of the tent.

I couldn't help the sudden sigh that escaped my lips when I left the tent. Immediately attacked by sunlight, I let my eyes shut briefly, tilting my head up. Today felt different. I felt different.

I walked around the side of Raen's tent but immediately frowned when I wondered where he could have gone. It was likely that he was filling in my father and brother – to which my stomach dropped.

My ears twitched however when I picked up on voices talking in a hushed tone not too far from where I was heading to Ana's house and I slowed suspiciously, going over to the corner of a nearby tent to listen on the other side.

Raen and Malakei's voices were distinct as they talked amongst themselves. Frowning, I listened to what they could be talking about.

"Are you sure?" Raen questioned. The worry and anger was evident in his speech. "You're positive that's what you saw–"

Malakei groaned in annoyance.

"Raen, I not make this up. It attacked us!"

Malakei raged silently and I furrowed my eyebrows at that before my eyes widened in recollection. I knew exactly what they were talking about that it had to be so secretive.

They were talking about the creature from last night

that attacked us in the forest. I couldn't help but shiver at the memory of the scaly creature and how Malakei – as strong as he was – couldn't defeat it. He almost lost his life last night if it weren't for Baja.

"I'm just making sure." Raen sighed out. "It shouldn't be here. This is not their sector. A murk can't just wander across without being seen."

"Do you think it is doing murders?"

Raen didn't answer.

"Possibly," He pondered in thought. "If not, we may have a bigger problem on our hands. We can't have creatures from *The Shadows* roaming the *Dry*–"

A hand suddenly clapped down on my shoulder and I let out a startled breath turning around.

Bow raised an eyebrow at me before suddenly pulling me into his arms for an embrace. I let out a sigh and hugged him back as I relished the greeting from my brother.

"Keylin. I didn't get a chance to do this yesterday." Bow sighed before he pulled back and slapped my cheek. I winced looking back at him in confusion only to see his eyes angry and full of betrayal.

I should have expected this.

"What were you thinking?! Sneaking out last night? *Really* Keylin. You–" I winced at Bow's loud voice and looked up at him expectantly when he suddenly stopped. He blinked quickly before he took me in his arms again into a bone–crushing hug.

"I thought you were dead Key. We *all* did."

He mumbled into my temple which made my ear twitch

slightly. He held me tighter before letting go then, pulling back to look down at me. I frowned at this.

"I did too Bow," I whispered out as I let my eyes cast down. "I don't know what happened, I–"

"Please Keylin, I... I don't want to know. Just promise me. Promise me you're going to stop looking for danger. You always seem to end up in the middle of trouble." Bow sighed, already starting to walk back, he shook his head at me in disappointment.

"Bow." I called out, hurt by his words but knowing that they were true. Ever since I came here, I have ended up somehow hurt. Last night – apart from the incident in the *High Peaks* – was the first incident where I was so close to death that it frightened him. It frightened *me*. It wasn't long ago he found out he had a brother, only for him to die suddenly in a freak soul–bounding experiment with an animal.

I watched Bow let out a sigh as he turned around and left me without another word. I shut my eyes at this, gritting my teeth.

"Dammit." I cursed before bringing a hand up to run through my hair, pulling in frustration before I sighed and turned around –

I collided with a familiar hard chest.

Raen stared down at me with an unamused look. Malakei stood beside him smirking.

"It's rude to listen to other people's talking." Malakei stated in amusement tilting his head at me innocently. I gulped, about to open my mouth and correct him when Raen suddenly sighed in frustration, he grabbed my shoulders as he looked down at me with furrowed brows.

"Why did you leave my tent? You should go back and rest."

"I–" I went to protest but immediately stopped to lift my brows in curiosity as I stared up at Raen pointedly.

"What's a murk?"

Both he and Malakei stayed silent. Malakei glanced at Raen with a wide–eyed expression before looking back at me. I kept my gaze on Raen however and waited for him to answer me. He only stared down at me, the same burning intensity in his eyes as I held in mine. When I didn't look away, he sighed in exasperation.

"A creature from *The Shadows*," He eventually gave in. "It's half–snake, half–human. They're dangerous because their nails are laced with poison, a scratch can be fatal. They don't usually appear in forested areas but they like water. The river must be where it wandered from."

"A creature from *The Shadows*?" My heart beat out of my chest as Raen nodded in confirmation.

"How… how did it get here? What is it doing here?"

"I guess we are going to river to check it out?" Malakei smirked.

Fear was an enemy of his. "Maybe there's more of them. If so, we need to keep them away from camp–"

Raen turned to Malakei with a pointed stare. I didn't know if he didn't want to go to the river in case there were more of the creatures inhabiting there, or if he didn't want me to hear that they were going to the river in case I wanted to go.

"I'm coming with you–" I started only for Raen to

tighten his grip on my shoulder. He turned back to me with piercing eyes and a clenched jaw.

"That is not happening. You're staying here. I heard what Bow said and I agree with him. It's best if you stay out of trouble."

My face fell at that as I looked down.

"You're staying Keylin. I'm sorry but it's for your protection–"

"What about you two?" I cut him off sharply as my eyes flickered between Malakei's and his. He frowned at that.

"Malakei is one of the strongest here..." I continued. "He almost got killed by one of them last night. How are the both of you going to manage if there's five of them at the river?"

"We don't know that," Raen counteracted. "There could be none–"

"I'm not taking that chance," I stated seriously, raising my voice slightly as my shoulders straightened. "I'm coming with you. Whether you like it or not."

Something blossomed in his gaze at my words. Before he could say anything, Malakei was breaking us out of our stare.

"He can bring Baja!" Malakei exclaimed suddenly, making us both turn to him.

"And what if something happens to his panther? Did you think she might get hurt?" Raen raised his brow at Malakei.

"She saved my life," Malakei shrugged. "She's only one that can kill murks. She would help a lot if we run into them."

Raen sent a deathly glare to Malakei at the suggestion and a small smile crept onto my features at my friend's words.

"It's settled then. When are we going?"

"Not tonight," Raen said pointedly and Malakei rolled his eyes. "First thing in the morning. You need your rest Keylin. You look exhausted."

He took his hands from my shoulder and I let out a small defeated breath.

"Okay."

Raen seemed to relax at that, nodding once at me before stepping back slightly.

"But if you leave without me–"

"We won't."

I noticed the small smile that played on his lips before he ushered me back to his tent.

I remembered my hunger when my stomach suddenly growled and I blushed in embarrassment as I clutched it. Malakei laughed loudly at this while Raen blinked down at me with a hint of a smile.

"Let's get you some food *dimples*." Malakei smiled as he slung an arm around my neck. I whined in protest at the nickname he had settled on for me while pulling me ahead. Raen followed closely behind, a ghost of a smile forming on his lips.

***

It wasn't long after Malakei, Raen and I were sitting down

on one of the wooden picnic benches that littered the outdoor kitchen when we began to hear screaming coming from some of the Dry Landers.

All of our heads turned to look at each others with a worrisome look. Thinking the worst, that the murk had found its way into the camp.

Raen immediately grabbed his axe as he stood up, about to head over in the direction of the screaming but something black made its way towards me and I fell back on the bench with a groan.

Baja reared up on her back legs, her front paws pushing at my chest which caused me to topple back before I could feel her head nuzzle into my neck with a low growl.

She was angry with me for leaving her.

I could see from the corner of my eye as Raen lowered his axe and sat back down onto the bench. Malakei stayed where he was and chose to look at Baja in awe.

"Baja..." I trailed off as I brought my hands around her back. My fingers gripped her black fur as I tried to push her down away from my body.

She whined in protest at this but I ignored her and turned my back, sitting down on the bench again to eat my food.

Malakei threw me a confused smirk as he started to eat his breakfast.

Baja whined from behind me for my attention and I took in a shaky breath, bringing a generous spoonful of the porridge up to my lips before crying out and letting the utensil drop back down into the bowl when her paw suddenly came out and scratched across my back.

I brought my hand down hard onto the wooden table and turned around to push her away. Her glowing eyes grew angry at this and she roared at me. I flinched back, breathing heavily as I looked down at her with gritted teeth.

Malakei chuckled from his seat behind me.

"You should not push her away. She only wants your attention."

My eyes turned to glare at him.

"I don't want to give her at–agh!" I let out a cry as Baja suddenly pounced on my back when I wasn't looking. Her claws dug into my shoulder blades as she licked the back of my head.

I brought my hands forward to clutch at the grooves in the table, eyes shutting in pain at her claws planting into my flesh and I let out a groan of pain.

"Come here girl."

Raen was quickly grabbing her attention. Opening my eyes, I saw he held out a bread roll in offer to her, snapping it in half while her nose sniffed the air.

She growled softly in my ear at the sight of Raen. This made my ears twitch and I brought my head forward to rest in my elbow.

Letting out a whimper when she unlatched her claws from my shoulder blades and lowered herself to the ground, I allowed my head to slowly come back up. My face scrunched in pain as I watched Baja warily make her way over to Raen holding the food out to her. She growled at him before swiping at his hand.

Raen immediately dropped the food and Baja took it in

her mouth, quickly retreating behind me to eat it silently near my back. I let out a sigh as I looked up at Raen, thankful.

"She will be good when you train her." Malakei noted hopeful. His eyes flashed with concern as he glanced at my clawed and slightly bleeding back.

"She's a wild animal." I protested. "She's not like a dog or a horse. She's different."

"You're different too. I guess you both have something in common." Raen interrupted with a raised eyebrow and I frowned at that, looking down at Baja who was busy licking her paws. Her eyes glowed as she looked up at me.

I sighed at that, bringing my hand down to rest on her head and she purred, immediately getting up. She pushed my hand off of her as she jumped up and curled into my lap. I frowned at this and looked back up to Raen unsure.

"I don't know the first thing about training an animal."

Raen smiled at Baja. His eyes met mine.

"I can help you train her."

"Thank you." I breathed out. An unknown emotion pooled in the pit of my chest as I did. He smiled at me and I couldn't help but return it, dimples appearing slightly as I did.

I scoffed down at Baja suddenly licking at the contents of my porridge bowl.

Rolling my eyes, I brought my hand down to her head. She quickly turned to look up at me, porridge lining around her snout and I couldn't stop the laugh that left my lips as I looked at her.

Baja tilted her head at the sound, her ears twitching as

she straightened her body into a sitting position beside me.

"No no *no*." My eyes widened when I noticed her moving forward to lick my face and I whined when she licked a clear line up one side of my cheek. Bits of oat stuck to my cheek as she did and even got in my ears and hair. I shivered at the sensation.

Malakei cackled at this, even Raen let out a chuckle. I closed my eyes and let Baja nuzzle into my porridge–covered cheek before lowering herself over my lap. I looked down at her with a small smile, my hand coming up to rub her head and she purred at that.

Maybe training her wouldn't be so hard.

XX

~*~

After breakfast, I decided I needed to clean myself up. Raen said he would allow me to borrow some of his clothes to put on after I finished cleaning my body of oats and panther slobber – and I thanked him as Malakei, Raen and I made our way back to the tent. Baja trotted silently beside me while her ears lifted and fell at the sounds and curious eyes of the Dry Landers.

I ignored their stares and tried not to listen to their judgmental comments as we made our way back to Raen's tent.

Baja immediately jumped onto his – what once was a bed, now consisted of several claw marks and ripped cloth. I frowned at this and turned to him while he was looking for clothes in his wardrobe.

"I'm sorry about your bed." I winced and Raen turned to look at me. "You can have my bedcloth back at Bow's house."

Raen walked over, handing me fresh clothes with a curious glint. My stomach erupted in butterflies when his hand brushed mine.

"No. It is fine, I have more clothes. I don't mind her – *or you*, staying here." He stated with calm eyes and I let out a sigh at that, nodding up at him gratefully.

Malakei didn't join us when we travelled to the small shallow bathing pool towards the edge of the camp because when Tara spotted him walking through the camp, she immediately darted towards him and pulled him along by the ears, ignoring his protests. She had mentioned something about teaching him a lesson for what he did and I could only assume it was how we both came close to death's door last night.

"Your sister can be scary." I found myself grimacing when I looked at her pulling Malakei along mercilessly.

Raen chuckled at that before giving me a small shove forward to continue walking to the bathing pool.

"Not all of the time. She's only scary when she's angry."

"Kind of like you." I noted with a small smile at the realisation of how similar they were. Raen sent me a look with pierced lips.

"You have not seen me angry."

My eyes widened at that and my heart pounded. He looked down at me with furrowed eyebrows.

"But I… you're always angry with me."

Raen shook his head at me. "Not always. Worried and frustrated, yes… but not angry. You will know when I am angry."

'I hope I never do.'

I nodded at that and bit my lip, looking down as we walked beside each other.

Baja was silent as she stalked beside me and didn't even attempt to explore like she usually did. Instead, she stayed at my side, afraid something would jump out and attack me.

"You're not angry that I snuck out with Malakei and almost died?" I asked him in a quiet voice and he sighed.

"What do you think I feel?"

I gulped.

"I think you're more disappointed than angry." He hummed at that. I looked up to notice more trees and rocks had formed – we were almost at the bathing pool.

"I am disappointed with you yes, it is Malakei that I am more annoyed with. He should have known not to go out when there was a warning to stay inside the camp – *all for a stupid journal."*

He muttered the last part. Malakei must have told him why we ventured out in the first place. I made a mental note to keep an eye out for his journal outside of the camp today, seeing as we were unsuccessful in retrieving it. At least the rain held off.

"I'm sorry." I found myself apologising as I kept my eyes on him, feeling suddenly idiotic. Raen stared down at me and nodded once before looking back at the shallow pool, the bushes and trees around it felt all the more private and a small waterfall from above filtered the water that splashed into the pool.

"Besides, it's not me you should be saying sorry to."

I let out a frustrated sigh as I brought my hand up to my hair, the beginnings of a headache starting to form.

I knew that he was right. I still needed to apologise to my father – and Bow – for disobeying his orders. I knew he would be the most disappointed.

"I know and I will. I just... I need time to get myself together and figure this out." I said quietly, glancing down at Baja and looking out at the pool.

Before Raen could scold me further, I pulled off my shirt, exposing the black paw print mark along my ribcage that resembled an inked tattoo and stripped down to my boxers before heading into the pool, leaving him and a whining Baja behind.

Baja followed me to the edge of the pool baring her teeth at the water as I stepped in. Relishing in its coldness, I walked forward until the pool water was up to my stomach and turned around to Raen.

Raen was still standing in his spot holding the fresh clothes that he bought for me tightly in his hands as he looked out at me. I spotted his eyes trailing my body before he shook himself and put the clothes and towel down on a nearby boulder. He moved to sit down on the edge of the pool a small distance from the wailing panther.

I frowned at this and turned to Raen first with slight confusion after submerging my body. I was already feeling the tension that had pent up inside of me begin to wash away.

"Are you not coming in?" I called over the trickle of the waterfall.

He opened his mouth and seemed to hesitate at that, shifting where he sat restless looking out at me all but naked in the pool.

He had seen me like this before, I didn't understand why he was being so shy all of a sudden. Maybe he was feeling uncomfortable with the thought of murks in the river outside of the camp and didn't want to come in because of it.

I frowned and let out a small breath as I focused my attention on the wailing panther. Her tail flicked once when my eyes found hers and she immediately stopped wailing. I smiled at her.

"Baja. Come in the water with me."

Baja sniffed the water and sneezed violently when droplets went up her nose. I chuckled at this.

"She is afraid of water." I heard Raen say from his position. My eyes travelled back to the panther dipping her paw in experimentally before recoiling at the coldness. She looked out at me longingly with sad eyes at the distance between us and wailed further.

"She will keep wailing until you come out."

I turned to him with a frown.

"I thought most big cats liked water?"

"Not this one." Raen threw a glance at the wailing panther inching back from the pool.

An idea suddenly made my eyes grow wide and I returned to the edge of the pool.

Baja flicked her tail at my actions and sat, waiting for me to come back patiently. Raen watched me in confusion but before he could say anything, I held my arms out to

Baja, still in the water so that the panther had to wade a small distance through it to get to me.

Baja noticed this and let out a small wail as her eyes travelled between me and the water.

"What are you doing?"

"I'm going to help her face her fears," I stated throwing a glance over to him. "Our bond is built on trust, right? Well, if I can get her to trust me then that's one step forward in training her."

I turned back to Baja, my eyes widening with delight when I noticed she made her first step into the water. I decided to encourage her.

"Good girl, come to me. Don't be afraid."

Her ears twitched at my voice, chirping at my soothing tone. She took another step forward and another until she was wading through the water while I quietly took steps back until she was paddling over to me with a wailing yowl. I smiled a toothy grin at her, feeling proud of her achievement.

"*Good girl*, that's it." I called making my way to her. She immediately jumped into my embrace and I brought my arms underneath to hold her up while her paws latched around the back of my neck. Her claws sank into my skin and I whimpered.

"I've got you Baja. I won't let you fall. Please unlatch your claws."

She immediately did as I said. I sighed in relief before she nuzzled my neck and licked me gently. I shivered at that, chuckling softly.

We stayed in the water for a few more minutes. Baja

trusted me enough to actually get out of my grip and wade around me. I smiled and laughed as she did this, enjoying our bonding time. I knew that we were getting stronger and more attached with every second we spent in each other's presence.

I decided it was time to get out after a while of this, Baja paddled beside me before her paws reached the ground. She darted out of the water, shaking off her wet coat and splashing me in the process.

I chuckled as I grabbed the towel resting on the boulder and pulled it around me. Sensing Raen come up behind me, I smirked proud of my achievement, turning around.

"You were saying before about her being afraid of water?"

Raen rolled his eyes at this while I smiled, feeling my dimples poking out of my cheeks as I chuckled. I brought a hand up to push him away lightly. He stumbled back but caught my hand.

He stared down at me with a raised eyebrow and I let out a light laugh at that. A small blush slowly appeared on my cheeks.

I noticed his eyes roamed my bare chest, sinking lower and lower to the towel around my waist and that glint was there in his eyes until they started to grow dark with an unknown emotion.

I bit my lip at him curiously, about to speak when he came forward, gently pushing me back against a nearby tree. His hands came around both of my wrists now to push them over my head and I gasped up at him wide–eyed as he looked down at me, our faces only centimetres from each other.

I felt his hot breath fanning my face, mingling with my short and quick pants. My ears twitched at the proximity and I let out a hitched breath when he stepped closer to me.

"Are you teasing me *Angelov*?"

"Angelov?" I gasped out, unsure.

"Did you not expect to have a last name?"

"I…" I stuttered out, avoiding his playful eyes and sarcastic tone as a deep red blush coated the apples of my cheeks and rose to the very tips of my ears.

'Keylin Angelov. Keylin Angelov.'

Raen pulled back from me when the sound of his name was being called through the tree line.

His hands left my wrists, allowing them to fall at my sides all the while I looked at him with wide and confused eyes but he didn't look at me. Instead, he allowed his eyes to shut as he breathed through his nose.

"Raen? Are you out here?"

My heart sank as I recognised the voice that had called his name, resulting in Raen stepping completely away from me.

It was Mila.

I immediately looked down at my slipping towel. Surprised it was still around my waist as I clutched it tighter to me. I looked back up in time to catch Mila coming into view. Her head turned to us in recognition before her eyes widened.

"Oh! I didn't realise I was interrupting some–"

"Is something wrong?" Raen asked, all trace of

playfulness absent from his tone when he looked at Mila.

"Maekin is looking for you. He is wondering when will be the best time to send out a search of the river."

I bit the inside of my lip as I felt Mila's eyes on me with a contemplating expression. Raen sighed and started to walk towards her, leaving me by the tree.

"I suppose now is good." He grumbled as he walked past Mila and disappeared into the treeline.

Mila glanced at me with a sympathetic smirk before she turned around and followed Raen.

I stayed put as I tried to will myself to move and put on my clothes to catch up with them but I couldn't seem to control my racing heart.

"Are you teasing me Angelov?"

"Gods…" I gulped, shaking out my traitorous thoughts and made my way over to the boulder where the fresh clothes lay, and back to Baja who sat waiting for me patiently.

I quickly pulled on the clothes belonging to Raen and immediately noted to myself that when I got back to Bow's house, I would change into something else. I didn't want to have his scent on me any longer than I already had and just wanted to be rid of them, rid of *whatever* was going on between us because he made me so *confused*.

Baja picked up on my foul mood when I sat down and put on the socks. She made her way over to me and sat down patiently behind me. I felt her chin rest on my head.

She knew that I was hurting and she was trying to console me. How pathetic must I be for an animal to take pity on me and try to assure me that it was going to be fine?

I stopped what I was doing and turned to her at this, bringing my hand up around her sleek neck and moving our heads closer so that our foreheads touched.

"I'm sorry for getting you into this Baja. I don't want you to feel like you have to protect me all of the time."

Baja pulled back at this, her bright and glowing eyes looking down at me seriously.

'Protect Trainer until Trainer is old enough to protect himself and Baja.'

Baja's soothing voice echoed clearly through my mind and my eyes widened. I looked up at her, breath hitching.

"I can hear you in my head..." I gulped, eyes growing confused. "This can't be possible."

Baja leaned forward and nuzzled my cheek affectionately, purring slightly as I heard her voice again.

'Trainer is young and doesn't know about world yet. Soul–bond grows stronger each day.'

I looked up at her and nodded my head before bringing our foreheads back to one another's. I let my eyes close briefly in thanks.

"Thank you Baja."

We were about to make our way back to the camp when I froze, remembering to pick up my used clothes. Quickly, I ran back and got them.

As I looked up, I noticed something beyond the waterfall.

Deep in the treeline was the shape of a man.

My breath hitched as I looked at him, only to blink repeatedly and wipe my eyes thinking that they were tricking me.

When I looked back up, the man was gone.

"I'm going mad." I whispered to myself as my eyes left the spot where I thought I saw none other than Corrin.

All of the memories of us together slowly came back and the sinking feeling of missing him again was suddenly setting in as Baja and I continued on our journey back to camp.

XXI

~*~

"There's no trace of any murks."

Raen said to my father after multiple Dry Landers spent half of the day checking the riverbanks on both sides. It was now verging on sunset. So far, the camp was clear for a thirty–mile radius and we needed to get back to its safety and protection before it grew any darker.

"Double the watch at the barrier," My father instructed to a nearby Dry Lander. "Something doesn't sit right with me about any of this. I'll send my concerns to *Dangho* and *Marbeya* when we get back to camp."

The Dry Lander nodded firmly before stalking off and no sooner my father was being whisked away to attend to other matters.

I let out a tired sigh as I brought my hands up and folded them over my chest. Looking down at the riverbank, hundreds of thoughts ran through my mind. Thoughts that only distracted me when I should've been searching.

Thoughts of Raen and his gentle touch, his stormy eyes and confusing words. My brother – who I felt couldn't trust me anymore. Baja, of course, and our newly found telepathy we discovered before leading me to the crux of my distraction.

Corrin.

I still didn't know if it was real or if I was slowly going insane, descending into madness seemed likely.

It gave me chills, I wasn't going to lie and found myself looking over my shoulder – in case Corrin was actually watching me right now.

The frightening thing was, I didn't know if I wanted to go back – if at *all*. It's all I had wanted since I got here but going home meant leaving my brother and father. I had only just discovered they existed, not to mention my new friends, Malakei and Tara. It was something I had longed for all of my life. Although I was grateful for my small family in the *High Peaks*, I always felt as though I was a burden to them.

Here, I felt like I had a purpose. I felt like I belonged.

Malakei had filled the vacant position of Corrin in my time here but in no way could he ever replace him. He had looked out for me and was there for me as a shoulder to cry on in times of need, as someone to talk to when I was down and to help toughen me up. Although he wasn't perfect, he was there when I needed him.

I didn't know if I could just leave them like that.

Especially when these murks were roaming the *Dry Lands* and killing people.

Could I leave Raen just like that too?

My heart sank at the thought. Would he find me again? He did it before. He could do it again.

"You are a part of this tribe. Wherever you go, the tribe will follow. If other sectors try to take you. It only means they have underestimated the will of the Dry Landers and what we will do to get you back. No one messes with family."

A hand patting down on my back startled me forward and my head spun around in fright.

"Hey," Malakei held his hands up in surrender, not expecting that kind of reaction from me. I sighed in relief at that. Glad that he wasn't Raen for some reason and let my shoulders untense.

"You alright? You do not look very good." He pressed his lips together in a thin line and stood beside me to get a better look at my face.

"I'm fine Mal, just tired." I assured him and looked back to the river, somewhat fearful of glancing over to the other side in case my eyes were truly playing tricks on me. I decided to blame it on my lack of sleep. I was hallucinating, that was it.

"I'm here, *dimples*."

I turned to Malakei at his words, seeing his soft eyes already trained on me and I dropped my gaze to the floor, taking a shaky breath.

"If you need to talk. I always here. We are brothers."

"Thanks Mal. I appreciate it. *Oh–*" I reached down into

my satchel and pulled out a slightly damp journal that I was lucky to spot on my search. It was perched on top of a branch where I remembered Malakei had left it to grab a water bottle.

Malakei's eyes softened in thanks as I held it out to him.

"Here's your journal."

***

"–Are you even listening to me?"

I blinked repeatedly, focusing my gaze on Bow's disappointed frown from where I sat against the wall of my bed.

I stared in confusion as I looked up at him, unable to register what it was he had been saying to me.

"I'm sorry… what?"

I yawned into my elbow, eyes watering in the corners as I did from tiredness.

It was a few days or so after we had left the river and since then, things had been uneventful.

Raen hadn't talked to me – more like avoided me as if I had developed the great plague since that day. I believed this was because of our awkward interaction by the bathing pool.

I hadn't seen Malakei since the other day either. Come to think of it, I hadn't really left Bow's house.

I also hadn't slept properly since the night we returned from the river. I found myself lying awake thinking about Corrin and the others. I still thought about them, only now

I was seemingly getting more frustrated with willing myself to give into exhaustion and sleep through the night but that wasn't the case.

Now, I didn't know why, but I felt angry all of a sudden, like I wanted to hit or throw something across the room. This anger only targeted Bow as he prodded and poked at me constantly in an annoying attempt to try and get me to open up to him, to tell him what was wrong with me.

I couldn't.

Even if I wanted to, how could I explain this? I had no proof and I was half convinced that I was just being paranoid.

'Was it hallucinations from unresolved trauma perhaps?'

I was too tired to talk to him. I just wanted to sleep but I couldn't. I didn't know what this feeling was.

I narrowed my eyes at Bow's concerned frown before rolling them and sinking my head onto my pillow. My arms folded over my eyes as I gritted my teeth.

"Stop looking at me like that. I said I'm fine."

"You don't look fine. You look tired. You should rest–"

"–You think I'm not trying to do that right now?" I hissed as my arms fell back at my sides, looking up at my brother with venomous eyes.

"I can't rest when you're fucking *pestering me*. Just get out!"

Bow was taken aback by my outburst and didn't hesitate in getting to his feet, coming over to where I was and pulling me up by my shirt with such strength I didn't know he possessed.

I kicked and shouted at him to get off of me but it was to no avail and he quickly swung me around to face him.

His hands moved down to hold my arms so that I couldn't lash out at him. That seemed to bring me to my senses.

Why was I fighting him? What were we even fighting over in the first place – him voicing that he was concerned for me yet I was hitting him over it? What was wrong with me? I was becoming someone I never wanted to be.

"Bow..." I breathed out in an apologetic tone, eyes–wide as I stopped my fighting. I noticed he kept the same neutral look on his face with the same concerned crease on his forehead when I looked back at him. He said nothing.

"I'm so sorry I–I don't… I didn't mean to. I'm just tired and I can't sleep. Bow I'm *exhausted*. Please, I think you should leave."

'For your own safety' I wanted to add but I only bit my lip and turned away from his thoughtful and concerned gaze.

"I know I've only known you for a few weeks, but this doesn't seem anything like you Keylin…"

He stopped for a moment and I looked up at him through tired and most likely bloodshot eyes.

"I think it has something to do with your bond with Baja." He furrowed his brows in thought. "Baja is a wild animal. It's only possible that she passed on some of her survival methods and instincts to you. They are rubbing off on you negatively. You're reacting to it and it's causing you to be this angry for no reason."

"I…" I started but quickly stopped and shook my head of tiredness, staring up at him with both serious and frustrated eyes.

Frustrated that Baja could have this effect on me, I turned to glare out the window at the stables attached to Bow's house, where I knew she was staying for the time being, until we sorted this mess out.

"How do I stop it?"

"You can't." Bow said quietly with a sad smile, his hands finally letting go of their hold on my arms and moving up to rest on my shoulders.

"But you can learn to control it."

"How?" I asked, raising my voice slightly. I caught myself and closed my eyes tightly for a brief moment, taking deep breaths through my nose before re–opening them. Tiredness seeped back into my vision as well as a look of defeat. Bow frowned at me sadly before bringing me into his embrace with a sigh.

"It's going to be okay, brother. I'll ask the crones. If anyone would know anything, it's them."

Elderly women who had a special talent ranging from herbal medicines to predicting one's future were referred to as 'crones'. They were different from witches, less powerful and creepier.

"Thank you. I'm sorry about before Bow. I didn't mean any of it." I apologised sincerely and Bow sent me a lopsided smile.

"I know. It's fine. We're alright."

***

It was a week later that I finally gave sleeping the middle finger. Seeing as though I was having none of it, I decided to blame it on Bow's room being too warm. In my discomfort, I threw something against the wall.

The concerning part was, I didn't realise I had done it until there was a loud smashing sound and a small ceramic pot laid in pieces directly under where the pot had collided with the wall.

Bow assured me that it was fine, he even went as far as to clean it up. He let me get some fresh air and all the while I hoped that it would clear my head and make me feel drowsy.

I was starting to have blackouts now.

Not major ones, just small but they were noticeable. This had something to do with my sleeping pattern, I knew it.

"Dimples!"

I turned my head away from where I stood silently looking at the forest to glare at Malakei, my jaw clenched at where he lay on the grass with Tara.

I blinked repeatedly and brought my fingers up to pinch the bridge of my nose.

How did I get here now? I couldn't remember leaving the house.

"Hey–"

I heard Malakei's voice, now closer and filled more with concern that made me want to huff in irritation. I could sense him coming closer, inching his way ever so slightly–

"*Dimples*?"

I looked up at him alert.

He went to speak but immediately took a look at me and his eyes widened, holding up his hands in silent surrender. Tara gasped from behind him and this made me let out an animalistic growl.

I had developed increasingly dark circles under my eyes, so much so that purple veins started to appear. I looked sickly with my worrisome bloodshot eyes but I didn't care about that right now.

All I cared about was *grabbing Malakei's axe from his belt loop and driving it deep into his ches–*

I clutched both sides of my head and shook the horrific thoughts from me as I repeatedly chanted no. Tears threatened to spill from my eyes as I looked away from Malakei. Afraid if I looked at him, I would get the sudden temptation again.

This… was a nightmare.

"Wake up already!" I screamed to myself in a rage, looking and feeling like a total psycho as I stumbled away from Malakei and Tara.

"Keylin!"

Malakei shouted and made the mistake of touching me, trying to make sure I was okay which I clearly wasn't. He should've known that. Maybe if he did, I wouldn't have spun around and grabbed his arm, feeling attacked – I twisted it painfully to where he let out a blood–curdling scream of pain.

I looked down at him in a blinking daze. My vision started to blur but I knew what I had done. Whimpering with fright, I immediately let go of his arm that I was sure I had dislocated.

"I'm – Malakei *fuck* I'm so sorry I don't… I didn't–"

"Keylin?"

I turned around at the voice. my eyes trailing away from a heavily breathing Malakei who clutched his shoulder. Tara now beside him looked up at me worriedly. She knew to keep a distance from me.

I didn't like to feel trapped.

Raen stood behind me at a distance. Too close for my liking, I screamed at him to get back.

He did as I asked with his hands up, showing me that he meant no harm. His face was neutral but his eyes were hard as he stared me down.

"You're not sleeping." He stated knowingly out of the blue with a low voice, almost as if that had solved his curiosity. I blinked at him and couldn't help the small sickening smile that played on my lips.

"Is it *that* obvious?" My voice cracked, dripping with sarcasm.

I spotted movement behind him and saw the hair of none other than Mila looking around worriedly.

They had been inseparable ever since Raen took off and left Baja and me at the river that day. I didn't know what I was feeling, but I knew it wasn't good.

My eyes darted over the small nosey crowd of Dry Landers that had started to form a distance away.

Raen suddenly came forward, taking my focus off of the crowd and shoved me back. Me – being as weak as I was, fell backwards and onto the ground. I landed hard as

I didn't even try to protect myself. I only let out a whimper as I rolled onto my side and thought for a moment, I wasn't going to get up. The ground was too comfortable.

"Let's settle this Keylin."

Raen's voice was stern above me. It made my ears flatten and my eyes fly up to his now full of anger.

"What?!" Malakei exclaimed from beside Tara as he looked between the both of us in fright.

"What is going on – why are you fighting?"

My attention immediately snapped to Malakei. My surroundings shifted to a purple hue as I screamed at him. The scream came out in a mixture of my own voice and an animal's roar. It took a lot out of me and I couldn't help but fall back onto the ground, whimpering as I tried to shield myself from them.

"I'm sorry! I can't… can't control it!" I screamed at them hoping they would understand but they didn't. They didn't know what was wrong with me.

Raen suddenly grabbed my legs and flipped me over onto my front. This caused my surroundings to glow purple again and my hand went out to swipe at his chest.

I managed to take him off guard. He stumbled back while I scrambled to my feet. My surroundings remained a glowing purple.

"Don't interfere," Raen said to the others as he circled me. "Trust me."

"Are you fucking insane!"

I roared at Tara causing her to flinch back. Raen took the opportunity to push me back down to the ground again. He was delaying the process of hitting me for some reason which only made me angrier as I got back up and kicked at his legs.

He grunted at this and leaned forward slightly in pain before I quickly pushed him back. His hands reached out to bring me down with him and I cried out. Our chests colliding knocked the breath right out of me momentarily.

It was long enough for Raen to roll me off of him. I only growled in frustration.

Clenching my teeth, I pulled myself back up so that I was straddling him. My fist came down hard on his cheek but he didn't react. I hit him again and again until my eyes caught something silver poking out of his belt loop.

He noticed this.

Immediately pushing me off of him, I scrambled to my feet, snatching his axe from his belt loop as I did and his breath caught at that.

"Keylin. Listen to me. Listen to my voice," He looked at me almost in pain. "*Fight this*. You need to fight this and regain control."

I held the axe up and went to swipe at him but he side–stepped me. I screamed out in frustration at this, turning around.

I tripped him up in a tactic, a quick swipe under the leg. He grunted as he fell onto his back. His eyes turned to me wide–eyed and fearful as I held the axe above him.

"You don't want to be a murderer."

Our conversation from weeks ago played on my mind. The axe shook in my hand as tears clogged my vision at the realisation of what I had just done – what I could have done.

I dropped the weapon and gained control of my body, taking deep breaths while backing away from a relieved–looking Raen.

I didn't even get a chance to speak when I felt my body start to shut down. Exhaustion finally took over as my legs buckled from under me. Someone caught me just in time before I fell and blacked out. Darkness, finally filled my vision.

***

When I finally began to stir awake, I realised I was in a bed.

I didn't know how long I had been asleep for or even whose bed I was in. Sleep called me, even though I had just woken up groggy and wanted nothing more than to go back to that blissful lull only moments ago.

All of these worrisome thoughts made me frown and I slowly peeled open my eyes. Memories from a few minutes ago – or was it hours ago? – flooded my vision and I began to panic.

I bolted upright in the bed.

"Woah."

Raen's hands darted out from beside the bed where he sat in a chair of sorts, looking like he was holding a bowl of something. His hand firmly pressed my chest back down onto the bed.

I immediately turned to him with a gasp, flinching away from his grip and narrowed my gaze.

Raen said nothing as our eyes met briefly. He looked

as if he was going to say something but shook his head at the thought. Quickly bringing forward whatever he was eating from the bowl into my line of view. My eyes trailed down to it.

"Here, eat this."

"What is it?" I asked warily and felt the scratchiness in my voice like sandpaper. I brought a hand out to rub my neck.

Raen quickly grabbed something from the floor and held it out to me, eyes landing on a glass of water and I didn't hesitate to take it in my hands, almost dropping it from weakness if it weren't for Raen – who somehow had a feeling it would happen – caught the glass before it could fall out of my grip. He helped me hold it up as I took gulps from the glass and quenched my dry throat.

I didn't realise I was so weak and when the glass was drained of its content, I frowned and turned to him.

"Why am I so weak?" Shifting on the bed slowly, Raen's eyes examined my every movement with emotionless eyes.

"You have not digested food in two days. Not to mention your poor diet before that and lack of sleep. Your body was starting to shut down."

"W–What?" My stomach dropped. "Where's Baja?"

"She is fine. Worried but fine. I'll get Malakei to bring her to you in the morning. But first, you need to recover." Raen explained, easing my worries but I didn't settle.

"I've been asleep for two days?"

Raen narrowed his eyes on me and looked as though he wanted to argue about the fact that there were worse problems than sleeping for two days but decided against it, instead, he focused his attention on the small bowl of green in his lap.

"Just eat this–"

"What is–"

"It's seaweed." He replied in what sounded like irritation before shutting his eyes and letting out a short breath.

"It will help you gain your strength back quicker."

I frowned down at the bowl as he held a spoonful out for me and my eyes widened, quickly shaking my head I tried not to vomit. I knew my stomach was empty yet it did nothing to stop the feeling of wanting to vomit at the horrid smell.

"I'm not eating that." I stated seriously and turned my head to the side, ignoring Raen's glare.

"You have no choice."

"Oh *really*?" I turned to him with a hiss. The sarcasm dropped from my lips.

"What are you going to fucking do? Force feed me?"

Raen blinked, startled by the malice in my voice before something twisted morphed on his features and blazed behind his eyes.

"Do you remember when I told you, I have never gotten angry around you – that you haven't seen me angry yet? Today may just be the day you do if you don't cut the attitude and let me help you get better."

I gulped at his words. The blush of embarrassment crept up on my cheeks before I turned my head to the side, biting my lip in contemplation.

"Yeah fine, but don't bother, I'm still not eating t–"

I cried out when Raen suddenly grabbed my chin and taking the opportunity, shoved a spoonful of crushed–up seaweed into my mouth.

I gagged at the horrid texture, shutting my lids tightly but tears still managed to escape the corners of my eyes from the awful taste.

When Raen took his hand away, I didn't hesitate in turning my body to the side. My head tilted over the bedside as I went to spit the horrible–tasting substance out of my mouth.

"*Oh* no you don't." Raen grunted to himself as he pulled me back down onto my back, his hand clamped over my mouth so that I couldn't spit it out and the only way he was going to let up was if I swallowed it.

"Swallow it Keylin."

Raen's dark eyes bored down into my wide ones. Something stirred in me at his words and I almost did as he said. I grew angry as I tried to shake my head and pry his hands from over my mouth.

I eventually swallowed the substance when it was becoming difficult to breathe, not wanting the taste of it in my mouth any longer and when I did I immediately started coughing.

Raen took his hands away from my mouth and allowed me to roll on my side, gasping and trying not to puke at the feeling of the awful seaweed. My stomach churned at the thoughts.

"See? It wasn't so bad."

Raen spoke through a smirk; I looked up at him

through hooded eyes, unmoving from my spot.

He got off of the bed now, a small, satisfied grin spread on his face while mine soured at the sight.

"Fuck you Raen."

If there was anything I regretted more at that moment, it was having said those words under my breath, thinking he wouldn't hear them.

He did.

There was a moment of silence above me with only the loud exhaling of breath before he grabbed my legs and pulled me down the bed, making me cry out in surprise.

I looked up at him, breathing heavily as he swooped down to pick me up in his arms – much like the time he had flung me over his shoulder when he caught me from escaping.

My head grew dizzy at the sudden movement and I could only register him moving out of the tent swiftly with a strong hold of me in his arms.

I started to grow sceptical, all confidence now suddenly shrivelled up like a prune when he took me out of his tent and into the pouring rain of the evening. I clutched his shirt near his chest in my hands.

"Put me down you fucking psycho!" I yelled at him as I looked up but his teeth only clenched tighter at my words, refusing to look down at me he continued to walk through the heavy downpour. Confused of where he was taking me all of a sudden, I glared up at him.

"Raen I'm serious, if you don't put me down–"

I gasped when my eyes fell on a large water trough quickly filling up with rainwater not too far away.

As he neared it, the more I clung to him. Believing he was going to dunk me in it, my eyes widened and I turned to him, noticing how he was trying to hide his smirk.

"Don't you *fucking*–"

He dropped me into the trough.

I gasped at the rush of cold water on my back and neck momentarily before the contents of the trough toppled to the side with me inside it, sending me barrelling onto the soggy mud ground.

I groaned as I curled up on my side, my shoulder now hurting from the impact it had made.

I could hear Raen chuckle from above me and I quickly glared up at him, eyes narrowing at his smirk.

"You find this funny?"

"We have a saying–" He continued speaking in Fasik. I all but growled at that.

"What the hell does that mean?" I tried not to slip getting to my feet in the mud but cringed at my dirt–covered body.

"It *means* elf–" He moved closer to me, biting his lip in an attempt to hide his smirk.

"You make your bed, you sleep in it."

I gritted my teeth as I got up from all fours, water dripped from the ends of my hair into my face from either the rain above or being drenched in the water bath, I didn't know. All I knew was that I was shaking from the cold and seeing red. Especially when Raen turned his back, beginning to walk away from me.

"I never asked for your help!" I shouted out.

I quickly got up and pushed his back, making him

stumble forward unbalanced – he landed on his front with a loud 'splat' and I smirked at this.

"That's what you get for dropping me in the water. We call that karma, *asshole*."

I repeated in his tone back to him, adding a little extra at the end because I knew it would make him mad.

He grunted at me and turned over onto his back. It was only then that I saw his front was completely covered in dark mud. It had managed to get as far as his face, neck and arms.

His eyes were now lit with a fire.

I couldn't help but gasp when I noticed him, bringing my hand up to stop the laughter from leaving my lips but it didn't matter. I was already laughing when I heard the sound of his body meeting the mud.

He shut his eyes at this and took a deep breath before opening them again.

"You better run. When I catch you, I swear I'm going–"

I was already running, not waiting to hear the rest of his empty threat as my legs travelled and took me passed tents within the camp, laughing as I did. I didn't care about either rain or the cold anymore. I was already soaked through my clothes.

I noticed through my running Tara had come out of her tent only to stop when she noticed me running straight to her.

"Tara!" I yelled jogging up to her in wide–eyed humour. She raised a brow at me in amusement and I slowed.

"What are you doing – you're drenched!" She couldn't keep the smile from her face. "I see you're looking better."

I winced at that and sent her an apologetic look but before I could say something, she was frowning at something behind me.

"Is that my brother covered in – what is going on?" She immediately jumped to conclusions, seeming now curious at the sight of her brother. She couldn't contain her laughter from leaving her lips.

"Oh, he's *furious*. What did you do Keylin?"

I gulped, holding my hands up and biting my lip as I blushed.

My eyes found Raen only to shriek when I noticed how fast he had run and was now only metres away from me. I immediately got behind Tara, using her body as a shield and shrieked out a 'hide me!'

"What are you two doing?" She chuckled as she shook her head fondly. Her eyes set on her quickly approaching and mud–laced brother.

I peeked over her shoulder to look at Raen and yelped when he was right in front of Tara, seeming confused as he wiped the mud from his face.

His eyes snapped to mine and he reached out to grab me but I yelped and took off running again. The laughter left my lips as I did and I almost fell forward from cackling when I heard him slip on more mud. The sound of Tara's laughter filled my ears.

I kept running until I found myself along the edge of the camp, several paces from the barrier and even further from the forest, but when my eyes caught on someone standing at the edge of the forest, I froze in my tracks.

"Corrin..."

XXII

~*~

I watched him as he stood unmoving against the edge of the forest, his gaze transfixed on something.

He wasn't looking at me. His eyes were on the camp as if he didn't notice me standing there. As close as I thought we would ever be again.

This had to be real.

"Corrin!" I screamed and this seemed to take him off guard, breaking him away from his trance to turn to me. His eyes were those familiar piercing blues that conveyed all I needed to know.

'Don't follow me.' They read.

I watched him suddenly back into the treeline disappearing from view and my eyes widened at that.

It wasn't a dream.

Before I could move forward, hands suddenly wrapped around my waist and Raen was breathing heavily down the back of my neck. My body tensed up.

"I got you…" He panted heavily into my neck causing

my body to shiver at his words.

He was no sooner removing his hands and pushing me to the side, straight down onto a muddy surface.

I groaned as my back came into contact with the now padded mud ground and my ears flattened at the squelching sound when my body moulded into it. I glared up at a chuckling Raen.

"Raen!" I gasped out at the coldness, attempting to get up and turn my head in the direction of the forest.

Corrin was long gone now, becoming one with the forest and all its inhabitants.

What was he doing in the *Dry Lands*? It was too dangerous for him to be here. If the Dry Landers found out… gods know what they would do to him.

I was so preoccupied with my thoughts, I didn't register Raen's body moving down to straddle me. Each leg rested on either side of my waist while he brought a hand up to wipe the dirt from his face. There was a mischievous look in his eye.

"Don't you–"

I started, but he only smiled down at me with false innocence before bringing his hand down onto my cheek. He rubbed the mud onto my clean cheeks and I squealed, turning my head to the side but he spread the dirt on the other cheek.

Child.

My eyes flew open to look up at him, amusement and mortification filled me when I took in his smiling form.

"How very leader–like of you." I grumbled, raising my eyebrows while he chuckled, smearing the dirt down my neck. His hands were freezing and I tried not to squirm.

"I like to set an example."

"So you make a habit out of rubbing mud on people's faces?"

"Only for you," His amused eyes found mine, taking away from his concentration to look down at me.

"You're special."

"Oh, thank you, I feel very special right now." I replied as he grabbed more mud from beside us on the ground. I whined when he rubbed it into my hair.

"*Gods* I hate you."

He let out a thunderous laugh at that, a crackling of electricity it sounded like in my ears.

I decided to pick some mud up at my sides. My ears flattened at the feeling of sogginess and I reached for his shirt, letting my hands snake under the material to rub the mud onto his bare skin around his back and torso.

Raen's breath hitched from the cold, his body arched closer to me in order to get away from my dirt–caked hands. I chuckled as he narrowed his gaze down at me, rolling his eyes while I brought my grimy fingers up into his soft hair.

"*Asshole.*" He mimicked me from earlier as he looked down with a small smile and I let my head fall back against the ground, letting out a boisterous laugh. I only gasped when he brought his hands under my shirt, holding a clump of mud to rub into my skin.

"No!" I yelled as I laughed harder, wiggling away from his cold hands massaging the dirt onto my body.

He laughed in fond amusement while I brought my

hands around the back of his neck, causing a chill to run down his body. His head buried in my neck after a while as he let his body lay on top of mine in the soaking wet mud.

It was still raining and it only got heavier now as my fingers tangled in his hair, my head rested back against the cold ground and I started to tremble, teeth chattering from the cold and wet.

Raen noticed this and took his head from my neck, his hands planted into the ground on each side of me when he slowly rose to his feet, being careful not to slip and fall on top of me. I chuckled as he got to his feet, looking at him covered in dirt, he was just noticeable in the darkening night.

Raen looked down at me with a toothy smile, laughing both at the situation and most likely at me, covered head to toe in mud.

"You look ridiculous."

I couldn't help but chuckle as I slowly got into a sitting position.

The treeline was just visible over his shoulders in the pale moonlight where Corrin once stood, now absent. I didn't know what to make of it. I couldn't go to him now or trust Raen not to hunt him down and do something reckless.

He reached out a hand to me, taking me out of my thoughts and I took it gratefully. He pulled me up and placed a gentle hand on my back, helping me out of the wet patch of ground we were lying in onto a drier and sturdy area of earth for us to walk on.

"So do you." He smiled down at me.

***

We were at one of the water pumps washing our bodies off near Raen's tent. We tried to remove as much of the encrusted mud from our skin before it dried and became impossible to clean.

Raen had tilted my head forward under the pump so that he could wash the mud from my hair. As much as I enjoyed the feeling of his hands in my hair, it was ruined by the bitter coldness of the water splashing down on my neck and sensitive ears.

I did the same with his hair and when we thought we had cleaned the majority of dirt from our bodies that was noticeable, we abandoned our ruined shirts and ran through the rain into his tent, shivering and teeth chattering.

My hands hugged my body as Raen quickly retrieved a towel from his bedside chest. He threw it over to me as he sought out one for himself.

I wasted no time wrapping it around my shoulders and shut my eyes to relish in the small warmth that radiated from the material. All the while I tried not to focus on the dripping hair down my neck and back.

Raen came over to me, looking up – I noticed him standing beside me moving the towel through his hair as he shook into it like a wet dog. When he opened his eyes, they took in my trembling form.

He immediately stepped closer, bringing his towel over

my head and shaking it over my hair – it made me laugh lightly. His towel massaged and dried my scalp before he moved down to dry my ears, neck and finally finishing at my cheeks.

I popped my head out of the corner of the towel with a laugh, feeling my dimples poke out as I did only to find him already looking down at me, amusement and fondness in his eyes. Only then did I notice how he had gotten closer whilst drying my wild and unruly hair.

I smiled up at him with my eyes as his thumb came away from the towel, softly brushing over my cheeks with a gentleness. I felt his thumb run over my right dimple before poking at it.

I chuckled at that, a blush creeping onto the tops of my cheeks as I looked down.

His hands came away from my cheeks to the back of my head, bringing me forward slightly as he pressed a soft kiss to the top of my head and took me into his arms, wrapping me in the towel as his hands rubbed up and down my back, creating warmth as well as drying me. It reminded me of that time in the mountains. How his body heat had saved me that time in bringing me back from death's door.

I gulped into his chest, smiling to myself. I turned red at the fluttering feeling in my stomach by his touch and the feel of his lips on my head.

It was a small gesture that could mean a lot of things, even an apology, not necessarily an 'I love you' type of kiss. That's not what it was. I knew Raen didn't love me. At least not in the way I thought.

Either way, it didn't stop the way my heart sped up when I was around him. How he seemed to suck all of the air from a room, making it difficult for me to breathe. My eyes frequently sought him out, even when I knew where he would be. Every sense of my being seemed to crave his touch, even my heart was beginning to yearn and call his name.

I was tethering dangerously close to the edge. If I wasn't careful, I fear I'd drown.

After we had dried and got into clean clothes, I made my way over to Raen's bed, immediately sighing with contentment at the warmth the fur radiated. I curled up in a foetal position on one side of the bed itself, allowing room for Raen.

Not a moment later, Raen sank down onto the bed with a sigh. I smiled at that and turned around in his direction, adjusting my head on the pillow as my eyes started to flutter shut.

I poked one eye open however a moment later when I felt Raen staring at me. He smiled at me gently before inching his head closer to me.

His hand reached over me to grab something and I frowned in confusion before I felt the soft fur of the blanket being pulled over me, over the both of us. He closed his eyes facing me, hand resting over me gently where he had been pulling at the blanket.

No words needed to be spoken. No apologies needed to be made. We were wrong on both ends but couldn't stay mad at each other for long. We had moved on from the argument.

When I was alone with my thoughts and hearing the gentle sounds of Raen sleeping, I thought back to what I saw earlier. It was no longer a dream now that Corrin was here – in the forest of the *Dry Lands*. He had crossed sectors. I knew he was planning something. I was going to find out what.

'Don't follow me.'

I gulped in worry, pulling the blankets closer to me and stared up at Raen's sleeping form.

It was becoming more difficult to want to leave you.

***

When I woke up the next morning, it was to an empty bed.

My hand had reached out as I shifted in my sleep, frowning however when all I felt was bed sheets between my fingers.

No Raen.

My eyes fluttered open slightly and I lifted my head off of the pillow for a brief moment before letting it fall back down, moving onto my front as I brought my fingers up to rub at my sleep–filled eyes.

"Raen?" I called out into the tent in confusion, not opening my eyes as I began to stretch.

"Yes?" I heard him reply from the couch and I jumped at that, not expecting him to be here and so silent.

I blushed and slowly sat up from the bed, looking around slightly before I spotted him in the far corner of the room, shirtless and with a bowl of something in his hands. He looked back at me with concern.

I blinked at him for a moment before bringing my hand up to rub at my cheek in slight embarrassment as I looked at him.

"Oh! I–I thought you... I didn't think you were here..." I trailed off before yawning.

Raen only stared at me with slight confusion and a small smirk tugged at his lips while he took in my form.

"Why would I not be here?"

"I just–" I looked back up at him before frowning slightly down at the tangled bed sheets, trying to hide my blushing face out of embarrassment.

"I don't know." I ended up saying shyly.

He chuckled at me from where he sat, amusement clear in his eyes and he shook his head at me, looking down to stir at the bowl of substance in his hands.

"You're cute Keylin." He said quietly. So quiet that my heart began to race at his words. My blush deepened.

I sensed him moving closer and looked up when he sat on the side of the bed, slowly pulling down the bed sheets with one hand I was using to cover my face, the bowl in his other.

Frowning at this, I rested my gaze on the seaweed within the bowl, only it was mushed up into a porridge–like matter.

"I tried something different with it." Raen remarked with a look of concentration. He stirred the concoction slowly before looking back up at me.

"I infused some *Dry Land* spices with it to make it more bearable."

I tilted my head at him in slight confusion as he showed

me by bringing the spoon up to his mouth and tasting it. He chewed it and swallowed without making a sour face and turned to me with a small smile.

"Tell me what you think."

He took the spoon from the bowl again with a fair portion of seaweed on it. I wanted to say no but he had me under his thumb, knowing that he went to this much trouble and not wanting a repeat of last night – I complied.

I slowly shifted forward and went to take the spoon from him but he shook his head at this which made me stop to look at him.

"Let me feed you."

He said with a glint in his eyes and I smirked at him. My dimples poked out as I brought my head closer to his outstretched hand, lips parting to wrap around the spoon. I let my eyes flutter closed at the familiar taste of the seaweed with the addition of spices I had never tried before – suddenly invaded my tastebuds, it took the sharp taste of the sea away.

His dark green eyes watched me with a look I had never seen before and I wanted to ask him about it but realised my lips were still around the spoon.

I pulled back and chewed the remaining pieces with contemplation, looking at him thoughtfully.

"It's nice." I smiled in assurance. His eyes were still on me as if hanging onto my every word. It was only when he gulped he seemed to regain himself, clearing his throat as he shifted on the bed under him.

"I mean, it still tastes awful, but you made it better. Thank you for doing that. You didn't have to." I smiled showing my appreciation, feeling a lot calmer than I was yesterday and he noticed it too. I was getting back to myself now that I was sleeping.

He was quickly looking up at me with kind eyes and a small smile, nodding once.

"I thought of it early this morning. My mother used to put cheese on my broccoli to help me eat my vegetables as a child. She told me they would make me big and strong but I didn't listen. I hated them – still do."

I couldn't help but chuckle softly at that. The image of a stubborn Raen as a child refusing to eat his vegetables flashed in my mind and his eyes glinted again as he looked at me, biting his lip to keep the smile from poking out. He looked away, letting out a breathy somewhat embarrassed chuckle.

"We know how to adapt well to our surroundings when we need to. You gave me a challenge. I guess I didn't want to force it down your throat again. That's why I did it."

I winced at the memory of yesterday and the memories of our argument causing him to *literally* force the food down my throat because I was being stubborn and rude. I said some hurtful things to him yesterday and may have caused not only him but the others too, a lot of stress and worry over the past few days.

Looking at him now, he seemed happier when he wasn't worrying about me being hurt or almost on the verge of death. When I was actually complying with him and doing as he asked instead of fighting him, he was less stressed but I knew this couldn't always be the case. Still, he always managed to surprise me.

He took a breath and placed the bowl in my lap before suddenly bringing his other hand up to the back of my head, pulling me closer to him so that he could kiss my temple.

My heart rate sped up as a blush deepened on my cheeks that he noticed when he pulled away. He didn't say anything, however, and only smiled as he moved off of the bed, going around to the opposite side of it to pick up his discarded shirt from last night and throw it on.

"Eat up. I'm going to get–"

Raen was cut off by a loud wail and I managed to catch a glimpse of something black rushing past him. Baja jumped up onto the bed and came over to lick my face.

'Hello Trainor.'

Baja spoke in my mind and I chuckled, holding the seaweed away from her as she did. Fearful she might take a liking to it, the same liking she took with my porridge.

I leaned into her and nuzzled my head against her neck, hearing her purr deep in her throat at my action.

When I looked up, I saw Malakei standing at the entrance with his arms crossed over his chest, looking on at the scene before him with an amused smile.

"Baja..." I sighed, closing my eyes. "I missed you."

Baja sniffed at my clothes and neck before lightly running her snout over my temple – where Raen had kissed me. I frowned at her when she gave a growl of disapproval.

'Trainor not smell like Trainor. Trainor smell like other Trainor and Baja not happy.'

Baja's words filled my mind and I turned to look at her,

just seeing her body slumped in a sitting position behind me, her head resting on top of mine as she looked forward unamused.

'She was sulking.'

She let out something similar to a huff at my thoughts and I found myself chuckling at that, her smelling Raen's scent on me the reason for her now foul mood, all because I was wearing his clothes and slept in his bed with him.

She was sulking over this and I frowned at her statement, shaking my head at her words. I told myself to teach her not to use the word Trainor for everyone when in reality, it was me who was the only Trainor around. Even still, I rather her use my real name instead of the term.

"That is cute."

I looked up and smiled in thanks at Malakei for bringing her to me. I could only imagine how worried she had been.

Raen scoffed at Malakei before turning to him.

"I thought you were my sister." Raen mused before a knowing look crossed his eyes.

"Speaking of her, you too have been hanging around each other a lot lately–"

"Well would you look at that!" Malakei let out a nervous laugh, directing his gaze anywhere but at me and Raen now. I frowned in confusion before a small smirk played on my lips. Baja's tongue darted out at a stray blonde hair sticking up near her mouth that had been tickling her nose.

"I should probably–"

Malakei didn't even finish his statement before he bolted past the entrance of the tent and away from Raen's murderous look of accusation. I chuckled at that while Raen rolled his eyes. He turned to me with a knowing smirk.

"My sister likes him and I like to tease him over it."

My eyes widened in surprise at the revelation, never did it cross my mind that Tara had a soft spot for Malakei. They seemed like opposites, yet they weirdly fit. They would make an odd couple but I couldn't think of anyone differently for Malakei.

"Are you kidding? He's petrified of you." I raised a brow at him, and his smile slowly began to disappear to make way for a serious look.

"Everyone is afraid of me. They know what I've been through, they know what I am... what I can do."

I shook away the sorrow from my eyes. He didn't want my pity. I knew what that was like and he didn't need that right now.

"I'm not afraid of you," I watched as he looked up at me with emotionless eyes. "Yes, *okay* I admit that I am afraid of your wrath, but not *you*. Even now, the more time I spend here being around you, I'm slowly starting to feel like I'm seeing the real you."

I looked down and chuckled to myself, hearing him let out a small sigh of what I could only guess was relief as he began to make his way closer to where I sat crisscrossed on his bed. The only sound made was Baja's warning growl as she felt he was getting too close for her comfort.

I looked up when he stopped to see him looking at Baja with a soft expression as he clenched his jaw, showing her that he meant no harm as he came to sit in the same position in front of me on the bed.

Baja's low grumbles seemed to fade as she allowed Raen to sit at such a close distance from me without lashing out protectively. This made me blink in surprise.

"She is very protective of you, you know."

"I know." I said quietly, bringing my hand down to tangle her tail around my hand. She purred at this and I let out a small laugh when she nuzzled again at my head. Raen looked on in amusement.

"She likes you and Malakei but she's protective all of the time when it comes to me." I said sheepishly as a small redness started to form on my ear tips. Raen smiled at this and nodded slowly.

"She must know that we only want to protect you too." Raen stated in a small voice, smiling when he saw me shift the bowl in my lap and start to eat the crushed seaweed. Baja sniffed and lowered her head down to look over my shoulder.

I held the bowl away from her and frowned, in the midst of chewing and oblivious to the bit of seaweed stuck to the corner of my mouth. She brought her head closer and darted her tongue out to lick it off, I whined, pulling away.

"Of course, you have to do that." I grumbled looking down at the seaweed. Raen chuckled at this while Baja purred, her tail flicked happily against my leg.

XXIII

~*~

"So you and Raen, yes?"

Malakei and I sat in the grass on the outskirts of the camp, our legs in a crisscrossed form as we both ate our lunch – a simple piece of bread with meat inside of it, nothing special. Malakei had finished chewing when he raised the question to me, a knowing smirk played on his lips while I picked at the last of my bread.

"Is this a sex question?" I asked flatly not in the mood to entertain my friend's curiosity – no matter how perverse.

Baja was outstretched on the grass sprawled by my side, unmoving in the warmth of the sun. It was hard to tell if she was sleeping or not.

Malakei only licked his lips as he looked me over, failing miserably to keep the smile from gracing his face.

"You both had sex yes–"

I let out an irritated moan. Malakei only chuckled at

this.

"Why is everyone so obsessed about sex here?"

"Come now *dimples*," He continued with the conversation, shifting forward slightly so that he was right in front of me. "You don't have to be embarrassed. Was he bigger than me? Everyone says yes and think Raen is ten inch but I don't think–"

"Malakei!" I cried out wide–eyed, growing more embarrassed and uncomfortable the longer this conversation went on. When would they realise that I had no interest in this sort of thing?

Not liking where this conversation was going, I quickly shook my head and went to get up. Malakei's face seemed to fall in realisation that I didn't want to talk about the subject and his hand immediately reached out to grasp my wrist, stopping me from getting up.

"Wait *dimples*, sorry. I do not intend to make you upset." Malakei pouted but I wasn't impressed. I frowned at him, correcting him on his grammar with a grumble before sitting back down.

"We didn't do anything Mal. *We're* – it's not like that. He's my *friend*."

I said the last part quietly. Ignoring the way my heart panged when I mentioned him being my friend. Raen was my friend, nothing more. That's all we were. Besides, I had a sneaking suspicion that he liked Mila.

Malakei nodded slowly at this, his eyes gazed upon me curiously as he seemed to dwell on something in his mind that may or may not have been troubling him for a while. I slouched forward and ripped the grass at my feet.

"Keylin?"

I looked up at his tone, all traces of joking and playfulness gone from his voice and my stomach dropped in anticipation of what he was about to ask.

"You never have sex before, did you?" Malakei came to the conclusion and I couldn't help but freeze up at his question, swallowing visibly as I looked at him. Bow's words rang in the back of my mind to keep that information a secret. No one could know about me being a virgin here, it could be dangerous and if the wrong person knew… I didn't want to think about it.

"What?" I scoffed. Unsure if a secret like this could be trusted with Malakei.

"Of course I had sex."

"Ever have blowjob?"

"Nah," I sent him a lopsided grin as I tried to relax my shoulders to show that I knew what I was talking about. I had no clue but if I bluffed, he might drop the topic.

"Never needed one."

"Really?" Malakei blinked in confusion. "Why not?"

Shit. "Well… I was too busy with school to have a… have one."

Malakei hummed, dimples poking as he squinted up at the sun.

"What did you have then?"

Fucking *shit*.

"You know…" I rubbed the back of my neck in boredom. "Some stuff here and there. I can't keep track of them all because I've lost count but you know!"

"I don't know what you are talking about." He

chuckled turning to give me a knowing look and I gulped, all colour drained from my face.

"But I know you are *liar*."

Malakei only continued to look at my pale expression, being patient as I failed to reply. He knew already that he was right about his assumptions and smiled softly.

"It is okay *dimples*."

"No, it's not," I cut him off, gulping to keep the nervousness out of my voice and glanced at him with defeat. "You don't understand Mal. I'm eighteen, I know it's not the same here but if the elves found out I had sex young..."

I could be shunned from my community. How could I ever return home if there was no home to return back to? Taking into consideration my 'unclean bloodline', Tobias once mentioned, the penalties could be worse for me. I could be executed over something like this.

My hands rested on my knees to keep from trembling.

I felt Malakei's hand place over mine in assurance, he frowned but his eyes were gentle as he assured me.

"You are Dry Lander now. If you want to have sex now or no, that is your choice *dimples*. No one will stop you and if anyone forces you – I will cut their dick off, cook it and make them eat it."

I couldn't help the small laugh from leaving my lips as he said this but he was completely serious. After a moment of laughing, I coughed and stopped to blink in astonishment, trying not to let the graphic images invade my mind.

"Do what you feel is right." Malakei stated leaning

back on his elbows on the grass, he let his eyes close briefly to relish in the high sun.

I bit my lip as I brought my hand down to pull at the grass. A question popped up in my mind that I wanted to ask Malakei, ever since Bow had talked with ill intentions about him, but I was unsure how to phrase it without sounding rude or like I was prying.

"How young were you when you..." I started but immediately trailed off, my cheeks blushing at the thought.

Malakei opened his eyes lazily and turned to me, raising a brow in amusement.

"When I have sex?" He was thoughtful for a moment. His eyes looked as though they had darkened deeper than their normal chocolate brown.

"Younger than you."

Bow didn't like Malakei because of his... escapades. It made me curious what was so wrong if having sex was okay here. Malakei's vague answer didn't help either. Instead of satisfying my curiosity, it only made me search for more answers.

"How... many times did you... ?"

He shrugged at that. "I do not keep tally."

"O–Oh." I gulped before biting my lip. "Does it hurt?"

"Do you want to find out?" He winked suggestively.

My jaw tightened at that and I went to get up.

"I am only teasing you *dimples*," He chuckled, grabbing my hand and pulling me back down to him. "You are cute when serious."

"Why do you always have to tease me?" I whispered

to myself, trying to avoid Malakei's grinning complexion.

I was surprised however when I felt his hand move to my jaw and he turned my head back to him. His touch was soft as his thumb ran over my chin.

"I like when your ears move and the colour your cheeks go when I speak." He replied honestly. Too honestly.

Burning heat flooded to my cheeks, rising higher to the point I shivered causing my ears to twitch. Malakei's smile widened at this and I shoved him away to hide my face.

We never spoke about anything like this to one another in the *High Peaks*, nor did we mention sex to begin with. It was all private and kept a secret. Mostly, because it was no one's business. The fact that Malakei shared all of this with me was remarkable and only made me more curious to find out more.

I groaned with embarrassment and brought my hands up to clutch my ears. My dimples poked out as I tried to stop myself from smiling.

Malakei laughed at me and brought his hands up to press over my hands, his head inched closer as he laughed. I opened my eyes and they widened when I realised how close we were to each other. Our lips were only centimetres from touching.

I glanced down at his lips before looking back up, resembling a rabbit caught in a trap. Malakei only smirked knowingly at this, having seen my eyes flicker down to his lips.

"Have you ever been kissed before?"

He asked quietly, voice just above a whisper as he

looked into my eyes and his hand moved from my ears to around the back of my head. His fingers tangled through my hair.

My breath hitched at the feeling and he moved closer to the point he was almost in my lap.

"N–No." I stuttered out before swallowing, my breathing started to pick up as I looked at him.

Malakei only smiled a small smile at this. His eyes were soft as he brought his lips up to my forehead, pressing them softly against my skin and I let out a small sigh. My eyes closed in slight relief before they re–opened in confusion when I felt him pull away.

He backed away. His hand unwrapped from around the back of my head and shifted away from me so that he could go back to the original position on the grass as he tilted his head back, closed his eyes and relished in the warmth of the sun. After a moment of silence, he spoke.

"I like sex," He confessed, eyes closed. "Too much actually. I like chase and get what I want. But I don't take. *Never* take. I am not that person."

He opened his eyes and turned to me with a knowing look. A small smile graced his features.

"Besides, I know you *dimples* and I know your lips off limits for someone special."

I gulped as I looked at him, eyes blinking repeatedly before looking down and feeling the familiar sting build in my eyes.

I knew he was talking about Raen. He didn't want to come between us because he thought that there was something – whatever it was between us. I couldn't see it.

The only time he was ever around me was when I was close to death, or hurt, or trying to run away. He was elsewhere any other time.

It made me feel like he didn't want to get to know me and only cared about me if my father told him to watch over me when he left on trips. It was not a nice feeling. He could never spend a day with me where it was just us and nothing else, no distractions.

I felt like a burden, a brat placed under his watchful eye because of my father. Raen probably saw me as nothing but an acquaintance, much less a brother.

'I guess that's complicated when the lips you want are off–limits too.' Even my own thoughts betrayed me.

Ever since that night in the rain, I knew this thing between us travelled further back than that. Back to that day in the bathing pool. I believed something was there between us, a spark.

Malakei bit his lip to keep from saying anything as he glanced away. Immediately he looked back with a thoughtful expression. He stalled for a moment, almost debating with the idea that seemed to have crossed his mind before he decided to go with it. He got up from his lying position on the ground and came over to me.

I frowned at him confused and my lips parted to ask him what he was doing when suddenly, he stared at me with determination.

"You need confidence. I can help you in becoming good kisser so that he falls into arms of yours. So you can know what you are doing when time comes." Malakei stated slowly with a beaming smile before it started to fall as he looked at me with hesitation.

"Only if you want to."

I bit my lip as I contemplated the idea. It was a good idea in the sense that I would know what I was doing when the time came with Raen. I could impress him and surprise him with the kissing skills Malakei would teach me instead of making a fool of myself. Who better than to learn from someone with experience?

The plan was flawless. It only meant giving up my first kiss. I didn't think of it as a first kiss, more like practice for the real one.

I knew Raen was busy with patrol duty near the river for the day, so there was no chance of him possibly stumbling upon us and getting the wrong idea. Taking a breath, I looked back up at Malakei, nervous but excited.

"Okay. Let's do it."

Malakei smiled a soft smile at this and continued to look at me for a moment in silence before he shook himself and clapped his hands loudly, startling me.

"Okay. Uhm… here –"

His hands reached out to take my own and I let him pull me into his lap. Blushing as he positioned my legs either side of him in a kneeling position, his hands travelled to place on my waist and I jumped slightly at this. He assured me with a smile.

"I am Raen." He furrowed his brows into an angry expression that made me let out a small chuckle. The resemblance was uncanny.

"Seems about right." I mumbled and he flashed me a toothy grin before his face turned serious once again. His hands moved from around my waist to my hands, holding them up to show me.

"Hands," He noted seriously. "Always have them doing something. Playing with hair, touching body or taking off clothes."

He told me as he motioned to what he was talking about and I nodded in understanding, intrigued by this, not knowing the action was so simple but so necessary. It was amazing how one could forget about their hands and in turn, lead the person to being more nervous and stiff.

Malakei brought my hands around the back of his neck – 'the perfect place' he said, because it allowed for the option of moving up and tangling in his hair or coming around his neck to down his chest.

I blushed the entire time. My heart pounded in my chest with both nerves and excitement as I listened carefully to his instructions. No sooner was he finished talking he let out a breath. His eyes bored into mine to check for any signs of wanting to back out, now that I knew what to do. All that was left to do was kiss him.

When he saw no hesitation or signs of backing out from me after I gave him a nod to continue, that I was okay with this. He sighed again.

"*Okay.*" He whispered as he brought his hands around my waist. My breath hitched slightly and my grip tightened around him, fingers gently played with the hair at the back of his neck and before I knew it, I was leaning down. My eyes fluttered closed when I noticed Malakei's shut also, leaning up to meet my lips.

When I felt Malakei's tongue dart out to brush along

my bottom lip, I gasped. The weird feeling made me jump, causing me to shift closer into his lap. His hands gripped my waist tightly, holding me in place as his tongue entered my mouth.

'So this was what kissing felt like' I thought to myself as Malakei and I kissed. His tongue licked the inside of my mouth before he broke away from my lips.

"You're unresponsive." He panted out slightly. His breath fanned my face as I looked at him, breathless also, not realising how much kissing could take out of you.

"I am?" I whispered slightly dazed against his lips and he nodded. His hands ran up my side before coming back down to rest on my waist. He suddenly pinched the skin and I yelped, leaning into him more to hide my face in his neck. This made him chuckle.

"That is better." He stated before one of his hands came up to my hair, pulling at it gently, making me come away from Malakei's neck to look down at him. I gulped and nodded, remembering to keep moving my hands.

"Hands. Got it." I breathed out and he nodded slightly.

"And don't be afraid to explore my mouth also. It better when both partners are into it." He whispered at my lips and I nodded, eyes already closed as I waited for his lips to touch mine again.

I could sense him smirk as he hovered over my lips. I mentally rolled my eyes as I brought my hands away from his hair and around his chest to above his back.

"Hey!" He yelped out between chuckles, his hands were still around my waist causing me to jerk forward as he pulled me down to the ground where he tumbled back.

I fell on top of him with a groan and I couldn't help feeling like we had been in this position before.

Before I could get off of him however he quickly sat up, knocking my head with his chest as his hands pushed at my waist.

His knee came in between my legs and before I knew it, he was pinning me down on the ground. One of his hands grounded itself beside my head while the other gripped my left thigh, bending it in such a way that he could fit his body in between my legs. His bottom half rested on top of me and I couldn't help but blush at the familiar training position we would use on each other, now being used for other purposes.

An unfamiliar feeling stirred in the pit of my stomach as I let my head fall back against the grass. Looking up at Malakei, I panted slightly. My hand came up to rest under his arm, curling around to his shoulder while the other gripped at his side.

He stayed silent as he looked down at me curiously, panting before all of a sudden he leaned down and captured my lips.

My head tilted up as I brought my hand away from around his shoulder and moved it across his chest up the side of his neck.

Malakei smirked into the kiss and I did too, knowing that I was improving now made me more confident. When I felt Malakei's tongue enter my mouth, this time I wasn't afraid to let our tongues battle with each other's.

I allowed my head to fall back onto the ground after a moment of battling, Malakei's grip on my thigh tightened as I felt his body completely lay on top of mine. I gasped into his mouth, clutching at his side and this caused him to hum in amusement.

I didn't know what came over me then but I brought shifted my hips upwards. My body erupted in heat and tingles.

He immediately broke the kiss.

His head hid in my neck as he took his hand from my thigh to ground my hips to the floor, getting me to stop what I was doing.

My face scrunched up suddenly and I couldn't help but whimper at the unfamiliar pleasure shooting through my lower region.

"*Stop*. We need to stop." Malakei panted into my neck and I opened my eyes at this.

They immediately widened when I noticed Tara standing a few metres away, a gobsmacked expression on her face as she blinked repeatedly, trying to register what she was seeing before her.

I gasped and sat up quickly. Malakei groaned as he brought a hand up to my shoulder to try and stop me from sitting up too quickly.

"Dimples, it's okay. You didn't hurt me–"

"I fucking will you *son of a bitch*!"

Malakei immediately froze at the familiar voice of Tara and quickly turned around. His eyes widened when he noticed her standing there with a look as though she wanted to strangle him.

"Tara!" Malakei exclaimed through a nervous laugh which made me wince. "You look very beautiful today.

Did you do something with hair–"

Tara immediately rambled off in *Fasik*, making Malakei's face drain of colour and before I knew it, Tara was coming forward and pulling Malakei off of me.

"It is not what it looks!" Malakei whined before she started to throw punches at his arms in rage.

"No stop!" My eyes widened and I quickly scrambled to my feet over to Tara to try and get her to ease up on taking her anger out on Malakei but before I could reach her, she turned back to me with a conflicted emotion across her face. Torn between wanting to strangle either Malakei or me – for kissing the guy she had a crush on.

I only now realised what we did was a very bad idea.

She showed disappointment towards me, as if she were not at all happy with my choice of kissing – not just Malakei, but someone else entirely that wasn't her brother. As if I betrayed Raen.

"Please Tara let me explain. It's not like that. He was helping me–"

"What? Helping you?!" Tara raged, making my ears flatten and Malakei groaned. Malakei got up from the ground and stood at a small distance between her as he cradled his sore arm.

"Not what you think Tara."

"You were helping him with what Malakei? His fucking boner–"

"He was teaching me how to kiss." I spoke quickly trying to diffuse the situation. Anxiety and worry built in my eyes as I realised how much trouble this had caused.

At the revelation, both of them turned to me. Tara with

a shocked look which immediately turned sorrowful and filled with regret as I brought my hands up to clutch my painful ringing ears. I winced.

"He offered to show me how to kiss because I didn't know how. I didn't think it would be a bad idea. We were just messing around and I'm sorry. I'm *so sorry* Tara."

Tara opened her mouth to speak but immediately shut it. Her eyes filled with concern before she turned to Malakei with a neutral expression. Malakei furrowed his brows at her with a knowing look as he took in a breath.

"He wanted to impress Raen. I told him I could help and we both went with it. Although, he is one hell of kisser."

"Okay Malakei." Tara gritted out before sighing, sensing her gaze to where I sat on the ground with my knees up, I hid my face in them, massaging the pain from my ears.

I ignored Baja's curious stare from where it looked as though she had just woken up, now moving to get up and come over to me but I stopped her, assuring her through our mind link that I was fine, just sad. I wasn't in danger.

I could hear Tara move forward, feeling her hand running soothingly along my shoulder blades as she sat down beside me.

"Honey, it's okay. I'm not mad." She hummed as she linked her hand with mine. Malakei sat down beside me with a small apologetic smile as he took my other hand in his. I lifted my head to her.

"I'm sorry."

"Don't worry Keylin, it's not your fault." Tara's voice

was soft but I could sense her staring daggers into Malakei who sat beside me. He noticed and blushed, mouthing a 'sorry' and I whimpered at that.

"Please don't blame Malakei. If anything, blame *me*. He was only trying to help me." I said quietly and Tara frowned at this, sighing tiredly before frowning.

"Honey. Malakei's an idiot that thinks with his dick. You didn't have to kiss him to try and impress my brother. In fact, you should have just kissed my brother to begin with." She grumbled the last part, ignoring Malakei's glare.

"I was only helping him. It not like I forced him into anything he not comfortable with." Malakei mumbled, looking away slightly angry. I clutched his hand tightly in assurance and he sighed, squeezing back and rubbing soothing circles into the back of my hand with his thumb.

"Fine." Tara huffed before closing her eyes. "Let's just forget about this and move on. Let's not speak of it again–" She quickly opened her eyes to narrow them at Malakei who froze and let go of my hand, showing her he wasn't doing anything.

"Don't think you're getting away with this. If you touch him again, I'm not going to kill you *oh no*, I'm going to leave that to my brother."

Malakei's eyes widened into saucers at that and let out a small nervous laugh, shifting on the ground as he tried to avoid Tara's menacing smirk. I chuckled at that.

"And my brother." I stated quietly making Tara chuckle and Malakei turned to me with a roll of the eyes, a small smirk on his face before he winked at me playfully. I chuckled again at this and shook my head at him.

***

It was as Baja and I were walking back to Bow's house –
I still refused to call it my home for some reason because
I knew that it would take time for me to get comfortable
with adjusting to this place. I didn't stay there much.
Usually, I would be at Raen's but this time when I went
over to his tent, he wasn't there.

My heart sank a little when I saw this, immediately
knowing where he could be besides here and I didn't want
to think of him with Mila as I turned around and walked
in the direction of Bow's house. Baja tagged along silently.

*"Why am I falling for someone I'm not even sure wants
to be with me? How could I be so foolish with my heart?"*

I whispered to myself as I walked up to Bow's home.
The moment however I went to open the door, it was flung
open to reveal Bow; standing there with a startled
expression before his tongue darted to the side of his
cheek and he crossed his arms over his chest. He leaned
against the door frame.

"Well well, look who decided to show up."

He said in a somewhat teasing tone and I flinched
backwards slightly letting out a breath and looking up.
Baja growled softly from beside me.

Bow's eyes flickered down to Baja before they came
back up to settle on me, he pointed at the panther.

"She can't come in. She has to stay outside."

"What?" I frowned at the rule as I looked down at Baja.

"Just this once? She won't do anything wrong. She's quiet."

"Mother just washed the floors and rules are rules. Sorry Keylin. No animals in the house" He smiled apologetically before biting his lip.

"Come on," He pushed away from the door frame and brushed past me. I turned and followed him with a sigh, knowing he was leading us to the familiar small stable at the back of the wooden house.

"She stays in here."

Bow opened the small door to the stable, revealing the spacious room with a bundle of straw in the corner where they kept the food for the horses.

I breathed out watching Baja sniff at the familiar entrance before hesitantly taking a step inside. When she was comfortable, she turned around and sat, staring up at me as she did. Her glowing green eyes shone in the black of night.

After I communicated with Baja through our mind link, explaining the situation to her. She wasn't too impressed to be staying in the stable again, she wanted to be closer to me but accepted the situation nonetheless, turning around and going to the far corner near the straw before flopping down. Her head rested on the ground as she started to relax. I sighed at that, turning to Bow and nodding at him.

He nodded back before closing over the door slowly. I let out a breath at that, frowning at the separation evident between Baja and I. Trying to ignore it, I followed Bow back to his home around the corner.

"Father is leaving for *Jhovst* tomorrow," Bow started and I frowned, looking back up at him.

"He wants to see you before he leaves."

"How long is he going for this time?" I questioned and Bow scrunched his face at the thoughts.

"Two weeks."

"I'll go to him first thing in the morning." I sighed at that, not saying anything more as I reached the door. I made my way upstairs to Bow and I's room, saying a quick hello to Ana as I passed her before retiring for the evening.

XXIV

~*~

"You wished to see me father?"

I questioned curiously, slowly making my way inside the large tent that belonged to my father for battle strategies. It was something of a private study where he spent most of his time lately, ever since the appearance of the murk came to light. The same tent where I had been in before with the others the first day I met him. That was the day he had mentioned I would be staying with Bow and Ana before stating that he would be leaving. This was just like that time but I kept my lips in a firm line.

My father turned around, his soft eyes landed on mine and I knew a look like this was only for Bow and me.

I felt as though he was not a soft man by any means. He was the leader of the camp. One of many leaders of the Dry Landers. This man didn't have time to be soft when it came to business.

This made me slightly concerned if all of this was some sort of mask, a front he was putting on just for me but I shook the thought out of my head.

I was his son.

I was the only thing left for him to remind him of my mother whom he loved with all of his heart. He broke the rules for her and he almost threw his life away to bring me here – could still throw his life away if the higher–ups from the *Sky Lanes* were to find out about any of this, knowing it was against the rules to cross sectors.

"Keylin." He breathed out in relief before raising his eyebrow, a small smirk made its way onto his lips.

"I thought I was going to have to leave you without saying goodbye."

"I'm sorry." I apologised tiredly, scratching the back of my head. "Baja insisted I feed her before she let me wander freely."

My father chuckled, shaking his head at my revelation. It was then that I noticed he had something in his hands. My eyes trailed down to them curiously.

"That panther has you on a leash. She does understand that you are supposed to be the one in control right?" Father questioned fondly and I blushed, fiddling with my hands nervously as I let the small smile creep onto my lips.

"Until I am old enough to defend myself, she calls the shots apparently. I am only a child in her eyes and need to fill into my boots."

"I do not think you are a child." My father objected softly. "You are young but I can see where she is coming from. With time, you will grow to be a warrior Keylin – the best Dry Lander. You are my son, after all, I have no doubt you will take after me."

He looked down at his clasped hands briefly. A sad smile graced his lips as he motioned for me to come over to him.

"Come here Keylin, I have a gift for you."

I furrowed my brows at this but walked over nonetheless, looking up at him curiously about to speak when he brought what felt to be a chain around my neck. He tied a knot behind me that hung the small object.

I looked down, observing the object in my hand gently.

It was a silver half of an angel's wing. The wing itself had very precise detail with small swirls and engraved patterns that made my heart thump in my chest. I recognised these patterns. This necklace was made by the craft elves.

Father had been watching my reaction the whole time, trying to hide his pain as he smiled down at me with his hands resting on my shoulders. I gulped at the sudden realisation and my lips twitched as I spoke.

"My mother gave this to you, didn't she?"

"Yes." He smiled at what I believed was a happy memory. "She bared her half, as I did mine."

He brought his hand up to my blonde hair and smiled as he touched it, running it through his fingers.

"You remind me so much of her Keylin. Every day you look more and more like her. She would be proud of you. I know I am."

I blinked. His words sent a wave of emotion through

me that I didn't think was possible.

He was proud of me. A father who I thought was ashamed I existed before. Proud of me...

"I–I do not deserve your kind words…" I found myself saying as I blinked in a sort of daze. My mind tried to register everything.

My father only chuckled quietly and brought my head forward. My face buried in his strong chest while he kissed my hair briefly before pulling away and looking down at me.

"Of course you do Keylin. You are my son. So is Bow, I love you both with my heart. The same goes for Ana and my camp."

"You must have a big heart." I chuckled as I stepped back, my fingers touched the necklace while I smirked up at him. He smiled at that.

"I only show it to my most trusted. If word got out of a soft Dry Lander leader, I would be challenged constantly. Neighbouring tribes would threaten to destroy me and claim my people. I show a kindness to you Keylin but keep in mind, I am anything but fair when it comes to protecting my people. They come first. I have no doubt you will see my other side with time and learn the reason why I am the leader. Although I am your father, I am your leader first. What I say, goes. Are we understood?"

"Yes, father." I recognised him asserting his status as my leader first, then my father. Back in the *High Peaks*, it was different. I cleared my throat.

"I understand."

He smiled at this for a moment before coming forward

and embracing me again, his hands came up and around to the back of my head as he took in a shaky breath.

"I will be gone for two weeks. If you need anything, Raen will be of assistance. I want you to feel like you can go to him. Although he is quiet and difficult to approach, he is smart. He is my best warrior. He always knows what to do if something were to go wrong while I'm away."

I frowned at that but nodded my head in understanding either way, ignoring how my heart rate picked up at the mention of the boy that had been playing on my mind lately.

***

"Try not to get into trouble this time boys." Father chuckled as he adjusted himself on his black stallion, his fur brown coat hung off his shoulders held together by a golden clasp I had come to understand was a symbol of status here in the *Dry Lands*. He looked down at me pointedly. I couldn't help but roll my eyes jokingly.

"Have a safe trip."

I called up to him as I watched my father and a fair majority of his warriors leave through the barricades of the camp on their horses, disappearing into the treeline of the forest. They rode effortlessly, without any fear of what was to become of them once they entered the unpredictable wood.

I wanted to be like that when I was older.

"Assholes."

I jumped at Malakei's voice from behind me, turning

around quickly to see him standing with his arms folded as he watched the last of the warriors on their horses gallop into the forest.

Tara elbowed him in the ribs making him groan.

"Don't be disrespectful." She scolded him, frowning.

"I guess you couldn't screw your way into first line this time huh Malakei?"

Bow snorted and I turned to him and frowned, the rest of the small watchful group either ignored the comment or curled their lips to snigger.

"The line was same as last trip Bowen. As Maekin stated before." Malakei gritted out and I turned to him, watching him silently, his fists on either side of him clenched and unclenched. He turned to Bow with a smirk.

"I suppose you did not notice that, you block out what he saying most of time, with having daddy issues and all."

"You *fucking*–"

"*Enough*."

Raen's voice was like thunder as it echoed through the air around us, making my eyes search for him. I sensed him coming forward towards the two boys.

"If you both refuse to get along then go home. I will not tolerate petty bickering."

Both Malakei and Bow groaned in frustration at Raen's words and I couldn't help but snicker, throwing Malakei a raised brow to which he returned with a roll of the eyes, smiling at me.

I didn't know Raen could be this bossy. I could see why my father left him in charge. Neither Bow nor Malakei seemed to challenge him, they knew their place while our father was away. They knew not to cross him in fear of him becoming angry.

I didn't look at Raen, even though every now and then I could feel his intense stare on me.

"If it wasn't clear in the meeting this morning, I am in charge until Maekin gets back and if both of you even so much as raise a hand to one another, I swear to the gods above; you will regret it." Raen threatened seriously and was about to speak again when Tara interrupted with a snort, finding her brother's frustration amusing. All heads turned to her.

"Calm down psycho, they were just teasing. Right guys?"

A bored agreement came from Bow while a not–so–enthusiastic 'right' came from Malakei.

I threw a worried glance at him, understanding the power something like Bow's words could have. I remembered Tobias' words and how they would often hurt more than a simple punch.

I observed as Malakei let his eyes fall shut for a moment before reopening them with that familiar 'Malakei' smile that I recognised.

A huff of annoyance came from Raen as he stood with a thoughtful expression. Looking as though he was debating on telling them off further but he chose against it and let it slide.

"Fine. Carry on with your business I guess."

"We should hang out." Tara suddenly suggested. "All of us, that includes you too, Raen. It would be like old times." Tara smiled at her brother as the others nodded enthusiastically, Malakei whooped with excitement.

"I got alcohol at my tent. We can go right now. It will be great!" Malakei exclaimed excitedly and Raen's eyes widened as he shook his head.

"No alcohol."

"Aw come now brother, lighten up." Tara scolded and I couldn't help but chuckle softly at that, resulting in all eyes turning to me.

Malakei's eyes fell to me in realisation as he moved forward and slung an arm around my neck, pulling me into his chest despite my protests.

"The little one can have first taste! It will be fun–"

"Hey!" I poked my head out of Malakei's arms and glared up at him.

"I am not little. Just because I am shorter than you, does not make me small."

Tara, Bow and even Mila chuckled at my statement while Malakei only smirked, rolling his eyes before bringing me into another headlock. He chuckled at my attempts to get free.

"Let him go Malakei." Raen said in an unamused tone. His emotionless eyes observed us with a frown.

"Hmm..." Malakei hummed and I elbowed him, making him flinch inwardly but continued to keep his hands around me. I whined and ploughed my head into his stomach in frustration causing him to chuckle as we stumbled backwards. His fingers tangled at the hair around my neck.

"I will if you hang with us. Have fun Raen, it will be great." Malakei said in between chuckles as I began to throw blind punches at his chest to get him to release me.

I could hear Raen chuckle after I brought my hand down on Malakei's chest hard, causing him to grimace but his hold tightened as he pulled me closer. I let out a huff of breath, my arms tiring already.

"It looks like you're feeling the effect." Raen sounded like he was smirking. "He'll be free in a moment or so by the way he's going."

Malakei snorted at that.

"He's tiring. I know every move he makes. I train him."

"*Katcha*!" I cursed him at the top of my lungs.

"Let me go already. My neck hurts!" I stated before smiling evilly and punching him hard in the belly button.

I suddenly felt Malakei's hands being ripped from around my head and two hands grabbed my waist tightly. I gasped as I was pulled away from Malakei, stumbling back into a warm body.

"Enough."

I panted slightly, exhausted as I looked up at Raen beside me. He narrowed his eyes as he and Malakei glared at each other.

"Finally." Tara chuckled as she made her way past us, grabbing Malakei's arm and pulling him along with her, causing him to stumble back slightly. I rolled my eyes and stuck my tongue out at him.

"Let's go already! I hope you saved the good stuff under your bed." Tara noted seriously as she turned around to Malakei who shrugged nonchalantly.

I went to move forward when the hands around my waist dragged me back, keeping me in place. I gasped when I collided with Raen's chest again. His grip on me never faltered as I twisted my head to stare up at him in confusion.

"Hey! What are you–"

"You are not drinking." Raen stated matter–of–factly before nudging me forward, I turned around as I walked to glare at Raen behind me. He began to walk too.

"Why not?" I asked confused. "It's one drink Raen. I'll probably hate it. I just want to try–"

"I said no." Raen raised a brow at me as he nudged me forward to move again after I stopped to speak. My breath hitched as I stumbled back.

"If you even take a sip, I will drag you home by your ears. Understood?"

He raised a brow at me and I narrowed my eyes at him, ignoring him. I went to walk forward but he pulled me back into him again and I groaned.

"Fine, I get it," I grumbled out. "No drinking."

I could sense his smile near my head and it infuriated me, causing a scowl to form on my face. Huffing when I felt his fingers remain on my waist unmoving, I twisted my head to look up at him.

"Can you let go please?" I raised a brow at him just as he did the same. He furrowed his brows down at me curiously. A glint appeared in his eyes as a small innocent–looking smile formed on his lips and it startled me slightly.

"Since you asked nicely–" He began before shoving me forward, I caught myself before I could fall face first. A small victory chant played in my head as I smirked triumphantly, sending him a dirty look.

"*Katcha*."

Smack.

I let out a high–pitched squeal when his hand slapped my ass, causing my body to lurch forward at the sensation. I threw a pointed and wide–eyed glare back at him. My cheeks and ears were tinted red from embarrassment. Raen glared back.

"D–Did you just–"

"Do not curse me in your language. I am not an idiot Keylin. Now *walk*."

I quickly turned around to hide my face as I walked quickly ahead. My face burned as I heard Raen laugh in amusement from behind.

'Gods, what was up with him today?'

***

We arrived shortly after at Malakei's tent. The others had already made themselves at home and got started with finding food to eat in various places around the tent hidden by Malakei. It was Bow that found the alcohol. Excitement and victory clouded his vision.

The rest of the evening went by much the same. The others drank and talked about random things, laughing and joking with one another.

Even Bow and Malakei were getting on well like long–time friends, as if all traces of fighting with one another earlier had disappeared from their memories.

Alcohol was strange. I could understand now when they said it messed with your head. Malakei's face turned bright red as he laughed at nothing. Tara did much the same but insisted on singing randomly while Bow talked nonsense.

Raen didn't drink. As much as the others had pleaded, they didn't push him. They knew better. Instead, Raen engaged in conversation with them, all the time keeping a watchful eye on me. I found him turning to look at me when he thought I wasn't watching and I could feel his stare on me the whole night.

Tara held her glass out to me in a teasing manner, ruffling her eyebrows at me in suggestion. She knew I wanted to try it but as much as I wanted to, I knew that a certain Dry Lander wouldn't allow it.

"No thanks." I sighed looking down at my hands to avoid her eyes, biting my lip. Raen's attention turned to me when I spoke, cutting Malakei off from his talking.

"Come on," Tara moaned as she rolled her eyes. She got up from where she was sprawled on Malakei's couch and came over to me – or more stumbled. She placed the glass in my hands.

"There's not much left. Have it. Tell me how it tastes."

"Tara." Raen warned and my eyes looked up in alert at his tone. Our eyes locked from where each of us sat at opposite ends of the room.

"I know." She huffed as I handed her back the glass of what I could only presume was red wine. Malakei and Bow whined.

"You have him on leash." Malakei chuckled, causing Raen and I to turn to him sharply. Raen's eyes narrowed as a blush crept onto my cheeks. I frowned afterwards at the statement while the others laughed in agreement.

"No, he doesn't." I protested with hurt evident in my voice. I knew that Malakei only meant it as a joke but I couldn't help but be offended.

Raen didn't control me. Just because he didn't want me to drink was reasonable; I was still young and there was possibly the effect that something could go wrong. It was my decision. If I wanted a drink, Raen didn't have a choice because it wouldn't be his to make, it was *mine*.

Bow scoffed, startling me out of my thoughts. His eyes held frustration as he looked at me.

"He's pretty timid for a Dry Lander but I guess that's the elf side. *Submissive*."

Tara spluttered from beside me, leaning forward and almost spilling her drink on me. Malakei gave a half–hearted laugh before finding the pillow interesting from where he lay on the floor.

My anger was slowly starting to bubble as Bow let his head fall back in hysterics, finding his own statement funny while I didn't find it the least bit amusing.

"Shut up Bow–"

"I think it's cute." Tara interjected and Bow rolled his eyes.

"You think everything he does is cute. I bet you're secretly hoping he gets with your brother so he can be a part of the *Daskalov* family."

'Raen and Tara Daskalov. Their last name.'

"Oh it's going to happen someday and when it does I will be the first to know." Her words were slightly slurred as she wagged a finger in his direction. Mila made a noise of disagreement from where she lounged on the opposite side of Malakei near the floor.

"He tells me everything. You wouldn't be the first." Mila informed in a sing–song voice making Tara roll her eyes and take another sip of her wine.

This conversation was starting to become really uncomfortable. Why did they have so much interest in what Raen and I did – or what we didn't do actually? It was none of their business in the first place.

Bow leaned towards me from where he sat on the couch. Six bottles of beer displayed like trophies around him as he cupped his mouth in a whisper formation, eyes glossy and far away.

"Does he know you're a virgin?"

"Bow!" I exclaimed in both shock and exasperation as I stood up. My face fell at Bow's words while Mila and Tara's eyebrows shot up in both interest and slight surprise. Malakei didn't react because he already knew. I didn't even look at Raen. The embarrassment was too much as my face flushed with anger towards my brother. Betrayal filled my eyes.

That was a secret. I told him that in confidence and he was the one that informed me not to tell anyone in the first place because it could be dangerous for me if anyone were to find out.

I watched as Bow only chuckled. The hurt on my face was amusing to him. If this was what he was like drunk, then I never wanted to drink alcohol.

I sensed Raen stand up and my eyes flew to him. His jaw was clenched as he threw on his coat and turned towards me. He looked ready to leave the messy situation before it could escalate further. His eyes said all they needed to say.

'I'll take you home.'

Was this why he didn't like drinking?

"Oh that's precious." Tara squealed suddenly beside me, making me wince. My ears became over–sensitive now as she tried to hug me but I pulled away from her, shaking my head.

"Get away from me." I whispered out in slight panic. Either she didn't hear me or completely ignored it and started to reach for me again. I stumbled back as Bow and Mila chuckled.

I quickly turned to Bow with a panicked look, sensing Raen move closer to me.

"Why?" I asked lowly, eyes now glassy as my heart thumped in my chest. "Why would you–"

"It slipped out!" Bow groaned before letting out a hiccup. I only frowned at him. He wasn't one bit sorry and it fuelled my anger towards him.

"Wow." Mila let out a scoff and my hands clenched into fists at my side. Malakei sat up with a frown, looking to have regained some sense of the conversation that turned south very quickly.

"That was not cool." Malakei stated as he glared at Bow. Bow stopped laughing and shoved Malakei back. His force was sloppy.

"You only care now because you want to get in his pants. If I didn't know any better, you're trying harder now just to be his first–"

"Fuck you Bow." Malakei shook his head and retracted his left leg slightly to shoot forward, kicking Bow in the shin which made him groan.

Tara's eyes widened at Bow's words before she frowned, looking past me to Malakei.

"Wait what? I thought you both were just friends, doesn't he like Raen?"

My ears rang and eyes bulged at Tara's words. Another secret exposed.

One that I didn't even have the privilege of saying to Raen myself. Now everyone knew I liked him, including Raen himself.

Breathing was becoming hard as my eyes trained on Tara's. When she spotted my tear–stricken eyes, her smile dropped and the realisation of what she just said sunk in. She brought her hand up to close over her mouth. Her eyes pleaded with mine, trying to convey the emotion of how sorry she was to me but I shook my head at her, backing away from the now silent room.

"I – no. I don't…"

I whispered in almost a daze as I began to back away to the entrance of the tent, past a frozen Raen. Malakei got up when he noticed me about to leave.

"Keylin wait."

It was Malakei's voice but I looked at Raen for the first time, shame and hurt on my features, embarrassment being the dominant emotion. Sadness, anger and fear also swirled around in them.

Raen's eyes were emotionless. I didn't even know what he was thinking as he looked at me. This news of a silly little crush must repulse him to no end.

There went our friendship – or whatever we had.

I turned around and left through the entrance of the tent ignoring the protests and calls of my name as I did.

XXV

~*~

"They are all horrible beings." I whispered out. My voice was dry and sore from crying relentlessly for what felt like hours.

Baja only puffed air at me, almost in agreement as she lifted her head up slightly, licking my tear–stained cheeks while I snuggled up to her side. I was cold and craved comfort from someone. Baja, as strange as it sounded – being the next thing to Mara.

I smiled a small smile as Baja finished cleaning my cheeks and let her head rest on top of mine. I shivered as her furry chin tickled my forehead.

'Only evil beings are those among The Shadows.'

Her soothing voice made me want to sleep as she purred deep in her throat. The sound vibrated through my head.

Somehow I ended up falling asleep in Baja's presence

knowing that I was safe with her, which must have comforted my mind into relaxation – I was exhausted.

I only stirred when a low and threatening growl rippled from her throat and the small wooden door to the stables behind Bow's house slowly began to open. It closed quietly and hesitant footsteps slowly made their way to Baja and me.

Baja let her body relax at the sight of the intruder, but her head shifted to the ground instead of where it nuzzled protectively against mine. I didn't bother to check who it was. I had a feeling that it was only Bow coming to apologise, he was the only one who knew where I could be, if not back at his house.

I didn't want to see anyone right now. So I clutched Baja's fur and gulped, refusing to turn my head as I spoke.

"I've got nothing to say to you Bow. *Please*, just leave. Right now I just want to be alone."

Bow stopped in his trek to me but no sooner did he stop he continued with his walk and proceeded to kneel by my side. I felt his hand on my shoulder and flinched away. My blood boiled as I let out a whine.

"I told you to–"

I stopped in the act of turning my body around to Bow and froze up.

My face paled when I realised it wasn't my brother standing behind me.

It was Raen.

He raised a brow at my speechless complexion and I let out a shaky breath, averting my eyes to the ground as I pulled myself up into a sitting position. I brought my knees up closer to my chest now with caution.

"W–What do you want?"

"You will freeze out here," Raen stated softly. "I looked for you. Bow told me you might be here."

"I'm not leaving." I shifted my hands from my knees down to my legs as I kept my eyes glued to the floor.

"I don't want to sleep in his house."

"It is your house too."

Raen informed quietly and I only bit my lip at that, not looking up at him because of how gently he spoke to me, as if me liking him had no effect on him and he just ignored it. As if my feelings didn't matter. He probably didn't care about it anyway. He was most likely used to this attention. I remembered Mila and I couldn't help but scowl at the ground.

"Mila is staying with Bow tonight,"

Speak of the devil.

I jumped when he placed his hand on my right shoulder. His thumb rubbed circles into the joining of my neck and shoulder and chills ran down my spine at the sensation.

He made me feel like this and he didn't even have to try. He did it unknown to himself. Either that, or he felt sorry for me.

"You can stay with me tonight."

I looked up at him in confusion before shrugging my shoulders. His hand slipped down to my collarbone.

"Are you sure you want that?" I gulped as my face fell and looked back down at the ground.

"You... don't mind?"

His hand moved from my collarbone to my chin. He pulled it up, making me look up to him.

"Of course not." He stated as if what I said was ridiculous.

"Stay with me tonight." He repeated as he got up. I looked up at him, confusion still on my face before he reached out a hand to me and helped me up onto my feet.

I was relieved that he didn't treat me any differently than before. If he did, I didn't notice because if this was his way of showing me hate, he had shown it to me multiple times before and I wasn't fazed.

It hurt that he didn't even acknowledge my feelings. As much as I wanted for us right now to go back to being friends, I needed to hear what he was thinking. I still didn't know what he thought of me and it scared me slightly. What I have been feeling lately, I needed to know if he felt the same.

"Why?" I found myself asking as he led me through the wooden door to the outside, Baja followed lazily behind and Raen glanced back at me but said nothing.

I jerked my hand back from him and we both stopped. He turned back to me with furrowed eyes that softened when he noticed the hurt in mine.

"Just tell me," I whispered tiredly and he blinked at me, refusing to budge. I brought my hand up to my hair, running a hand through it to calm me down and frowned up at him.

"I just want to know what you're thinking and I'm not crazy..." I mumbled as I brought my hands around my chest. A cold breeze blew as the windy night picked up.

"You are cold. Come on." He reached to grab my arm again but I stepped back shaking my head, eyes filled with frustration.

"Raen!"

"What?" Raen let his hand fall back to his side as he stared at me wide–eyed. He swallowed nervously.

He was acting weird around me, ignoring my questions and hiding something. I could tell. He looked conflicted most times and I just wanted him to speak his mind. To tell me what he was thinking.

"Talk to me," I pleaded. "*Please*. If this is making you uncomfortable I can go back and–"

"No." Raen cut me off confidently, and I shut my mouth, taking in his conflicted and agitated expression. This looked hard for him.

"No, Keylin. I–I want you to stay with me," He got out. "and I'm worried about you catching a cold out here."

I ignored my trembling from the cold of night but Raen didn't. His eyes immediately drifted to my shaking arms.

He suddenly sighed, reached forward and picked me up – placing me over his shoulders when he realised I wasn't going to move and trudged the rest of the way to his tent to get out of the cold of night.

"Raen!" I hit his shoulder and back – anywhere that I thought would get a reaction from him. As much as I didn't want to, I knew it was the only way to generate some sort of feeling from the man showing me he wasn't made of stone.

"You can't just pick people up and carry them away! What's your problem?"

Raen didn't respond to me or do anything else besides trudge forward.

The transition of cold to heat was noticeable as we entered his tent, it hit me like a wave and I let out a shaky sigh. My heart was beating wildly in my chest as he continued to stalk into his tent, not letting me down.

"Raen put me down already."

Not a moment later he lowered me down onto his bed. Raen brought both of his hands to either side of my head, his body moved in between my legs as his face came closer to mine. He had me pinned between his body and the bed and I didn't know how I felt about that.

All too quickly, Raen pulled back from me and brought space between us. I couldn't help but let out a breath I didn't know I was holding until I panted. My eyes never left him as I watched him retreat.

Was this why he wanted me in his tent?

"Take off your clothes." Raen demanded softly and I froze at his words, face paling as I went to shake my head and speak but he turned around to look for something in the far corner. I got to my feet and took a glance at the entrance.

Baja entered through the tent then, tongue out as she leapt onto the couch, licking her paws and blissfully unaware of everything.

I turned as Raen looked up from what he was doing. His eyes narrowed slightly as he must have noticed what I was thinking of doing.

"Take them off Keylin."

"Why?" I gulped. "W–What are you going to do?"

He let out an annoyed sigh and shut the chest at the end of the bed.

I stepped back slightly at this on alert, my face quickly hardening. I brought my hands up, ready to put up a fight if needed.

His eyes found mine as he walked closer. Soft but there was a pang of hurt in them, his lips pressed into a thin line as he held out some spare night clothes for me to wear.

I stared at the clothes in his hands before looking back up at him. My hard exterior fell as I let a tear slip from my eyes. I knew my face was flushed with embarrassment. He looked confused as he held out the clothes and I felt like a fool for doubting him, for thinking lowly of him. I hid my face in my hands.

"Here." He coaxed gently and I brought my hands away from my face to look at the clothes he was holding out for me to take.

"Clean clothes."

"Why do you do things like this? I thought… I thought you were going to..." I trailed off. My words died in my mouth.

Something flashed through Raen's eyes for a split moment before his jaw clenched. He looked furious at my suggestion.

"What led you to believe I would do such a thing?"

I took the clothes from him and his reaction alone gave me the security I needed to take off my shirt, putting on the new one immediately to cover my bare chest and stomach, feeling immediately better to be covered now. I scoffed at this pitifully and looked up with a vulnerability

I tried so desperately to hide.

"Why not?" I counteracted. "You found out a few hours ago that I'm a virgin and like you."

"You're right, it was a surprise," He bit his lip to keep the frown from showing. "But I am not the monster you believe I am."

"I didn't mean to upset you, Bow was the one that told me that it could be dangerous if other Dry Landers found out. I thought you–"

"I knew you were a virgin Keylin." He interrupted softly. His voice was nothing but calm ever since I started speaking my mind and showing a side of myself that he had not seen before. Either way, his words made me stop mid–sentence.

"You did?"

He let his lids fall in frustration as he took a breath to gather the words, only opening his eyes then when he exhaled looking far away as he thought back to a memory.

"You have ah... the sun in your eyes. Like a firefly. Innocent and pure light Keylin. It is hard to miss."

A sparkle?

I couldn't keep my dimples from poking out as I tried to hide the smile at his words of describing me and how he could've known. Now I knew why he didn't say much. He didn't have the words most of the time to describe how he felt or wanted to say. His actions spoke louder than words but sometimes, not the words he wanted to say.

"Keylin?"

I jumped slightly when his hand brushed against my cheek, his thumb ran under my eye at the stray tears. I looked up at him and noticed the small crease of worry on his forehead. Our eyes met and that glint returned to his.

I brought my hand up to cup over his on my cheek, my eyes didn't look away from his stunning green ones that marvelled at me like I was some shiny diamond. I needed to know how he felt about me and I needed to choose my words delicately. I sat down on the bed.

"Raen..." I started and gulped visibly. "I can't tell if there's something between us. Most of the time... I can't tell how you feel about me."

Raen blinked down at me and bit his lip thoughtfully, eyebrows furrowing before he slowly took my hand from over his, bringing it closer to him and holding it flat against his chest. Over his heart.

He looked at me with the same expression as he spoke. He formed my hand so that I was pointing at his heart now. He moved left slightly, sectioning his heart into three chambers.

"Tara."

He moved to the opposite side.

"Friends..." He moved down. "Camp."

He stopped for a moment and simply looked down at me. A small tug of his lips was evident before he frowned again. He dragged my finger in a circular motion, around each of the chambers, lining his whole heart instead of small separate sectors.

"*Keylin.*"

My eyes widened at the word, moving them away from his chest and up to his soft gaze that was already fixed on me. Maybe it was fixed on me the whole time. All I knew was my heart did cartwheels as he now laid my hand flat against his chest. His other hand came up to brush the hair from my forehead.

I didn't expect that.

From what I got from his warming gesture of hands and metaphors... Raen loved me. He loved me with *literally*, all of his heart. I was everything to him.

He looked down at me expectantly, but I couldn't muster any words. I was speechless.

Raen sighed and sank to his knees in front of me, grabbing both of my hands and holding them in his.

I blinked down at him. This was definitely a different side to Raen that I thought I had never seen but I was wrong. I had seen it. The fireflies, the lake, even when we were fighting in the rain...

"I will wait for you Keylin," Raen started. "I have waited this long – since I first saw you're beautiful green eyes. I will not ruin it now. You are what I want, *all* I want. I will wait as long as you want me to, until you are ready. Until you are *mine*."

Raen brought my hands up to his lips to kiss and I let out a hitched breath feeling the familiar sting behind my eyes as I pierced my lips at him.

"I will not take what is not mine."

I let my eyes close at that and moved forward to his surprise, latching my arms around him. My face buried into his neck as I let out a shaky breath of relief.

Raen's hands held me close to him, closing over the middle of my back. His nose was close to my hair and I could feel him inhale quietly before kissing the side of my head. I couldn't help but smile into his neck, tasting the saltiness from my tears as I did.

"Thank you for understanding," I mumbled into his neck and I felt him stiffen at my words. One of his hands came up to the back of my head and I pulled back from his neck to look at him.

"I think a part of me has always known…" I began, biting back my wobbly lip. "Us elves are strong believers in things happening for a reason. I believe our souls were meant to find each other. I don't know much about love or if it even exists. All I know is when you're near me my heart *sings* and cries when we are apart. I want to be close to you. It's a strange feeling to describe, I don't even know if my words make sense."

"I hear you." He whispered, voice cracking. "Loud and clear."

My lips wobbled into a smile when I noticed his glassy–eyed expression and I brought my hands up to thread through his hair.

He blinked repeatedly and I couldn't help the small chuckle as I too, blinked away tears falling from my eyes.

"We really should talk more. It gets us to places quicker." My voice cracked from how raw and dry my throat was. Raen sniffled as he looked back down at me, a small smile on his lips as he nodded.

Leaning down, he kissed my cheeks where the tears made my face damp and I smiled at that. He hovered slightly over my lips, eyes flickering between my eyes and lips and I smiled at his hesitancy before bringing him closer to me.

Our lips found each other's in a tangle of tears. I couldn't help but sigh into his mouth when my heart sang a familiar beat and felt relieved that this was happening, how I had wanted this to happen for a while now. It was finally happening.

The kiss was innocent and for the first time, I was kissing Raen, a real kiss. This one poured with passion and love.

Our lips moved in sync with each other's until we broke off panting, lips throbbing slightly from having been kissing each other for quite some time. I didn't even notice his hands had moved down to my waist.

Raen trailed his hands up my back causing shivers. I noticed his smirk and I knew right then that he knew of the effect he had on me.

He was the cause of the effect.

XXVI

~*~

I bolted upright from the bed just as a heart–wrenching scream left my lips, eyes scrunching tightly as I heaved for air.

"Keylin." Raen's voice was laced with worry and I didn't notice his hands around me, where he must have pulled me into his lap amidst my night–terror. Raen sat upright, with me laying across his lap. Once I regained myself from my loss of breath, I found him looking down at me. His worry–filled eyes matched his voice fuelled with concern.

"Are you alright?" He panted.

Why was he out of breath? And how did I get in this position?

"W–What..?–" I started as I continued to pant, looking around me in confusion.

I spotted Baja at the end of the bed staring at me silently. She bowed her head slightly when our eyes met and lowered herself onto the sheets, a feeling of relief filled my mind from her.

"What happened?" I asked quietly as I shifted into a sitting position on his lap instead of him holding me up. Raen gulped, brows furrowing.

"You tell me," He said quietly. "You were thrashing in your sleep Keylin. I was trying to wake you up for a few minutes now, but you didn't. You screamed."

I blinked in confusion as what Raen said began to sink in and my heavy breathing started up again.

Through my daze, Raen narrowed his eyes and quickly placed his hands on my forehead, checking to see if I had a high temperature or if I was brewing a fever. The last thing I needed right now was to get sick.

"*Nightmare.*" I mumbled as soon as Raen took his hand from my forehead before bringing my own hand up to run through my hair nervously. I gulped looking down and away from his intense stare.

"It was just a nightmare."

Raen didn't look convinced and voiced his thoughts as he let one of his hands rest on my knee.

"Are you sure you are alright? You worried me Keylin–"

"I'm sorry." I looked up at that. I swallowed back the tingling in my throat and brought my hand up to rest on his cheek.

"It was nothing. Just a dream. I'm fine Raen. We should get back to sleep."

I sent him an assuring smile as he moved his hand from my knee, up my thigh and to my side where he had a better hold to prevent me from falling backwards. He sighed at that and brought his forehead closer until both of our foreheads were touching.

He didn't say anything. He didn't need to. The small action was enough and I took in a calming breath, closing my eyes before re–opening them. A relaxed sigh left my lips.

"Thank you." The words went with my breath. His eyes never shifted from their concern and he said nothing. Instead, he placed a reassuring kiss to my lips before shifting me from his lap.

I slowly curled on my side facing away from Raen and I let the memory of the dream sink in.

It was the first time that I had a dream like that – one that was so real and almost like it wasn't a dream at all, but more of a warning.

"Rest Keylin."

I felt Raen whisper into my ear as his arm snaked around my waist making my body tingle at the sensation. It felt nice.

I sighed and decided to close my eyes for the night, knowing there was no use in worrying about it now. I would go to the forest tomorrow, even if only to put my mind at rest.

I needed to find Corrin.

Raen's breathing hit the top of my head. Soon, I was drifting to the sound of insects of the night and Raen's even breathing was the last thing I heared before I fell asleep. I didn't forget the dream.

***

"I'm sorry."

I frowned down at my breakfast where Raen, Malakei, Tara and I currently sat at one of the nearby food benches, Baja at my side. She aimlessly stared at my runny porridge when my brother suddenly appeared with his apology. The words tumbled out of his mouth the minute he was within reach of me.

"It's alright," I turned to look up at him, eyes squinting from the sun as I did so.

"What?" He gaped. "You... you're not upset?"

"I was, but not anymore. Honestly I really just want to forget it happened. It's done, I can't go back and change it. Let's just move on from it. Besides, it was the alcohol right?" I shrugged, looking back down at my porridge with furrowed brows.

"I still feel terrible about it, I'm used to fist–fights and tempers. We shouldn't even be talking right for another two days at least."

"I'm sure if you let out another one of my secrets in the future, you will definitely get that reaction from me. For now, apology accepted."

Seeing the relief on Bow's face as I said those words made the corners of my lips tug upwards and he took a seat on the bench beside Raen's sister.

Tara and Malakei had apologised for their actions of the previous night but I dismissed them. I didn't want this rift to settle between us or them to feel bad for having fun, even if that meant spilling secrets of mine. Although I didn't expect Malakei to apologise, he did nothing wrong if I remembered right. As much as he was drunk, he refrained from saying much. He barely teased me that night, which I would have expected from him.

All in all, I was glad they did spill my secret. Raen and I wouldn't be where we were right now if they didn't.

Raen sat on my right while Malakei sat to my left, already finished his porridge and was now shovelling toast into his mouth. Tara only looked on with a curl of her lip, indicating disgust as Malakei did this.

Raen and I were keeping our feelings for each other from our friends for now. At least, I thought so, the way he treated me hadn't changed and I was okay with that. I didn't want to tell anyone yet, I was still figuring things out. Raen needed to show strength and an ability to lead without a distraction.

Raen, however, wasn't afraid to hold my hand under the bench while he ate his porridge silently. It made me blush as I slowly ate mine. The only time I pulled away from him was to push Baja down from the table. Bow let out a strangled yelp when Baja almost dipped her head into his porridge.

The others chatted randomly amongst themselves while I gave the rest of my porridge to Baja, knowing it was her favourite food.

I quickly grabbed an apple from the centre table, almost choking on it when I felt Raen's hand rest on my knee. I blushed as I felt his hand move up to rest on the inside of my thigh.

I looked at him, startled by his actions. My ears twitched furiously as his touch seared my skin. He only smirked into his vastly diminishing bowl of porridge. I bit my lip at this, he knew exactly the effect he had on me and glorified in it.

After breakfast, Malakei and I made our way to the forest edge to continue with our training.

I was waiting for the precise moment to 'wander off' and wanted to search for Corrin but my attention was solely focused on the Dry Lander who insisted on coming with me.

I knew Malakei wasn't feeling it today because of his headache that he was constantly reminding me of, resulting in his slaking ability.

"We can stop if you need." I spoke, earning a scoff from him as if my words were teasing alone. He only stated that a trainee like me, with little experience in fighting, was almost mocking a fighter as skilled as Malakei.

"I've just got something on my mind." Malakei sighed and shook his head in a grimace.

"Do you want to talk about it?"

Malakei stepped back, panting slightly as he took in my expression. He contemplated my words before his gaze met mine, somewhat serious.

Suddenly, a smile forced itself onto his features and he shook his head lightly. His eyes left mine and refused to return. I frowned, opening my mouth to speak before biting my lip nervously.

"Is it my brother?"

A look of confusion made its way onto Malakei's face and I continued. A wave of anger took over me at the thought of my brother and his harsh treatment towards my friend.

"Is he giving you a hard time?"

"No it's–"

"Don't listen to him Mal. Bow can't hold his tongue and his words can be hurtful but I'm sure he doesn't mean it. He's just jealous of you okay?"

Malakei remained silent as he listened to me, to my words before he let out a small sigh. I wasn't sure if it was from relief or frustration.

"Why would he be jealous of me?"

I moved to sling my arm across his shoulder, mimicking how he had done so with me when I was usually down about something in an event to try and cheer him up and smiled at him.

"Because you're funny, kind and handsome. You can get someone so easily when he has no one."

Malakei chuckled dryly at that as he looked down, shaking his head lightly. I noticed the slight rosiness to his cheeks at my words.

"Is that so?"

I frowned at that and immediately stopped walking, bringing my arm away from Malakei's shoulder only to turn my body in front of his line of vision. My eyes searched his as I brought my hands up to rest on his shoulders.

I felt Malakei tense under my hands but he immediately

relaxed and kept a neutral face to look down at me with a raise of his brow.

"Well, whatever it is, you know I'm here for you. Whenever you need to talk. I'm always here. We're brothers remember?"

Malakei smiled at that, a smile that didn't quite reach his eyes but a gleam of understanding was clear in them. All I could process was the playful smirk coming from my best friend in assurance as he assured me that he was fine.

"*Brothers.*"

He emphasised as he brought his hand out in front of him in what appeared to be a Dry Lander handshake. I grabbed his hand firmly and we both squeezed tightly. Malakei smirked at my determined features but looked exhausted as if something was keeping him up at night. He looked like he was far from sad but also far from happiness…

"Keylin, I–"

Malakei started, bringing me out of my thoughts but when I looked up at him to continue, he had shut his mouth and was now staring ahead of me with an emotionless expression. His gaze landed on something in the bushes.

I frowned and turned around, only to let out a sigh of relief when Raen and Bow stepped through the bushes. I was glad it wasn't a murk.

Malakei retracted his hand from our grip and stepped back when he noticed the others. Raen's gaze landed on me and he nodded my way in greeting before doing the same to Malakei.

"What are you both doing out here?"

Raen questioned in confusion towards us, indicating that we were a little further than the edge of the forest beside our camp.

"They're sparring." Bow replied for us and my gaze turned to my brother. He smiled at me in greeting before quickly sending a punch to my arm.

"*Ow*," I grunted. My eyebrows knitted together in pain as my mouth fell open. My hand immediately went up to cradle my injured arm before focusing on a smirking Bow and they turned to slits.

"What was that for?"

"That was for running off with Malakei without telling anyone and leaving your cat in distress."

Bow said with a slight edge to his voice and I lowered my head at his words. My ears flattened as I apologised for my careless actions.

"What are you two doing here?" Malakei asked lightly from behind me, his eyes trained on Raen and ignoring the roll of the eyes from my brother. I frowned at that.

"Well if it isn't obvious, we're looking for you, stupid."

"Knock it off Bowen." I gritted out as I turned to him. Fed up with how he constantly treated my best friend, the thought that his actions could be taking a toll on Malakei's health made me sick.

"Stop treating him like shit."

"Calm down Key, I'm only joking–"

"It's strange..." I began with a humourless laugh and cast my gaze up to the trees curiously.

"This situation right here reminds me of how the other

elves used to tease me because of how I looked. They would reply with 'We were only joking' or 'it was just teasing'. Everyone knew it was more than that and it was true,"

I gulped and blinked furiously to erase the memories my mind replayed from my childhood.

"It's all just fun and games until one day, they try to kill you. They almost succeed too. If they weren't caught."

My eyes landed back on Bow to see him blinking at me in shock. He resembled an animal caught in a trap. The phrase suited his features right now as he gulped and the look of regret made its way onto his face.

"I have never and will never hurt Malakei. I tease him and I know I can go too far but that's it. Just teasing. I am not ill–minded like those elves that hurt you Keylin and I don't want you to see me like that because I'm not a monster. I feel horrible knowing that all this time you had a problem with Mal and I's interactions, I'm so sorry – to you too Malakei, really. I didn't mean to upset you."

Malakei nodded in acceptance as Bow reached out to bring me into a side hug, his face dug into my hair and I relaxed at this. I brought my hands around him to squeeze, assuring him that it was okay. He pulled back.

"I'm sorry, I'll do better." Bow whispered and a small smile made its way onto my features.

"Thank you."

"No problem."

***

"You didn't have to do that."

Malakei's footsteps fell in line with mine, we were all making our way back to the camp seeing as sundown was nearing and it was time for everyone to be heading back to the camp before nightfall.

I gave a glance to my side at Malakei, finding him staring ahead with a conflicted expression.

"I know." I breathed out and he turned to me with a raised brow.

Malakei opened his mouth to speak before letting a smile replace his words as he shook his head softly, bumping our shoulders together as we walked.

"You are something special *Angelov*."

My ears twitched at the use of my last name and I couldn't keep the smile from my lips as I looked to the ground.

"Hey," Malakei started thoughtfully, a knowing smile gracing his features.

"Did you know last name means 'son of angel' in our language?"

I looked at him puzzled, blinking in shock as the thought had never occurred to me.

"No. I guess I didn't."

I turned to Malakei with a smile to which he returned warmly.

"It fits you," He contemplated. "I have never seen angel but I know they lose when it comes to you."

I stumbled over my own feet at not just Malakei's 'almost' perfect grammatical sentence, but his comparison of me to something similar to an angel.

I never believed to have ever heard the word 'angel' and my name used in the same sentence together. That was until Malakei spoke and made the impossible possible.

He chuckled when I almost tripped, bringing his hand out to catch my wrist before he sent me a familiar smirk I was starting to grow fond of.

"Falling for me already *dimples*?"

He might just be the death of me.

***

Malakei and I parted ways when we entered the camp while Raen got whisked away to deal with a matter at the barricade. Bow and I walked back to his house.

Our house.

It still felt weird to say.

We conversed and laughed with Ana over dinner and for once, a family meal together made the place feel like a real home.

It was only when Bow and I were upstairs in his room, about to go to bed that a large horn was blown, acting as a sort of signal of distress.

It was cut short only moments later. As if it were never there in the first place.

But I had heard it, and so did Bow.

"What was that?" I asked, noticing how the air grew tense and silent. Bow hastily threw on his clothes, cursing in Fasik as he moved about frantically within the room.

"The signal…" Bow breathed out fearfully as if the

word was sacred and rarely used. I watched him realise as if the gears were turning in motion behind his eyes.

I got up from my bed in alarm as Bow turned to me. My stomach dropped.

"We're being attacked."

XXVII

~*~

This couldn't be happening.

Neighbouring tribes knew we were vulnerable without my father and his men. It was a cruel act to put us under siege at this time, especially at night when it was hard enough to see. It was clear that was the point.

My heartbeat rang in my ears as I all but sprinted down the stairs and into the kitchen, heading straight for the back door.

"Keylin wait – you can't go out there!"

"I can't leave Baja out there." I turned in frustration, already hearing her wails of fear, she could sense the danger looming.

"She will be fine," Bow's gaze softened. "She is safe in the–"

Something broke within the house and Ana's scream reverberated off of the walls. Both Bow and I twisted our heads in the direction of the living room, stomachs dropping.

Bow quickly acted and grabbed a knife from the kitchen worktop, heading out of the room and in the direction towards his mother's scream.

With a ruffle of frustration through my hair, I turned and bolted through the kitchen door into the garden, not stopping amid the attack filling the air as I reached the stable and unlocked the door. I quickly threw it open and almost fell over when Baja made contact with me. Her frantic voice filled my mind.

'So much anger and blood being spilled, all on Trainer's hands. Hands are covered. Can't wash clean–'

"Baja..." I stopped her rambling as I caught my breath. "We are under attack, there are already people in our house."

'Must leave now.'

I ignored her request and made my way back into the house. Much to her displeasure and low growls, she followed me. Her jet–black fur rose anxiously along her back as she growled around her into the threatening night at her surroundings.

"Bow!" I called out, hearing footsteps coming towards me. Baja quickly came beside me to take a stance, ready to pounce on the intruder.

Her body relaxed when she recognised Bow but growled at the bloody knife he held in his hand. My mouth became dry at this, moving to step back when Bow reached out and grabbed my hand. He looked out into the night before dragging me into the sitting room.

My eyes fell on a crying Ana, clutching the side of her bloody cheek where she had been attacked not too long ago. Her attacker laid on his front, face–down with multiple knife wounds puncturing his skin.

My stomach twisted as I felt like vomiting at the sight before me. My mind even played tricks on me as I stumbled back in panic.

Bow reached down and took the silver–designed bow and arrows from the dead elf and held it out to me with an unreadable expression, predicting that somewhere down the line, we would meet this fate.

"They're here for you Keylin,"

I shook my head at him repeatedly as my vision started to blur. My mind played back the memories of that terrible night.

Bow impatiently grabbed my arm, pulling me closer to him despite my protests as he shoved the bow and their arrows into my hands.

"You need to protect yourself okay? Listen to me! They're here for you. They're going to take you away from us, away from your family, friends–"

"I can't fight them!" I yelled in frustration, my voice wavering as a tear rolled down my cheek.

"They are my family too, do you expect me to murder the very people I grew up with?"

"You have to if you want to stay in the *Dry Lands*." Bow replied as he quickly scrambled for his sword secured in the wooden cabinet. 'For emergencies only', he showed me once. After retrieving it, he grabbed my hand tightly and led me out of the front door.

Baja followed suit on her guard.

We left Ana behind in her crying state but something told me she would be alright and Bow would be coming back for her.

This couldn't be happening.

"W–Where are we going?"

"I'm going to get you as far away from here as possible – we travel to *Jhovst*, where father is. They can't take you again this time. You're a Dry Lander Keylin. You belong with us–"

"I'm an elf too." I reminded him quietly and I felt Bow tense at that.

"Do you want to go back?" I heard the betrayal in his voice. My silence stretched too long between us and he turned to me then. All words failed me at the look in his eyes.

"It's not that simple."

"Do you want to go back? Back to your life as being seen as a disgusting, flawed, scum elf – those were the words you said to me. Do you forget your life before us?"

I was taken aback by his sudden anger. Tears spilt from his eyes as he yelled these words back to me. The very words that made my shoulders tense and my stomach knot because it had been so long since I had heard them.

"I don't know Bow."

"Then we travel to *Jhovst*."

I didn't say anything else and neither did he as we ran

forward, winding behind tents and trying to avoid the battle in the centre as much as possible, trying to keep out of sight.

We were yet to meet the first live elf. I wondered would I recognise him. Would he recognise me? What would he do when we encountered one another?

It was forbidden to cross sectors. Why would they cross for me and put themselves in this sort of danger? They knew the risks and have always hated me...

My grandfather came to mind.

Corrin–

A yell startled me from my thoughts and I immediately stopped in my tracks at the familiar scream.

Bow turned to me worriedly and pulled me forward.

"We have to–"

"Malakei's in trouble."

I clutched the bow and arrows tightly around my arm and I didn't let my fear or worry have a chance to enter my headspace.

I didn't hesitate.

"Keylin no!"

I ran through tents, following the scream of my friend and prayed it would lead me to him all in one piece. My friend, who could be enduring torture right now, all because of me.

This attack was different to when the Dry Landers invaded. It was dreary and filled with nothing but screams and fire.

Retaliation for their stolen prince.

Alfus must have given the Dry Landers up.

War, the elves had resulted to *war*.

This made me realise that the Dry Landers, known for their brutality and murders, were not the monsters everyone made them out to be.

The elves, known for their abstinence from war and gentleness, were doing the exact opposite, killing, destroying, terrorising... all because of me.

'This must stop.'

Baja's prints thundered onto the hard ground beside me, coat as black as the night itself. It made it easy to blend into the darkness around her.

I finally stopped at the scene in front of me and my heart all but stopped as my hands shook at the sight.

Bringing my bow and arrow up to my eye level, I aimed but didn't fire at the elven soldier dressed in plaid silver. His silver hair almost shone in the darkness.

His riding boots were pressed on Malakei's neck, squeezing and pushing him deeper into the dirt.

"Get off of him."

I demanded gripping my bow tightly, palms already clammy as I drew attention from the elf and tried not to focus on the litter of silver corpses that laid around me.

It had taken twelve armed elves to bring Malakei to his knees. I knew the number would have been higher if he had been armed.

The elf turned and looked shocked for a moment, likely thinking for a second that I was a Dry Lander in my dark brown clothing if it weren't for my light hair colour and sharp–tipped ears.

"My prince..."

The elf began, making the mistake of loosening his grip around Malakei under him. Malakei quickly reached up and pulled his leg down, bending it in an awkward, painful angle that caused a shrill cry to erupt from the soldier.

That was all that the elf could cry out before Malakei twisted his head.

A loud snap echoed in my ears.

My bow and arrow fell to the ground as my mouth formed an 'o' shape. My hands immediately flew up to cover it while I tried not to scream in horror at the sight of a pure elf dying before me, being killed before me. The sight was ungodly.

Baja growled from beside me when Malakei shoved the body of the elf away from him so that he could get up. Once in a sitting position, he looked up.

Something washed over his face resembling a mixture of emotions.

"Keylin..." He scrambled over to me and I tried to avoid looking in the direction of the dead elf.

I gasped as Malakei suddenly took my trembling hands away from my face, revealing tear–stricken cheeks and glassy eyes.

"Breathe *dimples*."

"My brother, I'm sorry." I whispered in my native tongue.

"Look at me." Malakei commanded softly, bringing his hands up either side of my cheeks and I let out a sob when I made eye contact with him.

"I'm so sorry." He whispered. His voice cracked with emotion as he spoke. "Believe me, Key. I had no choice.

We under attack. They would have took you and killed all of us. I can't let that happen Key, I *can't. You are my best friend* – my brother."

Baja chirped at this. Her tail flicked at Malakei in the process like a small cat would.

I let out a shaky breath as I nodded in reply but he continued to frown at me.

"Say something. I don't want you think I am monster."

"I'I'm… I think..–"

My vision spun and all too suddenly, I was moving to a nearby bush and hurling my dinner up. The stench of blood and ash triggered the wave of nausea. Malakei was immediately at my back, patting my shoulder before helping me up when I stopped vomiting.

I picked up on Raen's voice from far away and my heart stopped for a moment.

"W–Where is he?" I questioned as I turned in the direction of Raen's voice, right in the heart of death and screaming.

"Where is Raen?"

Malakei seemed confused for a second about how I could hear Raen from so far away but his eyes trailed to my ears and understanding washed over him.

"Front line," Malakei responded quietly after a moment. "He is by barrier."

I followed his movements and watched as he picked up a large axe from a dead Dry Lander. He twirled it in his hands before a moment later, he was impaling it in an incoming elf a few metres away that threatened to aim his bow at us.

'Please be okay Raen.'
'Much death Trainer. Baja angry.'

"I know Baja." I agreed out loud causing Malakei to glance at me worriedly, but I didn't care. The fire pooling in my stomach was enough to distract me.

***

We ran for a few minutes in the direction of where the battle was most prominent until we saw the spiked barrier that once used to be, now destroyed. Pieces littered across the forest floor set alight with fire but not close enough to cause a forest fire – thank the gods.

It was a bloody scene filled with weapons colliding and people shouting. The image of silver–caped elves on white horses filled my vision and I almost stumbled into an incoming axe if it weren't for Malakei pulling me to the side. He sent me an unamused look.

"Careful Keylin–"

"We need to find Raen!" I shouted through the screaming and sound of metal on metal, moving forward quickly only to have Malakei's arm snake around my chest and pull me back away from the crowd. Baja flattened her ears and lowered her body to the ground as she dodged an arrow.

"Malakei! *Let go*." I protested as I tried to prise his hands from my chest but he was too strong and dragged me back until we were backing into a tent out of sight. Baja darted inside the tent, relieved to escape the danger even if only for a short time.

Malakei flung me backwards and I stumbled slightly before regaining myself and turning around seething.

"You are suicidal!" He concluded before pointing at Baja. "If she is hurt, the end will come for you sooner than expect–"

"Tell me what to do then!" I screamed back at him in frustration, completely out of ideas.

"Because I don't know what to do! I'm torn between saving my new family and protecting my old one." I pointed a finger out of the tent at the bloodshed being spilt. "Those elves are risking their lives for me – their *purity*. And I'm supposed to stand by and watch them be slaughtered like *pigs*!"

"That elf you murdered…" I took in a shaky breath. "He called me his prince. We can't just let both Dry Landers and elves pick each other off in a stupid battle when all of this can be resolved–"

Malakei took a step forward in frustration.

"They not do this for you. They don't care for you. They care for king. They don't care if you live, die. The king – your grandfather wants you–"

"We can come to an agreement," I insisted hopefully. "He will listen to me. This can be settled without any more blood being spilt Mal."

Everything happened so fast in that moment I barely had time to register my surroundings.

Just as Malakei had opened his mouth to speak, four elves ran into the tent, immediately bringing Malakei to the ground as they aimed a bow at his head. Two others closed in on Baja, aiming at her ready to shoot. I screamed at this, my knees giving out.

I fell to my knees before I could hear the crossbow click.

I saw the purple lightning shoot out along the ground before I felt it and it was just as I remembered it would be.

My scream mixed with Baja's wail before it was gone and my head slumped forward.

There was silence above me. No elf made a move as they lowered their crossbows in confusion and astonishment. I felt their gazes on me as I slowly lifted my head, still on all fours from where I was brought to the ground.

They gasped as I looked up at them, too focused on my glowing complexion to notice the panther had made its way over to my side, glowing purple eyes now replaced the once bright green ones.

"Is that the prince?" One of the elf soldiers questioned. "What happened to him?"

"Do you think the savages did this to him?!" One bellowed as he dug the crossbow deeper into Malakei's shoulder making him wince.

I opened my mouth but what came out wasn't English. It wasn't even words, nothing but a mere growl which caused the tent to shake slightly.

I stood up. The energy coursed through my veins and I clung to it, slowly moving forward before I was able to walk normally. Baja was close behind me.

An elf raised his crossbow and being trigger–happy, accidentally shot at me. It was clear on his face that he didn't mean to and Malakei's panicked inhale filled the air for a split second.

I caught the arrow.

The arrow that was heading straight for my right shoulder at an incredible speed, no elf, let alone a human, could possess that power or speed to catch it. I held neither.

I looked down in bewilderment at what I had just done before snapping the arrow and throwing it to the side.

I moved forward, taking the nearest elf to me and throwing him to the side.

He catapulted through the air into a nearby bookcase. I watched him in astonishment fall to the ground and the bookcase fell on top of him. The remaining elves looked on wide–eyed before Baja carved the skin and eyes from the elf holding the crossbow on Malakei.

Malakei got to his feet and managed to grab one of the elves to strangle while the last elf backed away wide–eyed. Realising that he was the only one left. He bolted the same way he had come from, only this time, down three elves.

Malakei must have noticed the purple fading from my eyes as my strength was quickly depleting.

He rushed forward and caught me just as I was about to fall forward, knees buckling from under me as the surge of power left my body. I gasped up at him. Thankful he had caught me as I began to come to.

'Trainor not ready. Trainor still young.'

I heard Baja in my head but I ignored her as Malakei slung one of my arms over his in an attempt to support me. I groaned at this.

"Raen..." I began and Malakei sighed.

"If you can get energy to make eyes purple again, we will find him." Malakei stated as he looked down at me and I sent a lopsided smile his way as I moved off of him, stumbling forward.

"Let's go then."

'Trainor still too weak. Trainor cannot control purple lightning, purple lightning take Trainor if not careful.'

XXVIII

~*~

Through our journey – Malakei, Baja and I managed to find the spot where most of the soldiers on both sides were gathered. There were far fewer elves and Dry Landers now. Elves sprawled on the ground along with Dry Landers. So many had lost their lives and the remaining few had gathered near the blazing fire of the camp to finish the raid.

Baja and I took down the elves that wanted to attack Malakei and her; even multiple attempts of kidnapping me were made.

This was when Malakei decided to take a metal helmet from one of the deceased Dry Landers as a way of disguising myself. This turned things around to the point I was the one defending my life when it came into threat, along with Malakei and Baja's.

When I saw Raen alive and well, bearing only a few scratches here and there – I was relieved. He looked as though he had slain many elves and had taken several lives here tonight. It made me shiver before my gaze caught sight of a silver headpiece being flung off of an elven soldier.

My heart stopped when I recognised the long–haired elf not much older than me fighting with his life.

Corrin grunted as he swung the sword in his hands and struck his opposing Dry Lander.

I winced at that.

"Raen is fine," Malakei stated. "I don't know why you doubt him. He is great warrior."

My reply seemed to get lodged in my throat and all remnants of what I was going to say disappeared when my gaze followed Raen's.

His eyes had found Corrin's.

The glint of excitement was evident as he stared down at the distracted elf, too busy fighting another to notice the Dry Lander taking in his skill, almost looking as though he was a predator moving in on his prey.

"Keylin!" Malakei screamed as my feet took me forward just as Raen ripped his axe from the ribcage of an elf he had just killed.

His eyes were set on his next target.

Corrin looked up. His ears quirked in Raen's direction but he did not yet turn around as Raen moved in for the kill.

"Raen!" I screamed but it was muffled by my helmet, the screaming and the sound of clashing swords. Tears clogged my vision when Raen didn't hear me and continued towards Corrin.

My feet continued until I was shoved forward. Stumbling slightly, the helmet flung off to the side and revealed my blonde hair and ears. This resulted in nearby elves and even Dry Landers stopping what they were doing momentarily. They watched me make my way to the centre of the battle.

"No!"

Corrin turned his head in my direction. His exterior depleted as an unreadable expression made its way onto his features when he saw me.

Raen raised his axe.

I let out a breath as I grabbed the weapon. My other hand pressed against his shoulder to stop him as I lodged myself between Raen and Corrin, halting the bloodshed that was about to happen.

I let out a painful wince as the metal sliced into my hand but held it firmly in place, refusing to let it kill anymore.

Raen made eye contact with me, blinking in surprise before his sharp gaze turned to Corrin when the sound of the elf lifting his sword reached our ears.

"Don't!" I yelped as I brought my hand from Raen's shoulder down to grab Corrin's hand holding his sword. I twisted around and managed to pull the sword from his grip, throwing it to the ground beside me.

I stared at the boy who had been haunting my days for a while now, ever since I was taken that night in the *High Peaks* without so much as a goodbye. He was finally here.

Corrin took in a painful breath as he scanned me. His eyes grew glassy and he blinked them away. His lips tightened.

"Is it really you pipsqueak?"

My strong persona crumbled at his annoying nickname for me that I used to dread, now I couldn't be happier to hear.

"Corrin—"

Raen pulled me back. A death–like grip was held on my forearm as he pushed me behind him, holding the axe high in threat.

He watched Corrin warily take up the discarded sword, quickly regaining the position they once stood moments ago before I intervened.

"Stop!" I yelled as I squirmed in Raen's vice–like hold. Corrin's eyes darkened when he noticed me trying to break free.

"Let him go and I promise to take the elves back to the mountains. We will never step foot on this wasteland again."

"*Good.*" Raen snarled as he let go of his hold on me but held out his arm to keep me from going to Corrin.

"The boy stays." Raen all but growled out.

"Now leave and I'll spare you the delight I will take in killing you slowly."

Malakei and Baja approached to my left, halting in their step as they observed the scene before them. I turned to Malakei and sent him a pleading look to which he swallowed visibly before stepping forward.

"I'd rather die." Corrin snarled as he raised his sword, Raen did the same and I gasped.

"As you wish."

"We must keep elves prisoner until Maekin returns!" Malakei shouted, which made the two stop what they were doing.

Corrin glanced at Malakei momentarily as Raen continued to glare hatefully at the elf. I let out a breath of relief and moved between the two.

"Until he returns, we don't kill. We outnumber them now. Maekin will return in few days. He will decide what to do with them. He will want to know why elves come down from mountain for his son." Malakei continued and I stepped in front of Corrin to shield him, my heart in my throat as I looked up at Raen.

Raen noticed this and a humourless laugh left his lips.

"After *everything*." Raen glared down at me. Bitterness laced his words.

"You take their side."

"I take no side." My voice was firm as I narrowed my eyes up at Raen.

"I refuse to watch the people I love kill each other. Elves or Dry Landers. They are both family to me."

I could hear Corrin inhale sharply from behind at my words as Raen scoffed, roughly shoving his axe back into his belt loop.

He suddenly grabbed a fistful of my shirt and threw me towards Malakei with such force it had me staggering.

Raen grabbed Corrin after wrestling for his sword before bending the metal and throwing it to the ground.

"What are you doing?" Malakei asked in confusion as Raen dragged Corrin away from the centre to the front of the line, turning to address the remaining fighters from both sectors.

"Elves!" Raen voiced loudly, causing a few to stop what they were doing. In a matter of seconds, everyone was looking to Raen who dripped of power and strength while holding up Corrin.

"You are completely outnumbered. You will have two choices. Become our prisoner or die where you stand."

Raen paused to look down at me.

"Your prince would rather you surrender now and throw down your weapons. It would be a shame to disobey him after you travelled so far in an attempt to 'rescue' him."

"What the fuck is he doing?" I gritted out as I kept eye contact before turning to Malakei in desperation.

"I don't want this. Why would I want this?"

"It is only way to keep them alive for now. I'm sorry, I didn't know what to do." Malakei responded and I sighed before sending him a thankful smile, knowing I had no choice in the matter.

My forehead creased as I heard the clatter of metal hit the ground around us where the elves were dropping their swords, showing surrender.

Raen nodded in victory before he pulled Corrin along, leaving the rest of the Dry Landers to capture the remaining elves.

Tara and Bow were amongst the crowd, Mila also trailed not too far behind as their eyes swept the grounds. When Bow spotted me, he visibly relaxed before making his way up to us. The others followed him.

My attention, however, remained on Raen and Corrin.

I began to worry as Raen dragged a not–very–complying Corrin out of the crowd and through tents. I followed him as he brought my friend to the weapons stable before resurfacing and tying him to a tree near the back away from civilisation.

I watched him throw Corrin down beside it with a force that made my friend visibly wince.

"What in the gods are you doing?!" I raised my voice as Raen finished tying Corrin to the tree.

I dropped to my knees in front of my friend, my hand going to his forehead and cheeks worriedly.

"He will freeze out here."

"If he is strong, he will survive."

"Why are you doing this?" I tore my gaze from Corrin to look up at Raen. My vision became blurry as disappointment and confusion filled my eyes.

"He is an elf–"

"*I'm* an elf." I interrupted, not afraid to remind him of what I truly was.

They were so blind in believing that because I was their leader's son I was solely one of them but they forgot to realise my complexion.

I was still part elf, whether they wanted to believe it or not.

I got up from my knees in anger and Raen sighed, running a hand over his face.

"Keylin–"

"Give me a reason – other than him being an elf, why you're being cruel."

"*Look around.*" He moved closer to tower over me.

"Look what they did to our home. To *our* tribe. You say we are savages but we didn't raid your city and torch everything to the ground. We spared them. We didn't kill people."

"You *kidnapped* me." I snarled back causing Corrin and Tara to inhale sharply but I ignored their worried glances towards me, I wasn't near finished.

"You took their only heir to the kingdom and left them in shambles. You reduced them to something they swore on the ancient scrolls never to be. You didn't think for a second how it would affect them. Don't you *dare* play the victim in this. If *anyone* is the victim, it's *me*."

I brought my lips up to Raen's ear, allowing the flicker of fire within me to grow into a dangerous flame.

"You made your bed, now *lie* in it."

I pulled back from his rigid stance, took a breath and lowered myself down against the tree into a sitting position. Raen watched as I did so in silence.

"So if you can't give me a fucking reason or see me for what I truly am, I will be out here with them. For however long that may be until you see sense – or calm down, whichever comes first."

Raen said nothing, only letting out an exhale of air through his nose before his eyes fell on Corrin.

A darkness took over his gaze. He clenched his jaw tightly as he looked back at me. I had learned to adjust to Raen's mood swings and hot temperament but seeing him now. His blood was boiling and I was the cause this time, the cause of the effect.

"As you wish."

***

"Keylin?"

"Yes?" I answered into the night, ignoring the chattering of my teeth as the temperature dropped.

Raen tied me to the tree.

He had made sure to tie me to the opposite end of where Corrin was tied so that we couldn't touch or see each other.

"I hope you think about where your loyalties lie." He had said before leaving us here, warning the others that if they so much as talked to me they would receive the same treatment but upside down.

"Sorry," He chuckled. "I just can't believe it's you. You're actually real and alive."

I found myself smiling at that. My throat closed up in the slightest as emotion got the better of me. If only I could touch him. To feel the warmth of a hug from my best friend since childhood. It was all I wanted.

I tugged on the rope around my wrists and winced. They were tightly bound.

"You don't know how glad I am to see you Corry."

"Well, *hear me* I guess." He grumbled and I chuckled at that.

There was a rustling in the bushes and no sooner Baja's glowing green eyes protruded from them. When she spotted me, she yowled and stalked over.

"What was that?" Corrin asked out of fright and I chuckled.

"It's okay," I replied, noticing how Baja sniffed the air

and began to roam to the other side of the tree with curiosity.

"She won't hurt you."

From what I could hear, Baja was chirping at a heavily panting Corrin who had not seen an animal like this before. There was no such animal like Baja in the *High Peaks*. She was very intense up close. I remembered our first encounter.

"She's a panther," I called before biting my lip nervously.

"I uhm… bonded with her a while back."

"You what?" Corrin failed to contain the shock from his voice. "How is that possible?"

I was born to lead this life. It had been written.

"I–I'm her Trainor."

Silence.

Corrin didn't know how to respond. If I were in his situation, neither would I, to be quite honest. It was not common for an elf to be a Trainor in the first place, let alone one who held traits from more than one sector.

Ever since I arrived on the *Dry Lands*, everything had become so surreal.

"Who else knows about this?"

I frowned and took a moment to answer.

"Most of the tribe."

"Okay. It needs to remain that way."

"I know." I responded, knowing that he was talking about those of a higher power from the *Sky Lanes*. If they caught wind of me being a Trainor, I would possibly be executed on the spot.

"Your hair has grown longer since the last time we talked." His tone was lighter.

"So has yours." I smiled at that after a moment, dropping the subject but keeping his words in mind.

"You've changed so much," He started. "You used to be so shy and afraid. I nearly had to look twice when I saw you standing up to that monster. He looked like he wanted to eat you by the way. Even *I* was terrified of him."

"You didn't show it." I furrowed my brows in memory before letting out a sigh. My breath fogged in front of me with how cold the night was.

"Keylin, you shouldn't have stayed out with me. Although – I'm glad you did, you didn't need to."

I inhaled a breath of freezing air, like glass filling my lungs and shut my eyes.

"I wasn't going to let you freeze out here alone Corrin. It's the least I could do."

"Is the bastard at least coming back to check up on us?"

"I don't know." I frowned looking down at my feet. Baja had already retreated to my side but instead licked my cheek and crawled into my lap. As big as she was, she managed to get comfortable with her paws over my right leg and head resting on my shoulder. She dug her wet snout into the crook of my neck, blowing hot air and making goosebumps rise on my skin.

'Thank you.' I mentally said to her and she chuffed at that, her tongue kitten licking my neck in several cold places. Almost as if she was playing a game with herself to beat the cold from getting in on me.

"I don't like him." Corrin deadpanned and I rolled my

eyes at that.

"He's not fond of you either."

"Is he...? What is he to you?" Corrin asked, as if the words were hard to get out for him and I let my head fall back against the bark of the tree. The rough texture acted like a poor substitute for a pillow. It would have to do.

"Honestly..." I admitted quietly. "I don't know."

There was silence after a while and just as I was nodding off, I heard Corrin speak.

"Be careful Keylin... love, it's not as great as everybody says."

I blinked away the tears from forming in my eyes but managed a sniffle. I played it off as the cold getting to me even though the warmth from Baja was better than any blanket.

"I know."

XXIX

~*~

When I awoke the next morning, it was to the feeling of someone untying the rope around my wrists.

I blinked awake, my face scrunched up in slight pain from a pressing headache and the burn marks the rope had inflicted on my skin.

With a swipe of the knife, Raen untied me and the rope fell at my feet.

Baja was nowhere in sight. Most likely, she was hunting for food or exploring the camp – or what was left of it I figured.

I rubbed at my sore red hands as Raen silently cut the rope from around my middle that was securing me to the tree. When he finished, he tucked the small knife away in his pocket while I brought a hand around my middle. It was itchy and I knew rope marks would be littered across my skin.

Raen kneeled in front of me, taking my face in his hands as he narrowed his eyes to inspect me. I could feel a tinge of rosiness to my pale complexion and my red nose. I blinked tiredly in his warm hands.

How early was it?

Raen let my head rest back against the bark and I complied, almost falling back to sleep when I felt him pull me forward again. My face scrunched up in slight pain at the movement but it was distinguished when a warm fleece was pulled over me.

It was the warmest and softest thing I had ever felt. I couldn't help but let my head fall onto his shoulder as the warmth went up to my neck and ear.

Raen sighed from above me while his hands massaged my back, pulling me into his now bare chest. Was this his fleece?

"I didn't want to leave you out here." His voice rumbled and I blinked up at him. My eyes squinted at the brightness.

Raen's hand came up to the back of my head and ran his fingers through my hair.

"But I was angry with what you said. You made it sound like it was my fault. That *all of this* was my fault."

"I know." I mumbled and he exhaled.

"Your words stung, but they were words I needed to hear… I did what I believed was right, I am not proud of what I did that night in your sector – *none of us* are. The elves do not fight. We knew they wouldn't. We thought that by taking you quietly and in secret, they wouldn't suspect us. None of us could have predicted this would happen Keylin. We should have."

He brings a hand up to the back of my head, noticing I was growing tired in his embrace.

A yawn escaped me as Raen hoisted me up into his arms. I brought my hands up around his neck, letting my head rest on his shoulders but not quite falling back to sleep.

"I'm sorry for what I did. It was cruel and not fair to you. I am sorry, for putting you through so much."

We passed a sleeping Corrin. His elven features were prominent in the early morning dew. He looked at peace, as if he wasn't in the middle of being prisoner to the *Dry Lands*.

I wanted him to be okay. I only hoped he would be fine as Raen carried me the distance to what I presumed was his tent. I was too drained and cold to function properly for my mind to make sense of my surroundings.

I closed my eyes only to reopen them when I was placed on a fur–coated bed, I knew I had passed out and it felt as though sleep was going to take me under once again.

"Sleep Keylin," Raen stated softly as he took his hand from my cheek to bring the fur blankets up around me.

"I need to speak with Caito."

Caito. I hadn't seen him in so long, I wondered where he was… was he still alive? judging by Raen seeking him out to talk with him surely implied so, but why?

Raen placed his hand on my forehead and I furrowed my brows at this, not opening them as he whispered words off *Fasik*, lulling me into a slumber.

***

When I woke up again, I felt better. I didn't feel as tired as I once did and that gave me the energy I needed.

I pulled back the fur blanket and a displeased mewl came from Baja who now laid beside me as I accidentally hit her.

It was strange how she would leave me but be by my side in moments I needed her most. When I was most vulnerable. It made me realise that although I was her Trainor and she was my animal, she was not required at all times to be at my side but it would be better if she did. She reminded me of Mara, constantly worrying and fretting about me.

Baja tilted her head at my thoughts and chuffed as if she were laughing at me.

'Trainor has many thoughts. The thoughts are loud.'

"I will try to be more quiet then."

"Oh, you're awake."

I turned my head in the direction of the voice, smiling when I noticed Caito reading from an old book of sorts judging by the damp and stained yellow pages. Caito looked up from his book and smiled at me before packing the object away.

"How are you feeling?" He asked, coming closer to sit on the bedside near me. He twisted his body around to look at me.

"Fine... are you here to keep an eye on me?"

Caito chuckled at that before looking back with a knowing smile.

"I guess you can put it like that, yes. In case you take a turn like you did in the mountains. The night temperatures here do not agree with you." Caito concluded in a sympathetic tone and I couldn't help but look at him in silence as the gears began to turn in my head.

"You're a doctor?" I eventually breathed out in surprise and Caito scrunched his nose.

"I like medicine." He corrected. "I like to find cures and help people. If that is doctor, then yes."

I smiled in understanding at that before a frown creased my forehead and I let my eyes dart around the room, not finding what I was looking for.

"Where's Raen?"

"He's most likely dealing with new prisoners–"

My stomach dropped in realisation as Caito continued, oblivious to how I had reacted to the news.

"There are few who don't know the rules–"

I immediately began to pull myself up and out of the bed but before I could make it over the blankets, Caito stopped me. Immediately he jumped up and rested a hand on my shoulder, eyes alarmed.

"No Keylin, you must rest–"

"I'm fine really, I need to see Raen." I assured him as I struggled to get out of his grip. Caito only continued to shake his head and explain that I needed rest, but I had plenty of time for that later. Right now I needed to find Raen.

Just then, as if summoned by my thoughts alone, Raen walked through the pulled curtain entrance of the tent. His eyes travelled up at the commotion and immediately trained on Caito and me.

His eyes trailed to Caito's hand on me and his features darkened, jaw clenching as he motioned his head for Caito to leave.

Caito frowned but got up nonetheless, grabbing his things and making his way to the entrance. He stopped beside Raen who was yet to move from his frozen position.

"He needs rest–"

"Okay." Raen cut in sharply. His blank eyes were glued to me as his menacing voice pointed at Caito.

Both Caito and I flinched at his aggressive tone before Caito immediately nodded and walked briskly out of the tent. I brought the blanket closer to me, bunching the fur between my fingers as Raen stared at me from across the room.

"Stop looking at me like that." I eventually caved and glared at a patch of fur near the end of the bed. His eyes were unnerving as I felt them on me. I heard him clear his throat and looked up at him, suddenly feeling small under his intense stare.

"So the arrogant elf can look at you but I can't?" He questioned, almost in a grumble of words as his eyes narrowed at me. I blinked before registering what he said and my eyes grew stormy.

"Corrin?"

Raen's face soured at the name.

"He's my best friend." I stated softly and Raen immediately frowned at this, brows scrunching in discomfort.

A moment of silence overtook us and I could only sit there staring at him with my mouth slightly ajar from disbelief. I didn't see what was so important for him that he needed to know everything.

Then it suddenly occurred to me that Raen may have believed that Corrin and I were in a relationship, hence being the reason Corrin would lead the elves to the *Dry Lands*, to come and rescue me. I now understood why Raen was acting strangely. Even if I didn't say anything,

"I am not *in love* with Corrin."

Raen scoffed at this, turning his head away from me.

"Does he know that?"

He refused to look at me as he bit his lip in thought. My eyes softened at this. Upon seeing the real Raen. Not the one with the axe and dark persona that everyone was afraid of. He was vulnerable in front of me, unsure of himself. He was *jealous*.

"Why don't you ask him?"

"Keylin… tell me the truth."

"I told you the truth."

Raen pinched the bridge of his nose in agitation whilst I toyed with him. I knew there was a special place in hell for me to do this to him.

When I thought he had suffered enough, I wiped the smirk from my face and brought my hand up to rub the back of my neck.

"I'm not in love with him… I think I'm falling for

someone else. Actually, I have fallen for someone else…"
I let the words go with my breath before biting my lip.
Suddenly unsure when I noticed Raen's gaze shot up to
me, his brows furrowed and I looked anywhere but at him.

Shit. Why did I say that?

Shit. Shit. *Shit.*

"I–" I cleared my throat as I brought my hand around
my neck, letting out a small awkward chuckle. I was
completely aware of how red my face was and how Raen
had not moved yet from where he stood. I didn't look in
his direction as I avoided his gaze.

"I–I'm sorry forget I said that."

"Why?"

"I… I thought it would reassure you. That I'm only
looking at you."

Raen blinked as he crossed his arms and leaned against
a pillar, his eyes found mine and softened when they did.

"You caught me off guard." He said honestly as the
smile slipped from his face, his expression became
serious.

"You say it like it's a bad thing."

"It is... I am never like this when I am with you."

I frowned at this, noticing how he was inching closer
to me but paid no attention as his words echoed in my
mind.

"Like what?" I breathed out just as Raen sank to the
edge of the bed beside me, twisting slightly to look down.

"I feel... like every time I see you, with your big green
eyes laughing the way you do with Tara and Malakei..."
He cleared his throat and looked down sheepishly. I didn't

realise I was holding onto every word until I adjusted myself and looked down at my fiddling hands nervously.

"It's hard for me to open up," He continued, voice now distant. He turned to me and our eyes locked. "I wasn't always like this. One day I will tell you everything. I will open up to you because it is not fair for you to know me now but not me from the past. I want to share it with you."

He grabbed my nervous hand and held it in his, squeezing lightly.

"You already know how much you mean to me, hearing you say those words... " Raen smiled down at me and a small blush creeped onto my cheeks.

Before I knew it, Raen was leaning down. His hand came out to hook under my chin as he tilted my chin up slightly to meet his lips.

***

The days went by slowly.

It was obvious there was tension between not just Raen and I; but with everyone. Tara, my brother, even Malakei...

We all knew there was only one way to be rid of it and that was to execute the prisoners for not only trespassing on the *Dry Lands,* but also for the attempted kidnapping of their leader's son.

The only reason it was delayed for them to do just that was because of me.

I tried to tell them to wait, sometimes pleaded with them to just let the elves go, they'd be warned not to do this again and we could come to some sort of agreement with the sector.

Dry Landers were known for being stubborn and I finally understood why.

The tension during breakfast was so thick, a knife couldn't cut through it. Most of the time it was silence on my part as I ate my food and then left, not wanting to make things worse between my friends and me than I already had.

Raen and I had barely spoken since the time I told him I had fallen for him. He was being hard on not just me, but everyone recently, including Corrin. The more I stood up to him and helped Corrin, the more it infuriated him.

I scrunched my fist up at the thought as I stared down at my leftover rabbit stew, now grown cold. I shoved it away from my body with a sigh, causing the others to look up.

I was getting up from my seat when someone grabbed a strong hold of my arm. I looked down and met the determined eyes of Bow.

"Where are you going?" Bow asked – or more *demanded*.

"To the woods." I informed turning away but just as I was about to walk forward, Bow pulled me back. I glared at him.

"You may have forgotten what today is, Key."

He stated knowingly and I frowned at him, blinking repeatedly as the day had slipped my mind completely. I couldn't believe I forgot.

"Father..." The words went with my breath as my eyes

glazed over in thought.

He was coming home today. Today was the day that he would find out about the elves and apparently, his view would be the tiebreaker.

"Judgement day." Malakei stated before shoving a spoonful of stew into his mouth. I glanced at him with a blank expression.

"Not really since we know what he's going to think." Tara mumbled into her porridge and I narrowed my eyes at her.

"You're wrong." I gritted out making everyone look up at my furious gaze.

"He will show them mercy. His lover was a fucking elf. I'm also half–elf if you didn't forget. If he does this… he can forget about ever building a relationship with me. He will be dead to me."

"*Dimples…* " Malakei began with a pained expression but Raen cut him off, his eyes piercing as they glared into mine harshly.

"Your father is brutal in nature. He has killed friends and even other family members before. It may not be his decision at the end of the day if outside influence has anything to do with it. He puts the safety of the tribe first."

'I show a kindness to you Keylin but keep in mind, I am anything but fair when it comes to protecting my people. They come first. I have no doubt you will see my other side with time and learn the reason why I am the leader. Although I am your father, I am your leader first. What I say, goes.'

I didn't realise how quick and angered my breathing

was until there was nothing but silence at the breakfast table. I didn't have anything else to say as I took my arm from Bow and walked away without a word. Baja followed closely behind.

It was soon after that when father returned.

I had seen him arrive on his black stallion with his other soldiers as I sat in the grass near the forest. After that, I ran to his tent to make sure I could talk to him privately.

Of course, that wasn't the case at all.

Raen was already there waiting, along with Bow. They waited patiently for my father but when I walked into the tent, all of their gazes landed on me and I froze.

Just as I was about to say something, muffled voices could be heard from behind me and I turned around, backing up just in time for my father to fling back and enter the tent followed closely by a worried–looking Malakei.

My father's jaw clenched as he searched the tent. His gaze landed on each of us around the room, shoulders tense.

"What is going on here?"

XXX

~*~

Raen explained to my father everything that had happened since he was gone. Bow also had his say while Malakei and I stood quietly to the side.

Malakei chose to let his gaze drop to the floor in fright of my father whereas I had no choice. They were speaking in Fasik.

I fumed silently for another few minutes before I couldn't take it anymore. They could already be discussing when they were going to kill the elves and there was nothing I could do about it.

"Stop!" I yelled out to them in the middle of Bow speaking. He suddenly stopped as I said this. Everyone looked at me when I stepped forward but my eyes were only on my father.

"It is unfair," I began. "Unfair to think that you only care to hear one side of an argument."

"This is no argument Keylin," My father started

gravely in a dangerously low voice that made a shiver run up my spine. In all the time I have been here, I had never seen him like this. He was furious.

"Elves trespassed into my home and decided to kill and terrorise my people in search of my son. How else do you think I would react? What would the sky gods do to them if they found out they trespassed? I'm doing them a favour–"

"*You* did," I cut him off. "*You* started all of this. *You* trespassed into a foreign land. *You* kidnapped me; the *king's* grandson. You took advantage of their neutrality in battle and forced them to abandon their faith! How else did you think they would react?!"

My father must have noticed the tears beginning to form in my eyes and quickly turned his attention to the others.

"Everyone out *now*. This is not your conversation."

Bow blinked before nodding stiffly and walking out of the tent, Malakei followed suit. Raen hesitated at first but walked by me. He waited until the last second before looking back at me but I turned my head to the side refusing to let him see me cry this time. He was right about my father.

"There is no need to raise your voice at me Keylin." My father assured me, a hint of softness returning to his tone making me grit my teeth in anger as tears started to prick my eyes.

"I know you are upset–"

"I am *more* than *'upset'*," I sneered. The anger and hurt finally made an appearance settling on my father over everything he did and what he continued to do. All of this bloodshed was on his hands.

"It wasn't like I was your only son. You had Bow–"

"And turn my back on you?" His voice grew an octave. "To do so I would be turning my back on your mother–"

"You owe me nothing."

"And I owe her everything!"

A silence washed over us then, my father's words conveyed the years of bottled pain finally reaching the surface, spilling over as tears threatened to escape his eyes. The memories were painful for him.

"You are still young," His voice was full of emotion. "The day you have a child, you will understand that there is no end of Sorn you wouldn't walk to, no sector that could prevent you from being with your child. Having you here, I know you are safe. I know you are looked after and that is what helps me sleep at night. Keylin, you're grandfather kept you from me for eighteen years. He had no right to do that."

"You weren't there." I swallowed painfully. "He was all the family I had. You had no right to take me."

My father ran a tired hand through his hair.

"I wish more than anything things were different son. I'm sorry for all you have been through."

My heart constricted at his words, wondering how he had heard about me. All of this time, he never knew I existed until recently.

"How did you find out about me?" My voice was more gentle this time, losing its bite.

"There were whispers of an elven prince with Dry

Lander features coming of age in the *High Peaks*," He sighed, a sadness to his tone.

"I knew you were mine," He noted. "I sent a few of my trusted men to confirm the rumours… I didn't get my hopes up but when I saw you for the first time… you know the rest."

"Don't kill them," I pleaded with him. "Let them return to their sector. They don't understand, they shouldn't be punished for it."

My father was silent at this, refusing to look at me now as he turned to his oval table covered in maps and papers. The realisation sank in then that no matter what I said, it could never change his mind.

He had made his decision.

"You've already made your decision." I whispered out in defeat.

Out of everyone, I thought he would understand the most, but I was wrong. I was wrong about him all along. My father was nothing special. If anything, he was selfish.

"I know you're upset but we both know that this is the only way. They will never stop. Your grandfather will never stop searching for you and this is the only way to send that old *bastard* a message."

"This is immoral, and you know it," I let a tear fall from my eyes as I met his gaze.

"This is *wrong*. They don't deserve to die. I grew up with those people! They're innocent. If it was the other way around, they would show you mercy–"

"I don't want their *mercy*," Father spat the words as if they were venom on his tongue.

"I want revenge for keeping my son from me. For killing my people and for keeping me from your mother."

"My *mother*..." My voice broke as I took in a shaky breath and closed my eyes.

"She wouldn't want this. If she knew what you were going to–"

My father suddenly came towards me and my head flew up to him. Before I could take a step back, he stopped however and it seemed as though I had hit a nerve. His exterior was more breakable and his expression looked like it would crumble at any moment.

"*Don't* finish that sentence Keylin. Don't *use her* against me like that. You wouldn't know what she would have wanted."

That stung.

We continued to glare at each other in silence as I tried to piece our conversation together. I was finding it hard to grasp any more of the conversation and slowly turned around to place my hands on the leader table, on top of the large map of Sorn.

"We won't drag the matter to the *Sky Lanes* for their crimes against Sorn. To do so would raise suspicion of *you* and your existence. They will be beheaded on *Dry Land* in the morning," My father said after a few moments of silence between us. I shut my eyes.

"I will give you time to say goodbye to the ones important to you."

I nodded slowly. The tears fell hot and fast out of my eyes. I felt like I was in a dream. This couldn't be real. Corrin wasn't going to die. He couldn't. He saved me too many times...

I flinched away from my father's hand when it made contact with my shoulder and I turned around, face pale to see his hand in the air where it was only seconds ago, resting comfortingly on my shoulder.

It didn't comfort me.

In that moment I could feel myself turn to the darkest part of my very being. A place where I remembered Mara told me once never to go, that only those from *The Shadows* belonged. I knew if I allowed myself to go there, my father might withdraw his offer to say my final goodbyes.

'Comply. Comply.'

I didn't feel my feet drag me out of my father's tent and ignored my father's calls as I burst into the night air. My stomach churned and I could feel the remnants of my breakfast making its way up my throat.

I stood to the side of a tent and retched the contents into the wild grass. My body shook in a cold sweat. It was only when I finished, I wiped my mouth. The tears now dry but my eyes still blurred as I stumbled forward.

***

"I'm going to die, aren't I?"

I didn't say anything as I looked away from Corrin in shame. Utter shame and anger filled me that I couldn't do anything to save him. He knew he was right, he knew all along that he was going to die but kept a smile for me, giving me false hope in thinking that I could make a difference in this backward world.

Corrin was moved to a more public area within the camp. Still separated from the rest of the elves but he was deemed officially the 'leader' by Raen.

I thought at first it was Raen's way of getting back at him because he didn't particularly like Corrin, but Corrin disagreed and told me the truth.

He led the mission, with my grandfather's aid.

He volunteered to be the one in charge of bringing me back home. Of course, my grandfather couldn't come because he still had a kingdom to run. He did, however, supply the weaponry and with Corrin's help, created what could have been the rescue.

"I don't care what I have to do. I'll watch Sorn *burn* before I let them hurt you."

"Hey," Corrin started as he made a move to reach over with his hands outstretched to try and wipe the tears suddenly filling my eyes but the chains that bound his wrists pulled him back to the metal wall, preventing him from doing so.

He was in a cage.

Similar to the ones they used to transport slaves and animals through the black markets. The thought made the reality of what was going to happen a lot worse and I angrily wiped my tears.

"None of this is right." I sank to my knees in front of Corrin in tiredness. My knees started to ache from standing by the metal cage. I let my forehead rest against the bars just as I heard the rattling chains, indicating Corrin was sinking down to the ground in front of me.

I felt his fingers graze the tips of my hair before they vanished, and he sighed.

"It is *written* Keylin. If I die tomorrow then I know that the gods have made up their mind. I have lived a good life Key and I want you to know that I didn't die for nothing." Corrin said seriously, determination in his voice as I felt him stare me down.

My vision was blurry as I looked up at him before letting out a dry chuckle.

"You say that like you're saying goodbye."

"That's because I am." Corrin smiled a small sad smile and my face hardened as I tried to keep any more tears from leaving my eyes.

"Stop it. No, you're not."

"Keylin..." Corrin's voice was fond but really, he sounded as if he was not able to speak above a whisper. It was too painful.

I went to get up, my hand reached up to grab hold of the metal cage when the sudden jingle of chains rattled against it and my hand was yanked forward by my fingers until my whole arm fit through one of the many holes making up the cage.

My body pressed up against it as Corrin gripped my arm tightly, panting, looking wide–eyed. The most frightened I had seen him since he found out he was going to die in less than twelve hours.

"I won't die for nothing Keylin," He repeated firmly, looking seriously into my eyes and I blinked in confusion, he continued.

"I know you think that you can do something to stop

this but you *can't*. I don't want you to. Whatever you're thinking of doing that could put you in danger, *don't*. Do you understand?"

I bit my lip as it trembled. My breath hitched as I sucked in air.

"It doesn't matter if I get hurt, what matters–"

"*Please* Keylin, promise me."

When I didn't reply immediately, he tightened his grip on my arm and I let my eyes close shut out of frustration, my eyebrows furrowed before I nodded my head slowly, re–opening my glassy eyes.

"Okay. I promise."

I sluggishly walked back to Bow's house after a few minutes more of talking with Corrin; only I didn't go to my bed, instead, I went to the stables where Baja currently resided.

When I opened the door, I noticed her sprawled out on the hay around the stone room in the middle, her tail swooshing up and down as she seemed to be in a type of dream. That was quickly interrupted when I opened the door and her eyes opened immediately. Her head propped up to see who it was that disturbed her from her sleep.

When she saw me, she chirped and laid back down, moving positions to stretch.

I smiled a watery smile before lying down beside her. My head rested on her neck as she curled her paw around me protectively and purred. It wasn't long after that that I fell asleep.

~*~

I dreamt of a girl with fire for hair and eyes as clear as the water from the *Great Divide*.

She was calling my name. It was muffled – like she was far away, far enough away that I couldn't reach her but it didn't stop me from searching.

I didn't know this girl. This was the first time I had dreamt of a girl with these features. I was amazed at how my imagination could conjure up an image as interesting and beautiful as this one.

There was screeching so loud that I had to cover my ears.

A black shadow blocked out the sun above me and my heart quickened as I looked up.

Gasping, I turned and found myself in a deserted wasteland, ridden of life and nature. Everything was burnt to the ground and *bodies*. Bodies that were burned to charcoal covered the debris.

I quickly turned around at the sound of a name being whispered from the ground up. My head flew from one end of the land to the other as I searched for the cause of the whispering. Maybe the only person that could help me.

Unless… it wasn't human.

An image of a murk with its scale–like appearance made its way into my thoughts and my stomach dropped.

"Wake up Keylin…" I whispered to myself as I began clenching my fists at my side. *"It's just a dream. A nightmare, like the ones you always have."*

"This is no dream."

My eyes opened and immediately I spun around to find

494

the source of the voice. My heart almost jumped out of my chest when I noticed a woman standing a few feet behind me. She was older, but younger than Bow's mother. Her eyes were grey but held more secrets and mysteries than the girl with the fiery hair.

The woman smiled at me and I gulped, I knew exactly what she was. A witch.

"At last we meet–" She stopped herself to smirk and tilted her head to the side as she examined me, holding me captive with her intense eyes.

"*Trainor*." She concluded.

I shook myself out of whatever spell she had over me and furrowed my brows in confusion.

"Who are you?" I demanded softly. "And where am I?"

"It's sad isn't it?" She dodged my question, turning her head to look at the burnt pile of bodies to her side. I could still faintly hear the screams of agony from them before silence.

"Our ancestors were jealous creatures. Always wanting what the other had and going to such extremes. Going as far as to take other lives that meant nothing to them, but everything to someone else."

My stomach dropped in realisation.

This was the aftermath of the Great War. A time where all creatures of Sorn were prey to one another, this was the outcome when there was no order. The time before the sectors were created to prevent something like this devastation from happening again, to install peace between creatures.

"What?" I frowned. "I don't understand, can you tell

me why I'm here and what is going on please? Who are you?"

"It's sad isn't it?" She continued before turning to me. Her haunting eyes captured me once again before she smiled sadly.

"No matter how many years have passed, our ancestors may have passed on but the jealousy and hatred remains. It never goes away. It's there, like an invisible sickness. In the shadows."

I furrowed my brows as I mulled over her words, knowing that she was right. Sorn was supposed to be a world with structure and difference but it was tearing at the seams. We all tolerated each other yet hated one another. How could we progress from that?

"You are smart for your age elf." The woman's voice was in my ear and I turned around to face her, she smiled sadly.

"But not smart enough. Tell me, what do you see?"

"Everything is dead." My lip curled as I looked onward at the wasteland before me. The woman nodded in agreement.

"Yes. A war can cause such destruction and devastation, not only for people but for nature itself."

The woman mused as she crouched down to the black and burnt ground to feel the dirt beneath her turn to sand in the wind. I watched her for a moment before crouching down to her height and looking her in the eye pleadingly.

"What are you trying to tell me?"

"A war is coming Keylin."

The woman said seriously as she turned her head to me,

eyes letting out those secrets she had been hiding.

"What..." I gasped out in both fright and shock.

The last war was centuries ago. Now I understood why she was telling me this, but this war she was talking about, it couldn't be between the elves and Dry Landers.

"Bigger." The woman said.

"Sorn?"

She nodded.

I had so many questions. So many things I wanted to ask her. This woman – that I didn't even know who just appeared to me in my dream. If this even *was* a dream. I couldn't tell what was real anymore.

A loud screeching sound hit both of our ears like the one before and I flinched, covering them.

Her hands wrapped around my wrists, hoisting me up into a standing position. I opened my eyes to notice her in front of me, looking frantic and worried for the first time.

"We will meet again."

With that, the woman reached out with her hand and pushed my chest, sending me flying backwards as my balance faltered and I fell...

~*~

I jolted awake.

Panting and sweating as I felt Baja shift beneath me in her sleep before going back to unmoving, soft puffs of air left her nostrils. My mind was alert and eyes were wide awake. I didn't sleep because of all of the questions going through my mind.

Who was that woman? Why were there dead bodies everywhere? Where were we and who was that girl and that awful noise?

That was no ordinary dream. I knew that, but that could only mean it was something else.

An omen.

XXXI

~*~

I left Baja in the small barn to sleep. Every part of my being told me not to because I wanted her with me and this was extremely important. But I needed to find answers, and those answers didn't include Baja.

Something told me that bringing her with me would only make things more difficult.

I knew I needed to do this one on my own.

We would see each other again someday, hopefully soon.

I was leaving the camp, the *Dry Lands*, and going to find this woman.

This woman that I hardly knew the name of. Her name I could remember very clearly in my dream was the one being whispered by what sounded like a thousand voices.

It must be her name or even the girl's name with the fire–like hair. Either way, I was sure one of them could lead me to the other. They seemed to be connected in some way.

I planned to sneak out at night whilst every one was asleep. That way, they wouldn't suspect me. That way, I knew no one could stop me. I wouldn't have to face the heartbroken and confused faces of my friends and family.

Especially Raen's.

It was funny, before I wanted nothing more than to escape and go back to the *High Peaks*. Now that I was actually leaving, it hurt to leave my friends, my brother and the little family that I never knew I had – yet somehow created.

Despite their characteristics and nature being completely different from the elves, they treated me well.

They never put me down for my looks and treated me like an equal. Even though I was far from their strength, they made me feel like I was one of them.

I even fell in love with one of them.

I knew that I had to move on. I had to grow. I had to be better, stronger and if that meant being away from them for however long that may be, then so be it.

I quietly opened the door to Bow's house and crept up the stairs, soundlessly opening the door to Bow's room only to find he was in a deep sleep.

For a moment I just stood there and looked at my brother knowing this could be the last time I ever got to see him.

I quickly snapped myself out of my gaze and took a

small breath, immediately getting to work on quietly gathering a bag of clothes and my knife – that Malakei gave me to defend myself. I never went anywhere without it and I knew that wherever I intended to venture, I'd be needing it.

Once I was packed with everything I felt necessary, I left the room and went downstairs to fill a bag with some food from the kitchen.

I felt bad enough leaving without taking some coins from Ana, so I didn't. I'd find another way to get food when I needed to.

I left the house just like that and made my way into the night. Barely any light was visible apart from some torches that lit the trail down to the barricade. I followed it but knew I wasn't leaving just yet.

There was something I needed to do first.

Someone I needed to see.

***

"Keylin?" Corrin stirred in his sleep, bringing his hand up to wipe his face from where he slept on the ground. He blinked the tiredness away before looking up at me, shocked and disappointed.

"Keylin it's nearly bright," His voice was hoarse. "What are you doing here?"

"I'm leaving," I replied before successfully tampering with the rusted lock and pushing open the stiff cage. I made my way into it meeting Corrin's eyes.

"And you're coming with me."

"You're not leaving Keylin." He furrowed his brows and glanced at my bag before contemplating my attire.

I was dressed warmly knowing that where I was going was somewhere I wouldn't expect it. It was better to dress prepared for all weather when planning to roam across the *Dry Lands*.

Corrin frowned at this.

"You can't–"

"Yes, I am Corrin. Something happened and I–"

"What happened Keylin?" Corrin stood on alert, his chains rattled. I immediately walked forward to hold them in place to make sure they wouldn't make any more unnecessary noise. Corrin's nostrils flared.

"Did that bastard do something to you? What happened?"

"No! No – I'll explain on the way," I whispered, biting my lip in worry looking down at the chains. I knew exactly who he was referring to. He and Raen hated each other and for all the wrong reasons. Corrin sighed, giving in.

"If we get caught–"

"We won't, trust me." I assured as I followed the chain trail. I walked around it and crouched down to view where the chain was connected to the wood by a metal brace. I pulled on it hard but it didn't budge.

"I've tried that." Corrin stated matter–of–factly as he made his way over to me, folding his arms as he leaned against the wood.

"What now?"

"What is going on?"

My attention darted to the entrance of the cage where a

sleepy Malakei slowly became alert as he stared with a murderous look at Corrin.

My stomach dropped and I quickly stood from where I was crouched behind the wooden barricade.

Malakei's eyes flickered to me and I noticed confusion in them. He seemed to assess the situation in front of him and no sooner, his eyes filled with hurt and betrayal. It was gone in a second when his cold eyes and stoic features fell on me. I gulped, making my way around the wood.

"Malakei, please you need to understand–"

"You are setting elf free," Malakei voiced, harsh and low. "What is there not to understand?"

I contemplated on pleading with him not to tell any of the others, to just let us go but I knew Malakei wouldn't do that. Not because it was wrong, he couldn't care less.

He wouldn't want to see me go.

My shoulders slumped in defeat and I opened my mouth to speak. Malakei's eyes softened and he loosened the grip on his axe as he walked closer to us.

"What is it?" His brows furrowed, getting the sense that something must be wrong for me to act this way. My eyes slowly moved up to meet his and I couldn't lie to him.

"I had a premonition last night. A woman came to me, she told me there was going to be a war."

"That's impossible." Corrin said from behind me in a low voice but I didn't turn to him.

Corrin was the only person that knew about my dreams. I didn't usually dream but when I did, it was always something serious whether that be a warning of something about to happen, or someone trying to reach me.

Malakei didn't say anything as he looked between Corrin and I. Unsure of what to do, I continued.

"I'm leaving," I forced down my nerves. "I need to find answers and this woman. She knows something that could help me–"

"Help you what?" Malakei voiced his concern. His eyes showed no emotion as he looked at me. I knew he didn't believe me but I was telling the truth.

I walked closer, looking him in the eyes. I was scared. He could see that, but he didn't react.

"Help me in stopping the war."

"You are one elf," Malakei stated lowly with a surprising seriousness. "You cannot stop war."

"I have to do something Malakei. I can't ignore it. The woman, Vixen. She showed me things that have not been spoken of in hundreds of decades…"

I stopped speaking when I noticed Malakei's shocked expression. He looked panicked for some reason and I let out a breath at that.

'Now he believed me.'

"That name..." He started with a tone close to one of horror. "You heard it in dream?"

"Yes," I replied seriously. "I think… I was talking to her."

Malakei looked torn. He stood there for a moment twiddling his axe in his hands before he let out a growl, made his way forward and stalked passed me to Corrin. Corrin watched with wide eyes as he held up his axe and I panicked.

"No Malakei–"

He brought the axe down on the metal chain between Corrin's wrists and it snapped off with a loud 'clunk' before falling to the ground. Corrin only watched fearfully as Malakei turned back with a neutral expression, pointing his axe at me seriously.

"If Vixen reaches out to you like you say, then we have problem."

I let out a breath and brought my hand over my chest to try and slow my heartbeat from what I thought was going to happen. Malakei's furrowed brows reappeared as he stalked forward and stopped in front of me.

"I go with you."

"What?" I blurted out in confusion. "No way. You're staying here. What about Tara? My father... you need to assure people that I'm okay."

He winced at the mention of my father but quickly regained himself.

"We are brothers remember? You need protection. I go where you go."

I smiled softly at that, ignoring Corrin's confused look and ran my hand through my hair in desperation. Malakei took a breath before continuing with his persuasion.

"I can help you find Vixen. I know what sector she is in now. Let me go with you."

After a while I agreed, nodding as I bit my lip before reaching out to grip his arm tightly, a Dry Landers sign of trust. Malakei did the same with a smile. He taught me this after all.

We left the cage and were in the middle of walking

towards the entrance when I stopped.

To my left laid the bound, sleeping elves. Some were battered and bruised from the fight and others had tear–stained cheeks.

Seeing all of them sleeping... it unsettled me. Images of them in that position – only dead, flickered through my mind and I couldn't take it any longer. I gritted my teeth, remembering my father and I's conversation.

"What's wrong?" Malakei noticed I had stopped walking and came back to me.

"I need you to tell the guard his post is finished and you're taking over."

"*Dimples*," Malakei's gaze fell on the sleeping elves and his jaw clenched in realisation before he looked back at me seriously.

"We have to leave. We could get caught. They not worth saving."

"You were there when the Dry Landers attacked the *High Peaks*," I reminded him seriously, not forgetting. "I was taken from them. What else were they to do Malakei? The fact that they did something out of their nature and came to rescue me, knowing the risks, knowing they were outnumbered... I want you to look at them Mal. Look at them sleeping. Look at the blood. What do you see?"

Malakei was silent as he looked at them with furrowed brows, about to open his mouth to speak and I gulped watching him.

"Now remember when we were in the mountains. How I got hypothermia and almost died because of the cold. Remember how scared I was..."

Malakei's eyes changed at my words as he remembered. His eyes were softer now. He almost looked ashamed.

"Now look at me."

He swallowed before slowly turning to me.

"We have to set them free," I said softly and Malakei looked conflicted.

"They don't know *Dry Lands*," Malakei frowned at them. "They could die."

"They could live either Mal," I reassured him. "They've made it this far, they can make their way back. Taking a chance out there is better than what they will face if they stay here."

"Thank the gods we leave before they catch us," Malakei breathed out and my heart constricted as I took in his words. A thankful smile morphed onto my face as he let out a breath and turned his gaze to the unaware guard at the end of the sleeping elves.

"I'll signal you when okay."

I watched Malakei walk forward and couldn't help but send him a watery smile as I realised what he was doing. This was taking a lot for him to – in their eyes, betray his people, but I didn't see it that way.

Malakei was doing good. Righting a wrong that he made in the past. I knew when he looked at the elves, he saw them differently from how he had previously looked at them, he saw clarity. He saw the truth.

I had never been so proud of him in that moment. I knew that from now on, he was not just a friend to me. He was someone I wanted in my life for as long as I lived.

Little did I know, he planted something in my heart then, something that would grow with time.

"He's not like the others." Corrin mused and I didn't turn to him as I continued to watch Malakei talk to the guard in *Fasik*. The guard patted him on the back with a smile.

"You're right." I said in almost a trance as I looked at Malakei, trying to read him but whatever he did always surprised me. Even now, he kept me guessing. Unravelling the layers that made him who he was.

Malakei turned to me with a bite of his lip as the guard left and ushered us to come to him.

My heart fluttered ever so slightly but I assumed it was the adrenaline of excitement in anticipation of freeing the elves.

"He's different." I eventually offered up before Corrin and I made our way towards him, lightly shaking the elves as we began to break their chains.

***

Many elves wept and bowed, showing their knee to me as we freed them but I was quick to dismiss their thanks, making them get to their feet so that they could escape as quietly and as quickly as they could.

It was getting brighter now and it wouldn't be long before the rest of the Dry Landers would start to wake up.

Corrin told multiple elves to inform my grandfather of what had happened here when they got back to their sector and that his grandson was alive and safe with him but that we would not be returning to the *High Peaks* yet. There was a journey we needed to make but we would meet again when the time was right.

"Does the prince wish for me to pass a message onto the king?" An elf asked, bowing their head to me in greeting.

I smiled to myself, remembering my grandfather's words.

"Tell him I am finding my path."

The elf nodded at this, albeit confused as he retreated to the back of a quickly forming line where elves were gathering, awaiting orders.

The three of us ushered elves through a derelict, forested path near the back of the camp and watched as each of them made their way on foot, hurrying through the forest and disappearing. It brought my mind ease with each elf that passed me but it wasn't until I saw a familiar face that I froze.

I almost didn't recognise Tobias in his beaten and bleeding state, but our eyes met briefly.

Looking at him now, I wasn't afraid. I didn't want to cower away like I normally would have. His bullying was brutal but it felt like child's play to what I had gone through in the past few months.

I had grown up, and I knew I still had more growing to do.

Tobias gulped and opened his mouth to speak but no words came out as he looked at me.

"Get them home safely," I told him seriously. "Whatever you do, don't stop running."

He nodded wide–eyed before looking down at the ground. He cleared his throat.

"Thanks." He mumbled. "For saving us."

I nodded at this and watched him disappear into the forest. The moment was brief between us, it wasn't until he was out of sight that I blinked and realisation dawned on me of what just happened.

I didn't have long to dwell on it. Corrin's hand rested on my shoulder and I turned to him.

Did he see the encounter between Tobias and me?

"We have to go."

We didn't have to be told twice and made our way towards the horses tied up near the entrance of the camp. Each of us grabbed a horse to take.

I found it difficult to climb up. The last time I was on a horse was when I arrived at the camp. Now I was leaving on one.

Corrin managed to get on the horse without help but I felt Malakei's towering form looming behind me. His rough hands helped me up and I climbed over the saddle. My ears burned red at the embarrassment of needing help getting onto the horse but knew that with time I would be able to do this myself one day. I would grow taller and it wouldn't be so difficult.

I smiled down awkwardly at Malakei, showing my thanks and he chuckled at my expression before a curious look crossed his features.

"No Baja?"

The smile slipped from my face and I avoided his gaze.

"It's too dangerous. It's better if she stays. She's safe

here. Where I know she will be cared for."

'Safe with Raen.'

Malakei nodded at that. A knowing look crossed his face but he knew not to dwell on the subject.

Baja wasn't coming and that was it. If something were to happen to her out there, it would kill me. I wasn't strong enough to protect her. It was better if she stayed here where I knew she was with people who would take care of her for me until I was old enough. Until she didn't see me as someone she needed to protect. She stayed until then.

After Malakei got onto his horse, we headed towards the barricade where two people on guard were currently sitting down. When they spotted us coming they stood up on alert.

We stopped in front of them and they inspected each of us. The guards were accustomed to when Malakei and I would venture out to train in the woods. This wasn't out of the ordinary for them.

Malakei spoke to them in Fasik as I tried not to lose my nerve and glance back at Corrin.

I gave him my hood to shield his blonde hair and elven ears. His gaze was cast downwards when I last saw him. I hoped their eyes wouldn't linger on him too long to notice something was off.

The two guards nodded at Malakei, not looking completely happy but letting whatever he said go. One of them nodded at me as I left and I returned it as I passed them on my brown and white horse. They didn't so much as look twice at Corrin which slowed my rapidly beating heart in relief.

With that, we left the camp and travelled deep into the forest.

We left behind the chaos we knew would erupt in a few hours. By then, The elves would have scattered and created a distance between them and the Dry Landers, making their way back to the mountain the way they had come. They had escaped their cruel fate and my heart didn't feel as weighted by that as it did before.

I understood that my father wanted to erase all evidence that led back to me but as long as I was with him and alive, there would always be problems.

That was why I had to disappear.

**

We had travelled deep into the forest now to the point where I didn't even recognise the flora and tree bark. A blue tinge started to appear through the trees as the moon illuminated its last glow before the sun rose. Even though it was becoming brighter, this area of the unexplored forest was dark, shrouded in mystery. It felt unsafe. Still, although I was wary of including Malakei with Corrin and me, I was thankful he accompanied us. He knew these woods better.

"This witch is teller. She is known for seeing future," Malakei slowed down to where his horse now fell in sync with mine.

"Has she come to you in dream before?"

"No, this was the first time but she said we would meet

again." I trained my gaze on the forest ground in front as I shared this information with him.

"Soon?"

He grunted when I shrugged at this.

"Let us hope not. " I heard Malakei say under his breath and turned to him confused.

There was a clicking noise and the sound of something flying through the air.

Corrin let out a scream from behind us and I looked back in alarm to find him not on his horse anymore, but on the ground, withering around and caged in what appeared to be netting of sorts. My eyes widened in horror.

Malakei and I immediately got down from our horses. I ran to Corrin to try and rip the netting off of him using my hands, wincing as I felt them cutting into my palms like razors but I didn't care as I tried to pry the thing trapping my friend.

Malakei stood guard with his axe high and waited for sound. The thought of us being attacked made my insides rumble.

There was a rustling in the bushes to my left and Malakei turned in that direction. Black rusted boots suddenly filled my vision and I gasped.

My hand reached for my dagger when I felt something cold jab against my right shoulder from behind me.

"Ah ah ah. "

The low voice threatened from behind me in an almost teasing manner which made the man with the black boots in front of me chuckle.

I looked up at the black–booted man in front only to notice that he had dark ebony skin and almost black eyes. His black hair had been shaved to a buzzcut but growing back slowly. A piercing was visible in one of his ears and he wore a necklace of an arrow in a silver circle. A long brown coat and black boots were his strongest attributes. He looked like he was only fifteen when he smirked down at me victoriously.

Malakei was suddenly thrown down beside me and I jumped. He looked to be in pain but I couldn't see any blood on him as far as I could tell.

The man behind me said something to the boy in front who only nodded once. He grabbed Corrin and hoisted him up.

My breathing increased and I went to get up but a rough and cold hand pushed me back down by my shoulder. I whimpered at that and shut my eyes, trying to move away from the hand on me but it only tightened.

"Let him go you dirty pirate!" Malakei growled from beside me and I turned to him just in time to see another dark–skinned man kick him in the stomach. Malakei coughed and spluttered, spitting what looked like blood onto the ground. Fear grew within me.

"Now now, no need to be afraid."

The pirate whispered into my ear from behind and I shut my eyes, craning my neck away from him.

"What do you want?" I managed to whisper out as I willed myself to look around me.

To my horror, I found what looked to be a dozen men with similar skin tones rummaging through our bags, taking the satchels off of our horses and emptying them of their contents onto the forest floor before they led the horses away into the almost bright morning.

The man chuckled deeply from behind me, an evil type of laugh. It resembled a low rumble. One that made the hairs on the back of my neck stand upright.

"Little elf, you do not know who I am?" The man feigned hurt in his voice. I noticed that he had an accent. I shook my head and closed my eyes as the man made his way in front of me.

I kept my gaze lowered, afraid to look at the pirate towering over me but I gasped when I felt his rough hand tug my chin upwards so that I was looking at him.

His skin was similar in tone to the others while his eyes were the colour of tree bark after a rainstorm.

He had a silver piercing in his nose, his ear, and wore clothes that resembled the previous boy even down to the black boots.

This man looked down at me with such curiosity and confusion while he stared perplexed by my features.

"How strange..." He mused as he tilted my head to the side carefully and I gritted my teeth at that. It made me feel less of a person, like an object. Like I was a shiny toy to admire.

"Strange, but beautiful."

I turned to him fearfully and he laughed at my reaction before pulling his hand away.

I subconsciously went to touch it, not taking my eyes off of the man in front of me who smirked with a knowing look. He trailed his gaze on all of us before finally resting on me.

"Load them onto the ship!" He barked the order at the others which made my ears flatten against my head.

"It's almost light and we cannot be seen on these *Dry Land* areas."

He moved around me just as Malakei struggled but was hoisted up by two other men with piercings. I gasped as the pirate gripped my shoulder harshly.

"*You* are going to make me the richest pirate in all of the *Great Divide* – maybe even *Sorn*!

ACKNOWLEDGEMENTS

Where do I begin? I will keep this short. I want to thank my ARC readers for giving Keylin's story a chance and providing me with some very detailed feedback.

To my family, friends and extended family friends for always believing in me and never doubting my judgement. You have shaped me into the woman I am today.

To my editor and childhood best friend Shauna, thank you for helping me bring my book to life (and pointing out my dreadful spelling mistakes!)

Lastly, to all of those on social media who have been patiently anticipating the release of the book, thank you!

If you want to stay connected, become an ARC reader for upcoming works, see sneak peeks, character art and other book-related content, follow me on *TikTok* @emmahowlauthor

KEYLIN'S STORY CONTINUES IN
BOOK 2 OF 'THE SECTOR SERIES'

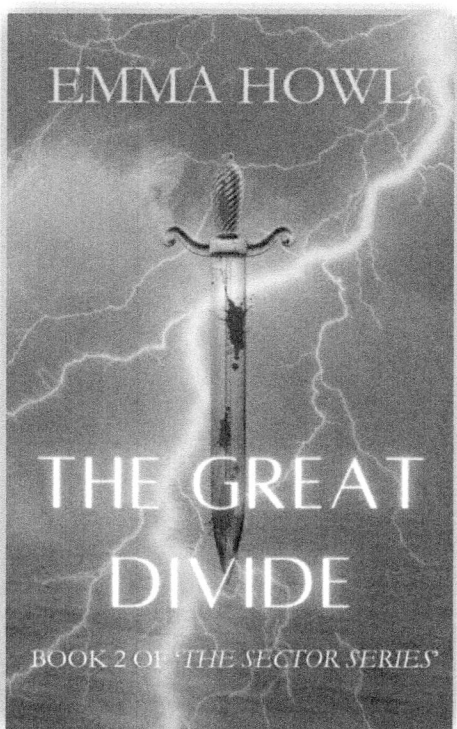

MARCH 2025

Read on for a sneak peek…

When I stepped foot onto the ship, the first thing that happened was me being tackled to the ground in a hug by Corrin.

Malakei rolled his eyes at the childish nature of the elf only a few months younger than him before heading off in search of Luis.

"You were longer than usual." Corrin said into my neck. My ears twitched at the vibration his voice was causing and chuckled in response as he held me momentarily tighter before moving back from me.

Corrin went to help me up but frowned when he did, remembering my bad foot and reaching down to hoist me to my feet instead. When I was on my feet, he furrowed his brows in pointed concern, looking at me expectantly.

"We got held up... I had to jump out of a window-"

"You *what*?!" Corrin's eyes bulged and he turned to Malakei – returning with Luis grinning knowingly at me. Luis helped me sit down on a nearby wooden crate while I frowned up at Corrin, glaring at Malakei.

"Something tells me this was your fault. *Again*." Corrin accused, venom laced in his tone towards Malakei. Malakei only turned to him with a scoff.

"It wasn't my fault he hurt his leg. I wasn't the one that pushed him out of that window."

"I didn't push him!" Corrin exclaimed in mortification, ears and face coated red before he turned to me with a pleading look.

"I didn't push you Keylin, I *promise* you. I would never do-"

"I would never do that to you Keylin because I love you and I want to-"

Malakei's mimicking was cut short by me crying out when Luis pressed down too hard on a particularly sore spot on my bad leg. His face lit up when he finally found the weak joint he had been searching months for. Now he finally found it, at an awkward moment, nonetheless.

Malakei and Corrin both reached for me in concern but stopped to glare at each other. I looked up at them when I recovered, feeling exhausted and sore. I was tired of their indifference.

One would think after over a year on the *Great Divide* together, they would have warmed up to one another. Became friends – acquaintances at the least, but no. They remained indifferent to this day. I hoped that their loyalties to me would have given them something to bond over, but it seemed to do the opposite. Now, it was like a competition for who could win the title of being my best friend.

A ridiculous pissing contest if you asked me. I loved both of them equally.

I narrowed my eyes at the both of them.

"Knock it off, both of you. Can't you both stop arguing for one day?"

"*No!*" They said in sync before narrowing their eyes at one another. I drag my hand across my hair in mild frustration before jolting forward, gripping the crate as an intense feeling of pain rocked through me and I stared down at Luis.

"*Shit*, my bad snake."

"It's fine Luis. How is it?"

Luis gave me a grim smile and I gulped at that, knowing that it couldn't have improved since the last time. It was getting worse.

"I think you have a torn ligament. You need a lot of rest Keylin." He scolded me as he got up, now looking down at me pointedly.

"Which means no more running or walking for long periods for the next few weeks *snake*."

I let out a breath at that, nodding nonetheless before I felt Luis's hand pat my shoulder in assurance and he disappeared up the wooden steps of the ship onto the main deck, most likely in search of his uncle.

Malakei and Corrin stood before me with the same thoughtful look on their faces, making a shiver run up my spine.

'How similar they were, yet utterly polar opposites.' I frowned at that and went to get up.

"I'll be in my cabin." I reminded them as I moved to limp forward past them, ignoring the pain shooting up my leg before curling up and settling in my lower back. Malakei was immediately at my side taking my arm and allowing me to lean my weight on him for support. I looked up and smiled at him tiredly. He returned my smile. His worry was evident but he helped me to my cabin with Corrin following.

When we got to my small room, Malakei helped me to the bed and I sat down with a grunt. I shifted on the bed and Malakei sat on the end with his elbows resting on his knees. Corrin folded his arms over his chest as he leaned against the door to my room looking in.

It was amazing how much these two boys had changed in the last year since we left the *Dry Lands*. Corrin had picked up training with the pirates. Mostly sword fighting, he was still to master fist fighting. He had gotten buffer because of the training, as did Malakei and me. We all learned a lot of new things that we wouldn't have had the opportunity to learn secluded in my father's camp.

The time away wasn't entirely spent in vain, however, when we weren't learning from the pirates, I was helping Malakei on improving his English. Not a day went by when the pirates wouldn't tease him for his bad grammar and lack of knowledge of certain words. To the point where I noticed he was starting to become withdrawn, the opposite of his carefree and confident attitude.

I noticed Luis' school books sprawled on his desk one

day. A book dedicated to 'English' caught my eye. Malakei and I started studying with one another from that day on. To the point where he was almost fluent – he still had a small accent, it suited him, made him… *him*. He also improved on his Timir and Talamahi immensely, with the help of Luis and François.

I got the opportunity to learn these languages that made up the *Dry Lands* and I was surprised how quickly I had picked them up. Corrin wasn't so quick to pick the languages up, but it didn't bother him.

I could understand Fasik now. Although I still needed help with structuring sentences, it was new to me and I was still learning, Malakei helped me so much and it was the only language that I could pick up the quickest. Most likely because it was the one I was most eager to learn.

I knew that to survive, I had to embrace the Dry Lander part of myself, not suppress it. So that was what I did.

"So what happened out there?" Corrin asked in a small curious voice, breaking me out of my thoughts. I turned my gaze on him, knowing that he was referring to the meeting with the Talami.

Malakei's jaw tightened as I let out a tired sigh and brought my hands up to my face.

"So, it didn't go well?" Corrin raised an eyebrow.

"It was a set-up," Malakei broke the silence with a knowing look. "They were there when Keylin was in the building. François and I had to get him out, else he could've been caught."

"*Fuck* Keylin." Corrin cursed lowly and a look of concern washed over his features. He made his way over to me.

"If I've told you once, I've told you thousands of times, it's too dangerous now. Your father has every Dry Lander looking for you. Even covered, they know you from a mile away."

That's why Corrin chose to stay on the ship. He knew that being in this sector as an elf with his blonde hair was very dangerous because he could be mistaken for me. I knew I should be doing the same and take more precautions but I figured it had been so long, they would have given up but the search was only getting worse.

'He isn't one to give up easily.' I remembered, fleeing the camp and running through the forest. He was the only one to keep up with the chase.

Raen was getting closer to me and I was nowhere near to finding Vixen.

"I know it's dangerous but this is nothing like it will be in the future unless I find her," I reminded them seriously, looking up at both of the boys.

"She knows I'm following her but she tells the Talami I would be there in the next few days, knowing that he will send word to my father immediately? *Why*?"

"Maybe she wants you to go back?"

Corrin questioned and both Malakei and I stiffened at that.

We couldn't go back now. We were traitors, runaways. If we stepped foot on the campgrounds, we would most likely be killed on the spot. I frowned and scratched my head, not liking the thoughts that plagued my brain.

"She would be sending us to our deaths." Malakei

responded lowly, voicing my thoughts exactly but Corrin shook his head.

"What if she isn't?"

We all waited for Corrin to elaborate further and he did with a sigh, leaning forward so that both of us could hear.

"She sends you a message in your dream over a year ago Keylin. But nothing else. Nothing until today. She knew the Talami would send word to the Dry Landers and your father. She wants you home."

Corrin's explanation of the presumption was believable but I couldn't shake the fact that he called *The Dry Lands* home for me, it was shocking. It made me wonder when he started to believe that I belonged with the Dry Landers more than the Elves. Maybe the water from *The Great Divide* had gotten clogged in his ears. Or maybe I had grown up more than I realised. I wasn't the same elf anymore and maybe that was what he believed.

"But *why*?" Malakei questioned in irritation. "Why now?"

"Maybe... something will happen?"

'*She's there.*' My thoughts intruded. The pieces all suddenly fit together. The thought that we had been traipsing *Sorn* looking for her when she was right under our noses was sickening. One I couldn't help but pay attention to.

What if she was there? Waiting for us...

"Corrin's right," I concluded through the pit in my stomach as both boys stopped their conversation, turning to me.

"We need to go back."

"*Whoa* whoa – are you sure?" Malakei questioned as he looked at me. The sudden realisation becoming real and the thought of being so close now to Vixen seemed almost bittersweet.

"No," I met his gaze determined. "But if she wants us there or if something is wrong, we need to go there immediately."

"I'll let François know you're ready." Malakei assured softly as he got up from the end of the bed, sending me a small smile before exiting my room and leaving Corrin and me alone to our thoughts.

"I'm not ready," I confessed. "I just know I have to do this sooner or later and I rather get it over with now because I'm not sure if I even have a later."

"You don't have to tell me. I understand." Corrin said before placing a hand over my knee and I jolted in surprise before relaxing and letting out a breath.

"Sorry." I apologised for my skittishness, knowing it couldn't be helped. I had always been this way but ever since we learned how to train with pirates, my senses were heightened. I was constantly aware of other crew mates stealing my food or socks. I was paranoid and always on edge when I went out.

"It's alright," Corrin stared at me with covered worry. "You've always been nervous, especially around me."

I snorted at that.

"Blame Tobias."

"I blame him for a lot of things, but this is something you have to overcome yourself Keylin. I can't help you, Malakei can't either. Only you have the power to control your emotions. You are strong. Don't let anyone tell you otherwise."

I lifted my head up from where I had it pointed downwards. Corrin's words made me feel stronger than I was and for a moment, I didn't feel the pain in my leg. I smiled at Corrin, making him smile back in return before he got up from beside me and made his way to the door.

"Thank you." I said quickly, making him stop at the doorway and turn around with a raised brow.

"For what? The crappy motivation speech?"

"For believing in me."

Corrin smiled at that. It made me realise how much he had changed over the years with the stubble forming around his chin. His hair was longer to where he could tie it into a bun now but no matter how old he got, he still had the innocence and childlike features an elf possessed. The same blue sparkling eyes that shone even brighter when I was around.

"You're my best friend. You know I will follow you anywhere."

With that said, he left me to myself, noticing now that the sun was going down and he had things to do around the ship. Of course, he had to pull his weight if he refused to do what was asked of François. He was a cabin boy after all.

I laid down on my bed and out of exhaustion, found myself falling asleep in a matter of seconds.

Printed in Great Britain
by Amazon